"Forget James Bond. Say hello to the real-life Miss Moneypenny, whose life was as replete with spycraft, adventure, and daring as any true hero's. Through Christine Wells's skillful storytelling, Paddy Bennett, aka Miss Moneypenny, doesn't just shine— she dazzles like the star she was. Just like you'll be cheering for the heroine of *One Woman's War,* you'll be cheering Christine Wells for writing this brilliant book."

—Natasha Lester, *New York Times* bestselling author of *The Riviera House*

"*One Woman's War* is the ultimate spy novel about the brave real-life women behind the Bond books. Christine Wells places us in the middle of the action with superb writing that will have your heart pounding through the adventures of these dazzling women. This gripping novel is one you will not be able to put down!"

—Madeline Martin, *New York Times* and internationally bestselling author of *The Last Bookshop in London*

"A pulse-pounding thrill ride of a read, *One Woman's War* pulls back the curtain on one of the most covert operations of World War II, while also immersing readers in the fascinating foundations of 007 lore. Powerful reading you won't want to put down!"

—Stephanie Marie Thornton, *USA Today* bestselling author of *A Most Clever Girl*

"A thrilling spy novel with a splash of glamour and plenty of intrigue, Christine Wells has penned an exciting WWII adventure of the real-life Miss Moneypenny and 007 that will keep you turning the pages until you reach the end. I highly recommend this exciting and daring book!"

—Eliza Knight, *USA Today* bestselling
author of *The Mayfair Bookshop*

"Christine Wells has crafted a spy novel worthy of Bond himself, bringing the unbelievable true story of Operation Mincemeat to life through the eyes of two unforgettable real-life female operatives. A must-read!"

—Bryn Turnbull, bestselling author of *The Last Grand Duchess*

"With a dazzling cast from history and a wild gamble of a mission, *One Woman's War* is a testament to the brilliance and daring of women and men in World War II. In true Fleming/Bond form, Wells has crafted a glamorous, engaging novel full intrigue, but one that also humanizes and brings to life many complicated people and terrifying situations. Mix a martini and settle in."

—Erika Robuck, bestselling author of *Sisters of Night and Fog*

"*One Woman's War* takes the reader on a breathtaking voyage to the glamour and edge-of-the-seat danger of London in the Blitz, as two very different women risk everything in a daring ruse that out-Bonds Bond. Christine Wells's latest is such a great wartime thriller that Ian Fleming himself would be envious!"

—Anna Campbell, bestselling author of
the A Scandal in Mayfair series

ONE WOMAN'S WAR

Also by Christine Wells

Sisters of the Resistance

ONE WOMAN'S WAR

A NOVEL OF THE REAL MISS MONEYPENNY

CHRISTINE WELLS

𝒲𝓂

WILLIAM MORROW

An Imprint of HarperCollins*Publishers*

HarperCollins books may be purchased for educational, business, or sales promotional use. For information, please email the Special Markets Department at SPsales@harpercollins.com.

FIRST EDITION

Designed by Diahann Sturge

Title page, part numbers, and chapter opener art © Yoko Designs / Shutterstock

Library of Congress Cataloging-in-Publication Data has been applied for.

ISBN 978-0-06-311180-6

22 23 24 25 26   LSC   10 9 8 7 6 5 4 3 2 1

For my brother, Michael, with love

PART 1

CHAPTER ONE

Point Verdon, Bordeaux, France
June 18, 1940

Paddy

The quayside at Point Verdon was in uproar. Women draped in furs and jewels perspired heavily under the harsh summer sun as they comforted distressed children or struggled with suitcases crammed full of their most prized possessions. Men laden with yet more baggage clutched fat wads of useless French francs and tried in vain to secure a passage aboard one of the ships that were idling at the port. Babies wailed in their nurses' arms; urchins darted about on errands or lifted treasure from the pockets of wealthy refugees.

Eight vessels of various nationalities—none of them British— were anchored at the mouth of the estuary. Word had spread that their respective captains refused to take anyone aboard at all, much less ferry them to safety across the English Channel.

Each German bomb that fell an uncomfortably short distance

along the coast whipped the crowd to a higher frenzy, and the Luftwaffe's machine guns strafed the countryside. Only the day before, the liner *Lancastria* had been sunk in the Bay of Biscay, killing thousands of British evacuees.

Victoire Patricia Evelyn Bennett—Paddy to her friends—set her jaw and made a beeline for the one man present in the melee who seemed to know what he was doing. Dressed in the trim uniform of an officer of the British Royal Navy, he strode along, head bent, hands clasped behind his back, while a slighter man in a shabby brown suit practically ran to keep up with him, chattering all the way.

Paddy weaved and squeezed herself through the crowd, judiciously using her elbows when she couldn't get through by polite means, "accidentally" banging shins with her suitcase, once or twice treading hard on the instep of a gentleman who wouldn't budge.

It was lucky her quarry was tall, because he was leaving her far behind in his wake. He had no trouble carving a path through his desperate countrymen and soon reached the edge of the quay, where the crowd thickened and a wall guarded the drop to the jetty below.

Paddy stopped short. The mob here was packed too tightly for her to get through. Before she could even get close enough to call out to him, the Navy officer had stood briefly at the narrow break in the wall where stone steps led down to the marina, given a few sharp orders, and nodded to the couple of burly uniformed individuals who were holding back the tide of people that surged toward the steps. Then the officer disappeared, presumably descending to the waterside below. When next she spied him, he was aboard a speedboat, motoring off toward one of the waiting ships.

Paddy's shoulders dropped. "All right for some," she muttered. It seemed every British citizen still in France was leaving today. Her mother was right: she'd been a fool to stay in Paris.

"Darling, it's not safe! Your father says the Germans will march on the city any day now. You must come home at once."

"Mother, I've spent three years at the Sorbonne, swotting my little heart out. I'm only a couple of weeks away from getting my degree. Herr Hitler is *not* going to stop me."

"You won't need a degree in architecture when you're interned as an enemy alien," Edith replied tartly. "I don't think you'll quite admire the prison camp period of design."

The words came back to Paddy as she stood, helpless, amid the confusion. Judging by the number of Bentleys and Rolls-Royces abandoned by the quayside, and the furs and jewels worn by the women, a great number of these evacuees were from the monied classes.

Yet here, no one had any influence. As far as Paddy could see, that was principally because no one had actually taken charge of the British evacuation. The ships moored off the coast were private craft, and the French ones might not be friendly to Britain. After all, if the French signed an armistice with Germany, they would be regarded as the enemy. Everything was upside down.

The French government had absconded to Vichy, so no help from that quarter; de Gaulle had flown off to London. And she was stuck here, nineteen, female, and alone, in this heaving crowd of desperates. All through her own stubborn pride.

The family she'd traveled with had taken one look at the crowds waiting to depart from this port and insisted on trying their luck farther south. For her part, Paddy saw more safety in numbers, and declared she'd prefer to take her chances at Point Verdon. Paddy had been adamant, and there was no time for protracted argument. Promising to send on the rest of her luggage, the Trevithicks had deposited her at the quayside with one suitcase and wished her luck.

"Oh, please! Please, somebody help me!" a young woman no older than Paddy cried out to no one in particular. "It's my mother. Please, I don't know what to do."

Judging by the girl's clipped accent, she belonged in Mayfair or Belgravia or one of the home counties.

"Can I help?" With a regretful glance toward the Navy man in the speedboat, who was now boarding one of the ships, Paddy fought her way over. "What's the matter?"

"Oh, thank you!" The young woman grabbed Paddy's arm and dragged her through the crowd so forcefully that Paddy's small suitcase banged painfully against her thigh.

"Steady on!" said Paddy.

"Sorry! Only I'm so distracted. Mummy's awfully sensible as a rule, but it's the heat and the bombs, and everything . . . She's terribly worked up, you see. Having some sort of attack." The girl hustled Paddy through the crowd, achieving with a smile and a polite "Excuse me, please" what Paddy had earlier accomplished by wielding of elbows and the sturdy heels of her leather Oxfords.

That was, until a pimply youth blocked their way. He took a peanut from a bag he was holding, threw it up in the air, and caught it in his mouth inches from the girl's face. At her surprised recoil, he grinned and turned to his cronies to make a crude comment but broke off with a yelp as Paddy's elbow connected with his solar plexus.

"Good show!" the other girl laughingly threw over her shoulder as they slipped past the rude youth and emerged from the crowd. "I'm Jean, by the way. And this is my mother, Mrs. Leslie." She indicated a middle-aged lady who sat on a large trunk, suitcases and hatboxes piled around her like a makeshift fortress. Swaddled to the throat in a mismatched mélange of sables and mink, she was clutching a lacy handkerchief, her fist to her chest, panting and gasping for breath.

Jean shoved some of the trunks aside to get to her.

"No, *don't* lose track of the luggage, Jean!" Mrs. Leslie managed between pants. "There are thieves everywhere." The thunder of a distant explosion made her give a faint scream. Her eyes bulged and her pretty face reddened as she clutched her chest, dragging in air with a horrible, strangled wheeze.

Paddy smiled reassuringly at the older lady. "My name's Victoire Bennett but everyone calls me Paddy. Let's see if we can make you more comfortable, Mrs. Leslie. Would you let Jean help you out of those furs, for a start?" *Honestly*, thought Paddy. *Anyone with a bit of common sense might have thought to do this.* But she could tell Mrs. Leslie required gentle handling, so she waited for Jean to unwrap her parent.

The removal of her furs didn't seem to calm the older lady, however. She was beginning to hyperventilate in earnest now. Rapidly reviewing and dismissing the contents of her own purse and suitcase, Paddy looked around for something into which Mrs. Leslie might breathe.

"Wait here." She made her way back to the rude young man with the bag of peanuts and snatched it from him.

"Oy!" he said.

"I need this bag. It's an emergency. Hold out your hands." Perhaps infected with her urgency or perhaps simply reacting to her tone of command, the youth did as he was told. She dumped out the peanuts into his cupped hands and took the bag with her.

Paddy approached Mrs. Leslie's heaving form. "Now, ma'am," she said in a calm, bracing tone reminiscent of her own redoubtable nanny from nursery days, "will you let me help?"

Mrs. Leslie's eyes were wide and trusting as she gazed up at Paddy and slowly nodded. That was the trick to inspiring confidence—never let anyone catch on that you had no idea what you were doing.

"You're going to breathe into this bag for me." Praying that theory would work in practice, Paddy pressed the edges of the bag up to the woman's mouth to form a seal. "In . . . and out." The paper bag ballooned and collapsed again as the lady obeyed. "Slowly. Slowly. That's right. Long, deep breaths, ma'am. Good."

Gradually, the lady's frantic pants slowed. Her shoulders relaxed and she slumped with apparent relief.

Paddy put an arm around her to support her. "There," she said, lowering the paper bag and watching Mrs. Leslie's face for any sign of relapse. "I think that's done it." She rubbed the older woman's back a little in a brisk, nanny-like fashion, then straightened. "You'd best keep this handy in case." Paddy flattened the paper bag, folded it, and handed it to Jean.

"How did you know to do that?" said Jean, tucking the paper bag into her purse. "Are you a nurse?"

"No, but I have the basics in first aid." Didn't everyone? Well, she supposed not. Once she was back in London, of course, she intended to do her bit for the war effort. Training to be a nurse seemed the obvious choice.

Paddy leaned down to meet Mrs. Leslie's gaze and spoke with firm reassurance. "Try not to worry, Mrs. Leslie. I have my eye on a Navy officer who can help us. If I have anything to say about it, we won't be stranded here for long."

Mrs. Leslie fretfully worked at her handkerchief. "The ambassador is here in Bordeaux. I know him a little. Surely . . ."

But every upper-class English family in Paris knew the ambassador "a little," and Sir Ronald undoubtedly had more momentous things on his mind at present. "I think this other gentleman is a safer bet. He seems to know what he's about." She wasn't quite sure why she was giving the Leslies what would probably turn out to be false hope. For all she knew, the Navy man had boarded one of those ships and sailed away in it, leaving them all stranded.

One simply had to trust in something, that was all.

Just then, another lady wearing a collar of diamonds that glittered madly in the June sunshine approached. "My dear Mrs. Leslie, is it you?"

Jean's mother stared up at the other woman, then broke into a relieved smile. "Oh! Oh, how good to see you, Daphne. Is Hartley here? Do you think he could possibly—"

It seemed the arrival of her friend and the promise of masculine support had dispelled any lingering shortness of breath Mrs. Leslie might have suffered. She broke into a stream of complaints, demonstrating the considerable capacity of her lungs.

The diamond-clad matron said, "Oh, you poor dear." She seated herself on another of Mrs. Leslie's suitcases and brought out a flask of tea from her capacious purse.

"If you'll excuse me," said Paddy. She wanted to be there if and when the Navy officer returned.

"I'm coming with you," said Jean.

Paddy didn't want anyone else slowing her down. She eyed the other girl. "Don't you think you ought to stay with your mother?"

"She'll be right as rain now," said Jean, with a nod and a smile in the direction of the newcomer. "Come on. Let's find this Navy officer and persuade him to help us. Oh, hold up!" She stopped short, cracking open her purse. "Just a minute while I . . ."

Paddy watched with interest as Jean slicked the deep red *rouge à lèvres* over her generous mouth. "Is that Chanel? Pretty."

"Isn't it?" Jean shot her an impish look. "Do you think your Navy officer will like it?"

Paddy chuckled. She was no stranger to masculine admiration herself, but it rarely occurred to her to primp for men. She had a strict beauty regimen, which she followed because it was simply what one did. Then she forgot about her appearance when she walked out the door. However, her new friend seemed to possess a clear-eyed awareness of her own allure, which comprised a complexion so perfect the word "alabaster" seemed an understatement, and an abundance of thick, wavy chestnut hair. Admittedly, Jean's talent might come in handy. Paddy wasn't above using every advantage, particularly in a situation like this.

Jean's handiwork complete, they made their way with some difficulty back to the water's edge—or at least, as far as they could go.

The guards at the top of the narrow stone steps that led down to the jetty seemed to have instilled some semblance of order. There was no more pushing and shoving, although there was a lot of noise and yelling out questions, to which neither man returned an answer—one as stoic and impenetrable as a soldier of the King's Guard on parade, the other juggling a clipboard and a megaphone, attempting to take names.

"I suppose this is as far as we can go," said Jean. From this vantage point, Paddy could gaze out to the estuary and spot the straight, tall figure of the Navy officer board yet another of the vessels that were moored there.

A commotion caught Paddy's attention. A ripple in the crowd . . . where was it coming from? "Oh, dear." One young woman had collapsed, perhaps from the heat, and her drooping form was being carried out. The mob surrounding the guards parted to let her through. As the people along the now-empty path craned their necks to see where the girl was being taken, Paddy saw their chance. She grabbed Jean's hand and darted through the gap.

After a struggle, they made it all the way to the wall, Paddy's feet throbbing from so many people standing on them, Jean's hat askew.

Paddy accosted one of the guards. "Do please tell us, is there any chance of our getting on board one of those ships today?"

The guard seemed younger than he had appeared from a distance. "Sorry, miss, I'm not at liberty to say. I'm to take names in an orderly fashion. Everyone is to remain calm and wait. That's all I can tell you."

Just then, someone behind Jean must have pushed her—or perhaps they hadn't. Jean stumbled and plunged forward, and the guard had no choice but to catch her. "Sorry!" she said with a rueful, flirtatious smile. "*Such* a crush!" Jean's hands were flat against his chest, eyelashes fluttered as she raised her gaze to his. "But oh, do be a dear and tell us what's going on. Is that officer going to fix it all, d'you think?"

Jean was definitely turning out to be an asset. Pushing her sunglasses farther up her nose, Paddy hid a smile. The guard had dropped his megaphone. While he half-heartedly attempted to extricate himself from Jean, Paddy bent to scoop it up.

The guard was saying, "I'm attempting to compile a passenger list, miss, but it's hell keeping this lot at bay, if you'll pardon my—Oy! What d'you think you're doing?"

Paddy wiped the mouthpiece of the megaphone with her handkerchief. "I'm good at lists," she said calmly. She had always lived by the principle that if you wanted something done, it was best to do it yourself. She took the clipboard from the guard's slackened grasp and filched a pen from his pocket as well. She inspected the breast-high stone wall. An excellent vantage point for someone as slight and small as Paddy.

She handed the megaphone to Jean and put the clipboard and pen on the top of the wall. "Boost me up, will you?" The bemused guard did as he was asked, easily lifting Paddy to perch above the crowd, her back ramrod straight thanks to all those years of ballet lessons. The stone wall was bumpy beneath her, baked warm by the sun. She glanced back at the drop below and thought, *If I fall, that won't be pretty,* but she wasn't afraid of heights, so she settled herself, crossed her ankles, and reached down. "Now, hand me the megaphone."

"I'll help!" Jean got a boost up, too. While the bemused but patently relieved guard found more paper and another pen, Paddy began issuing instructions through the megaphone in a clear, authoritative tone.

In no time, they had everyone lining up in two orderly rows. You had to hand it to the British: they did love and respect a queue.

"Please be reasonable, ladies and gentlemen," called Paddy through the megaphone. "There's room for everyone. If we all keep calm and cooperate, we'll get through this together." Paddy prayed her bolstering words would turn out to be true and that this list-taking exercise was actually leading somewhere.

They were making steady progress when, head bent over her clipboard, Paddy became aware of the next hopeful evacuee in line. "Last name first, please."

The ensuing silence made her look up, frowning impatiently, pen poised. Only to discover that the Navy officer she had been chasing all morning was standing in front of her, his head almost level with hers even though she was perched on the wall. He was handsome in a quintessentially English way—his face and jaw long and chiseled, his forehead high and his nose in proportion with the rest. Even the small imperfection in the middle of the latter feature—as if his nose were made of clay and someone had pressed their thumb down on the dorsum—seemed to add to his suave allure. His blue eyes had the hooded, lazy cast of a cynic, his mouth beautifully sculpted and firm with purpose.

Paddy wasn't often caught at a loss, and she didn't intend to let this man see that she was flustered. She jutted out her chin and said briskly, "I suppose you're going to ask what I'm doing."

"I can see very well what you're doing." He gave a curt nod. "Keep doing it. I want all of these people aboard and away before nightfall. And tell them they may only bring what they can carry in their own two hands. *No* exceptions." Before she could answer him, he strode off.

"Gosh!" Jean breathed as they watched him walk away, broad shouldered and straight backed. "It's awfully lucky I'm sitting down because my knees just turned to jelly."

"He must have managed to get all of those captains to agree to take everyone." Paddy couldn't help but be impressed. She'd rather thought the list making to be an exercise in futility—or at best, crowd control.

They watched the officer plow through the mass of refugees once more, tall and commanding, completely unruffled by either the panic surrounding him or the enormity of his task. One couldn't help but believe he would achieve his objective.

What a pity, Paddy thought. She hadn't even caught his name.

CHAPTER TWO

Estoril, Portugal
September 1937

Friedl

Friedl Stöttinger closed her eyes, wrapped one hand around the chrome microphone stand, and began to sing. The bittersweet melody had been a daring choice; the club was packed with noisy revelers who had spilled over from the casino, and the bandleader had advised against starting the set with something quiet.

But Friedl had sung in clubs from Vienna to Istanbul, and she knew how to command an audience. Her silver gown showered sparks as she moved in the spotlight; her scarlet fingernails and lips formed a striking contrast to the whiteness of her skin. Her short, honey-blond hair was crimped like a twenties flapper, and she let her large blue-green eyes smolder beneath thin, arched eyebrows.

No one in that crowd would guess that she was shaking inside.

He was here tonight. She saw him through the haze of smoke as clearly as if she sighted him down a rifle scope. She used to hunt with her father back home in Austria sometimes. Her sister Lisi was always squeamish, but Friedl wasted no sympathy on the deer. You survived in this world, or you were dinner.

The man wore no uniform, but he was a Nazi all the same. Just as her father had been before his recent death, not to mention her brother in Vienna, who was a rabid Hitlerite. Brought up in aristocratic comfort, surrounded by the elite of Viennese society, Friedl had turned her back on them all. She'd married an Orthodox Jew and run, left her cool green homeland for the dry, dusty heat of Palestine.

The marriage had been a disaster, as anyone might have predicted. She, too young and frivolous to settle easily into his earnest life; he, too good for her in every sense. Yet the letter "J" was still stamped on her passport, damning her in the eyes of most of her countrymen. She'd left Austria in 1934, three years ago now, and she would never set foot there again. Not if she could help it.

Now this German spy had found her, in Portugal of all places. Friedl let her body sway and loosed her death grip on the microphone stand to perform a few floating, expressive gestures in time with the jazz melody. She'd sung this number so many times, she didn't need to think about it, didn't falter on a single note.

But that left her mind free to worry about Kühlenthal. A fop and a poser and a ladies' man, yes. But still, he was Abwehr. German military intelligence. The bartender at the Hotel Palàcio had told her, and he was in a position to know. He'd said that

Kühlenthal had asked about Friedl, probing questions about her politics and her personal life, too. That was dangerous. From Kühlenthal to Canaris was a very short step. They were related somehow. And Canaris was King Spy, the greatest of them all.

Her chest began to tighten. Relax, she told herself. You're in Portugal, not Germany. This is not Hitler's Third Reich.

In Portugal, Friedl had thought she'd be free. But it turned out that for her, as for the deer in the Tyrolean forest, danger was everywhere.

Estoril was a hotbed of spies; everyone knew that. With impending war in Europe and intrigue around every corner, if something terrible happened to a mere cabaret singer, who would bat an eyelid? Despite the heat of the spotlight, she shivered.

But wait. If they wanted to punish her for having married a Jew, they would have arrested her already. And they wouldn't have sent their top man in Spain to do it.

Perhaps Kühlenthal wasn't here for her at all. Maybe he was here for the music, the gambling. They said he liked to throw his wife's money around.

She finished the slow song on a long, low note. Vaguely, she registered applause, shouts of approval from the audience, and marveled that a performance that had taken so little of her attention had still met with such acclaim. Automatically, she flashed a smile, used the lull to slow her breathing, fill her lungs. *Think, Friedl. Think.*

The next number picked up the tempo and Friedl clicked her fingers along.

Would Kühlenthal waylay her tonight? If he meant to stay in Estoril, they would meet at some stage, that was certain. Avoiding him would only arouse his interest. And anyway, he'd be sure to catch up with her sooner or later. High society in Estoril was a small and exclusive circle. Unlike the brownshirts and the bully boys who made up Hitler's S.S. and Gestapo, the more refined members of the Abwehr like Kühlenthal had the entrée everywhere.

Should she leave Estoril, join her sister in London? England would be safe.

Safe. The thought susurrated through her brain in time with the wire brush on the cymbals. And yes, it would be good to see Lisi again.

She saw Kühlenthal move to the exit and nearly laughed with relief. He wasn't there to see her tonight, after all.

The set went on and on while Friedl's mind skipped from problem to possible solution and back again. She had no clear memory of performing her finale, but she humbly accepted applause and blew kisses to the men who had leaped to their feet demanding an encore.

She demurred—*always leave them wanting more, liebling*—and walked off the stage, exhaling a long, shaky breath. The corridor outside her dressing room, which was usually filled with admirers carrying bouquets, was deserted. Friedl faltered and fought the instinct to turn back.

The door to her dressing room was open. She hesitated, licked her lips. Then she straightened her shoulders and made herself sashay forward. The Hollywood lights framing the mirror above her dressing table dazzled her eyes for a second after the dimness of the hallway outside.

"There you are." Kühlenthal's voice held a strange lack of resonance, like the rustle of the sea breeze through the date palms outside. The sound chilled her as much as the expression in his eyes. "I've been waiting for you, my dear. Your performance was truly magnificent."

Friedl had been away from home for so long that hearing her native tongue was usually comforting. Not this time. Not the way Kühlenthal spoke it—high German, with all the languor of an aristocrat.

She made no response, watching him warily as he moved past her to close the door with a controlled, definitive *click*. Kühlenthal's tall form was dressed in a light gray double-breasted suit with faint pinstripes, a lilac tie, a matching pocket handkerchief, and a gray felt hat with a light gray band. He took off his fedora, exposing a head of carefully swept back dark hair, and set it on her dressing table next to the bouquets laid out there. She wondered if he had collected them from her waiting admirers and told them all to clear out.

Kühlenthal observed himself in the mirror, and his brows drew together in a slight frown over his aquiline nose. He plucked the white rosebud from his buttonhole and discarded it. With great deliberation, he chose a pale pink bud from one of her bouquets, snapping its stem with a quick, ruthless nip of his fingers, then tucked it into his buttonhole.

She watched all of this with a wide smile, refusing to let him see how the small liberty infuriated her. What did he want? And how could she get him out of here without giving him whatever that was, or offending him unduly?

"Mrs. Gärtner." He smiled, adding, "Ah, but I believe you reverted to Stöttinger after your divorce, did you not? Very wise." He indicated the sofa by the wall. "Shall we sit? I have a proposition to make." His eyes lit up with a twinkle that some women might find engaging. "Oh, not *that* kind of proposition. Rest assured."

His words had the opposite effect from their stated intention. Friedl's skin crawled. She barely repressed a shudder.

Her unwanted guest sat down with more grace than she would have expected for such a large man. He patted the cushion beside him. Ignoring his mute invitation to join him, Friedl leaned back against the dressing table, gripping its edge tightly to stop her hands shaking. She knew better than to express relief at his lack of physical interest in her. "Oh? You disappoint me," she answered lightly. "What, then?"

"Your sister, Liesel . . ." Kühlenthal drummed his fingers on the arm of the sofa. "She has married and settled in England, I hear."

What on earth? This was the last direction Friedl had expected the conversation to take. "Yes," she said. It was hardly a secret. "She is married to Ian Menzies." The surname was pronounced "Mingiss" for obscure reasons only known to the Scottish, and probably not even to them.

"Your sister's esteemed brother-in-law, Stewart Menzies, works for the British government," said Kühlenthal. "He is a person of great interest to us."

Would it be disingenuous to ask? Friedl thought perhaps not. "'Us'?"

"The Third Reich," said Kühlenthal expansively. "My dear Miss Stöttinger, Stewart Menzies is a man very high up in the British security services. You didn't know?"

Stunned, Friedl stared at him. She would never have guessed that the quiet, reserved Menzies might hold an important covert role. Then the truth broke over her like an icy wave. It did not take too much ingenuity to guess what would come next. Clearly Kühlenthal wanted her to turn spy. Not only that, to betray her own flesh and blood.

A knock on the door made Friedl jump. Her gaze flew toward the door, then to Kühlenthal. He waved a hand. "Ignore it. They'll go away."

Friedl couldn't breathe, much less answer the door. This was far worse than being interrogated about her ex-husband. Surely Kühlenthal didn't expect her to harbor even a particle of patriotism toward the Third Reich. She wanted to point out that she was Austrian, and that as far as she knew, her homeland was still an independent nation. But that argument would be hollow coming from the daughter of a high-ranking member of the Nazi Party who had once been a powerbroker in Berlin. Besides, she was all too painfully aware of the way the cult of Hitler had swept her own nation like some virulent disease. It would not be too long before the two countries were united.

Get hold of yourself, Friedl. She needed to play for time while she figured out how to evade Kühlenthal's request without showing her fear and disgust—of both the man and of the regime he served.

The knock came again. "Miss Stöttinger?"

In a voice that shook a little, Friedl said, "If you don't mind, would you please get to the point, Herr Kühlenthal? I'm tired, and that's my dresser wanting to help me change. I don't wish to keep her waiting."

"The point?" Kühlenthal rose to his feet, a large, intimidating presence. "Why, my dear Miss Stöttinger. I want you to go to England to visit your sister, of course." He smiled. "It should be a most touching reunion."

"And if I refuse?" said Friedl, though she didn't know where she found the courage.

His smile broadened, then he assumed an expression of solicitude so false it sickened her. "I hear that your dear mother back in Vienna has grown very frail. What a shame you will not see her again before she dies." He shrugged. "But I suppose that 'J' stamped on your passport is damning, is it not?"

By marrying a Jew, Friedl had become one also, as far as the Nazis were concerned. Was Kühlenthal implying that he could remove this barrier to her return to Vienna? And would the carrot turn into a stick if she still didn't comply? The fact he knew about her mother was frightening.

Kühlenthal reached past her to pick up his hat, brushing close, and she fought the urge to shrink away. He moved back, and his shoulders shook, as if he was aware of her revulsion and amused by it. "But this has all come as quite a surprise to you, I'm sure."

"Yes," she said, clutching at the straw he dangled before her. "Yes, it has."

He set the fedora on his head and checked the mirror, then adjusted the brim to a more rakish tilt. With a small, satisfied nod, he returned his gaze to her. "Think it over." One well-manicured white hand came up to pat Friedl's cheek. She struggled not to flinch. "But I'm sure you'll find that your only option is to agree." Kühlenthal gave a faint smile and let his hand fall.

Get out, she begged him silently. *Just go.*

He paused, and menace seemed to gather in the room like a black cloud. Then the mood shifted, the cloud vanished, and he turned to leave. At the door, he set his hand on the doorknob, then looked back. "I'm in Estoril for a few days. I'll be in touch."

* * *

On the small crescent of golden sand that was Tamariz Beach at Estoril, one might see movie stars and royalty lazing beneath straw umbrellas or strolling the promenade toward the medieval fortress that stood sentry over the exclusive spot.

Friedl scanned the sun-kissed scene but failed to detect Kühlenthal among the beachgoers. She had slept badly. The vague threat Kühlenthal had made about her mother magnified the more she turned it over in her mind. She'd been tempted to distract herself in the arms of one of her admirers, but she was too upset to hide her fear beneath her usual gaiety, and she didn't wish to confide in anyone about Kühlenthal's approach.

Friedl set off across the beach, searching for a friendly face among the tanned bodies stretched out on the sand. She didn't want to be alone. She never wanted to be alone, of course, but today, surrounding herself with dozens of other sun worshippers seemed like a particularly good idea.

"Friedl! Over here!" Princess Stephanie waved from beneath a great straw umbrella. She sat with a group made up largely of minor European royalty, some of whose homelands were daily in danger of being overrun by fascism. Friedl wondered if, like her, they were only covering their anxiety with this brittle frivolity. Or were they so sheltered and pampered that they had no care for their countrymen at all?

She waved back and joined them. The men sprang to their feet and found her a low-slung deck chair, a spot in the shade. She allowed her bag to be taken and stowed safely. She shrugged off her short beach robe to reveal a swimsuit inspired by New York's Chrysler building, reflecting her love for art deco.

Lowering herself into the deck chair provided, she stretched out her long legs, conscious that every man's gaze had swiveled her way. She threw a grateful smile over her shoulder to the young Spaniard who was adjusting her umbrella so as to give her the perfect amount of shade, but that was an excuse to surveil the rest of the beach. She couldn't quite picture Kühlenthal donning a bathing suit and following her out here, but she didn't want to be taken unawares. He required an answer. Friedl never wanted to set foot in Austria ever again, but for her mother's sake, only one answer to Kühlenthal's request was possible.

A frosty cocktail was pressed into her hand. Like an automaton, she smiled then sipped. Rum-based, sweet. It was a little early in the day, and the flavor was not to her taste, but at that moment, the bracing hit of alcohol in any form was welcome. Her nerves jangled and twanged. Anything to calm them, to slow the thoughts that raced around her brain.

Sunglasses were such a blessing. One could appear to listen to the aimless chatter of friends and think about something else entirely. No one would know. She laughed along with the others at the appropriate places, always keeping an eye out for someone who didn't quite fit, someone who might make an approach. Perhaps Kühlenthal would not do it himself out in the open like this, but he might well send a messenger, or have a contact close by, perhaps even among her own circle of friends . . .

She couldn't avoid him; that was as bad as outright refusal. She didn't want to live in cold, dreary England, but perhaps it was safest there. After all, if Stewart Menzies was high up in the Secret Service, wouldn't he also be in a position to protect her? But then, she wasn't supposed to know what Stewart Menzies did—she still wouldn't know if it weren't for Kühlenthal. Lisi had certainly never breathed a word. If Friedl admitted to the British that she had been approached by the Abwehr, would they believe her to be a double agent and imprison her . . . Or worse? Would Stewart Menzies be able to protect her then, even if he wanted to?

She was less frightened of what the British might do to her than the consequences of refusing Kühlenthal's request. She loathed her fanatical Nazi brother—in fact, she didn't much care if she never set eyes on him again—but that didn't mean she'd want to cause him harm. Still, her mother was the problem. Friedl had heard enough about the ruthless methods the Nazis employed to know that her mother's frailty wouldn't save her if Friedl refused to comply.

The sea breeze picked up, flirting with the broad brim of her straw hat. Was it only yesterday that she'd stretched out on this beach, laughing and chatting without a care in the world? She'd thought she'd feel protected here, among these people she counted as friends, but the contrast between her dilemma and the concerns of the spoiled, idle rich made the blood pound in her ears until she wanted to scream.

She endured until it was time to go up for her massage, then slipped away. Perhaps the brutal hands of Johan, the hotel masseur, would settle her nerves. She wouldn't bank on it, but what else could she do?

Johan's pummeling turned out to have the desired effect. What with the sleepless night she'd spent, the sun and sea air and the drink she'd imbibed, Friedl's limbs began to succumb to the masseur's manipulations almost immediately.

Her mind drifted, the scent of coconut from the massage oil filling her senses. A soft, sweet melody played in her head. She winced as Johan dug into a particularly sensitive part of her neck. She'd told him never to go easy on her; he'd clearly taken her at her word. The pain was replaced by a warmth, then a flood of relaxation, and then he would pick another knot of tension and attack it, with . . . what? An elbow this time? "Ah!"

"Too much?" He eased off.

"No," she mumbled. "Keep going. I can stand it." She'd feel better in the long run as a reward for her present suffering.

But he still paused, and she wanted to turn her head to discover why, but her skull seemed to be made of lead. Johan started again, and she relaxed into the massage. He used a different technique this time, lighter and gentler, his big hands circling her shoulder blades, fingertips trailing down her back. She couldn't help feeling relieved. The torture part must be over.

And then she realized. The hands that kneaded lightly across her back weren't Johan's anymore. Friedl cried out and tried to sit up but a gentle hand pressed between her shoulder blades, holding her down. She was helpless, pinned like a dead butterfly.

"Fräulein Stöttinger," purred a voice in her ear. "I think, don't you, that it's time we concluded our little chat."

CHAPTER THREE

London, England
March 1938

Friedl

When Friedl first arrived in England, she lived in daily anticipation of being called into play as an Abwehr intelligence asset by some contact of Kühlenthal's. Thanks to Lisi, she enjoyed a glittering social life, mixing with aristocrats and royalty much as she had in Estoril. She took care always to be bright and amusing company, but she couldn't help viewing every overture of friendship with suspicion, particularly if the person making it was German.

As the months went by and no one made an approach, she began to relax a little. Perhaps nothing would come of Kühlenthal's recruitment attempt.

Friedl had only just settled in to life in England when another upheaval occurred. *Anschluss*.

She'd known it was coming, of course, but the pain she felt

when she heard the news was hard to bear. Germany had strong-armed her beloved Austria into agreeing to annexation, and now her homeland was lost to Nazi rule. Lisi climbed into bed with her and they huddled under the covers together and wept in each other's arms. Europe would soon be at war—Friedl knew it, even if the British prime minister was blind to Hitler's plans.

"You know you'll have to do something," Lisi said to her eventually, stroking her hair in a motherly fashion even though Friedl was the elder of the two. "Ian says they will intern enemy aliens when war comes, and now you are one of them." Lisi was a British citizen married to an influential member of the establishment, so she would be safe. Friedl was a different matter.

Friedl wiped her eyes with the heel of her hand. "Can't you ask Stewart to do something?"

As Kühlenthal had so rightly pointed out back in Portugal, Lisi's brother-in-law was a powerful man, head of the Secret Service. If anyone could protect her, surely he could.

"I'll do my best," said Lisi cautiously. Friedl shifted on the pillow to scan Lisi's face. Was her little sister in awe of Stewart Menzies? Lisi would have died a thousand deaths rather than admit it. She was an extraordinarily beautiful woman. To all outward appearances, she had both brothers wrapped around her little finger. This was the first inkling Friedl had received that perhaps this wasn't entirely the case.

"You might have to offer them something in return." Now Lisi's voice had a small quaver in it, as if she was nervous, and the speech sounded just a little rehearsed. Had Menzies put her up to this?

"Yes?" said Friedl lightly. Her encounter with Kühlenthal in

Estoril came to mind, and her stomach lurched. "Do you mean information? Become a spy?"

That was a little blunt for Lisi. She tensed, and in the dim light from the bedside lamp, Friedl saw her eyes widen a fraction. Lisi pushed the strap of her negligée up over her shoulder in a nervous gesture she'd used as a child. "It might be a good thing to make the offer before they ask," she said. "Show them clearly where your loyalties lie."

And where was that, exactly? Friedl's loathing for the Nazi spymaster and all he stood for notwithstanding, she had not outright refused his proposition back in Estoril. She might be forced to tread a dangerous tightrope if she agreed to spy for the British as well.

The sisters had been speaking in English, a habit into which they'd fallen to avoid dirty looks from Lisi's staff, but now Friedl switched to German. "Will you set up a meeting, then?"

Lisi's face shone with relief. "You'll do it?"

"I'd do pretty much anything to avoid internment," said Friedl frankly. "Wouldn't you? Besides, being a spy should be amusing, don't you think?"

"But what if it's dangerous?" said Lisi, clutching her arm, her eyes wide with alarm.

A tiny thrill speared through Friedl. She didn't consider herself particularly brave. Reckless, perhaps, always seeking that edge of excitement, whether it was in a performance or in a lover. "Oh, I doubt it. These British are such gentlemen, after all, and what trouble can I get into here in England? Please go ahead and set up a rendezvous."

* * *

A full month passed before the meeting came about, and it was not with either Menzies brother, but with another man from one of the intelligence services, Major Maxwell Knight.

An attractive, efficient young woman named Joan Miller, who introduced herself as Major Knight's secretary, came to collect her at noon one day. "You'll call him 'Major Knight' in public, but at the firm, we call him 'M,'" said Joan.

"Oh. I see." This already sounded quite thrillingly cloak-and-dagger.

Joan got behind the wheel and Friedl climbed in next to her. "I expect you're wondering what you've let yourself in for," said Joan, as she pulled away from the curb. "Don't worry; you'll find the major charming."

Joan transitioned smoothly into a tactful and subtle interrogation that Friedl answered frankly enough to make Joan chuckle several times—although what precisely Joan found so amusing, Friedl wasn't entirely sure. Friedl refrained from mentioning Kühlenthal, of course, and steered the conversation onto less serious but more amusing topics than her contacts in Nazi high command.

"You have had a very interesting love life," Joan commented at the end of these confidences. She glanced at Friedl. "I suppose it's no wonder."

"Yes," said Friedl on a sigh. "I am always in love but it rarely amounts to anything." She observed Joan, who was dark and trim and possessed oodles of what the society girls called "S.A.," or "sex appeal," though perhaps her allure was more subtle than Friedl's. "What about you?"

Joan smiled with determined cheer. "I'm afraid it's just the one man for me."

Friedl detected an edge of sorrow to this statement. "He doesn't return your feelings?"

Joan's smile went awry. "Married, I'm afraid."

"Ah."

"Here we are," said Joan as they turned into Whitehall Court, before Friedl could inquire further. "This is the Authors' Club," she added, as they drew up outside a handsome building. "It has a colorful history."

She pulled in and handed the keys to an official-looking in-dividual wearing a dove-gray suit. As she led the way around to a short staircase, Joan went on to explain about all the famous literary luminaries who had been members of the club, including Oscar Wilde and Sir Arthur Conan Doyle.

Friedl listened with only half an ear. She was thinking hard, planning what to say. She needed to be unequivocal in her alle-giance to Britain, but not too eager to pursue a career in intelli-gence. Lisi had told her that those who yearned desperately to be spies were rarely recruited. Kühlenthal had said much the same.

Well, Friedl knew how to play hard to get.

They reached a small lobby, and Friedl repressed a shudder. What on earth was there to like about this mausoleum? Every-thing looked very old and a little shabby: worn furniture draped with antimacassars, faded rugs, and occasional tables covered with knickknacks and lamps with fringed shades. Shelves of leather-bound books lined one wall, and a series of portraits of old-fashioned-looking men, some of them autographed, were scattered throughout—no doubt the more venerated members of the club. One rather expected to find Sherlock Holmes himself sitting in one of the armchairs, chewing the stem of his meerschaum pipe.

When she mentioned as much to her companion, Joan chuckled. "I don't think the place has been refurbished since it opened in 1891." She lowered her voice to a whisper. "The food is quite appalling, too, always served cold. But you won't mind that, I daresay."

This was true. Friedl rarely ate a midday meal. Right now, she was certainly too nervous to swallow a bite.

She peered around curiously. To her left, down a hallway, was a closed door with a sign on it that read: "Wait for the Stroke." The stroke of what? she wondered. A clock? A pen? It was the Authors' Club, after all.

But just as she was about to inquire of Joan, an imposing man entered the lobby from the other direction.

"Ah. There you are, Miss Miller. And Miss Stöttinger. How do you do?" He shook hands with Friedl, his grip pleasantly firm, his dark eyes holding an expression of smiling sympathy, which took Friedl by surprise. She had not expected to meet with any kind of understanding from this British spymaster.

Friedl surveyed Major Maxwell Knight, known to his colleagues as "M." So this was the man who held her fate in his hands. At least, this was one of them. Kühlenthal's face rose briefly to mind but she banished it.

Major Knight certainly possessed a warm, masculine vigor the dandified Kühlenthal lacked. Trim and fit looking, the major

wore his expensively tailored dark suit well. His hair was ruth-
lessly parted in the middle, winging backward with a slight wave
to it, paired with a short back and sides that made his ears appear
rather large and sweetly vulnerable. The rest of him was quite
formidable, including a very big nose, a feature that both dominated and enhanced his face, balanced as it was by thick, black
eyebrows.

It was lunch time and the club seemed well-attended at that
hour. Major Knight ushered Friedl and Joan to a table in the corner of the dining room. When they were seated, he ordered for
them without glancing at the menu.

Friedl said, "I am intrigued, Major, at your choice of club. Are
you a writer yourself?"

"I dabble," he said, with a faint, almost regretful smile, and
touched a napkin to his lips.

Joan lightly touched Knight's forearm. "The major is being
modest." She would have continued, but Knight deftly steered
the conversation away from his literary efforts, whatever they
might have been. Friedl was grateful. She rarely opened a book
if she could help it. Real life was so much more interesting. In
her experience, books tended to be dull, and talking about books
even duller.

After the meal, Joan Miller discreetly disappeared, but Friedl
scarcely noticed her departure. She was focused on the major.

He was intelligent and amusing, and he knew an enormous
amount about wildlife, which seemed an incongruous hobby
for a spy. He had even at one time owned a pet bear called Bes-
sie, which he used to take for walks around London. Knight was

attractive—the nose did not detract from his charms at all—and he had a voice that would melt a glacier. Deep and rich and mellifluous, it was the voice of a mesmerist, and Friedl wondered if that was a tool of his trade. With that voice, surely, he could persuade anyone to do almost anything. *Ach du lieber*, she could listen to him all night. She'd very much *like* to listen to him all night . . .

However, in the short exchanges between Knight and Miller before the latter's departure, Friedl had sensed a marked degree of intimacy, and a watchful quality to Joan's countenance that spoke of possessiveness. Trust Friedl to know a romance when she saw one. Well, she didn't poach on another woman's territory—at least, not when she liked the woman in question. With a regretful inner sigh, Friedl let the vision of taking Knight as a lover fade away.

"You have traveled extensively," M observed after an exchange of anecdotes about the kinds of hospitality one met in different European cities. His gentle gaze betrayed nothing more than faint interest, but she was aware that now they'd got down to the business of the day.

Well, she had nothing to hide—she hadn't agreed to do anything specific for Kühlenthal, after all. "I have lived all over Europe."

"Born in Austria . . . Your late father a card-carrying member of the Nazi Party . . . Brother the same . . ." The pause was suggestive.

"As is almost everyone in Austria these days," Friedl pointed out coolly. Did he think she was one of them?

M's gaze became distant, his fingertips steepled together. "Spain . . . France . . . Before that, *Palestine* . . ."

She shrugged. "I married an Orthodox Jew. We saw how things were in Germany, and in Austria, too. We got out." A great many others had not been so lucky. The knowledge was like a lead weight in her chest.

"And your husband? Where is he?"

"Ex-husband," she corrected. Carefully divesting her voice of emotion, she said, "I imagine he is still in Palestine."

"I see." There was a long pause. She didn't fill it. Then he continued. "Last stop, Portugal." He said it as if he were mentally flicking through her passport. Was there a file on her somewhere? She supposed there must be.

Something in M's thoughtful gaze told her he knew everything about her—even the things that weren't recorded anywhere on paper. Kühlenthal's approach, his threats, his plans for her. All of it.

She smiled in a bid to ease the tension. "That's right. I sang at a nightclub in Estoril for a while, stayed at the Hotel Palàcio."

M relaxed back in his chair and took out his cigarette case. Opening it, he offered it to her, and she accepted one of the long, hand-rolled cigarettes with alacrity. Ordinarily she avoided smoking. It wasn't good for the vocal cords. But she wasn't in England to continue her profession as an entertainer; Lisi was trying very hard to put her own past behind her and had begged Friedl to do the same.

He lit her cigarette for her, and she drew on it greedily, but instead of calming her, the hit of nicotine amplified her anxiety. Her nerves were like plucked wires, the face of her German would-be handler rising up before her mind's eye, an arrogant, brilliantined specter at the banquet.

She must have hidden her sudden tension well; something about the silence turned companionable. M gestured with his cigarette. "Your sister is holding a house party down at Worplesdon this weekend. I'd like you to go. See what you can find out."

Find out? About what? she might have asked, fluttering her eyelashes for good measure, but there was little point in such disingenuousness when dealing with a man with M's perceptive gaze. "Anything in particular you had in mind?" she asked instead. "Anyone?"

"There is an element in England sympathetic to the Nazi cause. Several elements, in fact." He waved a hand, trailing smoke. "The Right Party, for example . . . Mosley's black shirts . . . The National Socialist League . . . White Russians." The major eyed her speculatively, then tapped ash from his cigarette. "You are close to your sister, are you not? Then you're aware of her recent, er, history?"

Cautiously, she nodded. Lisi had worked at the London Casino, posing seemingly nude in a full-length flesh-toned body stocking. Venus in the half-shell. Regulations had prohibited Lisi from moving—that was a different kind of show.

Lisi's beauty had attracted Ian Menzies, a wealthy member of the establishment. They had married, and now Lisi hosted lavish parties at Dassett, her mother-in-law's house near the unpronounceable Worplesdon in Surrey, to which, of course, Friedl had been invited on many occasions.

M flicked ash from his cigarette. "Your sister will fill you in on who's who. I'll leave the targets to your discretion, see how you do."

Friedl hesitated. She hardly liked to mention it, but the nest egg she'd brought with her to London wouldn't get her very far if she had to work for free.

She licked her lips. "Ah. And . . . If one might be so bold as to inquire . . . Expenses?"

The corners of M's eyes crinkled, as if he found her request amusing. "If you come through this first test, we'll set you up in a tidy little flat somewhere. As for spending money—you'll need a bit of that, of course. I'm sure some arrangement can be made." His gaze traveled over her, not in a lascivious way, but more with the critical assessment of a professional. She became conscious of the flattering cut of her hunter-green suit, the bright scarlet she'd painted her lips. "After all," he said, "you'll need to keep up appearances if you wish to run with that set."

Knight drew heavily on his cigarette, blew smoke out of his nostrils. "You will need to give up your passport and your Austrian citizenship."

Friedl swallowed. "Is that strictly necessary?"

"I'm afraid so," said M. "You'll revert to your maiden name on your passport and your nationality will be listed as German. We will, of course, omit any reference to your visits to Palestine, as well as the fact you married a Jew. There must be no question in the minds of these pro-fascists about where your loyalties lie."

She thought of the "J" that was stamped on her passport. She'd hated that Nazis saw fit to brand people that way, but at the same time, somehow she felt it wasn't right to have the Jewish designation so easily expunged. The reversion to single status was less problematic. She'd been so unhappy with her husband and the restrictions his sober way of life imposed upon her, the idea of reverting legally to Fredericka Stöttinger held strong appeal. And then there was the idea of giving up her Austrian citizenship in favor of Germany. She never wanted to see either country ever again.

M had already moved on. "In the meantime," he said, "we need to get you a job."

She blinked. "But I thought *this* was to be my job. Spying, I mean."

"It is, it is," said M in a soothing tone. "But you also need an ostensible occupation. What we call a cover."

Friedl didn't like the sound of this. "What sort of occupation?"

"Hmm." His heavy brows drew together. "You were a stenographer in Vienna, I believe?"

Ah, she did not want to go back to that dreary life. But then, the alternative was even less appealing, so she made herself smile brightly. "I'm a bit out of practice, but yes."

Perhaps sensing her deep reluctance, M smiled. "All right. What about posing as a mannequin?" When she frowned, he added hurriedly, "A very high-class one, of course. Top drawer."

"No, I don't want to do that." Mannequins were considered by the British to be on the shady side of respectable, much the same as actresses when it came to morals, and she'd promised Lisi she'd behave.

"No? Ah." He cocked his head. "Well, perhaps I have something else that might suit you." He paused. "I've had an inquiry from the author Dennis Wheatley—heard of him? No?"

Friedl shook her head.

"He's a novelist, writes very popular books. Thrillers, adventures, that sort of thing. Needs some background on the Nazis for his current book. And perhaps you might do some secretarial work for him, as well."

That didn't sound too frightful. She liked it better than the mannequin idea.

M jotted something down on the back of his card. "That's his address. Go around tomorrow afternoon at four. I'll tell him to expect you."

Excitement rose in her chest. No internment for Friedl! She was still wrestling with the expectations of the German spymaster, spending every minute of every day on tenterhooks, fearing that some Nazi spy might make contact and put an end to her freedom and muddy the clear waters of her conscience. That fear wouldn't diminish now that she was working for M—if anything, it would grow exponentially—but at least she could feel fairly confident she wouldn't be interned as an enemy alien once war came. Right now, that seemed a worse fate than the prospect of being a double agent. "Then I have the job?"

M puffed on his cigarette, his expression noncommittal. Again, he said, "Let's see how you do."

"I'll be very good at this, *liebling*. You'll see," Friedl promised. She was excellent at the art of conversation, and even better at getting people to confide their secrets in her. This assignment suited her perfectly. She would go out tonight, celebrate with champagne and dancing, and perhaps a nice warm man in her bed.

"Oh, and by the way," said M, as she was turning over in her mind which of her current beaux might be free to escort her at such short notice. "The first thing I would like you to do is to visit the German embassy."

Beneath the table, Friedl's hand clenched into a fist. *"Bitte?"* He wanted her to walk straight into the lion's den?

M smiled faintly and she inwardly berated herself for having betrayed her consternation. Could he possibly guess the true cause? What if her visit became the catalyst for Hitler's spies at the embassy to activate her as an agent?

"No need to be alarmed." M's voice was as deep and soothing as the caress of a mink glove. "It is a mere courtesy call to congratulate them on the Anschluss, show your colors as a staunch supporter of the Third Reich. Nothing more."

She tried to swallow but her throat was dry. She had heard of people disappearing into embassies and never coming out again. And could she possibly bring herself to applaud the thing that had brought her more anguish even than the dissolution of her marriage? But she understood: M wanted her to establish credentials with the Germans so that it would be easier to infiltrate those groups who were working against British interests. It was all part of the game of deception that she'd naïvely been so eager—no, *thrilled*—to undertake.

"Of course," she managed to say. "I shall make it convincing, don't worry."

But as she left the Authors' Club that afternoon, Friedl felt like a child huddled under the covers in the blackest of nights, with monsters under the bed and the walls closing in.

CHAPTER FOUR

London, England
September 1940

Paddy

*P*addy hated nursing. That was a sentiment she would never, ever utter aloud because there was a war on, and one must do one's bit without complaint. But still, she hated it. Having joined too late for anyone to train her properly, or teach her anything at all, really, she was basically a dogsbody around the hospital. The menial tasks, the lack of responsibility, the total absence of mental challenge grated on her. She would stick it out because of course she would, but she couldn't help envying Jean Leslie for finding more interesting work at the War Office.

She wasn't sure precisely what her friend did and it was not the done thing to inquire, but Jean seemed to look forward to work with eager anticipation, whereas Paddy grimly forced herself to toil at the hospital, hour after hour, day after day.

This evening, however, they would both forget their work and the war. They had arranged to dance the night away at some club or other with a group of Jean's friends. Paddy's suggestion that they invite a couple of nice young men to escort them was met with kindly scorn by Jean. "Too dull, darling! Let's go out in a group. It will be more fun."

Paddy had an inkling that Jean had been running with a fast crowd lately, but she agreed because, why not? She had to admit she was curious. She'd lived her own life in Paris, by and large, and she rather missed the days she'd spent far away from parental scrutiny. Oh, there had been supervision, of course. She was billeted in Paris with a dear friend of her mother's, but Tante Véronique had deemed Paddy a sensible sort, well able to take care of herself, and generally let her go her own way. Whatever trouble Jean might get them into, Paddy deemed herself perfectly able to handle.

The night began well. Paddy had managed to get away from the hospital on time for once and Jean had arrived at Paddy's house in the Boltons to get ready only a little later than predicted.

"Are you leaving for Dorchester in the morning?" said Paddy. Jean's mother had moved out of London and rented a house on the Thames.

"Oh, yes. Mummy has a luncheon party on tomorrow and I absolutely must be there." Jean pulled a face. "I'll have to be up at the crack of dawn to get back in time." She searched among her things and came up triumphant. "Here it is!"

She was holding a packet of powdered gravy mix, which wasn't going to grace anyone's roast dinner. Feeling a little ashamed of the very real silk stockings she had slipped on tonight, Paddy watched as Jean mixed a little of the powder with water, then carefully applied the resulting beige-colored stain evenly to each leg. "There!" said Jean proudly. "You wouldn't know the difference, would you? Certainly not in the dark."

They walked to the Ritz and each ordered a champagne cocktail at the bar. By the time they'd finished their drinks, a crowd of Jean's friends had gathered, among them a couple of people Paddy thought looked vaguely famous. Or notorious, perhaps. It was difficult to decide which.

One, she did recognize: the young poet Dylan Thomas, who was making quite a name for himself. He certainly looked the part, handsome as any of the doomed Romantic poets who had fired Paddy's imagination in her teens, with soulful brown eyes and tawny hair tumbling over his brow in thick, curly abundance.

"Darling!" Jean greeted Thomas with a kiss on each cheek. "Where's MJ tonight? I thought she was coming with you."

Paddy had heard much from Jean about Marie-Jaqueline Lancaster and her set. Rather a wild bunch if the rumors were true.

"That she did, my lovely Jean," he replied in his rich, deep voice, "but she was turned away at the door for wearing Lucian Freud's sailor's suit. Pity," he added, nodding down at his drink as if it would agree with him. "She looked absolutely smashing. I think she went off to find somewhere that would let her in."

A slight, pale, dark-haired man, with the heaviest, blackest, most perfectly arched eyebrows set above melancholy deep-set brown eyes, came up to them. "Oh, hello, Brian!" Jean jumped up. "Paddy, this is Brian Howard. Brian, I'd like you to meet my friend, Paddy Bennett. We escaped from France together, flee-ing from the Hun. It was terribly thrilling."

"Ah, any friend of little Jean's . . ." Howard leaned in and said in a stage whisper to Paddy, "Jean and I escaped from *jail* to-gether, you know."

"Brian!" Jean reared back as if he'd slapped her, and Brian gave a sour, sneering sort of smile. Paddy tilted her head and looked back and forth between them. What was this about?

Howard waved a hand. "Don't worry, pet. I'm not going to spill any state secrets." Again, he leaned in to Paddy, saying ear-nestly, "There's a war on, you know." He pursed his lips. "D'you know what they call Jean and the rest of the little girls in the sec-retarial pool at the firm? The beavers. Isn't that just the limit?"

Jean frowned, puzzled. "But what's wrong with that? Person-ally, I take it as a compliment."

"I'm sure you do, pet." Brian's eyes danced madly above the rim of his glass as he drained his drink in one gulp.

Paddy wasn't sure why this amused Brian so much. She sus-pected a double entendre that she'd prefer wasn't explained to her and decided it was best to ignore him.

Flustered, Jean turned to Paddy for support. "But you know, they call us that because we're eager beavers. We girls work hard and we're keen as mustard." She threw Brian a darkling look. "Unlike *some* people I could mention."

Brian gave a little wriggle of feigned delight. "And I'd bet you're the eager-est beaver of them all."

Paddy wished she could get up and leave without seeming as rude as Brian Howard. What an utterly obnoxious man. He had the reckless, restless air of the spoiled aristocrat and seemed to enjoy needling people in tender places. On top of that, his insufferable smile made Paddy's hand itch to slap it off him. But of course, that was the effect he so clearly desired, so she curbed her temper and changed the subject.

Before she'd uttered a complete sentence, however, Brian interrupted her. "Now, what fine establishment shall we grace with our presence tonight, hmm?" He eyed Paddy and Jean. "I suppose *you* little girls want to go to the Four Hundred Club, do you? Well, off you trot, then. Don't let us stop you."

Paddy shrugged. "I do like the Four Hundred Club, as it happens, but I'm open to new experiences."

"*Are* you, indeed?" Quick as a flash, Howard pulled up a chair and sat beside her, peering into her face as if she were a rare new specimen for his collection. "Then where shall it be?" He tapped his chin with one slender white fingertip. "The Conga? The Music Box? The Nuthouse? Hmm." He shook his head. "No. I think the *Gargoyle Club* for you, my dears."

Somehow they found themselves outside the hotel and getting into a car that Brian had magicked up from thin air, all cramming themselves in together with much laughter and flailing of limbs. They were let out at a place in Soho, and Howard led them around to the back of the building, where they squeezed into a rickety old elevator that was surely too small to accommodate them, but somehow they managed to fit. Paddy was reminded of games of sardines at Christmas time.

They arrived at the top and poured out of the elevator. It was like entering a different world. A Moorish influence pervaded the club; its walls were covered in mosaics created from shards of mirrored glass that reflected the chancy light. The coffered ceiling was covered in what looked to be gold leaf, and wooden lanterns shaped like gargoyles hung here and there.

"There's MJ," called Thomas over the noise of the band. "*Not* in the sailor suit. Pity. And Freud's here, too." He stopped short, then whistled. "Who is *that*?"

The third member of the group seated in one of the booths was a sparkling blonde dressed in a scandalously low-backed dress, whose bare shoulder blades gleamed in the half-light of the club. A band played some old tune and her body swayed along—a subtle sway, true, but it was as if she couldn't help but move to the music.

Paddy's group all piled into another booth, much as they had crammed themselves into the elevator. A few moved off to dance, while Paddy found herself wedged into a corner by the arrival of Guy Burgess, who shoved a glass of whisky into her hand, then turned his back on her and proceeded to ignore her for quite some time. Trapped by his bulk, with no one to talk to, Paddy grimaced at the mirrored glass on the wall next to her. An advantage of the decor was that one might safely check whether one had lipstick on one's teeth.

"Henri Matisse," MJ shouted across the table at Paddy over the din, as she slid into the seat opposite. She waved her hand to indicate their surroundings. "Tennant asked him to decorate the place. Isn't he a genius? There's a painting or two of his here, as well."

As the evening wore on, Paddy accepted several invitations to dance. Wartime had made everyone live in the moment because there might be no tomorrow, but this club seemed to reach for a new level of decadence. She couldn't help but be fascinated by the freedom and the outrageous, reckless air of this set of people.

At one point, Paddy happened to be passing a table of Army officers when Brian Howard lurched toward them, clearly drunk and spoiling for an argument. Oh, dear! Should she intervene? The Army officers looked like hardened men of action, while the willowy Howard would blow over in a gust of wind.

Brian cleared his throat in an obvious attempt to attract their attention. "My dears!"

The officers didn't seem to hear him and went on with their conversation.

"Ahem. My *dears!*"

Now the men looked up, puzzled, perhaps wondering if they were at all acquainted with the odd-looking gentleman who accosted them.

Brian smiled and shook his head. "Members of a rather unsuccessful profession, my dears." Howard wagged a finger playfully at them. "Dunkirky-wirky!"

Fortunately for Howard, the officers looked too astonished to react with the fury this utterly shocking statement ought to have provoked. Britons were still red-raw over their ignominious retreat after the Battle of France.

Paddy, feeling that any intervention on her part would only make matters worse, hurried back to their table to fetch Dylan Thomas. She stopped short before she reached the booth, however, because the poet was engaged in some scandalous behavior of his own. He sat next to MJ, who was turned side-on in the booth with her back to the wall. The poet was holding the heel of MJ's extended leg in his palm and inspecting it closely. As he bent over that shapely long leg, Paddy stared, hardly knowing where to look but unable to tear her gaze away. Was he going to kiss MJ's slender ankle, right here in front of everyone? That was a bit much, wasn't it?

She was aware of the music, a slow, old tune, playing in the background as for several heartbeats, the poet contemplated the leg he was holding, his unruly auburn hair flopping forward over his eyes.

Then he dipped his head, and licked MJ's leg from ankle to knee, repeating the action in time with the music. A strange, hot feeling that might have been revulsion squirmed in Paddy's stomach. MJ, on the other hand, threw back her head and laughed, seeming to enjoy the attention. Then, Paddy realized: Dylan Thomas was licking the gravy stain off MJ's leg. She'd used the same trick to imitate stockings as had Jean.

When Jean came over and asked, "Are you having fun, darling?" Paddy answered quite truthfully and succinctly, "I am, now that I am no longer quite sober." She wouldn't go beyond this pleasantly tipsy state, however. She had standards, and those didn't change no matter what company she found herself keeping.

The rest of the evening passed without major incident—except when Guy Burgess refused to stand for "God Save the King" and nearly got into a fight with the Army officers at the table nearby.

The military men seemed to have reached the upper limits of

their tolerance, so MJ deemed it best to take their party else-where. They took another car, but when Paddy asked politely to be let off at her home in Kensington, MJ said, "No, no! You're all coming home with me." She gave the order to the driver and Paddy thought, why not? She'd probably never see most of these people again, and she wasn't quite ready to end the experience.

As they got out of the car and groped their way to the front door of More House in the pitch-blackness, the air raid sirens wailed out. Searchlights strobed the sky.

"To the cellar!" cried MJ, brandishing a bottle of unidentifi-able liquor she'd swiped from Stephen Tennant, the Gargoyle's owner, as they'd left the club. "Come on!"

She led them through the grand old house like some sort of drunken Pied Piper, and soon they found themselves in a large ballroom that was covered in mattresses like a makeshift dormi-tory. "Grab one of those and bring it with you," she called, haul-ing up her own mattress and leading the way.

"Where's Brian?" asked Jean, when they reached the cellars, where MJ's mother and the staff were already gathered. "Did we lose him?" For some reason, Paddy felt anxious, too. There was something vulnerable, something wounded, about Brian that made one worry about him even when he was at his most ob-noxious.

"Oh, Brian," said Freud. "He'll be wandering the streets, no doubt."

"Death wish," agreed MJ, swigging from her bottle. "Poor old Brian's heart is in—where's Anton at the moment? Austria? Ber-lin?"

The air raid was a bad one. Even from the relative safety beneath MJ's house, they heard the whistle of the bombs, the *ack-ack* of anti-aircraft fire, the explosions that rocked and shook the ground above.

However, the occupants of the cellar at Tite Street refused to show their fear. MJ led the company in a jolly sing-along that couldn't help but lift the spirits, even while the shelling raged overhead.

Dylan Thomas was giving them a stirring rendition of a Welsh folk song when someone clattered down the stairs. Thomas broke off and they all sat up, alert and watching, as Brian burst into the cellar and staggered toward them. "Mayfair. Kensington. Westminster," he cried hoarsely. "They've all been hit."

Paddy's head felt light. She put her hand to her temple. "Please," she muttered. Not her mother. Not their house, their neighbors, friends.

She took a deep breath and let it out. There was no need to panic about things that weren't certain and could not be changed if they were. She put her arm around Jean, who was trembling. Jean's mother was in the country, but of course they knew people all over London. They would be hearing of deaths and casualties among friends and family very soon.

But Paddy refused—utterly *refused*—to let the Germans make her afraid. She forced herself to call out with determined good cheer, "How about another song?"

* * *

The next morning, Paddy took the Tube home and came up out of the station with dread gripping her chest so tightly she could scarcely breathe. She passed several disaster sites, giant piles of bricks and rubble that had been buildings only hours before.

As she turned the corner, St. Mary's came into view. "Ah, no!" She started toward the church, her heart aching at the sight of that dear old building with the glass from its windows blown out, its roof ripped in places like an old, tattered blanket. Still, it could have been worse.

Had her own house been hit? St. Mary's was close by. Before she knew it, Paddy was running, sprinting toward home in the previous night's dancing pumps. When she finally got to the eye-shaped block of Victorian mansions where she lived, she stopped, letting out a ragged sigh of relief. Their street had been spared the blast that had damaged the church. Hands on her thighs, bent over, and panting, Paddy paused a moment to collect herself. Heart still pounding, she let herself into Number 12.

The tired but smiling face of their housekeeper reassured her. "Oh, thank goodness, Mrs. Rivers!" said Paddy, gripping the housekeeper's hands. "Is Mother all right? Is everyone?"

"Mrs. Bennett has gone to St. Mary's to see what's to be done," said Mrs. Rivers. "Everyone's well. In this household, at least."

The housekeeper's mouth was tightly closed and turned down at the corners, a clear indication of suppressed feeling. Cautiously, Paddy asked, "Is something else troubling you, Mrs. Rivers?"

The other woman looked as if she might burst if she didn't speak. "I told Madam!" she blurted out. "I told her she must shut up the house and remove to the country, but she won't leave London."

"I should rather think not," said Paddy. Her family didn't skulk away from a fight, leaving others to stick it out. Besides, Edith was heavily engaged in supporting the war effort, running committees, arranging for aid to the countless citizens rendered homeless by German bombs.

Delicately, because Paddy knew the housekeeper would rather stick pins in her eyes than leave the family, she said, "Do you wish to remove from London, Mrs. Rivers? Because I'm sure we could arrange a leave of absence, or . . ." She trailed off, positive that they could not possibly do without the housekeeper, not with Paddy working such long hours and her mother scarcely less occupied.

"The idea!" Nostrils flaring, the housekeeper drew herself up to her full, commanding height. She towered over Paddy's diminutive form, and Paddy might have smiled at the comical picture they must present if the subject of their discussion hadn't been so serious. "I'm not going anywhere, Miss Paddy, and that's flat."

"Well, that's all right then," said Paddy. "We stay."

"Why don't you try to persuade Madam to move to the Dorchester?" Mrs. Rivers persisted. "They say it's the safest place. Or Claridge's? You know she loves it there."

"But then what about you and the rest of the staff?" said Paddy. "Oh, we couldn't. No, Mother's right. We'll stay right here, at the Boltons, where we belong. Göring and his cursed Luftwaffe are not going to scare us off."

CHAPTER FIVE

London, England
October 1940

Paddy

Fresh from a twelve-hour nursing shift, Paddy went to the hospital cloakroom to collect her hat, coat, and purse. She was supposed to have had the night off—it was the evening of her birthday dance, after all. Mother would be upset if she was late to her own party—but what could one do? There was a war on.

"Bennett!" The strident tones ripped across the cloakroom. Sister Bromley fixed Paddy with a narrowed gaze. "Do not even think of leaving before you've emptied those bedpans."

Paddy suppressed a sigh. Trainee nurses were always given the scut work on the ward—rolling bandages, sorting soiled laundry, and so on—but Sister Bromley seemed to save the absolute worst jobs just for Paddy.

Blame it on the plum in her mouth. The other girls sniggered that Paddy would never stick it out as a nurse, given her la-di-dah background, but she'd shown them. She might not have the right accent, but she was half Yorkshirewoman and half Irish, grit and fire. The part of her that called the bleak north country of England home was grimly determined to persevere—and triumph— even more so because of all the doubters around her. However, it must be said that when Sister Bromley delayed her departure for her birthday dance purely out of spite, Paddy's Irish temper began to gain the upper hand.

She forced herself to smile brightly. "All done, Sister."

Bromley's mouth puckered and her cheeks blew in and out, like a dragon who'd run out of flame. "Then you can get on with changing Mr. Hennessy's dressing, like I asked you to do half an hour ago." She hadn't, but what could Paddy do but obey? She put back her hat, coat, and purse. Mother would be disappointed, but she'd understand. If it wasn't the overtime, it was the trains, and failing that, it was an air raid. There was always something.

Mr. Hennessy was recovering after receiving burns to a particularly sensitive area. Paddy approached the bed, adopting her briskest manner. "I've come to change your dressing, Mr. Hennessy."

He must have been in considerable pain, but he was frisky for all that. "Cor blimey, love. Thought you'd never ask."

Grimly ignoring him, Paddy lifted his hospital gown and set about snipping away the bandages. The wound was mercifully clear of foul matter—unlike Mr. Hennessy's language. Paddy tried to block out both the sight of his semitumescent appendage and the suggestions about what she might do with it while she was down there. Really, the past three months at the hospital had been quite the education, in ways her mother would not approve.

In her severest tone, Paddy said, "Now, now, Mr. Hennessy. That's *quite* enough of that." But she re-dressed the wound with a gentleness that she considered showed truly heroic restraint.

"Now that you've finished that," said Sister Bromley, "you can give Mr. Richardson his enema."

Paddy gritted her teeth.

* * *

The hour-long train ride into London seemed to take forever, but at least they weren't delayed along the way. Paddy took a taxi from the station to Claridge's Hotel and arrived about an hour and a half late.

Claridge's was an impressive structure built from a fine-grained red Mansfield sandstone, and with its white pillars and window frames, it always reminded her of the iced ginger biscuits Cook used to make. Inside, the decor dazzled—gleaming glass and brushed steel, geometrical patterns and sleek, curving lines. From the black-and-white marble floor to the smooth art deco arches, to the glittering chandeliers, everything was utterly modern and perfectly chic.

"Evening, Saunders," Paddy said to the porter as he held the door open for her to pass through.

"Good evening, Miss Bennett." He touched his top hat with the tip of a gloved finger. "And may I say, many happy returns on your birthday."

"Thank you." Paddy had been born at Claridge's. Her pregnant mother, alone in London while her husband was still in Germany negotiating the Great War peace, deemed the nursing home in which she was to deliver her first child too uncomfortable, and had removed to a suite at the hotel for Paddy's birth.

As their housekeeper had intimated, it might have been safest to remove once more to the exclusive hotel to see out the rest of the war. Paddy's father, Colonel Joe Bennett, was off sitting on the Control Commission in Africa, so two women fending for themselves might be forgiven the indulgence.

However, stubbornness was a characteristic both Edith and Paddy shared, and they utterly refused to leave their home. This evening was a special occasion, though, so they had taken a suite of rooms in the hotel for the night.

The Claridge's staff could have no recollection of the squalling infant who entered their domain in the autumn of 1921, but they pretended they did, and they greeted Paddy with the affection of old retainers. They even seemed excited about the dance her mother was giving for Paddy's birthday tonight.

"Evening, Miss Paddy," said old Mr. Franks as he opened first the door and then the metal grille of the elevator for her to step inside. "Straight to the party, or will you change first?"

"I rather think change, don't you, Mr. Franks?" said Paddy with a twinkle in her eye. "Mother would have a fit if I appeared at her party in this get-up." The white nurse's uniform beneath her coat had been neatly starched and pressed at the beginning of her shift but was now sadly stained and wilted.

"Right you are, then, Miss." Franks hauled the grille closed and took them up to her mother's floor. She let herself into the room and dashed for the washbasin.

Jean Leslie appeared in the doorway to Paddy's bedroom, a drink in hand. "There you are! I've been waiting ages, Paddy. Where've you been?"

"Sorry! You should have gone down without me." Paddy kicked off her shoes.

"Oh, I don't mind at all. But Brian's picking me up later. We're off to the Café de Paris if you'd like to come."

Paddy wasn't overly enamored of the occasionally witty and often poisonous Brian Howard, but she merely said, "Sounds tempting, but I can't leave Ma in the lurch, you know. Another time." Unlike Jean's crowd, she wasn't the sort of person who left in the middle of her own party. It was poor enough form to arrive late.

She pulled on a gown of deep indigo that complimented her blue eyes and dark hair.

"Paris, I presume," said Jean, chin in hand.

"Worth," said Paddy, quickly fixing her hair. She leaned in to apply lipstick in a daring shade of red.

"Well, you look marvy, darling. Too, too marvy for words."

Paddy eyed her friend with misgiving. As evidenced that night at the Gargoyle Club, Jean had taken up with a wild set of people—the Bright Young Things, everyone used to call them, though perhaps the years had dimmed their luster as well as their youth by now. And just look at what a mess that Diana Mitford had made, getting into bed with Hitler and Oswald Mosley's fascist black shirts, clapped up in Holloway for her convictions.

However, tonight was not an occasion for worrying about the company Jean kept. Paddy was a little more concerned about the company her mother had invited this evening. Edith had taken charge of the guest list, and Paddy darkly suspected a ruse of some sort. Ever since she'd returned from Paris, her mother had been introducing her to one "nice young man" or other, but Paddy hadn't paid much attention. They were all so very young and not very interesting. Not their fault, exactly, but she felt decades older than these fresh-faced youths.

She wasn't sure she wanted to give her heart to a man in the armed services in any case. That could go so tragically wrong. Then again, any of them could be dead at any time, the way the dratted Luftwaffe pummeled London night after night. She hoped there wouldn't be an air raid to spoil the party this evening.

They entered Claridge's ballroom, and it was like stepping into a socialite's idea of heaven. Despite the call for every available garden to be dug up for produce, Claridge's had managed to source flowers from somewhere—lilies and stephanotis, all in white. The chandeliers twinkled and the silver gleamed and the guests drank fine wine from the hotel's apparently bottomless cellars. If not for the uniforms milling about, one would scarcely know there was a war on at all.

"There you are! I was starting to worry." Edith Bennett swooped on Paddy the minute she entered Claridge's ballroom. "Oh, hello, dear," she added to Jean. "You'll find your set over by the dance floor." With a smile and nod of polite dismissal to Jean, her mother took Paddy's hand. "Darling, do come along. There's someone I want you to meet."

Paddy winked at Jean in apology and allowed herself to be dragged away. "Sorry I'm late. The dragon kept me emptying bedpans."

"Well, now, that's why I want to introduce you to Admiral Godfrey," said her mother. "He's looking for a secretary. I told him you're just the girl he needs."

"An admiral?" Paddy followed her mother. "Gosh, that's flying high, isn't it?"

"Rear admiral," said Edith, though what difference that made, Paddy didn't know. "Far more interesting than nursing, and you don't have to get your hands dirty, either. Emptying bedpans, indeed."

"We all have to do our bit," said Paddy automatically, catching sight of two tall men in full Navy uniform. Both looked intimidatingly distinguished. One, a great, burly older man—fair and handsome in his way—who must be the admiral. But it was the younger officer who caught and held Paddy's attention. Tall and lean, dark hair, hooded blue eyes, long nose. She'd seen him before . . .

"Bordeaux!" she exclaimed, before her mother had the chance to make the introductions. "Fancy meeting you here."

The admiral's eyebrows shot up. He glanced from Paddy to his subordinate.

"Admiral Godfrey, I'd like you to meet my daughter, Victoire Bennett," said Edith.

"And this is Commander Ian Fleming," said Godfrey, glancing between Paddy and the younger officer. "But I take it you've met?"

"Not formally," answered Fleming, drawing out a silver cigarette case from his pocket.

"Bordeaux, eh?" said Godfrey, cocking an eyebrow at Paddy. "Ah, of course. You must have been one of the evacuees."

"That's right," said Paddy. "I'm surprised Commander Fleming remembers me."

"Of course I remember. Your effrontery was only matched by your efficiency." He turned to Godfrey. "Tell her she's hired."

The admiral's eyes lit with amusement. "Sounds like the two of you will get on splendidly."

They spoke for some time about France and Paddy's education there before returning to the subject of her employment with the Admiralty. Paddy was immensely impressed with Admiral Godfrey. Here was a man who asked intelligent questions and listened to the responses, made incisive remarks, and who even seemed to possess a sense of humor beneath that stern facade. The idea of working for him held strong appeal.

Guilt crept over her at the thought. She'd been determined to stick it out with nursing, particularly as it was so unpleasant. When she said as much, the admiral was silent for a moment, before saying, "Nursing is important work, of course. But I don't know of anything more valuable than the work you'll do for us."

And that was that. No more bedpans for Paddy. Without fuss or fanfare—or any training to speak of, Paddy started at the Admiralty the following week.

CHAPTER SIX

London, England
October 1940

Paddy

*P*addy left home full of nervous anticipation on her first day at the Admiralty. Hard to know what to expect, in view of the terse explanation of her duties Godfrey had given her. She took the Tube to Charing Cross, then headed along the Mall and on through Admiralty Arch.

Despite the ravages of the Blitz, the old Admiralty building was still an impressive sight, with its turrets and cupolas and walls of red brick and Portland stone. The mixture of styles, which Paddy recognized from her architectural studies, seemed to be English Baroque and French Grand Siècle. Sandbags were stacked high against every wall and a forest of barrage balloons hovered overhead, but the building remained an impressive edifice.

She'd been told to enter via the door behind the statue of Captain Cook that graced the Mall. It was a cold autumn morning, and her breath clouded in front of her as she passed the monument to the famous explorer. Once inside, the air was scarcely warmer, and her voice echoed in the drafty, utilitarian hall as she stated her name and business and showed her papers at the reception desk. She hoped her place of work would be a bit more cheerful than this space.

After a considerable wait, a young man in uniform came to collect her, introducing himself as Lieutenant Grant. "You're in Room Thirty-Nine," he informed her as they went down the cavernous corridor, which was rather less impressive than the exterior of the building and reminded her very much of a local town hall. On the tiled floors, tiny mosaics depicted anchors with lettering on them, but she couldn't make out the details as they moved swiftly along.

The young lieutenant seemed the chatty type. "You'll be working for seven of us, I'm afraid," he said. "Busy office, lots of juggling deadlines. Fleming's work takes priority, of course. At least, he's the most punishing of them if you don't get his done immediately. And he has the ear of the big man, so he's not one to cross."

"The commander doesn't seem to suffer fools," she agreed. "But then, neither do I. We should get along swimmingly."

Grant gave a sort of sniggering snort. "Not too well, I hope!"

Paddy had several "looks"—a selection of which she had inherited from her mother. The look she gave this young fellow now wasn't the Grade A Look, employed to shrivel a man where he stood. It was a widening of the eyes, and a lift of the brow and the slightest jerk of the chin. It said, *Can I have heard you correctly? Did you actually just speak to me like that?* And it usually worked on anyone with the least sensitivity.

The lieutenant reddened but he didn't retreat entirely from his position. As if duty-bound, he furrowed his brow and added, "That's to say, whatever you do, Miss Bennett, don't fall in love with Commander Fleming. He's fatally attractive to women, but it will only mean trouble if you do."

Ha! No chance of that. "I can safely promise you I won't." She wasn't the kind of girl to fall for a handsome face and an air of command. If she had wondered sometimes about the officer who had sorted out everything with such arrogant and ruthless efficiency back in Bordeaux, it was only with a detached, professional interest.

They came to a sort of transept, an intersection where a short corridor crossed the main hall. To her left was a large room filled with men in uniform coming and going and pile upon pile of files, papers, boxes, and trays. Amid the chaos, she noticed a tea-making kit: kettles, milk bottles, cups. She would be spending quite a bit of time in that room, she imagined. But that wasn't where Grant ushered her.

"Here we are," said the lieutenant, flinging open another door. "Directorate of Naval Intelligence. Room Thirty-Nine."

Paddy balked at such a dramatic entrance—surely everyone would stare—but she needn't have worried. No one so much as glanced at them. The occupants of Room 39 were too busy to bother about her.

Relieved, Paddy took her time to look around. A map of the

world the size of an entire wall dominated the space, spiked with a variety of pins marking the oceans at various points. She would need to learn what it all meant. There were desks everywhere, phones ringing, papers shuffling, a low hum of masculine conversation. An ugly black marble fireplace boasted a real coal fire and iron radiators were scattered throughout, but most of the heat seemed to dissipate into the high ceiling. Sitting by a window nearest a rather important-looking green baize-covered door was Commander Fleming. An island of concentrated calm amid the chaos, he was annotating a typewritten page with bold, precise strokes of his pen.

"Impressive, eh?" said her guide, and it took a moment for Paddy to realize he thought she was contemplating the three massive windows opposite, rather than the very man he had warned her about. With a wave of the hand, the lieutenant indicated the window on the right. "Foreign Office through there. That's St. James's Park lake, of course. To the left, we have the Horse Guards, the Treasury, and the Old Admiralty. Center, the garden of Number Ten."

It was hard not to feel that in working in Room 39, Paddy was as close as she might ever come to the seat of British power. Such a different prospect from working at the hospital, where the gaze turned inward, to the shattering effects of Nazi bombs on the human body. As a nurse, she had felt useful yet at the same time utterly helpless in the face of the stream of casualties that came in each night of the Blitz, her small, unskilled efforts akin to shoveling sand in the desert with a teaspoon. Hard, honest work though it was, she never had and never could make much of a dent in all that must be done.

Here, at the Directorate of Naval Intelligence, might she play a very small part in great and momentous events? Even if her remit was typing and filing, Paddy meant to learn as much and be as useful as she possibly could.

"Now, Miss Bennett, you're over here." Grant indicated the desk beside Fleming's. It boasted a typewriter, pad and pencil, and four trays overflowing with papers, maps, and reports. There was yet another stack of papers and dockets on the floor beside her chair. She needed to sort that lot immediately. How long had it been since her predecessor left? Or had that girl spent her time mooning over Fleming rather than attending to her duties? Perhaps that was why this young fellow had given her the warning.

"'Scuse me." Someone nudged her aside, strode across to the desk that was now hers, and dumped another pile of dockets on her chair.

Paddy tried not to appear daunted by the work that continued to stack up even as she stood there. She indicated the heavy baize-covered door in the corner of the room near Fleming. "And is that . . . ?"

"Right. Admiral Godfrey's office. Usually he summons staff with a buzzer. One buzz for Fleming, two for one of us, and so on. Come. I'll introduce you." Grant lowered his voice. "He can be a bit abrupt, you know, but stand your ground and you'll do well."

Paddy didn't mind abruptness. In fact, she appreciated men who didn't waste time explaining things that she grasped perfectly well the first time.

"Ah! Miss Bennett," said the rear admiral when Grant had introduced her. "Come in, will you?" He nodded to her companion. "Thank you, Grant. Shut the door on your way out."

Paddy bit back a smile at the lieutenant's chagrin at being so summarily dismissed. She gave him a nod in thanks as he left.

The rear admiral's lair was like any study you might find in a gentleman's house, with its heavy mahogany furniture and leather-tooled books, but the walls were covered with charts and maps.

Paddy advanced into the room but remained standing. She wondered if she ought to salute but she was a civilian, so she rather thought not.

"Now, Miss Bennett," said Godfrey in his clipped no-nonsense manner. "You've signed off on the *Official Secrets Act*?"

"Yes, sir."

"So you know that nothing—not even the most insignificant detail of your work here—can be divulged to anyone. Not to family or boyfriends, not even to husbands." He raised his eyebrows. "You don't have any of *them* lying around the place, do you?"

"No, sir." Like any of the debutantes she knew, she had several boyfriends on a bit of a rota, young men who might be counted on to escort her to dinner or parties and, later, to the clubs. All terribly respectable—at least, Mother approved of their families—and none would ever dream of crossing the line. "No one serious." No one to whom she'd be tempted to spill state secrets, anyway.

"No? Good. Well, I expect Fleming will occupy as much of your time and capacity as he can, but you will be expected to keep up with the rest. Any problems, come to me."

"Yes, sir." Of course, she would do nothing of the kind, and they both knew it. She banked on the willingness of the men outside the door to show her the ropes. Men loved explaining things, didn't they? One simply had to be patient with them until they realized one's mind was as quick—if not quicker—than theirs.

She hesitated, unsure whether the interview was now at an end.

Godfrey didn't dismiss her, but he bowed his head over some papers. After a discreet interval, she left.

Glad to know where matters stood, Paddy removed the stack of dockets from her chair, plonked them on the floor beside it, then sat down at her desk. Without a glance at Fleming, whose presence radiated some kind of magnetic pull even though he paid her not the slightest attention, she straightened her shoulders and made a start.

Sorting the files and papers that seemed to have piled up between her predecessor's finishing and her beginning would take some time, and more work flowed in constantly, which kept putting her further behind.

It was nearly the end of her first day before Commander Fleming acknowledged Paddy's existence. "Oh, you're here," he said, handing her a stack of memoranda with his corrections all over them. "Good. Type these up, will you, Miss Bennett? I'll need them before you leave tonight."

Paddy didn't allow her smile to falter. "Certainly, sir." She'd completed a short secretarial course a couple of years ago, but she hadn't expected to deal with such a large amount of work in such a short amount of time. She glanced at the clock. It was nearly six. How long would this lot be likely to take her?

Determined to look like she knew what she was doing, Paddy checked the ink ribbon and fed paper into the typewriter carriage. So far, so good. She focused on the first page of the memoranda Fleming had given her and began to type.

Paddy was only half an hour into her task, when out of the corner of her eye she saw Fleming gather his cap and coat and stride out of the room.

At seven, Lieutenant Grant stopped by her desk. "Still here, Miss Bennett? Why don't you leave that till tomorrow and come with us for a drink? We'll toast your first day on the job."

Paddy's smile was perfunctory. She'd just spotted a spelling error in the last page she'd typed so she'd have to do it all over again. Maybe that wasn't strictly necessary but she wanted her first task for the commander to be perfect. "Afraid I can't, sir. But thank you for the offer. Perhaps another time."

Grant jerked his head toward Fleming's empty desk. "He's out with one of his lady loves. Won't be back again tonight, you know."

Much as she would have liked to cap off the day with a drink in the company of her new colleagues, it wasn't in Paddy's nature to shirk a task—particularly when she felt her skills at the task weren't up to par. Besides, Fleming had said she needed to get these done that evening, and he struck her as someone who wouldn't take kindly to an underling disobeying orders. On her first day, at that. "Sorry, sir. I really do have to get on."

As she punched away at those typewriter keys, Paddy could feel her speed beginning to improve. It was all coming back to her now, like riding a bike. Still, by eight o'clock she was only a little over halfway through the pile of documents.

Even at this hour, there were plenty of people about. Room 39 hummed along, lights dim and blackout curtains in place. Doggedly, Paddy kept going, and still Fleming hadn't returned. Her stomach growled and she threw his empty desk a sour look. He was probably eating Dover sole at the Ritz or sipping champagne from his mistress's navel or something, while she was still here, slogging away.

When Paddy finally finished, it was close to ten. Now she wasn't merely irritated—she was irate. Where was Fleming? If he hadn't returned by now, he wasn't likely to do so.

Paddy checked her work and deposited both the marked-up pages and the retyped ones on Fleming's desk with two satisfying *thumps*. The knowledge that if she'd been a decent typist she'd have finished that lot in half the time only maddened her more. Fueled by a stubborn desire to see for herself whether she had just worked late for nothing or whether the commander really had needed this typing done right away, Paddy did not leave the office, but dealt with several piles of dockets with ruthless efficiency. She became so absorbed in her task that another hour passed without her noticing. It was after eleven when the door opened and Commander Fleming strode in. Paddy's jaw literally dropped, her righteous anger deflating like a popped balloon.

Fleming went to his desk and flicked through the memoranda,

signing and initialing each one. "Go home, Miss Bennett," he said, without looking up. "The war will still be here when you get back."

* * *

Over the weeks and months that followed, Paddy became accustomed to the rhythm of the NID and to the eccentric ways of her colleagues and of her superiors in particular. Clearly, Fleming was indispensable as the rear admiral's right-hand man. He was everywhere, coordinating interdepartmental initiatives, smoothing ruffled feathers, delivering bad news with swift diplomacy and driving action and compromise.

He showed a marked lack of deference toward his superior officers, including Godfrey, which the rear admiral seemed to take in stride. "There are only two people you should ever call 'Sir,'" he once told Paddy. "God and the king."

She was scanning a docket containing the minutes of a very dull Joint Intelligence Committee meeting when she heard Ian Fleming on the telephone, speaking around the short cigarette holder in his mouth. "Darling Mu, about last night . . . yes, wasn't it lovely? Shall we again tonight? Good. I'll see you at seven. And don't forget my cigarettes, will you, darling? I'm almost out."

The phone receiver went down. Immediately it was picked up again and he was dialing. "Ann, darling, shall we meet? Lunch at the Carlton Grill? No, not Quo Vadis, I was there last night with Mu. Yes. Yes, I'll see you then, darling. Bye."

Paddy rolled her eyes and sent him a pointed glance, but Fleming went on with his work without an ounce of awareness or shame. She'd learned very quickly after her arrival just what sort of man Ian Fleming was when it came to his dealings with women, and one might as well fling one's garter at the moon as expect him to change his ways.

She hadn't been disappointed—not exactly. She was in Room 39 to work, not to find love. She couldn't help feeling sorry for this "Mu" person, whoever she might be. Buying him cigarettes while he romanced another girl . . . Just how smitten was she? Paddy glanced at Fleming, who was jotting down notes of some kind.

After another half hour, he leaned over to place on her desk a fifty-one-item memorandum covered in comments and corrections. "Retype that, will you, Miss Bennett, and bring it in when you're finished."

"Certainly, sir." Her typing skills had improved markedly since her first day in Room 39. She lowered her eyes to the page, then looked up at Fleming. "The *Trout* Memorandum, sir?"

One corner of his mouth lifted. "We're going to do a spot of fishing."

She watched Fleming saunter into Godfrey's lair, then lowered her gaze to the document he'd handed her. Fleming possessed a brisk, energetic style of prose—direct and to the point. Well, he'd been a journalist at one stage, hadn't he? She seemed to recall her mother mentioning it. Edith had been full of the Flemings and their doings since Paddy had taken the job at the Admiralty.

Scanning the memorandum, Paddy raised her eyebrows and let out a silent whistle. This was by far the most fascinating piece of business she had come across since her arrival. A list of possible operations Naval Intelligence might carry out—each more outlandish and daring than the last—to deceive, misdirect, sabotage, and otherwise confound the Nazis.

Paddy suppressed a snort. *Someone* had clearly grown up on a strict diet of Kipling and Biggles books. Her hand flew to her mouth when she came across one that even Fleming commented was not very nice. The dead body of an airman with pockets full of top-secret dispatches to be dropped off somewhere along the Spanish coast for the Germans to find. This idea was one he *had* filched directly from fiction. She'd read *The Milliner's Hat Mystery* by Basil Thomson, so she recognized the highly improbable ruse. Of course, the dispatches would be falsified, designed to mislead the Germans about troop movements, invasion strategies, and so on. Surely Godfrey wouldn't entertain such fanciful plots for an instant?

But when she gained admittance to the rear admiral's office with the retyped memorandum, she realized her mistake. Godfrey took the pages she handed him and frowned over them with fierce concentration. A short bark which she interpreted as laughter escaped him at one point. Which item had he found so amusing? It was hard to tell. They'd all been quite extraordinary.

"Well?" Godfrey slapped the memorandum with the back of his hand. "Which of these has legs? What do you think, Miss Bennett?"

Paddy decided to tell the unvarnished truth. "I think they are all completely outlandish, sir."

"Ha!" He cocked an eyebrow at Fleming. "What do you say to that?"

"They are imaginative, certainly," said Fleming, apparently unperturbed by her challenge. "But the more you think about them, the less impossible they appear."

Paddy had to be impressed. In Fleming's position, many men would have dismissed or belittled her for stating an opinion at all, much less disagreeing with him. She had to award him points for doing neither.

It emboldened her to counter dryly, "They seem to me to be possible only between the covers of a novel."

Fleming smiled. "Well, of course, these are all in the order of romantic daydreams, but they contain the germs of very workable plots."

"Capturing German code books . . ." Godfrey fingered his chin, clearly tempted by the idea.

That gambit had to be the most dangerous of all. Flying a group of commandos out over the sea, having them and the pilot parachute into the water while allowing the plane to nosedive as if it were crashing with everyone on board. Then the commandos were to lie in wait in the water for a German vessel to come along to pick them up, hijack the vessel, and capture its code books.

"Forgive me, sir," said Paddy, "but how on earth is the pilot supposed to crash a plane into the sea and live to tell the tale?"

Godfrey sighed. "Bennett's right. It's far too dangerous. It'll never be approved."

"But the intelligence coup if we pull it off!" insisted Fleming, and Paddy sensed the coiled energy in him, his entire body tensing with it. She rather thought Commander Fleming wished he could be one of the commandos in question, parachuting free of a nose-diving aircraft, lying in wait for a hapless German navy crew to come along. Was he frustrated to be stuck behind a desk while other men were engaged in such feats of daring?

The rear admiral shook his head, summarily dismissing that point of discussion, and picked out a few more items of interest, which were duly debated. Paddy was surprised and thrilled to find that the two men actually listened to her opinions, treating her as if she were an equal, as long as she had something sensible to contribute.

"This one. Number twenty-eight," said Godfrey, circling the item on the paper. "Planting false papers on a dead man. I doubt we'd get it through, but just for argument's sake, where would we get the body?"

Fleming shrugged. "The Naval Hospital has no shortage." He fingered his chin. "Though we'd need a fresh corpse . . ."

Paddy said quickly, "You wouldn't use a Naval casualty, would you, sir? I mean, the poor man's family—"

"No, no!" said Godfrey, shaking his head. "We could never do that."

"He'd have to be someone no one would miss," Fleming agreed. He removed his cigarette case from an inner coat pocket, opened it, found it empty. A spasm of irritation crossed his face and was gone. He slid the case back inside his coat. "Could we use a vagrant, perhaps?"

Paddy suppressed a shudder. Vagrants were God's creatures,

just like any other person. She didn't like the thought of using someone's body this way when they were not in a position to object.

Still, the admiral was a man who dealt only in the practical, so she found another tack. "Would the Germans not do an autopsy?" She was unwillingly fascinated by this gruesome discussion.

Fleming shook his head. "No, that's the beauty of doing it off the coast of Spain. The Spanish are pro-German but they're officially neutral, so they have to make it seem as if they are doing things by the book. They won't let the Germans near that body, and we'd have a British official hovering nearby to make doubly sure they don't. Roman Catholic population—they don't much like the idea of autopsies—plus, the kind of place I have in mind is a small, seaside town with only a local doctor on hand. We should be able to find a body that would pass a cursory examination."

"Relying on a lot of ifs, aren't you, sir?" countered Paddy, quirking an eyebrow. By now, she'd lost any sense of deference toward the commander that she'd previously felt. Godfrey glanced at her and back at Fleming, clearly enjoying the exchange.

Fleming shrugged. "What's the downside if they discover the ruse? But succeed in misdirecting them—about where the Allied invasion will take place, for instance—we could save thousands of lives. Tens of thousands."

The argument was compelling. Paddy had to admit she was swayed by it, despite the uneasy suspicion that her morals were being slightly corrupted by debating ways and means to make use of a dead body. "And if the Spanish are so keen to play things by the book, how will the Germans get their hands on the planted documents?"

"Ah," said Fleming. "This is where the key to the plan lies. There is a German agent in Huelva who is very good at getting intelligence out of the Spanish. Name of Clauss. If there's a dead Naval officer washing up on a beach somewhere in the region, he'll pick up on it straight away. And from there, he will report to Kühlenthal, who is the top Abwehr man in Madrid."

"And up the chain of command it goes," murmured Godfrey. "We hope." He was silent for a moment, his pen tapping the desk. "All right," he said. "The Twenty Committee will hate it but I'll bring it to the next meeting. Fleming, you're dismissed. Miss Bennett, a word?"

Paddy waited while Fleming strode from the room and Godfrey jotted some notes on the memorandum. Then he looked up. "Settling in all right, are you, Miss Bennett?"

"Yes, sir." She considered telling him she intended to make a complete overhaul of the filing system but thought better of it.

With dogged determination, Paddy worked long hours to wrestle the filing system under control, while also dealing efficiently with new material coming through to Room 39. Her in trays would never be empty—she might as well accept that from the outset—but now she could see the surface of her desk. It was a start.

However, no matter how early she arrived, nor how late she left, Fleming was almost always there before her and there when she called good night—with frequent absences for wining and dining his women, of course, and several foreign trips in between.

One might wish to write Fleming off as a dilettante because of his proclivities with women, but no one worked harder or more efficiently, or produced such concise, insightful reports. Paddy soon realized something else: that by virtue of her position as Fleming's assistant, she was privy to highly sensitive information that not even the officers around her knew.

"You place an awful lot of trust in me," she said to Fleming one day. "And on very slight acquaintance."

"Hmm?" He glanced at her, his teeth clamped on his cigarette holder, then he smiled. "Well, it's always a trade-off, isn't it? Trust no one, and nothing gets done. Besides, I'm an excellent judge of . . ." He broke off, a wicked gleam lighting his eyes as his gaze traveled from her head to her feet and back again.

". . . women?" she supplied, her voice dry as the desert.

"*Character*," he corrected smoothly. "And Miss Bennett, character is something that you have in spades."

She decided to ignore the suggestive undercurrent in those words. Lowering her voice, she asked, "Do you really think that operation will go ahead?"

He frowned a little impatiently. "Which operation?"

"The one with the dead body off the coast of Spain," Paddy whispered.

"Oh, no. Probably not." He said it with apparent carelessness, as if he hadn't argued forcefully in favor of the mission in front of her very eyes. "The old man tries his best, but they're a bunch of blinkered fools upstairs. If one in a hundred of our proposals makes it through, we count ourselves lucky."

As time went on, Paddy heard nothing more about the gruesome operation, and secretarial work became the least of her duties. Room 39 received, analyzed, and reported on a massive flow of information from countless different channels. Intelligence gathering was one thing; sorting, categorizing, and analyzing the importance of that intelligence was another, and for Naval matters, that function was primarily the purview of the officers at Room 39. Paddy soon became the main conduit through which the most vital intelligence flowed, first to Fleming, then to Godfrey.

She was scanning a report on American shipping movements one morning when a small parcel landed with a light *hush* on her desk. She looked up to see Ian Fleming standing there, smiling. "For you, my dear."

Paddy smiled back at him, eagerly ripping open the wrapping. She gasped. "Stockings! *Silk*." She ran her fingertips over the soft, light weave. Where had he found them? America? He'd taken off on some secret jaunt somewhere that even she hadn't known about and hadn't returned for weeks. "Beautiful. Thank you, sir."

He perched on the edge of her desk, a burning cigarette in hand. "No need to be so formal, is there? Call me Ian."

Oh, no, you don't! thought Paddy. She fixed him with a cool stare but she kept her voice light. "If you don't mind, sir, I have work to do."

"Fleming!" The admiral's roar ripped through the room. "If you've *quite* finished, I'll have that report."

Paddy could have sunk through the floor, but Fleming continued to smile down at her. Over his shoulder he tossed at Godfrey, "Didn't know you were in, Admiral." At a leisurely pace, he slid from her desk, dropped his still smoldering cigarette into the dregs of her teacup, and sauntered into Godfrey's lair.

Blowing out a slow breath, Paddy shoved the stockings into a drawer, then fed a new sheet of paper into her typewriter.

Fleming was an inveterate ladies' man—she'd known that from the first. While she might not be completely immune to his charm, she wasn't going to put up with any nonsense that lowered her in the admiral's estimation, nor in the eyes of her colleagues. She'd worked too hard to be dismissed as a giggling debutante.

Aside from the fact that he seemed to have a different woman for every day of the week, there was an element of ruthlessness to Fleming's charm. He did not treat women well—she had learned that from being privy to his side of numerous telephone conversations, not to mention acting as the unwilling recipient of confidences from his girlfriend, Muriel Wright, after meeting her at various social occasions in his company. Oh, no. Paddy Bennett was too clever to get caught in Commander Fleming's snares.

Having lived in Paris for three years, Paddy was quite accustomed to dealing with masculine flattery, and she'd been obliged to depress the pretensions of more than one young man who had tried to take advantage. She could not help but like Fleming and respect his abilities. But as for pining after him, as Lieutenant Grant had expected her to do, most certainly not. She wanted more substance in the man she fell in love with. More kindness, too. But in the meantime, silk stockings were silk stockings. Paddy wouldn't discourage that kind of thing, as long as Fleming didn't expect special favors in return.

* * *

Paddy mentioned the incident of the stockings to Jean when they met one evening at the Café Royal.

"Don't tell me the divine Commander Fleming has been flirting with you?" said Jean, her eyes as wide as the saucer of her champagne coupe. "How utterly marvelous, darling. He seems like he'd be a lot of fun."

"A lot of *trouble*," corrected Paddy dryly, unable to think of anything less "fun" than being one of a string of women who seemed largely interchangeable and wholly disposable as far as Fleming was concerned. Except, perhaps, for one. She leaned in and lowered her voice. "I have it on good authority that he's smitten with Ann O'Neill. I wouldn't get on her bad side for anything."

"Poisonous, I know," Jean agreed. "They say she's cruel to him and that's why he's mad for her." She pulled a face. "Poor Muriel. She really should give him the heave-ho."

"Don't look now, but there she is," said Paddy, raising her glass to the svelte blonde who was smiling and waving at them from the other side of the balcony.

"She really is stunning, isn't she?" Jean sighed. "Used to model swimsuits, I hear. And she's a terrific skier. Plays polo, too."

Paddy rolled her eyes. "All that seems not to make any difference to the way he treats her."

"She's taken a job as a dispatch rider for the Admiralty," murmured Jean. "Said the air-raid warden uniform was too ugly. Must be quite a lark, riding around on a motorbike all day."

"Dangerous, though," said Paddy. "I heard one girl had to ride through an air raid and nearly got herself killed."

"Oh, how awful!" said Jean. "Makes you glad of a desk job, doesn't it?" Jean was a secretary at MI-5, though she hadn't told Paddy as much. They both took the *Official Secrets Act* very seriously. Jean worked at the War Office and Paddy worked at the Admiralty, and that was that.

But Paddy had been privy to a very interesting docket that proved her friend was not just a pretty face. Jean was responsible for reading all the transcriptions of interrogations of captured spies conducted at a certain detainment facility in a large Victorian mansion in Surrey. She had discovered some glaring inconsistencies in the story of a Belgian operative. Further investigation revealed he had been acting as a triple agent against the British all along. Paddy could only imagine how thrilled with herself Jean had been . . . until she'd heard that her brilliant discovery meant execution for the traitorous Belgian.

Death was all around them. It had become commonplace to remark that X or Y had *bought it,* as if such brutal language could ever make anyone grow accustomed or hardened to loss. They just had to get through it, didn't they, this war? And if Jean's work led to a traitor's death, well, then, how many people had that Belgian betrayed to theirs?

No hint of any turmoil appeared in Jean's demeanor that evening, however. "I've got an early start tomorrow." Jean stretched her bare arms above her head and twinkled her fingers. "Until then, I'm free!"

Jean wasn't the only one who danced the night away at the clubs only to turn around and work the next day. Flocks of young women did the same, some of them traveling from the country into London and back again before work. All of them operated on very little sleep, as if compelled to wring every ounce of enjoyment out of life while they could. They existed in the moment, brushing thoughts of the future aside. Any one of them could be caught in a surprise air raid, obliterated from the earth in an instant. Tonight, they would dance as if there would be no tomorrow.

For some of the people here tonight, that might well be the case.

CHAPTER SEVEN

London, England
July 1939

Friedl

In the summer of 1939 with war rumbling on the horizon, Friedl worked harder than ever before, spurred by the constant fear that if she didn't prove her worth to the spymaster, M, he would cease employing her. That would mean losing her British work permit and being deported—most likely to Germany—because she had given up her Austrian citizenship for a German passport. Friedl would do anything to avoid living under Hitler's Third Reich.

M had warned that once war broke out, the consequence of failure would be equally dire: she would be interned as an enemy alien. So it was with desperation lacing her usual verve and sparkle that Friedl talked her way into all the right circles—and high-flying circles they were.

Sympathy for Nazi Germany was rife among the British elite.

Ever fearful of the communist threat, many saw fascism as the one thing that would stem the red tide that was poised to engulf Europe. That summer, Friedl flitted from one aristocratic house party to another, gathering information as she went, depositing tidbits of gossip and surmise and some tiny grains of solid intelligence with her handler like a bee taking pollen back to the hive.

Her target this evening was the secretary of the London branch of the Nationalist Socialist German Workers Party—the Nazi Party, as it had become known. Fräulein von Ahlefeldt was from a noble German family, well-connected and utterly devoted to the Party.

Friedl had been cultivating the friendship for months now, to the point where the two women had pet names for each other. Friedl was "Fritzi" and von Ahlefeldt was "Schatzi." Unfortunately, although capable of waxing lyrical about Hitler until Friedl longed to slap her, when it came to secret Party business, Schatzi became inconveniently tight-lipped.

They were both attending a rather dull house party hosted by a prominent member of the Right Club when Friedl decided to make her move. Considering the guest list, this pleasant country weekend was obviously a blind for secret meetings between those sympathetic to the Nazi cause. As Party secretary, von Ahlefeldt was likely to have in her custody all kinds of interesting documentation. After dinner, while the company was enjoying billiards or cards, Friedl would take the opportunity to search von Ahlefeldt's room.

Apprehension shivered down her spine. If she was discovered snooping like this, the cover M had given her might be blown.

That would be disastrous. On the other hand, the morsels of intelligence she'd managed to gather so far hadn't quite amounted to a full meal. She needed to take a chance in order to get quality information.

The evening was stiflingly hot and the company in the ugly Tudor banqueting hall tedious. After dinner, having assured herself that Schatzi was fully engaged in a rubber of bridge, Friedl winkled a bottle of champagne and a couple of glasses out of the butler and slipped up to Schatzi's room.

For a moment, Friedl listened at the oak-paneled door but heard nothing. She knocked softly in case a maid was there, then turned the handle and peered inside.

No one. Friedl eased into the room and closed the door behind her. She set down the ice bucket containing the champagne and glasses on a little pie crust table and looked around.

The room was small but richly furnished, decorated in rose velvet and chintz, with a mahogany four-poster bed that took up most of the available space. Friedl darted to the desk by the window and swiftly searched the drawers. A leather compendium with its owner's initials tooled in gold was the only item that seemed of any interest, but it contained nothing but personal correspondence. Hmm. Friedl leafed through the letters and skimmed them, just in case. Nothing that might interest M.

She sifted through the contents of Schatzi's wardrobe and luggage, taking care to put everything back as she'd found it. Nothing there, either, although she did commend Schatzi for her taste in lingerie. Friedl tapped a finger on her chin and surveyed the room. Maybe the more sensitive information was hidden somewhere.

She spent some time hunting for hidden caches, even getting on her hands and knees in her evening gown to peer beneath the bed, but came up empty. Dusting herself off as she straightened, Friedl sighed. It would have to be the personal touch, after all.

She dashed off a message to Schatzi and sent it with one of the footmen. Slipping out of the stuffy house by a side entrance, she carried her champagne bucket on her hip as if it was a small child and headed toward the gazebo by the lake.

The endless summer twilight had fallen like a gossamer veil over the sky. The air was still and warm but several degrees cooler than inside the house. The ice bucket sat, deliciously cold, within the circle of her arm. Ignoring the well-furnished gazebo, Friedl walked out to the small wooden landing where a little green rowboat was tied to a post. She set the champagne bucket down, then kicked off her shoes and shed her stockings, bunched up her skirt, and sat on the edge of the dock. The water below was still and soft and cool, enveloping her feet and ankles in a silken caress.

She was contemplating opening the champagne when Schatzi's harsh voice shattered the spell. "There you are! Fritzi, you naughty, naughty girl! You are such a bad influence on me."

Friedl turned to waggle the champagne bottle in Schatzi's direction and laughed up at her. *My dearest Schatzi,* she thought. *You have* no *idea.*

* * *

Friedl thrust the fare at the driver, leaped out of the taxi, and hurried up to the Wheatleys' front door. Ordinarily she would submit a written report to her handler after a house party such as the one she'd just attended, but what she'd learned from Fräulein von Ahlefeldt last night had her haring back to town as soon as she could decently take her leave. She needed to speak to Billy Younger in person.

It was Sunday afternoon, so Billy was likely to be at his stepfather's house in St. John's Wood Park. This also happened to be Friedl's ostensible place of work. All very neat that her MI-5 handler should also be the stepson of her employer, Dennis Wheatley. That was the spy trade for you. They liked to keep it in the family.

True to his word, M had secured her a position as translator and research assistant to the famous novelist. Initially, Friedl had provided background information on the Nazis for a straightforward thriller Wheatley was writing. However the author's interest in the occult was wide-ranging and pervasive, and Friedl found this side of his nature disconcerting, to say the least.

Not content with writing about such activities, Wheatley had cultivated several sources who encouraged him in the most unsettling habits. There was the Catholic priest with a vast knowledge of witchcraft, the Egyptian called Ahmed who had become an expert on voodoo while in the Caribbean. Aleister Crowley was even said to practice Satanism. It was rumored, though the novelist denied it, that Wheatley himself had dabbled in many of the dark arts about which he wrote. Friedl wouldn't be at all surprised.

She arrived at the Wheatley residence to find one of the writer's unusual acquaintances preparing for a séance in the small parlor the family used as a breakfast room. On a Sunday? That was blasphemy, surely. Though sadly lapsed, Friedl had been brought up a Catholic, and she had to fight the urge to cross herself as she tried to catch Billy Younger's eye.

Her MI-5 handler was seated at the round table, gazing fixedly at the Ouija board and looking as if he'd rather be anywhere else. Dear Billy was such a *mensch*. He had quite a crush on Friedl, and she wasn't averse to encouraging him. He might not be as dashing as some of the other men in her life, but he was kind and dependable, qualities Friedl ought to appreciate more than she did.

She hovered at the doorway, raising a hand to attract Billy's attention without Wheatley seeing her. She didn't want to join this party, and she didn't want to have to come up with an excuse as to why she couldn't. Luckily, Wheatley was seated with his back to the door, and he was peppering the medium with questions, the answers to which would no doubt find their way into his next book.

Billy caught sight of Friedl and his shoulders relaxed with apparent relief. "Will you excuse me? I'm afraid duty calls."

Heads turned to look at her, but Friedl quickly retreated from the doorway.

Someone in the parlor called, "Curtains, please!" and the parlor was plunged into darkness. Billy stepped out and firmly closed the door behind him.

"Thank you, dear Friedl," he murmured. "There didn't seem to be an easy way to extricate myself from that circus." He looked at her more closely and seemed to sense the excitement she was trying hard to contain. "What is it? Or, no, wait. You'd better come to the study so I can write it all down."

They went to Wheatley's library, which was decorated with all manner of ephemera, from voodoo dolls and skulls to witches' poppets, chalices, pentagrams, bottled specimens, and other items Friedl would prefer not to think about.

As soon as Billy was seated at the desk, Friedl began. "You know I've been meeting regularly with Fräulein von Ahlefeldt?"

"That Nazi Party secretary?"

Friedl nodded. "She's just come back from Germany."

Drawing a sheet of paper toward him, Billy began to write. "Go on."

"She mentioned to me last night that she was traveling through Cologne and met a friend high up in the Party. She didn't say who, but this person told her that negotiations were underway for a rapprochement with the Russians."

"*What?*" Billy's large eyes widened farther as he stared up at her.

So it was the first he'd heard of it, too. Thrilled with herself, Friedl added, "And when she mentioned this to another highly placed person in Berlin, he told her that it was information of the utmost secrecy and that her friend had better watch his mouth or he might be eliminated!"

There was more, but this piece of news was the gem in the collection, a diamond of the first water.

"Must pass this on to M," said Billy when she'd finished, gathering up his notes. "Well *done*, Friedl." Sobering, he added, "I mean, it's terrible news, of course. Devastating if the negotiations lead to an alliance. But if we have the information, at least there might be something we can do about it."

As Billy stood, Friedl moved closer and fixed him with a melting look. "You'll tell M it was me who brought it to you, *liebling*, won't you? You won't leave that part out?"

He smiled and rubbed her arm reassuringly. "Of course I will. *And* I'll tell him we were right about you! Excellent work, my dear."

When Billy had gone, Friedl performed a celebratory shimmy around Wheatley's study. This news, this one piece of information gleaned after attending Party meeting after Party meeting and listening patiently to so many stultifying political ravings in private, made it all worthwhile.

This must surely prove Friedl's worth as an asset to the British. She was free and safe from deportation or internment—at least, for the time being.

London, England
November 1940

"You *bitch*! I'll kill you for this!" Anna Wolkoff struggled against the restraining hands of the court constable, her face so close, Friedl smelled the Russian's foul breath and felt a shower of spittle hit her cheek.

The other woman's round face and hard, dark eyes came into focus again as the constable regained control and yanked the prisoner back. Anna Wolkoff was a white Russian, the daughter of an admiral. At one time a couturier who dressed such high-flyers as Wallis Simpson, now she wore a mask of hatred that had lost all traces of sophistication. Chills raced down Friedl's spine. At that moment, she believed the woman capable of anything. *Lieber Gott im Himmel*, let Anna receive a *very* long jail sentence.

Thank goodness there were no reporters about to witness the exchange. Wolkoff's trial had been held at the Old Bailey in camera, closed to the public, with Friedl as a key witness, her true identity protected, as it had been by the use of an alias throughout the operation. Friedl's mission had been to keep tabs on the former members of the fascist Right Club who met at the Russian Tea Room in South Kensington, which was run by Anna Wolkoff and her father.

Anna had been sending intelligence to Berlin via a contact at the Italian embassy, most recently copying communications of the most sensitive nature between Churchill and Roosevelt which her accomplice, a cipher clerk at the American embassy, had stolen. Both the cipher clerk and Wolkoff were charged under the *Official Secrets Act*. Today, Anna had been convicted.

Friedl stepped back, thankful for Billy Younger's steadying arm around her waist. He handed her his handkerchief, but she waited until Anna was out of sight before she carefully patted her cheek dry of the woman's spittle. Friedl smoothed a thumb tip over the raised edge of the embroidered monogram on the large square of white cotton. She would keep the handkerchief as a reminder of Billy.

Joan Miller, who had also given evidence at the trial, gave

Friedl's arm a bracing rub. "Come on. Let's get a drink. I think we deserve it, don't you? Billy? Where shall we go?"

They chose a cozy pub nearby, and Friedl resigned herself to the very poor-quality wine they served there. The wine, when it came, was indeed terrible, but once the alcohol hit her system, she began to relax.

"Best be going," said Joan, picking up her purse and sliding from the booth. "Work tomorrow."

Billy only had eyes for Friedl. "Must you?" he murmured, not even glancing at Joan. "Poor you."

Friedl smiled at Joan, jumped up, and kissed her on both cheeks. "Sleep well, *liebling*. Thank you for the drink."

Soon afterward, Friedl and Billy also left the pub, strolling arm in arm toward St. Paul's Tube station. The night was seeping in, but the streetlamps would not be lit due to the blackout. Soon it would be dark, but a half-moon would give them enough light to see their way home.

"I'll tell Dennis to give you tomorrow off," said Billy, patting her hand.

Friedl laughed. "No need. He's away at the moment, anyway. Didn't you know?"

She slid a glance at Billy. He was not the most handsome of men, dark and round-faced, not as tall as she'd have liked. And he had a large mole at the corner of his mouth that was impossible to ignore. But he was clever and kind, and he adored her. And she rather thought she might love him, too. Really love him, not the kind of infatuation she fell in and out of almost constantly.

Billy pressed her hand. "You don't mind it, all this?" She took "all this" to mean her intelligence work. "You must miss performing."

Friedl tilted her head. Did she miss singing in the clubs? Perhaps, but then spying produced a similar thrill. She had discovered she was quite good at it, and so far, she had not been forced to make the desperate and dangerous choice she had anticipated after her meeting with Kühlenthal in Estoril. Despite his warning that someone would make contact with her once she reached England, no one ever had.

"I find it stimulating," she said. "And working for Mr. Wheatley is never dull, either. Besides, I never know what dear M has in store for me next."

"I wonder . . ." Billy hesitated, then cleared his throat. "I have something . . ." He coughed again. "That is, I wonder if you'd like to, ah, come to tea with my mother tomorrow?"

Excitement tap-danced in Friedl's chest. "Really?" Very few young men ever took Friedl to meet their parents, and while she was already acquainted with Billy's mother, it was only through her work for Billy's stepfather. Joan Wheatley had rarely given Friedl more than a polite greeting in passing. But this hesitancy, the significance with which Billy seemed to invest this invitation, indicated that a proposal might be imminent.

Friedl opened her eyes wide and searched his face for a clue that his intentions weren't sincere, but she found nothing but pride and yearning in those earnest, dark eyes. Then she'd been right to hope. Billy Younger was serious about her.

A strange feeling of comfort washed over Friedl, a feeling she hadn't experienced since childhood. Security. As the wife of

Billy Younger, daughter-in-law of Sir William Younger, a wealthy brewer who owned a castle in Scotland, she would never need to worry about Kühlenthal, or internment, or British intelligence, or anything, ever again.

"Oh, *Billy*! I'd love to." Friedl threw her arms around him and kissed him passionately, right there in the street.

* * *

The next day, Friedl spent an eternity debating what to wear to tea with Billy's mother while she waited for Billy to telephone to make the arrangements.

Regardless of the venue he chose, she ought to wear something modest, certainly. That was a given. But did the green floral tea gown look better against her skin than the lemon? And which of her precious lipsticks would best inspire the trust and confidence of a prospective mother-in-law? Oh, and her hair. If she dressed it in a victory roll, would it be too severe? Something softer, perhaps?

She frowned. Usually she was more decisive when it came to matters of style. But knowing Billy loved her and wanted to marry her was one thing. Winning the approval of his mother to the match was a different prospect altogether.

Friedl had canceled her luncheon appointment and stayed in all morning in case the telephone rang, admiring her manicure as she leafed through the latest magazines. A tiny doubt needled at her. Was Joan Wheatley the sort of mother who would like a girl who painted her nails scarlet? She bit her lip, then decided that forgoing polish was a bridge too far. The scarlet nails could stay.

Time seemed to crawl as she stared at the shiny black telephone. Was there anything more annoying than the sound of a ticking clock when one was waiting for something? She picked up her little ormolu carriage clock and stuffed it in her underwear drawer to muffle the sound.

Bored, restless, Friedl even attempted to read Dennis Wheatley's *The Devil Rides Out*, which the author himself had autographed and presented to her. What a strange, twisted mind that man possessed. But even the lurid plot of this potboiler couldn't hold her attention for long. She moved about her little flat aimlessly, until suddenly she realized that teatime had come already and Billy's call had not.

As the temperature on that November day dropped with the going down of the sun, so did Friedl's hopes. Ought she simply to call Billy and ask him what the matter was? There could be any number of explanations as to why he hadn't made the promised arrangement. No need for despair.

The telephone rang out stridently, making her jump. She leaped for the instrument and snatched up the receiver, heart pounding. "Billy?" She let out a sigh of relief when she heard his greeting. "Darling!"

"Look, I know it's late notice, but are you free for dinner tonight, old thing?" There was something strained about Billy's voice, as if his collar was too tight.

She gave a small, uncertain laugh. "Yes, as it happens, I am." She hesitated, twiddling the phone cord between her fingertips. "Just us, darling?"

There was a pause. A telling one. "Yes, darling. Just us."

After saying goodbye, Friedl put down the telephone receiver very carefully. She knew what that short exchange meant. Joan Wheatley had vetoed the marriage. She might have guessed it would not be that easy!

Would Billy be man enough to defy his mother and marry Friedl anyway? Experience told her the answer to that question.

Wrapping her arms around herself, Friedl surveyed the outfits that spilled across her bed through a sheen of tears. She had a sudden urge to gather everything up in a heap and fling it out the window. Instead, she blinked back her tears, squared her shoulders, arranged each garment carefully back on its hanger, and stowed them away in her wardrobe. Then she got out the slinkiest, most revealing gown she owned—a scandalous Schiaparelli she'd bought in Paris—and laid it on the counterpane.

That evening, Billy took her dancing at the 400 Club, and she let him hold her close, brushed her lips against his ear when she whispered into it, ran her scarlet nails lightly down his back. When, at last, he presented her with a slim, velvet-lined jewelry box that was too large to have an engagement ring nestled inside it, she smiled widely and kissed his cheek and asked him to clasp the tasteful pearl necklace around her throat.

But when Friedl departed the club that evening, she left on the arm of another man.

* * *

Friedl hadn't left the next club on the arm of the man she'd entered it with, either. In fact, as she sashayed along the Soho streets alone in the dark, her brain a little blurred from all the fizz she'd drunk at other people's expense, it occurred to her that she had no earthly idea what time it was. As an enemy alien, her curfew was earlier than other Londoners', so the fact that she wasn't the only reveler out and about at this hour didn't mean much.

The straps of her dancing shoes cut into her heels with the merciless precision of a surgeon's scalpel. Her flat wasn't terribly far off but she didn't want to limp all the way there.

She exchanged a nod with the working girls she often saw on that particular corner. "Any cabs about, *lieblings*?" But she knew the answer to that. One only got anywhere fast at this hour by hitching a ride.

"Nah, love. Won't get one of them for love nor money this time of night."

Friedl hunched a shoulder. She should have let that middle-aged man who claimed to work at the War Office take her home. He'd looked like the sort who could command his own chauffeured car.

"Cripes!" one of the working girls shouted. "Rozzers!"

A van had pulled up beside them. The peep of a policeman's whistle sounded and there was a bit of a scuffle among the girls. Friedl watched curiously as a couple of uniformed constables proceeded to manhandle the women into the back of the van.

"Come on now, girls, no fuss. In the back there. Right you are."

After their initial attempt to escape, Friedl's companions submitted docilely enough to their arrest. Satisfied that they weren't being mistreated, Friedl was about to go on her way, when a big hand took her arm in a firm grip. "Where d'you think you're going, my lovely? Come on, in the back with the rest of the tarts."

"But I'm not a tart!" She wasn't especially insulted by the insinuation, but she didn't want to be arrested in case it affected her residency. Besides, M wouldn't like it if she drew attention to herself. "Officer, darling. There's been a mistake."

The bobby flicked on a flashlight that had been dimmed with masking tape and shone it from Friedl's feet, up her body to the plunging neckline of her dress, and lingered there, then flicked to her face, making her wince and blink against the sudden brightness. "You expect me to swallow that one, you must think I was born yesterday. Now, don't give us no trouble, sweetheart. See your mates there, all coming along, nice and gentle. Like little lambs, they are."

"But—"

"No explaining, no complaining. You can tell it all to the magistrate at Bow Street in the morning, love. In you go!" He shone the flashlight into the van to light her way.

"Come on, ducky." The redhead peered out at her and gave her a wink. "Don't keep us all out in the cold."

So Friedl shrugged and allowed herself to be helped into the waiting van. She accepted a nip from a bottle of something truly horrible one of her companions offered her as they were transported to the cells and sighed. At least she wouldn't have to walk home in these heels.

The following morning, Joan Miller came to get Friedl released.

Friedl had slept sitting up on a hard wooden bench, her back against the cold, damp wall. When she saw Joan, she scrambled up. Her stomach lurched and her head swam as she crossed to the iron bars of the cell and reached out her hand for Joan to squeeze briefly. "Thank goodness, *liebling*! You came."

Joan made a face and stepped back. "Golly, Friedl, you reek! What *have* you been doing? I thought you went out with Billy last night?"

Friedl gave a self-conscious laugh. "I did, but then I met such interesting people and . . ." She waved her hand a little, indicating that the inevitable conclusion to an evening spent with interesting people was a morning in jail.

"Honestly!" But Joan's bottom lip quivered, as if she wanted to giggle. "Can't the police tell the difference between you and . . . and . . ."

Friedl laughed and shrugged one shoulder. "Clearly the constabulary don't recognize a Schiaparelli when they see one. And anyway, I didn't want to make too much fuss." She lowered her voice. "Out after curfew. You know how that might go." She let her mouth droop into a pout. "But *liebling*, why are we still standing here? Aren't you going to get me out?"

Joan looked at her watch. "Sorry. You'll have to wait for the magistrate." She rolled her eyes. "Typical! This lot won't take my word for anything. I've had to call a chap I know at Special Branch to sort it for you. Billy will be along to take you home once the hearing's over." She eyed Friedl. "You're shivering. Didn't they give you a blanket, at least?" Joan shrugged off her coat and handed it to a nearby guard. "Give that to Miss Stöttinger, will you?" To Friedl, she added, "Won't be long now, old thing."

Billy was less inclined to laugh off the incident than Joan had been. His face was pale and unsmiling when he escorted Friedl from Bow Street Magistrate's Court. The drive back to her flat was accomplished in silence and Friedl, feeling sick in both body and spirit, didn't attempt to break it with her usual stream of amusing chatter.

From his stony expression and his habit of avoiding Friedl's gaze, she gathered Billy had received the message last night, loud and clear. That was good. He would feel better about the whole thing if he considered himself the injured party. She could do that for him, at least. And it went some way to soothing her own wounded pride.

Settling back against the leather-upholstered seat, Friedl suppressed a sigh. She would be obliged to see Billy all the time for work and that would be painful. But he wouldn't cause a scene. He might throw her the odd darkling glance now and then after her outrageous behavior last night, but he was too proud to reproach her, and too professional to let his feelings interfere with his work.

Certainly there was no shortage of activity for Friedl to report in the weeks leading up to Christmas. She was well-connected and moved in the highest circles among the rich and powerful. She had known about the Soviet nonaggression pact before Churchill's advisers caught wind of it, and she continued to monitor pro-fascist activity in London.

"I keep seeing Anna Wolkoff's face in my dreams," she said, rubbing her upper arms as she paced the living room of her flat one bleak December day. Billy was seated at her little desk, poring over her latest report. True, she had used an alias to spy on Anna Wolkoff's group and no one had been allowed to watch the trial itself. She'd made sure never to have her photograph taken in the company of the Wolkoffs and their set. Still, what if Anna managed to get word to those who were still at liberty about Friedl's part in her arrest and conviction? Friedl didn't feel quite safe anymore.

Billy didn't seem to hear her. He raised his eyebrows. "The Duke of Bedford has been busy." He gathered up the pages of the report and clipped them together, then tucked them into his briefcase. "I hear there's to be a party down at Dassett on New Year's Eve. You're bound to pick up a lot there."

Friedl had considered not going to Lisi for New Year's. She'd received an invitation from friends in Scotland, and it rather suited her mood to celebrate the occasion among a group of people who had nothing to do with subversive activity, and who would undoubtedly see in the new year with innocent, if drunken, gusto. However, this was the price someone like her paid for freedom, wasn't it?

"Yes, I'll be there," she said. "I'll do my best." But thinking of New Year's Eve made her think of kissing, and the knowledge that it would not be Billy's lips pressed to hers as the clock struck midnight only sharpened the ache in her heart.

CHAPTER EIGHT

Surrey, England
December 1940

Friedl

Friedl glanced about her at the preparations for Lisi's New Year's Eve party and accepted the fact that, like many of her class, her sister did not do austerity well.

The Blitz had decimated London. Around every corner were ration queues, scarred and ruined buildings, sandbagged doorways, blown-out windows covered with newspaper—all the bleak reminders of war. But at this New Year's Eve party in nearby Surrey, Lisi would create a new reality, where the Blitz was merely a figment of the imagination or a fleeting bad dream.

Dassett would be full of Greek shipping magnates with pure silk shirts and gambling addictions, mixing with the elite and titled of British society—all of them swigging the finest champagne and sampling black market caviar. Somehow, despite unashamedly mixing brashness with breeding, Lisi's parties always combined refinement, raffishness, and glamour to a perfect degree.

The house itself was owned not by Lisi's husband, Ian Menzies, but by his mother, whose second marriage to Sir George Holford had brought her the wealth and happiness her first marriage to Ian and Stewart's father had not. The very walls at Dassett seemed to exude luxury. Everything, from the decor to the napery, was of the finest quality and in the best possible taste. Not an easy feat, to strike the perfect balance between opulence and excess, but Lady Holford had managed it.

Friedl would work for a few hours, then she would "clock off" and start enjoying herself. She'd do her duty by MI-5, subtly extracting information from this guest and that, letting slip a pro-the-Fatherland statement here and there to see whether the seeds of intrigue fell on fertile ground. There was an advantage to beauty: people—*men*—simply assumed she wasn't very bright and let down their guard. Or, at least, they took one look at Friedl, and her brain was the last piece of anatomy they considered.

The thought of a midnight kiss made anticipation hum through her body. She didn't have a serious lover at the moment, and the uncertainty of who might be at her side at the arrival of a new year thrilled her. At least, that was what she told herself. Determinedly pushing aside the hopes she'd once harbored of a different ending to this night, Friedl mentally reviewed the guest list. She had her eye on Hugh Forrester, a dashing pilot who had miraculously survived countless dogfights and was as different from Billy Younger as it was possible to be. Hopefully Hugh would attend tonight. If not, there were always others . . .

Well, she might not be an acceptable wife for Billy Younger in the eyes of his family, but there was no reason to despair. Look at the brilliant marriage Lisi had made. She wanted for nothing and was accepted by her mother-in-law despite her recent employment at the London Casino. Lady Holford even conceded the role of hostess to Lisi on evenings like this.

"Miss Stöttinger. A word?" The quiet request came from behind her. Friedl turned to meet the assessing gaze of a man she recognized but had never formally met. She'd heard Joan Miller and M refer to him as "Tar" and wondered at the nickname until Joan had explained it was simply made up of his initials and was not some obscure sobriquet, which the British seemed addicted to bestowing upon each other to the bafflement of everyone else. Early forties, slim, dark, and handsome, with a perceptive gaze, Thomas Argyll Robertson clearly expected her to know who he was. She also sensed that his request for an audience must not be denied.

Even more so than with M, Friedl felt at once that Tar was not a man one could distract with meaningless chatter or flirtation. Yet she did not mean to make things easy for him. She merely raised her eyebrows and said with a hint of hauteur, "Have we met?"

"Forgive me. Robertson's my name," he said with an urbane smile. "We have a mutual acquaintance, but he doesn't appear to be present, so I thought I'd presume . . ."

Friedl decided to give in gracefully. "Of course. M—I mean,

Major Knight—has mentioned you often." She held out her hand to him. What now? she wondered. Had she done something wrong?

A European man would immediately kiss any female hand offered to him, but Robertson gripped hers and gave it a brief, businesslike shake. "I'd like you to meet someone," he said. "We heard that you've been doing some work for M, and we thought you'd be the very person for a little job that we're planning. Will you join me in the study for a moment?"

She glanced around her. Most of Lisi's houseguests had returned from playing golf on the course nearby and retired to their rooms to get ready for the party. Tar was already dressed for the evening. Perhaps he had more of these interviews planned.

Excitement skittered down Friedl's spine. Truth be told, she was getting bored with the work she'd been doing for M and Billy Younger, even though it only entailed enjoying herself at parties like this one and reporting back to them on what she discovered. She was more than ready for a new challenge.

"I'd be delighted." She followed Tar to a small study off the main entrance hall. The room lay in semidarkness, lit by just one jewel-toned Tiffany lamp, and Friedl had the impression of cozy shabbiness at odds with the rest of the house. Friedl peered at the gold-tooled lettering on some of the books that lay piled up on the handsome mahogany desk, quite as if her mind wasn't raging with speculation about what Tar could possibly want with her.

As soon as the door clicked shut, a sudden nervousness flooded her system. She sensed a change in the atmosphere and began to wish she hadn't agreed so readily to this meeting.

At Tar's invitation, she sat in one of the worn leather armchairs by the hearth. She crossed one leg over the other, then leaned forward a little, all avid attention. Tar's gaze never shifted from her face. She rather wished he would offer her a drink from the decanter on the small sideboard, but he didn't seem in a hurry to set her at ease. Prickles of apprehension raced across her nape.

Robertson leaned forward also, elbows on his thighs, and clasped his hands together. "Let me preface this by saying that we know all about you, Miss Stöttinger."

Her gaze flew to his but she kept her cool. "What does *that* mean?"

As if she hadn't spoken, he continued, "We know, for instance, that you were approached by the Abwehr in Estoril. We know that an officer by the name of Kühlenthal asked you to spy for him."

Friedl stared at him, her heart beating so hard she felt the pulse in her throat, and in her head and her stomach, too.

"And we also know," continued Tar tranquilly, "that you agreed to do as Kühlenthal told you."

All the breath left her body. Hoarsely, she said, "Mr. Robertson, I—"

"Please." He spread his hands, palms upward. "Call me Tar."

She tried to swallow, but her throat was thick with fear. "Tar. I know how it looks, but I haven't—I mean, I never . . ." She trailed off, trying desperately to interpret the enigmatic expression in his eyes. "You must understand, Kühlenthal threatened my family, so I agreed to come here, thinking it would be safer that way. But please believe me. *Please*. No one has made contact or given

me instructions of any kind. I have done nothing whatsoever
to harm this country." Quite the reverse. She had done everything in her power to aid the British war effort. Had it all been
for nothing?

Tar was silent for a moment. Then he said, "Do you know what
my job is, Miss Stöttinger?"

She shook her head in answer. "Please. Call me Friedl." Even
through her daze of fear, instinct made her turn on the charm.

He nodded. "Friedl, then. My job is to find German spies and
either turn them and get them to work for our side, or . . ." He
smiled. "Well, let us not go into the alternative." He paused.
"I've heard excellent things about your work for M, Friedl. He
has given you a glowing recommendation, in fact. That you were
approached in Estoril is actually a *good* thing from my point of
view."

Relief made Friedl a little dizzy. She wasn't going to be arrested and carted off for interrogation and execution, which was
undoubtedly the "alternative" to which Tar had alluded. "Whatever it is . . . whatever you want . . . I'll do it," she said fervently.

"I'm delighted to hear that," said Tar, though surely he had
never doubted that she'd comply. "We are running a very important deception against the Germans in Portugal at the moment. Among other things, it involves providing intelligence to
the Germans via agents here."

"False intelligence," said Friedl, nodding. The reverse of what
she'd been doing for M.

Tar folded his hands together. "Our aim is to feed the Germans small pieces of a puzzle. Some will fit, some won't. Some

will give the truth, and others will distort that truth. Some will be false. By the end, we build up a complete picture in their minds that, in reality, is no more than a mirage."

Friedl tilted her head as a thought occurred to her. "But how do you know whether the Germans are being fooled by this mirage?"

Tar was silent for a moment. "That part needn't concern you. What we want from you, Friedl, is to set yourself up as a German informant in this particular circuit."

Her throat tightened again. "You mean you want me to contact Kühlenthal?"

Tar raised his eyebrows. "Would that frighten you?"

Was she afraid? She felt edgy and alert, perhaps, but no, she was not afraid. There wasn't much Kühlenthal could do to her in England, after all. She pushed away the thought of the threats he'd made against her mother. "Should I be?"

A gleam lit his eyes. "That's the spirit. In fact, it won't be Kühlenthal you'll deal with, although he will undoubtedly be informed about the intelligence you provide. You will be part of a three-person circuit, the head of which should be here tonight. One of ours, working as a double agent. His name is Duško Popov. Code name: Tricycle. He's a Serbian businessman, and the Germans trust him implicitly. Popov is the man who will arrange contact with the Abwehr and monitor how your intelligence is received. He'll also instruct you on the kinds of things you should pass on, the tone and style of your correspondence, and so forth. What we need is for the Germans to accept that your allegiance is with them, so that they will rely on the intelligence you pass on."

"So this man, this Duško Popov, operates in Portugal."

"In that region, yes. He is in London for a short stay. I hope you'll get to know him in that time, before he returns." Now Tar's gaze traveled over her body. "I think the two of you will hit it off admirably."

She narrowed her eyes at him. Was this a subtle request for her to show this unknown agent a "good time," as the saying went in Hollywood movies? She didn't do that sort of thing, and she didn't like the idea that this new handler might expect more from her than intelligence work.

"At all events, meet him tonight," said Tar mildly, perhaps correctly interpreting her expression. "See how it goes."

As a consequence of this exchange, when Friedl did, finally, meet Duško Popov, she was not in the mood to be particularly charming. Instead of the flame red gown she had planned to wear that evening, she chose a column of pure white that screamed *Don't touch* and clasped cold, hard diamonds around her throat.

That evening, she entered Lady Holford's drawing room with all the grace and poise of a queen. The second she crossed the threshold and swept her gaze over the assembled guests, she knew which of them Duško Popov must be.

He was the most dashing and sophisticated man she'd seen since she'd come to England. His brown hair was brushed back from a high, broad forehead and his skin bore the glowing, golden tan of someone who had spent the summer somewhere on the Mediterranean. Most likely sunning himself on Tamariz Beach, just as she'd done what seemed like a lifetime ago. He would have been surrounded by pretty women, his gray-blue eyes and sensual lips seducing them all.

Oh, yes. He had magnetism, this man. He was trim and broad shouldered and wore his expensively tailored suit with an urbane elegance that was wholly European. Duško Popov radiated the kind of self-confidence that was neither arrogant nor offensive. He had nothing whatsoever to prove to anyone, much less to these English.

Ordinarily, Friedl would have fallen for him there and then.

But the suggestive undertone she'd detected in Tar's recommendation to her to spend some time with Popov while he was in London still rankled. Friedl might fall in love easily and often, but her lovers were always taken freely, and not at the behest of anyone, much less the British intelligence services.

When Lady Holford none too subtly took Friedl's arm and led her directly to Popov himself to make the introductions, Friedl returned his greeting coolly enough to make his dazzling smile falter.

"So you are Duško Popov," Friedl said without inflection, leaving him to wonder how—and what—she knew about him already. She gave him a dispassionate once-over, then turned to greet an acquaintance. Despite taking care not to glance too obviously in his direction, she was aware that his gaze followed her when she walked away.

Of course, part of Friedl knew that she couldn't have behaved in a manner more calculated to arouse the interest of any dedicated lady's man.

Joan Miller, who hated these parties and greeted Friedl with an expression of relief, took a glass of champagne from a passing waiter and tilted her head in Popov's direction. "Not like you to play hard to get, Friedl."

Friedl was forced to admit the truth of that statement. Life was short. The danger of war made life all the more precious, and why waste time pretending indifference when she was interested in a man? "Perhaps I've made a New Year's resolution." She shrugged. "Perhaps he's not my type."

Joan gave a little snort. "He is absolutely your type. What's the matter? Has he offended you in some way?" They both watched as Stewart Menzies, head of MI-6, also known as "C," spoke a few words to Popov and shepherded him from the room. Joan murmured, "C wants you to show him about in London, I hear. Take him to parties and such."

"Hmm." She could do that much, certainly. But no more.

"I wonder how long he'll be in London." Joan echoed her own thoughts.

Friedl sighed. It would be fatal to fall in love with a man who was only there on a fleeting visit, and one who would spend the time he was away working as a double agent, neck deep in unimaginable danger. A wise woman would keep Duško Popov at arm's length despite the hot look in those steely eyes whenever his gaze rested on her—which seemed to be almost constantly. Throughout the evening, she took care never to steal a glance at him, but whenever he came into her line of sight, she caught him staring at her as if he couldn't drag his eyes away.

No, she should not get involved with Duško Popov.

But oh, that kiss at midnight . . . Suddenly, the idea of the strapping RAF pilot's embrace lacked appeal. Friedl was only flesh and blood, and not terribly good at resisting temptation at the best of times. On several occasions that night, she caught herself imagining what it would be like if Duško Popov took her in his arms.

However, true to the vow she'd made, Friedl held herself aloof. Even if she hadn't been annoyed about being treated like one of the MI-6 "popsies," it was never clever strategy to fall into a man's arms too soon.

So, when the clock struck twelve, Friedl didn't kiss Duško Popov.

But she didn't kiss anyone else, either.

London, England
January 1941

"Gelatine." Friedl stared at Duško Popov, puzzled. "What sort of code name is that?"

She was sitting on the edge of his desk, perusing a briefing paper while Popov marked up a letter she had drafted for him to pass on to the Germans.

As part of his cover, Popov had been assigned an office on the sixth floor of Albany House, just off Piccadilly Circus. The sign on the door said, "Tarlair Ltd.—Export-Import." "A little joke on the Germans," Popov had said, playing on Tar's nickname. He certainly seemed to enjoy the British sense of humor, and Friedl had heard he was often to be found enjoying a cigar with C or a game of billiards with Tar at one of London's exclusive gentle-men's clubs.

Friedl smiled. Before she had become more acquainted with the mindset of the secret services, she might have been discon-certed by the levity with which the British approached such important business, but she'd discovered that the more serious matters became, the more these men made light of the situation. Instead of worrying about their likely competence if everything was such a lark to them, she'd learned to derive comfort and re-assurance from their odd sense of humor.

That afternoon, she and Popov had been working out a pro-tocol for the letters she would write to the Germans under a new cover name, Mrs. Ivy Trevallion. Internally at MI-5 she was henceforth to be known as "Gelatine."

At her querying of the code name, Popov shrugged and shook his head with similar bafflement. "They said it was because you are such a jolly little thing." He glanced up at her, smiled rue-fully, then returned his gaze to his work. "Clearly not the side you have been showing to me these past few days."

She let the remark pass, watching as Popov finished annotat-ing her letter. He would be gone all too soon, departing for the sunnier climes of Spain and Portugal, leaving her behind in gray old London. He would have a woman over there. Several women, most likely. Her fingers curled and tensed at the thought.

Ah, she had promised herself she would not fall for this man! She certainly shouldn't let herself feel possessive over him, but it was already a lost cause, and probably had been since the mo-ment she'd met the Serbian spy.

As instructed by Tar, Friedl had dragged Popov hither and yon around London to this party and that, all of them "top drawer," as Tar would say. She'd introduced Popov to all of the most influential people of her acquaintance so that he could credibly claim to have received information from them that would be of interest to the Germans. Friedl had steadfastly refused Popov's invitations to enjoy a nightcap back at the Savoy, where he was staying, but with every passing day she felt her resolve slip a little more. Popov was charming, attentive, and apparently smitten, and his stay in London would be all too short. The knowledge of the constant danger he would face as soon as he arrived in Portugal gave her desire for him an urgency that was becoming difficult to deny.

"I expect you find London parties a bore," she commented.

"It is hard not to feel my time might be better spent," he agreed. This time, Friedl could not pretend to be unaware of his meaning. His gaze was direct and suggestive, and she all but fell, limbs flailing, into those fathomless eyes. Quickly, she bent her head to peruse a pile of invoices and receipts on his desk.

One receipt for four suits at W. Millen of Savile Row, one invoice for eighteen custom-made monogrammed silk shirts with matching monogrammed handkerchiefs from A. J. Izod. She lifted her eyebrows and brandished the small sheaf of papers. "Claiming for expenses?"

He laughed. "No. Let me show you." He rose from the desk and came around to where she sat, took out a gold lighter from his pocket, and removed the invoice from her grasp. Friedl sucked in a breath as he stood beside her, his head bent close to hers as he waved the lighter flame beneath the invoice. As if by magic, writing appeared, spreading outward from the source of the flame.

"Oh, secret writing. I see," said Friedl, her voice a little shaky. He smelled of expensive cologne and damp wool, and something else . . . Sandalwood, perhaps?

"Best to use innocuous papers a man might carry on him for these kinds of things," said Popov. "No one looks twice at a bill." He moved to the desk, set the invoice alight, letting it burn, then dropped the smoldering remains in the ashtray before they could scorch his fingers.

As her breathing returning to normal, Friedl checked her watch. "I have an appointment, but I'll see you tomorrow."

He nodded. She knew he was going to dine with C tonight at Quaglino's, probably go from there to White's Club. She wondered what the two of them found to talk about beyond the mission. They were men of very different characters, although Popov had said once that talking with C was rather like having someone peer directly into your soul.

Popov said, "What do you have planned for us tomorrow, my dear Friedl?"

"Lunch with the Tavistocks at the Carlton Grill," she said, picking up her purse and gloves. "After that, a cocktail party, and then dinner at the Ritz with a party of former Right Club members."

His mouth twisted. "Must we?"

She suppressed a smile. "I'm afraid we must." He seemed about to say more but she cut him off. "Call for me at noon, all right, darling?" She waved her gloves. "'*Wiedersehen*." Before she could weaken, she whisked herself out the door.

Friedl spent a restless night. One ought to be sensible, but then where had making the sensible choice led her in the past? One failed marriage, one painful rejection. At least, with a man like Popov, she wouldn't fool herself into believing he was serious about her. Then again, when had her heart ever responded to cold logic? It was dangerous to become entangled with Duško Popov, but the danger of it was half the attraction.

She kicked off the covers in frustration and hugged her pillow tight.

When Popov arrived to collect her the next day, all of Friedl's good resolutions flew out the window. He turned up considerably before the appointed hour, when she'd only just stepped out of the bath. Friedl was a great believer in spur-of-the-moment decisions prompted by these little twists of fate, and the entire set of circumstances seemed to decide the matter. She wouldn't waste any more time. Duško Popov would leave her soon to live among Nazis, to dance on the edge of discovery every minute of every day. She couldn't let him go without showing him how she felt.

So when he pounded on the door of her little mews flat a second time, she didn't make him wait any longer. She wrapped herself in a terry-cloth robe that barely covered the essentials. Hair damp and tousled, eyes wide with feigned surprise, she opened the door.

His face registered shock, delight, and then it darkened with some other emotion. "Friedl, I can't stand it anymore. I'm mad for you. Utterly mad."

That speech was straight out of a bad movie, but there was something about the way he said it, the fire in his eyes, that rendered it more poetic—and far more thrilling—than Göthe or Shakespeare to Friedl's ears.

She smiled a slow, sure smile, then turned on her heel and padded barefoot to the bedroom. After only a short hesitation, Duško followed with quick, impatient footsteps, storming into the room like a man whose patience has been tried to the limit. "Friedl, we need to talk."

She lay there on the bed, smiling up at him, her hands clasped behind her head.

"Go ahead," she told him. "Talk."

They missed lunch, then the cocktail party.

They never made it to dinner.

CHAPTER NINE

London, England
Spring 1941

Paddy

Despite the long hours and pressure of work at the Naval Intelligence Division, Paddy played tennis at the Hurlingham Club in Fulham whenever she could get away. Famous for its polo matches and manicured cricket grounds, the Hurlingham was an exclusive sporting and recreational club, dominated by an enormous white Palladian mansion that closely resembled the American White House.

The atmosphere had changed considerably since the beginning of the war, however. Once a tranquil and rarefied oasis, the Hurlingham's extensive grounds now played host to hundreds of Army and RAF officers, many of whom were billeted in the stables or in the grandstand. The officers' mess was situated in the clubhouse itself. One polo ground was given over to an anti-aircraft battery and the RAF kept one enormous barrage balloon at the other polo ground, and a second looming over the cricket field.

Added to that, a wall of the swimming pool by the river had been blown out by a German bomb, so there wasn't an awful lot of traditional sporting activity going on at the Hurlingham at the moment. Fortunately for Paddy, however, most of the tennis courts still remained intact. Despite the buzz of activity and the ugliness of war that surrounded them, belting a tennis ball about in the fresh air was the perfect form of relaxation as far as she was concerned.

Invigorated after a particularly hard-fought five-seven set loss to one of the top players at the club, Paddy was heading back to the house to change when Muriel Wright caught up with her.

"Oh, hello!" Impossibly tall and slim, rather sick-makingly resplendent in her tennis whites, the former model slipped her arm through Paddy's and fell into step with her. "Fancy a drink? I'm *parched*!"

It was, indeed, a sunny, clear spring day and what could be better than sitting out on the lawn, sipping a refreshing glass of Pimm's No. 1 Cup while they gossiped about their friends and exchanged news? They both changed into tea gowns in the makeshift cloakrooms—Paddy's a poppy red georgette with tiny white flowers and Muriel in cool mint green crepe—and went along to the tea lawn, where drinks were being served. Paddy hadn't even taken her first sip of Pimm's when Muriel heaved a huge sigh and ran a hand through her thick blond curls. "I don't think Ian's ever going to make an honest woman of me."

Paddy refrained from pointing out the obvious—that if Commander Fleming hadn't popped the question after five years, he wasn't likely to do so any time soon. "I hear there was a bit of unpleasantness last weekend," she commented. The incident was the scandal of the town, so it seemed disingenuous not to mention it.

Muriel was practically living with Fleming at his Belgravia flat, and her very proper upper-crust family was appalled. Apparently, her brother had vowed to sort this Fleming fellow out and avenge his sister's honor and had caused a ruckus about it—surely the opposite of what he'd set out to achieve.

Muriel's eyes widened. "Bloody Fitz! Do you know, he came after Ian with a horsewhip? I mean to say, what sort of antiquated behavior is that? Positively gothic! As if Ian were the stable boy having it off with the lord of the manor's daughter. My brother is *such* a fuddy-duddy old fool."

"Good Heavens!" said Paddy faintly. The mind positively boggled at the thought of the debonair commander fending off a thrashing from Fitzherbert Wright. "What did Commander Fleming do?"

Muriel shrugged. "Oh, luckily, we'd gone off to Brighton for the weekend, so Fitz didn't get the chance."

Paddy felt a touch of regret. "I would have liked to have seen the commander talk his way out of that one." But then, she rather thought her superior officer capable of just about anything. The man was abrupt to the point of rudeness most of the time, but when he wanted, he could charm the birds from the trees. He'd probably end up inviting Fitz in for a drink and a glance through his collection of erotic etchings, at the end of which, they'd become the best of friends.

Muriel curled her lip. "I told Fitz it's absolutely none of his business. I'm old enough to earn my own money, live my own life. What with this horrid war, we could all be dead tomorrow."

A chill of horrible presentiment danced down Paddy's spine. It was the most unsettling feeling, and the Irish part of her took heed, beating back the hard-headed northern good sense on which she usually prided herself. It made her say sharply, "In that case, I do rather wonder at your wasting what precious time you have left, Muriel. I like and respect him very much as a colleague, but Ian Fleming is a horrid boyfriend."

The other girl stiffened, glass in hand, and Paddy thought for a moment the contents would be dashed in her face, cucumber, strawberries, and all. Muriel refrained from that gesture, but her voice rose to a volume loud enough for those around them to hear. "Honestly, Paddy! I thought at least *you'd* be on my side. You know how hardworking and clever, and . . . and amusing he is."

"A man can be all those things and still be a thorough scoundrel when it comes to women," said Paddy, keeping her tone quietly reasonable, willing Muriel to follow her lead. The better part of valor would have been to appease, but she liked Muriel too much to sugarcoat her opinion.

"*Well!*" Muriel's face worked and she sputtered a bit, but it seemed she couldn't come up with anything more adequate in response. She leaped up and slammed her drink down, making the little bud vase of violets in the center of the table totter. Then she snatched up her purse and stalked off, still managing to look beautiful and elegant, even in her rage.

"It's nothing I haven't said to his face, after all," Paddy muttered, aware now that all eyes were swiveling between her and Muriel's retreating back. Good Heavens, she hoped the gossips didn't think the two of them were having a catfight over Ian Fleming.

Much as she liked Muriel, she found her defense of the commander irritating. Where his "Mu Mu" was concerned, Fleming was callous to the point of brutality, picking her up and dropping her again when it suited him, like a child with an old toy. Well, despite the attention their spat had attracted, Paddy wouldn't slink away, even though all eyes were now upon her. She would sit there, hold her head up, and calmly finish her drink.

"Excuse me," said a deep voice. "May I join you? My party seems to be late."

Paddy looked up into the pleasant, smiling face of a uniformed Army captain. Tall and blond, with high, rounded cheekbones, he reminded her of a friendly lion, and he had a definite twinkle in his eye.

Paddy lifted one eyebrow. Rescuing a damsel in distress, was he? Well, Paddy didn't need rescuing, but she rather liked the good humor that seemed to radiate from this exceedingly tall man.

"Please do," she said, gesturing to the chair Muriel had so dramatically vacated. "Do we happen to be acquainted at all?" Her mother's rather Victorian ideas of proper introductions and warnings against encouraging strange men—especially men in uniform—came to mind.

"No, but I know who you are," he said, turning his head to

summon a waiter. He ordered another Pimm's for her and a gin and tonic for himself. "My name's Ridsdale," he added as the waiter bowed and glided away.

"And how do you know me, Captain Ridsdale?" asked Paddy. The name was familiar, of course. The Ridsdales were a prominent political family, connected to a former prime minister, no less. Paddy debated with herself. The captain didn't seem in the least like a bounder or a shady sort of character, but one couldn't be certain. True, his pedigree was reassuring, but it wasn't a guarantee.

"I saw you here once before and asked my friend Charles Doughty about you," he answered, breaking in on her speculations. "He utterly refused to introduce us, being, I think, half in love with you himself."

Paddy blinked in surprise. Ridsdale's manner was more pleasant than flirtatious, but he seemed to possess more directness than most Englishmen she knew. "Did he?" she said, her tone turning crisp as it often did when she felt a little flustered. "I trust he told you only the good things."

"What he told me made me all the more eager to meet you," said the captain lightly, and she felt a strange warmth rise to her cheeks, as if she'd just come off the tennis court.

The waiter returned with their drinks then, giving Paddy a moment to recover from her confusion. What was wrong with her? She didn't usually blush and simper like a silly little girl, but this man, with his charmingly self-deprecating manner, had somehow caught her off guard.

"I hear you work for the NID," said Ridsdale once the waiter retreated. He cocked an eyebrow in the direction of the doorway through which Muriel had departed in high dudgeon. "Fleming's a hard taskmaster, eh? Godfrey, too."

Paddy had picked up her drink but at his last words, she paused, the glass halfway to her lips. Frowning a little, she watched half a hulled strawberry bob and jostle against a straw of cucumber in her punch, then took a long sip. What was this Captain Ridsdale trying to pull? Could he possibly be a spy? Unlikely as that seemed, why else would he ask her about her work immediately upon making her acquaintance?

"Oh, you've been misinformed," she said, laughing and waving away the suggestion with a nonchalant hand. "I work in the secretarial pool at the Admiralty, that's all. I hardly ever even set eyes on the big man." She shrugged. "It's all terribly mundane, really, typing and filing, but one must do one's bit." And now *stop*, she told herself. Overexplanation was always a sign that someone was hiding the truth.

Captain Ridsdale was watching her with a disquieting gleam in his eye that told her he didn't believe a word of it. She lifted her chin and steered the conversation away from dangerous waters. If he wasn't a spy, had he been sent—perhaps by the intelligence services—to test her discretion? It did seem the more likely alternative. Rather a deflating thought.

Inwardly, Paddy sighed. It did seem rather unfair that the first man she should come across who made her feel—what?—a little breathless, a little excited, a little unsure—should turn out to be a man she might be wise to discourage. But her job meant everything to her, and the trust Godfrey and Fleming placed in her was too valuable to jeopardize. If Godfrey had sent this Captain Ridsdale to test her, then she would make sure she passed with flying colors.

She brought the conversation to a close as soon as she had finished her drink, then rose from the table, pulling on her short white gloves. "Well, I must get on. Thank you for . . ." She made a gesture intended to encompass the drink, the conversation, and his gallantry in rescuing her from prying eyes, unnecessary though it had been.

The captain got up when she did, and Paddy found herself offering her hand for him to shake. He reached out and gripped her hand lightly, yet she felt the strength in those long fingers. And there it was again, that odd little tilt of her very stable, sensible world.

His smile lit up his eyes in a most attractive way. "I trust we'll meet again, Miss Bennett."

She hoped the glow that warmed her chest at the prospect of seeing him once more did not show on her face.

"Perhaps a game of tennis?" His expression was guileless, hopeful. He still held her hand.

"Perhaps." She slipped her hand free.

"Then shall we say, this time next week?"

"You are persistent, Captain." If he was here to tempt her into indiscretion, surely he'd done that, and she'd resisted. If he was a spy, well, she simply couldn't imagine it. And then she thought of her earlier conversation. Muriel had spoken the truth, after all. Life was too uncertain and too short to deny one's inclinations—particularly on the strength of such wild imaginings as Paddy had been indulging in about the captain.

So she didn't send him to the right about as she'd initially intended but said, "I am an excellent tennis player, as it happens. And I take the game *very* seriously." She picked up her purse and slid the short strap over her wrist. "Just a friendly warning. I wouldn't want to embarrass you when I thrash you off the court."

He laughed. "Then perhaps we ought to play together. Doubles. That way, you can make up for my shortcomings. They are, I fear, considerable."

She liked that he didn't bristle at her ribbing or boast of his own prowess. "Very well, then. Why don't you set up a match with Charles and his partner?"

"May I telephone you to make the arrangements?"

Without quite realizing what she was doing, Paddy took out her card and handed it to him. His face brightened, as if he had just won a prize at the tombola.

For the first time, Paddy allowed herself to smile back at him, and was rather delighted to see the captain blink and swallow hard. "Miss Bennett—"

"See you on the tennis court, Captain." She gave a little mock salute. "Be sure to bring your best game."

As she returned home that afternoon, Paddy realized she had not stopped smiling since she'd parted from her new acquaintance. Captain Ridsdale. What an unexpected and delightful encounter. Then she recalled his questions about the NID and her smile faded. He did seem like rather a lovely man, but she ought to be on her guard. She wasn't about to risk her future for the sake of a love affair. She wasn't at all like Muriel Wright.

* * *

As it turned out, it was some weeks before Paddy saw Captain Ridsdale again. First of all, she was caught up in the frenzy of the fallout from the capture of Crete by Göring's Eleventh Airborne Division. Then Fleming, after a stint abroad—which she suspected included a trip to America, if the gifts he brought back with him were anything to go by—wanted to know everything he could about what had led to the British defeat. It was Paddy's job to collate all of the reports that came in and to present them in some coherent format for the commander to peruse.

"Fellow by the name of Skorzeny," said Fleming, perching on the edge of Godfrey's desk one late summer's day. "Landed with the first wave of German troops, but he didn't join the fight. Took a small team and headed straight for British headquarters at Maleme and Heraklion."

Godfrey sat back in his chair. "With what objective, I suppose we can guess."

Paddy spoke up. "Intelligence." She knew all about it, having researched the details. The Germans had pulled off an amazing coup that left the British at a complete disadvantage in the region.

"Right," said Fleming. "The fellows who went in, the members of Skorzeny's team, must have had special training. They knew exactly what they were looking for. Maps, codes, equipment, divisional orders. The lot. They got in and secured everything before our chaps even knew they were coming."

"And?" Irascible as ever when contemplating a defeat, Godfrey raised his eyebrows. "Get to the point, Fleming. I'm sure there is one."

"Intelligence commandos," said Fleming. "We need some of our own."

Paddy frowned. "You mean we don't have any?"

"No, and it's a wasted opportunity," said Fleming, warming to his theme. By the light in his eye, Paddy deduced he'd give anything to be one of those commandos himself, racing in ahead of the troops with a cover force made up of just a handful of Royal Marines. Blasting his way into German headquarters, rifling through papers and files while his men provided cover fire. Perhaps a small firearm for himself and a desperate fight to the death in hand-to-hand combat with the officer-in-command . . .

"The idea has merit," said Godfrey. "But let's get one thing clear, Fleming. On no account will you be the one to lead any crack team like that."

"Really? I should have thought—"

"Out—of—the question." Godfrey shook his head. "Good God, man, the sheer volume of sensitive information that's swimming around in that head of yours . . . What would happen if you were captured? Might as well lead those men myself."

Fleming moved restlessly, as if about to argue the point further. Seeing Godfrey's choler rise, Paddy sought to forestall them both, lightly touching Fleming's sleeve. "That's a compliment, Commander, in case you didn't notice." She smiled at both men, holding up a docket that had come in immediately before their meeting. "Could you both spare a moment to look at these dispatches? I think they're rather important."

Summer came and went, and Paddy heard no more about intelligence commandos. As was his habit, once the matter was dropped, Fleming appeared to forget all about it. Godfrey might be quick to see the advantages of training an advance assault team of the nature Fleming described; the First Lord of the Admiralty and the Joint Intelligence Committee were slower to catch on. But Fleming wasn't one to try to persuade people who wouldn't listen, and in any case he was far too busy to try. He went about his business with his customary ruthless efficiency, and Paddy swam along in his wake.

Generally speaking, there was quite a bit of joking and easy bonhomie in Room 39, particularly when Admiral Godfrey was absent. Commander Slade was a particular favorite of Paddy's. He would dash off amusing stanzas of verse here and there about the personalities of Room 39. One memorable poem began "Do not mark that paper to me, Sir," bemoaning the river of paperwork that flowed into Room 39 without cease.

One impatient glance from Fleming was enough to douse any high spirits, however. The rear admiral's right-hand man never engaged in the friendly banter that went on between the others at the NID. He was rather a lonely figure, Paddy thought. She shrugged. Fleming was hardly a fitting object for pity. He seemed to have no shortage of friends outside of Room 39.

She had been unable to broker a friendship between Fleming and Julian Ridsdale, though she'd made the attempt. She and Julian had managed to clear up the misunderstanding over his intentions when asking her about her work at the Admiralty. "It was inappropriate to raise the subject," he said to her when they'd become better acquainted. "Do, please, forgive me. I was so dashed nervous, you see. I'd been wanting to meet you for months, and suddenly there you were. I'm afraid I said the first thing that popped into my head. Bad form. I realized my mistake as soon as I said it." He smiled. "And you were so cool to me, too. I thought I'd blown it there and then."

His self-deprecating honesty disarmed her. Of course, the entire speech might have been disingenuous, but Paddy prided herself on being an excellent judge of character. Then, too, she had taken the precaution of mentioning Captain Ridsdale to Ian Fleming after their first meeting at the Hurlingham Club, and Fleming had grunted in response. "Bit of a dull dog, isn't he?"

"I found him rather amusing and sweet," said Paddy. "But that's not what I wanted to know. Is he . . . ? *You* know."

Fleming frowned. "Is he what?"

She lowered her voice. "Well, Captain Ridsdale seemed to know that I worked for you and Admiral Godfrey. I mean, *how* does he know, and what ought I to do about it?"

Fleming looked down at her, amusement sparking in his hooded eyes. "Oh, don't worry about that. Load of old gossips, intelligence service men. He probably heard about you from one of the chaps here."

Paddy blinked. She didn't even speak to her own mother about what she did at the Admiralty, and here these fellows were, blabbing to all and sundry! Exchanging anecdotes over the brandy and cigars at their clubs, no doubt.

Well, she'd think about that later. "So he's all right, then—Captain Ridsdale, I mean?"

Fleming shrugged. "As far as I know, he's not an enemy spy or anything. But I think you know what I'm going to say. You're dealing with high-level stuff here, Miss Bennett. In many ways you're privy to more sensitive information than most of the officers in Room Thirty-Nine. You can't tell Ridsdale any of it. Not even something as seemingly innocuous as whether or not you've had a good day at the office."

"Well, that's what I thought," said Paddy, glad that her caution had been justified.

At first, keeping her own counsel had been a simple matter. Now that she'd grown to like and admire Julian so much, however, separating the personal and the professional became increasingly difficult. How did married people manage?

Oh. That's right. As soon as she got married, she would have to leave the NID, so it wouldn't be an issue—at least, not on a daily basis the way it was now. Paddy pursed her lips. Fortunately, she did not intend to get married for a good while yet.

London, England
December 1941

From the same officers who had no doubt gossiped to Julian about Paddy, she discovered one more point in Captain Ridsdale's favor. It transpired that he worked in the War Office in some capacity and was therefore in a similar position to Paddy as far as secrecy went. He had been posted to Japan as military attaché at the time Japan declared war on Britain, and he'd been obliged to get out of the country in rather a hurry or risk being arrested as a foreign spy. From this, Paddy deduced that Captain Ridsdale was currently engaged in some sort of intelligence work focused on Japan and the Pacific region, though he never said as much.

The shock Japanese attack on Pearl Harbor only the day before had distressed Julian, though he tried his best to hide his feelings behind his usual bonhomie. Paddy burned to ask him all about it, but of course she couldn't. Trying to act as if Captain Ridsdale had no inside knowledge of the matter was like picking one's way through a conversational minefield. He had been working around the clock in the days leading up to the catastrophe, but tonight he had insisted on fulfilling his promise to escort her to a party before returning once again to the War Office.

"I think it best if we avoid talking about work altogether," said Paddy as they strolled into the foyer of the Dorchester Hotel. Although it was hard to see how that would be possible tonight. No one talked about anything else. Surely the Americans must enter the war now?

"Oh, absolutely," said Julian. "There are so many more interesting things to talk about, after all. For instance," he said, lightly touching the jewel-studded arrangement in her hair, "what are we calling this?"

"It's a snood, if you must know," said Paddy, laughing. "Though I can't imagine why you should care."

"I want to know everything about you," said Julian so matter-of-factly that it took her by surprise. "Everything you do interests me."

It was times like this, thought Paddy, when one simply

couldn't think of what to say. Almost from their first meeting, Julian had shown the serious nature of his interest in her. She was more cautious and, she supposed, a touch more phlegmatic, when it came to matters of love. She wasn't terribly interested in settling down too soon. Her work at the NID was so varied and fascinating, it completely consumed her at times. She felt useful, her opinions respected, her intellect engaged. Marriage—if marriage was what Julian Ridsdale intended—would put a stop to it all. She'd have to give up her job at the NID and that would be that.

That evening, they were attending a party thrown by none other than Ann O'Neill. The same Ann O'Neill who was rumored to be having a torrid affair with Commander Fleming.

"Awkward," Paddy said to Jean when they met later in the evening. "Muriel was threatening to gate-crash, but I don't see her."

"I do hope she doesn't," said Jean. "That would not end well."

"What wouldn't end well, my sweeties? You intrigue me!" The voice of Brian Howard came from behind them. He was weaving a little, as if drunk, his dark eyes larger than ever beneath those emphatic black eyebrows.

Not for the first time, Brian Howard reminded Paddy of a wounded panther, continually striking out, never allowing anyone close enough to tend to his wounds. Tonight, tail lashing, he was ready to pounce. Paddy, who had developed an unwilling liking for the wayward and troubled soul, said, "Never you mind."

"Don't look now," muttered Jean. "Fleming's arrived."

But of course, Paddy did send a covert glance in the commander's direction. He was wearing his uniform, having come late, presumably direct from his duties.

"My *dears*," murmured Brian in his signature waspish tone, "if it isn't the chocolate sailor."

"Brian!" said Jean, swatting his arm.

Paddy sent him a sharp glance. "Don't start spreading that name about."

"Why, I didn't coin the sobriquet, darling. I heard it somewhere." They watched Fleming converse with their hostess, both of them looking as if butter wouldn't melt in their mouths. "I also heard that Ann O'Neill laughed her head off when someone said it in her hearing," Brian added.

Paddy swallowed a blistering retort. Ian Fleming could fight his own battles. She didn't know quite why she was protective of him when it came to Lady O'Neill. Surely his falling for a woman like that was some sort of poetic justice.

Julian returned to them then and followed the direction of their collective gaze. Smoothly, he appropriated two glasses of champagne from a passing waiter and handed one each to Jean and Paddy. "Gossiping about our hostess? I can't think why everyone is so obsessed with those two."

Commander Fleming was something of a touchy subject between Paddy and Julian. The knowledge—though Paddy herself had never confirmed it one way or the other—that the girl he loved worked closely with a man like Ian Fleming would give most boyfriends a few qualms. When the two men met—which was seldom, as Fleming seemed to take as much care as Julian did to avoid any such encounters—they never seemed to hit it off.

Which was understandable, of course, at least on Julian's side. But it was rather a pity. The two men had quite a lot in common if only they could set prejudice aside.

"Well, I'm not interested in that affair in the least," said Paddy, not entirely truthfully. "Oh, look! There are the Troubridges. We must say hello."

"Rather you than me, pet," drawled Brian, sauntering off.

"Don't mind Brian," said Jean in an undertone. "He just got sacked from his job, so he's in one of his moods."

"Brian has a job?" said Paddy. "I'd always thought him purely ornamental." Somehow, she'd forgotten that long-ago allusion he'd made to working with Jean until now. She couldn't quite imagine Brian Howard actually working for a living or taking orders from anyone.

"Well, he doesn't have a job anymore," said Jean, sighing. "I've always adored him despite his little ways, but even I have to admit it: Brian's turning into a bitter, bitter man."

A young fellow approached Julian and murmured into his ear. With a quirk of the eyebrow, Julian gave a curt nod and turned to Paddy.

"You have to go." She smiled at him and tried not to feel disappointed. "Good night, Captain Ridsdale."

She watched as he made his way through the crowd. Some time later, the music stopped abruptly. The bandleader announced, "Ladies and gentlemen, the news we've all been waiting for. The United States of America has declared war on Japan!"

A whoop went up all around them. *Finally!* Finally the Americans were going to join the fight. Paddy and Jean hugged each other and jumped up and down. The band played "Yankee Doodle Dandy," and everyone kicked up their heels and danced. Now surely, the tide of the war would turn.

CHAPTER TEN

London, England
July 1942

Paddy

*T*he matter of Fleming's intelligence assault unit did not arise again until early in 1942, when plans for full-scale commando raids on the French coast got underway. And even then, it wasn't until July that he seized the chance to make up a team to storm German headquarters in advance of a raid on Dieppe.

"Two Navy lieutenants. A small force of Royal Marines—ten of the best," said Godfrey. "That's all I can give you."

"If I went in with them, Admiral—" Fleming began.

"This again!" Godfrey threw down his pen. "I told you in no uncertain terms, Fleming, you will *not* undertake any mission where you put yourself at risk of capture. If you must be on the spot, you can observe from a safe distance aboard one of the carrier ships."

"But Admiral, if you'll simply—"

"The *good* news, however," Godfrey interrupted, raising his voice a little, "is that your intelligence assault unit has been given the go-ahead. You are to undertake and supervise all of the selection, training, and planning for your team in preparation for the North African invasion."

Paddy blinked. The Torch landings—a three-pronged Allied attack on French North Africa via Casablanca, Oran, and Algeria—were slated for November. That would not give Fleming much time. She didn't need to glance at the commander to know that his entire body had tensed like a pointer when it scented game. He was poised and ready for action as soon as Godfrey dismissed them.

The second the baize-covered door to Godfrey's lair closed behind them, Paddy whipped out her notepad and pencil to take Fleming's rapid-fire instructions.

"Telephone Ryder and tell him I want to see him immediately. And Watson, Friels, and Simpkins, too."

"Yes, sir."

He dictated several lists and memoranda to her, and the messages flew about the country, as Fleming gathered to him information, expertise, and personnel. "We'll need to involve Scotland Yard," he said, pacing back and forth in front of her desk as she took notes. "The unit must have instruction on blowing safes, picking locks, and breaking and entering. Field work, use of explosives—both plastique and gelignite—booby traps, minefields. Weapons training, hand-to-hand combat, and silent killing."

She could see Fleming warming to the prospect of learning

all of these skills himself. Paddy had to admit, it sounded like a lot of fun to her, too. Maybe she could persuade him to let her join them.

"And the intelligence training?" she prompted, as he stood gazing out the window at the gardens of Number 10.

"Right. Yes," said Fleming, beginning to pace again. "I'll cover that side of it and work up a comprehensive syllabus. For now, list these items: capture of radar sets, ciphers, code books, intelligence reports, secret orders, new weapons specifications . . . Very well, Miss Bennett, that's it for now. No, wait. Get me all the information you can on Algiers—aerial pictures, maps, models, all the intelligence we have. I need to know everything there is to know about the place."

If Fleming had been a machine before, now he was a powerhouse, energized and excited by the prospect of commanding his own elite unit and enjoying the utter freedom Godfrey gave him to design and recruit the team and plan their operations as he saw fit.

* * *

"I never see you," Julian complained to Paddy over the telephone when he finally reached her at home late one evening. It had been all hands on deck in Room 39 lately, and this time she'd been forced to stand him up for dinner at the Ritz, couldn't even spare a moment to ring to tell him she wasn't able to go. According to a reproachful Mrs. Rivers, Julian had called for her, and, finding both Paddy and her mother absent, had waited in her father's study for almost three hours for her return. The housekeeper had offered him a light supper but he'd declined and eventually left.

Of course, there had been occasions where the positions were reversed, too, particularly in the frenetic time surrounding the Japanese attack on Pearl Harbor. However, Julian had always been able to send her word that he was tied up and couldn't come.

"I know! I'm so sorry," said Paddy, kicking off her shoes and flopping down on her bed fully clothed. "I miss you, too." Slowly and surely, over the past year, Julian Ridsdale had become the most important person in the world to her. But it had to be said that her work for the NID was so hectic and absorbing that there were long periods every day when she forgot about everyone outside of Room 39, including Julian.

Guilty at the thought, she added, "I have the night off tomorrow. Do you think we could go to dinner at the Étoile, just the two of us?"

"That sounds lovely, darling." His voice was warm and comforting, like a cup of cocoa, and she snuggled down into the pillows for a long and comfortable chat. They would still have plenty to talk about tomorrow evening, never fear—they simply didn't ever run out of conversation. That was one of the things about him she liked best. Jean and Muriel might prefer men like Ian Fleming, who were dangerous and full of mystery and ignored them entirely more often than not, but give Paddy her dear Captain Ridsdale any day of the week.

The next evening after dinner, she invited Julian in for a nightcap. He had been on edge and fidgety the whole time they'd been together, so when he took her glass of sherry from her and set it carefully on an occasional table, then kneeled down and clasped her hand in his, she ought not to have been taken so completely by surprise. "Oh!" she exclaimed, as he opened a small velvet box to reveal a gleaming diamond ring. "Julian! *Really?* Are you sure?"

He laughed up at her. "Yes, really! And now you've made me forget what I was going to say. I had an absolute ripper of a speech all prepared."

She chuckled. "Well, whatever it was, when you remember, you must write it down for me and I'll stick it in my scrapbook. Darling." She took his face between her hands and bent to kiss him. "Of course I'll marry you."

She took his hands and drew him to sit beside her on the sofa. He slid the ring on her finger, and they both admired it as it sparkled on her left hand. Then he put an arm around her shoulders and drew her close, saying into her hair, "Let's set a date as soon as possible."

Paddy's voice rose higher. "I was rather thinking spring might be nice."

He drew back, his expression crestfallen. "Spring? But that's almost a year away. I'd marry you tomorrow if I could."

Tomorrow? Paddy's eyes widened and her mouth dropped open. Of course he was joking, but still . . .

He laughed. "Don't look so alarmed. I know you ladies must have your big weddings and all the fuss. But surely with your powers of organization we could manage the arrangements within, say, a month?"

Scarcely less appalled by this prospect, she forced a smile.

"I doubt a month would be long enough, but I'll do my best. In good conscience, I ought to make sure everything is in order and ready to be passed on to my successor at the Admiralty before I leave."

Desperation clutched at her chest. It was all very well for Julian to talk about getting married tomorrow. His life wouldn't alter much once they were wed, while hers would change completely.

A flutter of panic made her mind race. How could she go from dealing with matters of national—*international*—importance every day to . . . wifedom? Designing menus and entertaining, running a household, knitting balaclavas, for goodness' sake. Or would Julian expect her to move out into a flat with him, just the two of them, and cook and clean and wash his socks? That sounded like a deeply uncomfortable way to begin married life.

Don't be ridiculous! she told herself. Julian wouldn't dream of asking her to wash his socks. He'd better not, at any rate! Nevertheless a deep reluctance to leave Room 39 became a small, tight knot in her stomach.

"How about September, then?" asked Julian. "Won't that be enough time?"

"Hmm." At this moment, it felt as if there would never be enough time to accomplish what she wanted to achieve at the Admiralty before she left. Suddenly, it struck Paddy that she'd wanted to be right there in Room 39 when the war was won.

But how could she wait that long to marry Julian? The war had dragged on for years, and even if the Americans had joined in the fight, it might be many more years before the Allies emerged victorious. She loved Julian. She wanted more than anything to marry him and start a family. She couldn't wait years for that.

Well, if this war had taught them anything, it was that life is short, and she adored this man to bits. She would marry him, and trust in her own resources to create an interesting life for herself outside the four walls of Room 39. There were plenty of other jobs a married woman could do in the current climate, after all.

Before Julian could wonder at her hesitation, Paddy smiled brightly. "September sounds divine, darling."

* * *

"Married?" Admiral Godfrey rubbed at the creases on his forehead as if attempting to clear away the headache Paddy's news had brought him. "Must you?"

Paddy clasped her hands behind her, rocked onto her toes and back. "Sorry, sir. Afraid I must."

"I *mean*," said Godfrey, throwing out a hand, "we're about to invade Africa. How in the world will we do it without you, Miss Bennett?"

Paddy knew he was not even half joking, but she chuckled. "Never fear, sir. I've left plenty of time to train up my replacement." Jealousy was a most unattractive quality, but every time she thought of the eminently capable young woman she was about to hire to take her place, Paddy could not help gritting her teeth. Fleming had given Paddy carte blanche to engage whomever she thought suitable, only saying, "No harridans, if you please." That drew one of her Grade A withering looks, but his back was turned so he didn't see it.

Fleming had taken Paddy's defection in stride, giving a curt nod, as if he'd expected nothing less of a mere female than that she'd place such a vapid institution as marriage above her duty to crown and country. He seemed to deal with Paddy's expected absence by treating it as if it had happened already, largely ignoring her unless he needed something. Though Paddy would rather die than admit it, his behavior hurt—particularly when contrasted with the reaction of the other men in Room 39. They were far more outspoken, feigning heartbreak, calling Julian a lucky dog, and asking if he knew how greatly he was setting back the war effort by stealing her away. But somehow, all of that flummery didn't quite make up for Fleming's seeming indifference.

On her final day in Room 39, Paddy packed up the very few personal items on her desk into a little box. For a moment, she took a good look about her, drinking in the scene of organized chaos, the ringing telephones, the clatter of typewriter keys and the zing of the bell, the insistent *buzz . . . buzz . . . buzz* from Godfrey's office that brought one of his officers running. It had been the scene of such tension, of late nights, of triumphs and crushing defeats, and at times, it must be said, of excruciating tedium.

From this day on, Room 39 would close its doors to her. She would never again be privy to the secrets of the NID, never step inside Godfrey's office and debate matters great and small with him and Fleming, never sit at her desk and type a memorandum filled with outlandish plots to confound and misdirect the Germans. What had happened about the *Trout* Memorandum?

Thank goodness the scheme with the dead body floating somewhere in the Mediterranean had never come to pass.

A rush of nostalgia edged with sadness made her swallow
hard against threatening tears. Paddy forced herself to lift her
chin and square her shoulders. With a determinedly cheery "Bye
all!" Paddy picked up her little box, turned, and walked out of
Room 39.

London, England
February 1943

Despite her qualms about leaving the Admiralty, Paddy could
hardly claim married life was dull. What with the household
to run, various committees and good works initiatives to take
her time and energy, and the never-ending problem of how to
stretch the rations to feed the household, there was plenty to occupy her. Then, too, the Luftwaffe kept things interesting, peri-
odically returning to rain down more brimstone on the city of
London.

By this time in early 1943, Paddy and Julian had stopped
traipsing down to the cellar every time there was an air raid. If
they happened to be home at the time, they would simply put on
a record and dance, or busy themselves with the crossword or
in discussing the latest political developments. Following in the
footsteps of his uncle, the former prime minister, Stanley Baldwin, Julian had ambitions to enter Parliament one day. Paddy
was all for it. She was even now seeking out political connections

and forging alliances that would stand Julian in good stead after the war.

Rather than try to find a new place to live, as well as new staff, the couple had chosen to move into the Bennett house at Number 12 The Boltons with Paddy's mother.

This arrangement suited all three of them. Edith Bennett certainly did not match the typical idea of a mother-in-law. Even had she the inclination to interfere with the newlyweds, she was far too busy to do so, and Paddy wouldn't have stood for it, anyway. The three of them rubbed along well together, and if Paddy found her days disorientingly free from the thrilling tension and high-level activity of the Admiralty, she was not the sort of person to sit about repining or twiddling her thumbs. She got on with what was in front of her and counted her many blessings. Not least of these was that her husband worked at the War Office, so she was able to see him every day.

"You must promise me," said Julian, taking her hands with an expression of seriousness he rarely wore, "that if . . . well, *when* the time comes that you're expecting a baby, you must go to your family in Ireland. Get plenty of fresh air, good food, and rest."

This was something they'd spoken of before, and Paddy had almost unthinkingly agreed, because a baby seemed far off in some misty future, a mythical sort of future that did not include the war. Now, she said, "Of course. I've read that the stresses of London air raids aren't good for babies or their mothers." She kissed Julian on the nose. "I'll be good, I promise."

One evening in February, the German bombs came too close for the crossword to take Paddy's mind off the shelling. The whine of plane engines could be heard clearly from the sitting room on the second floor, where she and Julian were ensconced, rugged up against the cold.

A blast that was far too close for comfort actually shook the house, rattling the sitting room windows. Paddy was about to suggest—quite casually—that perhaps it might be wisest to repair to the cellar on this particular occasion, when a loud *whump* overhead made her jump, heart pounding.

As one, she and Julian raced upstairs, and up again to the attic, where the dormer windows were free from blackout masking because the family so seldom ventured up here.

"Should I get a torch?" said Paddy, peering about her. The moon shone brightly, but inside the attic, light came only in patches, shafting through the windows in the roof.

"No, we can't do that," said Julian. "Let's wait a bit for our eyes to grow accustomed to the dark." Paddy heard a dragging sound and realized Julian was pulling a large piece of furniture over to the space beneath the dormer window.

Looking up, she could see searchlights panning the heavens and heard the nearby anti-aircraft guns cracking away in defense of the city. "Oh, do be careful!" she called as Julian climbed up onto the table to look out the window. She could make out his shape better now that he was silhouetted against the sky. What was he going to do?

"Now, I want you to stay calm, Paddy," said Julian in a matter-of-fact tone.

"Calm? Of course I'm calm," Paddy snapped. "What do I need to be calm *about*, precisely?"

"Well, my dear, it's just that there's an incendiary bomb on the roof. It doesn't seem to have caught fire, though."

"Oh. Well." Paddy forced down the panic. Incendiary bombs were fairly common and usually not dangerous if they did not ignite on impact, but that didn't mean she wasn't terrified to have one on the roof. "What do we do about that, then?"

"It's caught in the guttering, too far down for me to reach from here. Maybe I can climb out . . ." He was opening the dormer window but it was far too small for a man of Julian's size to squeeze through.

"I'll do it," said Paddy without hesitation. If she thought too much about it, she might lose courage.

"Absolutely not. It's far too dangerous." But Julian's response was automatic. The entire terrace of houses was at risk if the bomb ignited while on their roof. Julian was physically incapable of accomplishing the task without Paddy's help.

"Well, it must be done, and we can't ask the staff to do it," said Paddy. "Let me try."

And so it was that Paddy soon found herself dangling out of her attic window, her faithful spouse gripping her by the ankles, while she attempted to push an incendiary bomb off the roof of Number 12 with a broom.

The device didn't look like much—a foot-long cylinder of metal, shaped like a baseball bat with most of the handle chopped off. As Julian had said, the bomb had lodged in the guttering, where it seemed quite determined to remain.

Paddy stretched out as far as she could, using the bristled end of the broom to try to sweep it up and over the side of the gutter.

"It doesn't seem to want to move," she called back to Julian. "I'll try the other way."

The broom handle seemed as if it would work better. She almost had it underneath the device when an explosion shook the house and lit the night around her. The broom slipped in her grip. With a cry, Paddy clutched it harder, put her head down and squeezed her eyes shut, waiting for the end to come.

The terrible noise of the bombing subsided to the dull roar of a raging fire some streets away. "You're all right, darling. I've got you." Julian's voice, determined and calm, floated down to her. His grip on her ankles was firm and reassuring.

Gasping for breath, perspiration slicking her palms, Paddy lifted her head, adjusted her grip on the broom, and tried again.

After several failed attempts, she managed to wedge the end of the broom handle underneath the bomb and lever it up . . . and . . . "Over!" she yelled in triumph. The device dropped down and landed with a *thump* in the garden below. Paddy waited, tensed for an explosion of some kind, but none came.

"Reel me in, Captain!" cried Paddy, nearly dropping the broom as Julian obeyed orders with alacrity, pulling her up and helping her over the windowsill and into his arms. Both of them laughed their heads off as they hugged each other tightly, full of victory and the joy of being alive. Paddy's shins and knees were bruised and she might have pulled a muscle or two, but she had triumphed.

"I'll get the sand bucket," said Julian.

"What a night!" Paddy poured them each a glass of whiskey and threw herself into an armchair. Julian, having dumped a bucketful of sand over the incendiary, arranged for someone to come and make sure the bomb was deactivated properly.

It was at times like this that she was particularly glad she'd married Julian. Oh, the wedding itself had been perfect—St. Margaret's for the ceremony, Claridge's Hotel for the reception. She'd worn a picture gown made of duchess satin with a train and a veil of Brussels lace. The gown had been sewn from a bolt of fabric her mother had bought in Paris and put away years before. The veil was a family heirloom. It had all belonged to a fairy tale, and she'd enjoyed every second of it. But this—*this*—was real, working together to solve life's difficulties, even if said difficulties involved pushing an incendiary device off one's roof.

After all of that excitement, Paddy slept in the next day, a luxury she would never again take for granted after her stint at the Admiralty. She was woken by Mrs. Rivers, who indicated the telephone beside Paddy's bed. "Call for you, Miss Paddy—Mrs. Ridsdale, I should say."

"This early?" Paddy sat up. "Is something wrong?"

"Nothing wrong, I'm sure," said the housekeeper. "But it's the Admiralty. I thought you'd want it put through. Said his name was Fleming."

"Gosh!" Paddy blinked a little owlishly. "What sort of time does he call this?" The clock told her it was only a smidge after eight.

Truth be told, she was a bit annoyed with Fleming. He had politely declined her invitation to the wedding, sending an expensive yet impersonal gift of a silver entrée dish instead. Well, if she'd had any doubts where she stood with him, she didn't anymore. She'd rather thought it would be a case of "out of sight, out of mind" between them henceforth—at least on his part. On her side, Paddy had made up with Muriel long ago after their spat at the Hurlingham Club, and was still obliged to hear all about Fleming whenever she saw her friend.

With a nervous twist to her stomach, Paddy turned to the telephone and picked up the receiver. "Hello?"

"Mrs. Ridsdale," came that familiar voice, clipped and direct. "Are you free for a twelve o'clock lunch at the Savoy today? We have a small favor to ask."

Before she could answer, he rang off. Paddy held the receiver away from her and stared at it, indignation rising. Did he simply expect she'd be available? Or worse, that she'd drop everything else and come running the second he crooked his finger? She was a very busy person, she'd have him know. And even if she *was* free, how could Fleming expect her to want anything more to do with him and his schemes?

She frowned. He'd said "we." Fleming wasn't one for identifying himself with the Admiralty, or for using the royal "we," either, so he must be talking about someone else. It couldn't be Admiral Godfrey. He had been replaced as director of the NID the previous year. Which was a complete travesty, as far as Paddy was concerned, but that was internal politics for you.

As it happened, Paddy was *not* free for lunch that day, and she would have liked to have been granted the opportunity to tell Fleming so. However, he must have known wild horses couldn't have kept her away from this meeting. What on earth could they—whoever *they* were—want with her?

With a slight, wry smile at her own weakness in the face of raging curiosity, she telephoned Muriel Wright to cancel their lunch appointment. "Dreadfully sorry, old thing. Could we re-schedule for next week? All right, then. I'll ring you later."

Paddy jumped out of bed and hurried to get dressed.

CHAPTER ELEVEN

London, England
Spring 1941

Friedl

*W*ithout Duško Popov, London had lost a little of its sparkle, but Friedl wasn't one to sit about at home, pining. She went out more than ever, to nightclubs, the theater, to parties and concerts. Anything for distraction, anything to pretend she didn't miss her Serbian spy quite dreadfully.

When she drank too much, which happened often, Friedl lost track of time, and her evening ended in a jail cell with the working girls on more than one occasion. "Honestly, Friedl!" said Joan, rolling her eyes. "We ought to issue you with a little tag that says, 'If found, ring this number,' like a lost puppy or something."

One evening, it was late, and Friedl had decided to walk the short distance back to her flat from Claridge's Hotel, only to discover that this was more difficult than it sounded. The night was moonless, and because of the blackout, London was so dark that she had to feel along the railings outside the buildings of Mayfair for guidance.

Still, her flat was only a block away, and she wasn't too concerned about the lateness of the hour. Despite the threat of air raids, which had eased off considerably after the initial pounding of the Blitz, to Friedl, London at night had always felt safe.

Now, as she inched her way along the mews toward her apartment building, she blinked hard in an effort to see something, anything, but she couldn't even make out her hand in front of her face.

She reached the block of flats that adjoined hers. Nearly there. Just two more sets of railings to go. Then she saw it. Or rather, she sensed it. A presence. A darkness more profound than the rest of the darkness around it, looming in the doorway to her building.

She blinked, then squinted. It was just a trick of her overactive imagination—wasn't it? Surely it must be. Then she saw a small flame hover briefly in midair, as if someone in that doorway was lighting a cigarette. The merest glimpse of a man's profile, illuminated by the lighter, before it disappeared. The glow of a cigarette tip, like a firefly, marking the stranger in place.

Friedl's heart lurched and began to pound. She hadn't been exaggerating when she'd told Billy and Joan she still had nightmares about Anna Wolkoff, the Russian spy she'd helped put in jail. She could never quite erase the image of Wolkoff's face, so close to hers, her features twisted with rage. Since then, Anna had been sentenced to seven years in prison, but Friedl had no doubt that if Anna Wolkoff could have carried out her threat to murder Friedl, she would have done it. And if she couldn't, she might well order someone else to do it for her.

According to M, most of Wolkoff's coconspirators had been rounded up, but Friedl and Joan needed to be a little careful to avoid the places where the remainder of Wolkoff's supporters might be found. Both Joan and Friedl—or rather, the aliases they'd used when frequenting the Wolkoffs' Russian Tea Room—were on several blacklists, so while M didn't anticipate trouble, it paid to be cautious.

This man in the doorway might well be entirely unconnected with the Wolkoffs, but Friedl couldn't convince herself to take another step toward him. She wanted to turn and run, but that would be foolhardy in the darkness. Slowly, silently, she retraced her steps until she found the recessed doorway of the building next to hers, then drew back into its shelter. She groped behind her for the handle and tried the door, but it was locked. Shaking with fear, she crouched on the small landing, waiting for the man with the cigarette to go away.

Something Popov had once told her about self-defense came to mind. "If you find yourself in a tight spot, and all you have is your purse, make a fist and put pennies between your fingers. Then hit the fellow as hard as you can in the tenderest spot you can reach."

Desperate, Friedl rummaged in her purse for pennies, but she only came up with one. With a whimper, she waited, and waited some more; she didn't know how long. The blackness seemed to swallow all sense of time.

After what seemed like half the night, Friedl steeled herself and peered around the corner to see if a cigarette still marked the man's presence, but there was only darkness.

Friedl never knew how she mustered the courage to inch toward the doorway to her building once more, her hand in a tight fist, that single penny clutched hard between index and middle fingers. Finally, she could make out the front steps clearly enough to tell that the man with the cigarette had gone.

The relief was so overwhelming, Friedl's knees buckled beneath her and she had to clutch the railing for support. She never wanted to go through something like that again.

The following day, she told Joan how terrified she'd been. "I was sure he was going to kill me," she said. "Just like that Wolkoff woman promised."

"Probably some perfectly reasonable explanation for his being there," said Joan. "However, I think it might be best if we do something about this." From her large handbag, she took out a roughly cylindrical leather item. "It's a cosh," she said, smacking her palm with it. "Just a small one, but it's filled with ball bearings and really packs a wallop. M gave it to me for Christmas."

"Darling M. Such a romantic!" said Friedl with delight.

Joan offered the weapon to her to try. Friedl tested the cosh on her own palm with a *whap*. That *did* hurt. "Yes. I would like one of these, please. Where did M get it?"

"Tom Hill's in Knightsbridge," said Joan, returning it into her bag. "He had it custom-made just for me."

"Tom Hill's?" said Friedl. "You mean the bootmaker?" Well, that explained the leather, which was at a premium these days and very difficult to find.

Joan nodded. "Let's order one for you, shall we? Probably best I do it through M." She fished around in her handbag again. "And then there's this!" With an air of triumph, she held up the tiniest handgun Friedl had ever seen.

"It looks like a toy," Friedl said with a touch of disdain, thinking of the shotguns and rifles she had handled at home. "Point that at any self-respecting villain and he'd laugh at you, darling."

Joan shrugged. "It might be little more than a stocking gun, but it works. I've been practicing down at Camberley. M made me shoot it over and over until I was perfect." She laughed. "I've become quite deadly, you know. As long as my attacker stands still and is within range, his goose is well and truly cooked."

Friedl eyed her. "*Do* you keep it in your stocking, darling? I know some men who'd find that exciting." When Joan simply laughed and shook her head, Friedl said, "Can I have one of those, too? It would make me feel so much safer."

"But you can't be caught with a gun, Friedl. You're an enemy alien."

Friedl pouted and pleaded, but Joan shook her head. "Really, I don't think it's possible. I mean, I can ask, but I know what the answer will be."

"Never mind, darling," said Friedl. "Don't bother M about it. You're right, of course, and the cosh will be something, at any rate."

But the cosh would be a little difficult to conceal, unlike the tiny pistol, and Friedl thrilled to the idea of keeping a deadly weapon tucked in her girdle while she swanned about at social events, her acquaintances none the wiser. A cosh also necessitated getting close enough to your attacker to use it. And a pistol could be wielded with greater menace than a blunt instrument, especially when handled by a woman.

She knew well enough the risks of being found in possession of a deadly weapon when she was registered as an enemy of Britain. But as far as she could see, the risk of being murdered in cold blood by one of Anna Wolkoff's people outweighed that by far.

She hadn't considered this solution before, but now that Joan had given her the idea of the handgun, Friedl couldn't quite let it go.

London, England
July 1941

"*Liebling*," said Friedl, stretching out on the bed in a way that she hoped might induce Popov to forget his business appointment and go back to what he'd been doing earlier. "I'll be so lonely when you're gone."

She watched him button his shirt, preparing to depart her little mews flat for the office of Tarlair Ltd. Duško always dressed impeccably, which wasn't surprising given the totals she'd seen on his tailor's bills. She'd expended a considerable amount of thought on the gray silk tie she'd picked out for him and she was glad to see him remove it from its box now and tie it around his neck with swift, practiced grace.

While no one would have guessed it to watch Friedl dance the nights away, she'd missed Duško dreadfully while he was gone. This visit to London would be all too short.

She sat up, her face brightening. "Why don't I come back with you?"

"What?" He seemed to be thinking of something else. "To Estoril?" He reached for his jacket, shrugged it on.

"Yes, why not?" Friedl happened to know that her principal rival for Popov's wayward affections, the French movie star Simone Simon, was off somewhere filming at the moment rather than sunning herself on the Portuguese Riviera, so Popov might be glad of Friedl's company. She stretched out her legs, observing their luminous whiteness, and pointed one toe. "I could use a little time in the sunshine. I'll see old friends and you can do your work . . . We'll spend a couple of lovely evenings together and then I'll come home."

He eyed her thoughtfully. "That does sound like a delightful idea." He shot his cuffs and reached for one of the gold cuff links he'd left in her china pin tray.

A surge of happiness filled her chest. She'd been very much afraid he'd hate the proposition and show it. Then she made a moue. "I suppose it will be difficult to convince Tar to agree."

"He'll agree," said Popov, affixing the second cuff link. "Leave it to me."

True to Friedl's prediction, Tar wasn't best pleased when Popov made the suggestion about her tagging along. Too many people knew Friedl in Estoril. If she used the false identity she'd adopted for the purpose of passing intelligence to the Germans via Popov, one of her acquaintances was certain to ruin that cover. She would have to go as herself, thus muddying the waters if she were questioned by Popov's contacts, or, God forbid, ran into Kühlenthal while she was there. It was all a lot of bother, and Tar would really rather they didn't.

Then, too, they were still in the process of convincing Popov's German handler in Portugal, a clever and ruthless intelligence officer named von Karsthoff, that Friedl's information was sound, her allegiance pure. Could she pull off that deception in person, with no one looking over her shoulder to advise her what she should and shouldn't say?

"I'll keep her out of von Karsthoff's way," Popov promised. "And frankly, Tar, no man looks at Friedl and thinks about war work."

That wasn't true in Friedl's experience, and clearly Tar didn't believe it for a second. However, Popov was one of their most valuable assets, and both Tar and Stewart Menzies devoted themselves most assiduously to keeping him happy. Popov wasn't above trading on that when he had to.

"I'd consider it a great favor," he said mildly.

Tar seemed to wrestle with himself. "Very well," he said at last, in a clipped tone. "I'll make the arrangements. You'll both be on the first Pan Am flight the day after tomorrow. But stay out of trouble, will you?" He addressed this to Popov from beneath lowering eyebrows. "No shenanigans that might put our Gelatine in danger."

His face solemn, Popov promised that he absolutely would not engage in shenanigans of any kind. Then he broke into a dazzling smile, white teeth brilliant against the tan of his skin, but he shook his head when Tar asked him, frowning, just what was so damned amusing.

"Shenanigans!" repeated Popov with a snort of laughter as they left the offices of Tarlair and headed down the stairs. "Ah, these English. I like them very much."

When their flight took off two days later, an incredible sensation of lightness and freedom buoyed Friedl's heart. She hadn't realized how caged and confined she'd felt, being stuck in dreary old England during this interminable war when her soul was so essentially continental. Estoril might not be Paris or Vienna, but it was full to bursting with aristocratic Europeans who thought and acted like she did. She couldn't wait to be reunited with her acquaintances, although she had to admit, she hadn't given even one of them a moment's thought while she'd been away.

To her delight, she spied several familiar faces as well as some interesting new ones upon arrival at the Hotel Palàcio. Friedl greeted them all eagerly as soon as they'd checked in, kissing cheeks and clasping hands, before rejoining Popov, who had followed the luggage up to their suite.

After confirming that their accommodation was to his liking and that Friedl wanted for nothing, Popov said, "I'm afraid I must leave you, darling. I have business that can't wait."

Friedl suspected a visit to yet another lover lurking somewhere about the seaside town, but she was too wise to accuse him of it. Instead, she gave him an impish smile and an airy wave. "Until this evening, darling. I'll have a massage and perhaps a little drink by the swimming pool with my friends. Don't worry about me."

That seemed to give him pause. "Be careful, won't you? Remember what Tar said."

"Yes, yes, of course. Off you go." She broke through the doors to the balcony, lifted her shoulders, and breathed in the fresh, salted air with a feeling of tranquility she hadn't experienced since . . . Well, since that evening Kühlenthal had come to see her in her dressing room after her show at the casino nightclub. Their room overlooked the hotel gardens, which were set out in geometric patterns after the formal French style, but with date palms adding an exotic touch here and there. Beyond the gardens lay the golden crescent of Tamariz Beach and the heavenly Mediterranean.

She sensed Popov behind her, and her blood tingled, sparkling beneath her skin as he pressed a lingering kiss to the nape of her neck. Then he left, taking a briefcase with him.

Mentally, Friedl shrugged. She didn't know what was in that case and didn't much care. She was taking a vacation from intrigue. According to inquiries Popov had made, Kühlenthal was safely ensconced in Madrid, and she would be here in Estoril for too brief a time for anyone else to undertake serious investigation into her recent movements.

Friedl drifted around the suite, enjoying its size and elegant appointments, the lightness of its white walls, and the gauze curtains that floated and danced in the strong breeze. It was pleasant to be with a man as free and generous with his money as Popov. He begrudged her nothing, and she was a woman who liked beautiful and expensive things. How could she stop herself falling madly in love with him?

With a wistful smile, she traced the lines of a bronze statuette on the sideboard that was cast in the form of a stampeding bull.

There was power and movement to the figure that evoked the excitement and terror of the bullfights she'd witnessed in Cádiz years before. She closed her eyes. Had it been less than a year since she'd yearned to settle down with earnest, adorable Billy Younger and forgo forever the excitement of being with someone like Duško Popov? How fortunate, and how uncharacteristically neat of her, that she'd managed to end that affair before the one with Popov had begun.

A knock fell on the door, startling her. She padded across the room, pushed the hair out of her eyes and bent to spy through the little peephole in the door.

A tall man with a very handsome face stood on the other side. He was frowning and checking his watch, clearly impatient to be admitted. He glanced down the corridor, then stared back at the spyhole, narrowing his eyes as if he could see her peering through it. Squinting downward, she made out a large black attaché case in his hand.

The visitor seemed vaguely familiar. However, given his manner, most likely he wasn't there to see her. Still, Friedl was curious . . . Where had she seen him before? She flipped through a mental catalog of her acquaintances in Estoril but couldn't locate this man.

Then she placed him. She'd seen him once or twice—not in Estoril but in London—dressed in the uniform of a British Navy officer. Now, he was in civilian garb, a dark blue suit that shouted Savile Row, and a conservative striped tie.

Hmm. If this man was meeting Popov here, it was probably important.

She yanked open the door. At the sight of Friedl, a pronounced change came over the visitor's expression. The look of irritation lightened, and he smiled with his eyes, if not with the rest of his face. He looked, she thought, rather like a boy about to unwrap a highly anticipated Christmas gift.

"Miss Stöttinger, I presume," he said in German.

"Yes," said Friedl, also in German. "And you are?"

"The name is Fleming," said the stranger. He glanced past her shoulder. "Popov not here, I take it? Mind if I come in?"

* * *

By the time Duško did return, Friedl was getting on famously with Commander Fleming. Probably too well, if the bland expression on Popov's face was any indication. "Thank you," said Popov when Fleming recommended a jaunt to the casino, "but we have other plans tonight."

Friedl wasn't aware of any plans, but she didn't argue, and graciously left the men to talk while she went to dress for dinner. She chose a black, cowl-necked sheath that was elegant and alluring and made her skin look pearly white. She sighed. She wouldn't have enough time here in the sun to develop a tan. Besides, she wasn't officially in Portugal at all, so even if she had the leisure to acquire a healthy glow, explaining it to her friends back in London would be a touch difficult.

Still, it was a blessed relief to be staying in a neutral country, away from the threat of bombs and the sight of the terrible destruction that had become part of the bleak streetscape of London. She couldn't wait to sample the local cuisine again. The hotel itself served French fare, but at the many restaurants in Estoril one could sample traditional dishes—fresh shellfish and rice in a spicy tomato sauce, mussels in white wine.

When she returned to the sitting room, she found Popov alone, dressed in black tie, leafing through a small sheaf of papers. When he saw her, he quickly refolded the pages, slotted them into a packet the approximate size of a cigarette case, and slipped that into the inner pocket of his dinner jacket.

"Ready?" He smiled, his expression devoid of any trace of reproach about her earlier warmth toward Commander Fleming. Friedl didn't know whether to be glad or sorry. She never set out to make her lovers jealous; it was simply her nature to be extremely friendly to men and women alike. That often resulted in misunderstandings that were both incomprehensible to Friedl and, admittedly, rather exciting to watch. Was there anything more thrilling than two handsome, virile men fighting over one?

Popov, however, displayed not the slightest hint of jealousy. He had been ardent in his pursuit of Friedl and charmingly attentive once he'd captured her. She suspected, however, that if she left Duško for this Commander Fleming or someone else like him, Popov would shrug and move on. He refused to be faithful, but he wouldn't share, either. Friedl sensed that about him, and it was horribly unfair, but she couldn't seem to get mad about it. She simply didn't want anyone else. She cared that he did want other women, and she hated that he acted upon his desires. But she was helplessly in love with the man, so what could she do?

All in all, instinct told Friedl to give herself over to enjoying her time with Duško Popov to the full. She exhaled a tiny sigh as he guided her so smoothly through the foyer of the hotel, toward the door. She was constitutionally incapable of setting a guard over her heart. He would break it, that was for sure. It was only a question of when.

They ate spicy Arroz de Marisco and drank a local Vinho Verde that was cool and crisp on the tongue, then strolled in the moonlight along the seafront. Friedl tried to relax, but she sensed tension beneath Popov's calm demeanor and furrowed her brow. Despite her earlier resolution to take a vacation from intrigue, she couldn't help but wonder what the papers in his breast pocket might be, and whether he intended to pass them on to some other operative—friend or foe—that evening. She didn't object at all in principle to his carrying out his mission with her present, but she had rather hoped that his business might have been concluded that day, that they could enjoy an evening floating in a small champagne bubble of their own, free from the stresses of intelligence work.

It was late when Popov finally guided their steps in the direction of the Estoril Casino. Friedl raised her eyebrows. Had he decided to take Fleming's advice, after all? But despite Popov's penchant for high-stakes gambling, they didn't move through to the baccarat tables but instead to the casino's nightclub, where Friedl used to perform.

She sucked in a long breath as she stepped inside the dim, smoky club. Even though she'd spent countless happy hours there, the shadow of Kühlenthal seemed to loom large.

She stole a glance at Duško, who was tipping the waiter and indicating with a graceful gesture that Friedl should precede him to the best table in the house. She squared her shoulders as if to throw off the troubles of the past and followed the waiter. After a few deep breaths, she really did begin to relax and was able to smile and nod as several acquaintances hailed her.

They took their seats at a candlelit supper table with an excellent view of the stage. The band struck up a lively tune—something new that she didn't recognize—and couples spun and hopped and swung around the dance floor with energetic abandon. As usual, Friedl couldn't stay still for long when music stirred her soul. Her body began to sway a little, and the tense muscles in her shoulders to soften. Popov leaned in to her and said, "You are far and away the most beautiful, sensual woman in the room."

She was quite sure he said that same thing to Simone Simon when he came here in her company, but she smiled and glanced sideways at him under her eyelashes. Who cared about that French kitten? Tonight, Duško was all hers.

The band ended the number with a rousing crescendo of brass, then the leader announced a break. The noise level in the room heightened to fill the void as people swarmed off the dance floor to their tables, mopped their perspiring brows, and ordered more drinks.

Some acquaintances of Popov's accosted him and took the vacant seats at Popov and Friedl's table. Others joined them, dragging over more chairs. Friedl leaned in to enjoy the conversation, which was conducted first in French and then in German, then switched back to French again.

A screech of laughter came from a table near the bandstand. Friedl glanced over, then turned back to the conversation. But

Popov straightened and stared hard at the offenders. "Who are those people?" Of all things, he abhorred bad manners, and these revelers were making quite a spectacle of themselves. Friedl widened her eyes and shrugged. Did it matter? "Live and let live" was her motto.

"Oh, them!" said one of Popov's friends with a roll of his eyes. "They're journalists from London's *Daily Mail*. Rowdy lot, aren't they?"

"Hmm, I don't think—" Popov was about to say more, but was cut off by an earsplitting squawk of feedback on the microphone. Friedl looked up. A woman in a fussy yellow frock stood, tottering, on the stage, drunkenly gripping the microphone stand for support.

Popov winced as the woman in yellow began to sing a capella. *If* you could call that singing, thought Friedl. It sounded more like a stag's mating call.

Still, what could one do but wait for the band to return and oust the usurper? Friedl became aware, however, that Duško's surprised irritation was turning to intense disgust. Suddenly, he lifted a finger, summoning a waiter to his side. "Take this to the lady at the microphone, will you?" Popov placed something on the waiter's salver. By some sleight of hand, a tip disappeared into the waiter's pocket, and he duly bore whatever it was that Popov had placed on his silver tray over to the struggling songstress.

The young woman in yellow didn't notice the waiter at first, absorbed as she was in her performance, until, finally, he tapped her on the shoulder and presented his salver. Breaking off mid-note, she turned her head and blinked at the object the waiter proffered as if it was out of focus. Then her eyes widened, her lips compressed, and her face turned crimson.

In no time, a couple of the men from the singer's table were on their feet, shouting and gesturing at the waiter. The waiter, unperturbed by the ruckus, answered them. Whatever he said caused the unruly group of journalists to turn, as one, to stare at Friedl's table. Popov held up his hand and gave a casual wave, as if to acknowledge that he was indeed the root cause of their outrage.

The men who had stood up were large, and their faces took on a menacing pugnacity that had Friedl plucking at Popov's sleeve. "What did you do, *liebling*? Those men look as if they want to kill you."

"I expect they will try," he replied, reaching into his coat. Popov took out the papers she'd seen him put there earlier and slipped them into her purse, clasping it shut. He stood, shrugged out of his jacket, and carefully draped it over his chair. "Keep those safe, will you? And get out of here. I'll meet you in the garden."

His manner was calm and measured, but Friedl didn't mistake the urgency of the situation. Without hesitation, she left the table, the packet of secret papers burning a hole in her purse. Before she reached the door, she looked back, to see Popov duck a flying fist and wade into the fray. Would any of those lounge lizard friends of his come to his aid? She wouldn't bet on it. But she couldn't worry about that now. She suspected they'd both be in bigger trouble if someone found what was in her purse.

What was in these papers, anyway? Something that meant Popov didn't want them found on his person, that was for sure. She moved unhurriedly past the casino tables and out into the warm evening air. It was dark but flambeaux burned throughout the gardens, illuminating nearby date palms and throwing pools of light across the path. Friedl glanced over her shoulder. Despite the activity inside, there weren't many people about in the gardens tonight.

She kept walking in the direction of the Hotel Palàcio. The light spray of water from a fountain up ahead felt pleasantly cool on her skin. She was just deciding whether to loiter by the fountain and enjoy the sensation when footsteps sounded behind her. Not the click of high heels that might have been reassuring, but the softer pad of masculine brogues.

Already on high alert due to the important papers she carried, Friedl felt the hairs rise on her nape. Wishing that she'd brought some kind of weapon with her and regretting the cosh and the pistol she had yet to obtain, she quickened her pace, moved past the fountain, and ventured a glance over her shoulder. Forget meeting Duško; she'd make for the hotel, and safety.

But a scuffle of footsteps told her that the man behind her had sped up, too. She whirled around, to see him rushing at her. Friedl screamed at the top of her lungs, hitting out blindly.

Her assailant was big and strong, and she had no chance against him. Brutal hands caught her flailing wrists, then her purse was wrenched from her grasp and a shove sent her, flying, to the ground. Winded by the hard fall, she coughed and gasped for air. She felt the sting of scraped elbows and palms, tasted blood in her mouth. Her hair was tumbling down from its chignon, clouding around her face, obscuring her vision.

She stared around, dazed, then her mind snapped into focus. Her purse. The papers! Panting, Friedl scrambled to her feet to take off, hobbling as fast as she could after the thief. Of course, she could never catch him—not in these heels—and not out of them, either.

But the thief's flight back in the direction of the casino was cut short by a trim figure in black and white who came sprinting toward them. Friedl sped up, cupping her hands around her mouth. "Duško, get him!" she screamed. "He's got my purse!"

She wasn't sure whether he heard her, but Popov was confronting the thief, who was larger than he was and, she thought, considerably meaner, too. Friedl bit her sore lip as she saw the assailant rush toward Popov. What happened next was so quick, she wasn't sure how he managed it. Popov's foot somehow connected with the thief's head, sending both the thief and her purse flying.

Calmly, Popov stooped to pick up the purse and walked toward her, past the supine form of his adversary. He opened the clasp, and she thought he would retrieve the papers, but he closed the clasp again and turned, as if a sixth sense had alerted him to another person's presence.

Mr. Black, the manager from the Palàcio, came hurrying toward them, glancing worriedly from Popov to the sprawling, unconscious thief, and back again. Popov handed Friedl her purse, then buttonholed the newcomer and drew him aside. Friedl heard Mr. Black say, "But you must understand, sir. This is a police matter. I'm obliged to report it."

"Yes, yes, of course you must," said Popov in a soothing and slightly congratulatory tone. "You were positively heroic, my dear Mr. Black, running down this fellow after he assaulted one of your guests. But I'm sure the lady's name need not be mentioned to the authorities." He smiled. "Her presence here with me is a matter of some delicacy, shall we say? And keep me out of it, too, will you, yes? There's a good chap."

Friedl noticed that no money changed hands this time, and wondered why the manager should do Popov's bidding, in this instance or any other. However, if they were to be let go without having to explain the situation, she wasn't going to argue about it.

Popov put his coat around her shoulders as he led her back to the Palàcio. "Are you all right, darling? You must have had quite a shock."

Friedl was feeling exhilarated more than anything else, but she allowed herself to be cosseted and caressed once they were back in their suite at the hotel. She made no reference to Popov's fighting prowess, nor to the documents he'd slipped into her purse. That seemed to be the way he wanted it. However, this reticence took considerable restraint on her part. She wanted to pepper him with all sorts of questions: How had he learned to fight like that? What, exactly, had happened back at the club? She examined him covertly as he changed into more casual clothing, but there didn't seem to be a mark on him apart from a bruise on his cheek and a split lip that gave him an attractively rakish air. He refused to let her tend to the small wound, saying it was nothing.

Later, when she was bathed and dressed in a peach silk peignoir and feeling rather as if she wished to reward her hero with something other than words for saving her, Duško returned to her with a glass of brandy, which he pressed into her hand.

With an apologetic look that she was beginning to know very well, he said, "I'm afraid I have to go out again now, my dear. Will you be all right? Shall I telephone one of your friends to come?"

Disappointed, but determined not to show it, Friedl reassured him and sipped her brandy. The drink caught in her throat and made her eyes water—or perhaps that wasn't the brandy. She widened her eyes and looked up to the ceiling so that the threatening tears didn't spill over. It was just the reaction from the events of the evening setting in, that was all. She wasn't silly enough to weep because he was leaving. Not in the ordinary course of things.

"Good girl." Popov kissed her forehead—*her forehead!*—and left.

When she went to look inside her purse, she found that, of course, the documents he'd put there were gone. And she still hadn't discovered what it was that Popov had sent over with the waiter to that girl in the yellow dress.

CHAPTER TWELVE

Estoril, Portugal
July 1941

*F*riedl hadn't seen Popov since breakfast. She'd spent the day at the beach and later, she'd dined on shrimp salad and fillet of beef at the hotel with friends. The evening had ended at the casino, as so many evenings did in Estoril.

The casino's interior reminded her of a Viennese opera house, but here the music was the clack of the white ball on the roulette wheel and the libretto was the croupiers calling for bets. Friedl kept a weather eye out for Duško, and the thought crossed her mind that it would be all too sordid and embarrassing if she caught him there in the company of another woman. Surely he wouldn't . . . No, he was nothing if not discreet. More than anything else, Duško Popov loathed a scene.

Friedl had dressed to kill in a backless, floor-length gown of oyster-gray duchess satin, paired with long, white gloves. Several men turned their heads as she moved through to one of the baccarat tables and pretended to watch her friends play. Her mind wandered, that familiar feeling of being quite alone in the midst of a crowd returning to her in full force.

What was Duško up to now? She suspected he was responsible for far more important matters than running a couple of British agents. Their circuit was limited to three. Popov had been given the code name Tricycle for that reason, although Friedl had overheard one wit remark that it was because Popov liked to have a threesome in bed. Truly, the mind boggled.

The indefinable sensation that someone watched her made Friedl look around. No one that she could see on such a quick, sweeping glance. She straightened her shoulders, attempting to throw off the feeling, but it persisted. Eventually, she excused herself from her friends and took a quick surveil of the area on the pretext of going to the powder room.

No one suspicious, or not that she could tell. Was she jumping at shadows? After the events of the previous evening, perhaps it wasn't surprising that her senses remained on high alert. Had that been a common thief who'd assaulted her? Or had it been someone who'd followed Popov and seen him slip those secret papers into her purse?

These were questions she might have asked Duško himself, but something guarded about his manner since his return to the Hotel Palàcio made her feel as if any further discussion of the subject would be unwelcome. He certainly hadn't volunteered an explanation.

Friedl refreshed her bright scarlet lipstick and fixed her hair, then left to rejoin her friends. The powder room gave on to a small, poorly lit vestibule, which was out of sight of the main passage to the casino floor. She'd taken only a couple of steps when a figure moved to block her path.

Fear stabbed her gut. Defensively, she raised her hands and opened her mouth to scream, before she saw who it was. Duško grabbed her wrists and pinned her to the wall. His face inches from hers, he whispered, "Darling Friedl, I've missed you so."

His mouth came down on hers with a passion that was hot and urgent and just this side of corporal punishment. Breathless, Friedl said, "I missed you, too," and gasped when he attacked the tender skin of her throat with kisses and a sharp nip of his teeth.

"Oh, no! How can you, Duško? That might leave a mark." Flustered, flattered, excitedly aware of the danger of someone catching them, Friedl whispered, "What's got into you tonight?"

He took her hand and moved it inside his jacket. Her fingertips met paper, the size and texture of money. Lots of it. "What?"

"Shhh." In between kisses, Popov said, "I . . . have . . . eighty thousand American dollars . . . in my pockets."

Now she understood his excitement. What was he doing with all of that money? Did he plan to use it at the casino?

He took her hand and kissed its palm. "Come. Let's have some fun."

"Wait." She plucked his handkerchief from his pocket and wiped the red lipstick smudges off his mouth. "You go. I'll have to freshen up after all that." She shook her head. *"Ach du lieber,* Duško, you are an animal sometimes." But she said it without a trace of rancor. Her blood was pulsing in her veins, her lips tingling and pleasantly bruised. She hoped he wouldn't be too long at the casino. She was impatient to have him to herself.

After freshening up, Friedl returned to the baccarat tables to find Popov contemplating one particular game. Her heart sank. She knew that look. It was the same one he'd worn when that woman in yellow had monopolized the microphone yesterday evening at the casino nightclub. Scathing disapproval bordering on disgust.

"What is it?" she murmured.

"Look at this fellow," he said to her, indicating the man who held the bank. "The most vulgar display I've ever seen."

"What is he doing that's so wrong?" Friedl wasn't terribly interested in baccarat. Roulette was more her style. Baccarat required enough skill that it fooled players into believing they had control. At least, with roulette, one was under no illusion that it was a game of pure chance.

At first, Duško made no reply and Friedl gave a mental shrug. She didn't care too much, but she hoped this wouldn't be the second night in a row when Popov got into a physical fight at this establishment.

Then she saw that he was staring, not at the table but somewhere beyond it. She followed his gaze and gasped in surprise. Commander Fleming sat nearby, nursing a martini.

"Oh!" said Friedl, but Popov put a warning hand on her arm and she remembered that they weren't to acknowledge Fleming in public, since Popov was supposed to be working for the Germans.

"No limit!" The boor at the baccarat table, whom Friedl

now recalled was a wealthy Lithuanian by the name of Bloch, was yelling to anyone who would listen. "Unlimited stakes, my friends. Who has the stones to take me on?"

Even Friedl knew this was the height of bad manners. The accepted practice was to discreetly give the croupier an acceptable limit. The Lithuanian, however, was clearly filthy rich and determined to be ostentatious about it. He could hardly have behaved in a manner more offensive to Popov's sensibilities.

"This fellow," said Duško, "must be taught a lesson."

With a significant glance over at Ian Fleming, Duško took a seat at the baccarat table and reached into his pocket.

"Fifty thousand," he said, slapping a fat wad of bills on the table. And then another, and another until the Lithuanian spluttered and protested, his face reddening with fury. The stake Duško proposed was five times what most people earned in a year. There was no way anyone could afford to cover that bet.

Friedl glanced at Ian Fleming. His face had taken on a ghostly pallor, faintly tinged with green.

So . . . Friedl quirked an eyebrow. It wasn't Duško's money he'd thrown down, but perhaps the British government's? A gurgle of horrified laughter bubbled in her chest.

"Well, sir?" Duško prompted the Lithuanian, his expression neutral.

"This is outrageous! I don't . . . I can't . . ." Bloch spluttered. Friedl pressed her lips together to hide a smile. Clearly he could not cover such a preposterous stake and everyone knew it.

Duško turned to the croupier. "Is the casino standing surety for this gentleman?"

The croupier shook his head.

With a disgusted snort, Popov swept up his money, saying, "This kind of thing is a disgrace and an irritation to serious players. I trust that in future, management will prohibit such irresponsible play." He pocketed the cash and stood to leave, having achieved what he wanted: Bloch's utter humiliation at no cost to MI-6. And as a side dish, an effective tease of his minder from British intelligence.

Was Fleming furious? He had every right to be. But as Friedl was about to turn and follow Duško out, she caught the expression on the commander's face.

Fleming smiled. Definitely, he smiled.

* * *

The same edge of danger that had made Friedl's encounter with Popov outside the powder room at the casino so exciting had carried over to the bedroom at the hotel. She shouldn't make it so easy for him, probably, but the magic of Duško Popov was that no matter what doubts about his fidelity lodged like glass splinters in her heart, one night spent basking in the light of his full, undivided attention made those jagged shards simply melt away.

In the morning, he was gone again, but Friedl didn't mind. Too exhilarated to sit down to breakfast, she went out alone for a stroll along the esplanade. Her silk beach pajamas, printed in blues and greens, swirled and flapped around her in the breeze. The sun still hung low in the sky, but its rays were strong enough to warm her to her toes, and her sense of well-being was complete and perfect.

She passed several people who were out for their daily constitutionals, but it was too early for most of her acquaintances to be abroad. Friedl grinned, feeling smugly virtuous. She was due to leave for England today, and she wanted to wring every last drop of Portuguese sunshine from her visit before she left.

The fresh sea air filled her lungs. She yearned to run but contented herself with slipping off her shoes and walking down the sand to the harbor's edge. The water was cold, a pleasant shock to the senses, a gentle balm on her skin. She rolled up her trouser legs and stood in the shallows, toes curling into the wet sand. The gentle waves came to greet her, then slipped away again.

The sense of utter freedom made her want to laugh out loud. She wanted to dive into that water and swim away.

With a sigh, finally Friedl turned back, dangling her espadrilles from her fingers as she watched the sun make sparkles in the sand. A shadow fell across her path. She looked up, and lost her balance, stumbling back a pace. "Herr Kühlenthal." Joy abandoned her in an instant, and she turned cold.

She regained her footing, but not before the Abwehr officer reached out to grip her elbow. To steady her, or to prevent her from running away?

"Thank you. I'm fine," she said, pulling free with a decisive movement that she hoped didn't bruise his delicate pride. She glanced up and down the beach, then pushed the hair out of her eyes, tucking it behind her ear. "I didn't expect to see you here."

He was wearing a light cream suit and a panama hat, a man dressed for leisure, but his eyes wore an expression that said he meant business. "No?" Kühlenthal's smile was thin. "But when I heard you were in Estoril, my dear Miss Stöttinger, I was drawn like a moth to a flame."

Of course. She'd known he'd have spies everywhere. That he would fly to Estoril immediately upon hearing she was there was something she hadn't expected, and it did not augur well. Again, she glanced about her. What if Popov or Fleming or some other British spy witnessed this exchange?

"Well, flattering as that is, I hope you'll excuse me," said Friedl. "I have an appointment to keep."

"Have you indeed?" murmured Kühlenthal. "One wonders what brings you back to Portugal at such a time."

"Duško Popov brought me, if you must know," she said. He would have discovered that much already. "I was sick of England. I wanted some fun and persuaded him to let me tag along."

Kühlenthal shook his head, as if to say she ought to know better than to try to deceive him. "You are working for Popov."

It was a statement, not a question, but she remained cautious. After all, she had used an alias in those letters to Popov's German handler. "*Working* for him? What on earth do you mean?"

"I've received copies of the intelligence briefs." He shrugged. "You used a cover name, of course, but the fact that you came here in his company helped me put two and two together."

He must be certain of his facts because if she wasn't working for the Serbian spy, Kühlenthal had just blown Popov's cover. Still, Friedl couldn't afford to waver. Kühlenthal might be bluffing, after all. She made a show of turning over his words in her mind, then feigned shocked disbelief. "What? Do you mean to tell me *Popov* is working for the Abwehr?"

"I applaud your patriotism, and your initiative in attaching yourself to him of your own accord," murmured Kühlenthal, brushing aside her question. "But I trust you will accommodate me as well."

Instinct urged her to refuse. But how could she do that without sounding to him like a traitor? She was supposed to be only too willing and eager to assist the Abwehr. She decided to go on the offensive. "You said you would have a use for me, that I could help the Third Reich. I even went to the embassy to see if you'd left word for me there. You never made contact."

His gaze froze her to the marrow. "I've been holding you in reserve, shall we say." He paused. "But now that I know you are able to travel freely between England and Portugal, you become all the more valuable to me."

"I might not be able to get back here again," she said truthfully. Tar had been so reluctant to grant Popov this favor, she'd assumed it was a one-off.

Kühlenthal stared out to sea, as if admiring the view, and the casual note in his voice made his next words all the more chilling. "Then you must find a way, Miss Stöttinger. Otherwise . . ." He shrugged. "Your mother is doing very poorly back in Vienna, I hear. It would be a shame to cause her further distress."

PART 2

CHAPTER THIRTEEN

London, England
February 1943

Paddy

*U*nlike Paddy's former place of work upstairs, the Admiralty's Room 13 hunkered down in the bowels of the building, at the end of a dingy corridor lined with so many exposed pipes, it resembled a map of the London Underground. This small, overcrowded den was presided over by Captain Ewen Montagu and Flight Lieutenant Charles Cholmondeley. ("Chumly. Spelled C-H-O-L-M-O-N-D-E-L-E-Y," as he'd introduced himself to Paddy the previous day.)

A fog of cigarette smoke clung to the ceiling of Room 13 and the walls were papered in maps. Small desks were crammed wherever one would fit, and a large refectory table dominated the space. Around the table sat twelve people—secretaries in civilian clothes and uniformed officers, mostly from the Navy.

The room was so cramped that Paddy was obliged to wait in

the corridor outside until a place was found for her to sit. Patricia Trehearne, the pretty secretary who had come to fetch her when Paddy signed in at the front reception, found her a chair and said, "Do come in, Mrs. Ridsdale. Tea? Coffee?"

Paddy politely refused. Miss Trehearne had better things to do than fetch refreshments.

What is *all this?* Paddy wanted to ask, but habit kicked in and she remained silent. They would tell her what she needed to know, and no more. But she couldn't help allowing her gaze to travel over the maps, the most detailed of which showed the southern coast of Spain. A large red pin marked the port of Huelva. Paddy frowned. Now where had she heard Huelva mentioned before?

The luncheon she'd attended at Fleming's brusque invitation had been remarkable in several ways, but primarily for the absence of its host. Fleming's reserved table at the Savoy Grill had been occupied by three other people, all in plain clothes. There was Patricia Trehearne—perhaps brought along to give the party a more sociable air. There was a tall, thin, brown-haired man with a waxed moustache and round eyeglasses who introduced himself as Charles Cholmondeley, and there was Captain Ewen Montagu, who now stood at the head of the refectory table in Room 13, gathering some papers together and clearing his throat as if preparing to give a lecture.

At the Savoy, they had eaten lamb cutlets and Scotch woodcock while the two men danced a delicate two-step around the object of their meeting. They referred to the job they wanted Paddy to do in such veiled terms that she had no clear idea of what on earth might be expected of her if she agreed. Montagu had closed the odd little meeting by saying that if she decided to help them with a matter that involved "a little play-acting and field work" she ought to report to Room 13 at the Admiralty at 0900 hours the next day.

"We do hope you'll say yes, Mrs. Ridsdale," said Cholmondeley. "We've heard such glowing praise from Fleming about you."

That last comment came as quite a surprise to Paddy. She couldn't imagine Fleming waxing lyrical over her competence—he'd always seemed to take her efficiency as the basic requirement of her role. But Cholmondeley needn't have looked so earnest and entreating. Nothing on the planet could have kept Paddy away. She'd been obliged to tell some white lies both to her mother and to Julian in order to clear her schedule that day, but if they knew the truth, both of them would surely understand.

"Right! If I could have your attention, please?" called Montagu, whose egg-shaped head and receding hairline didn't altogether detract from his mature good looks.

"Some of you know most of what I'm about to say. Some of you know very little. But what I want is for us all to be up-to-date with this operation as it now stands by the end of this meeting." He stared around the room, making eye contact with each and every person before continuing. "Now. This is an operation that was conceived some time ago by the NID. After many months of persuasion, we have finally convinced the Twenty Committee to let us take the preliminary steps."

Paddy suppressed the urge to roll her eyes. Committees of

one sort or another had been the bane of Admiral Godfrey's existence. Originally called the Double-Cross Committee, set up for counterespionage, catching and turning foreign spies into double agents, this group had been renamed because the double cross "XX" was the Roman numeral for twenty.

Ewen turned with his pointer to the map behind him, indicating each region as he spoke. "At this very moment, more than one hundred and fifty thousand Allied troops are amassing in North Africa, ready to invade the soft underbelly of Europe as part of Operation Husky. This will take place in a few months' time, with the planned landing point being Sicily. Well, anyone with half a brain would deduce as much, and the Germans have the place heavily fortified. We came up with our operation with the aim of misdirecting the Germans and convincing them that the invasion will not take place in Sicily but rather, in Greece and the Balkans instead." With the pointer, he circled the spot around Salonika. "That way, we hope the Axis powers will move the bulk of their forces to that region and leave Sicily more lightly defended for the Allied attack."

Montagu cleared his throat and went on. "Now, because this idea has been floating around for some time—" At a snort from Cholmondeley, Montagu paused, and Paddy saw his lips twitch. "Ah! Poor choice of words. At any rate, it is rather a fantastical sort of plot, and one you ladies might feel just a little squeamish about. I'm sorry for that, but when you think it over you'll see that if it works—and we aim to do our utmost to see that it does— this operation will save thousands of lives."

A feeling of déjà vu stole over Paddy. She stared at Montagu, then glanced at Cholmondeley and back again.

It wasn't. *Surely* not.

Montagu set his shoulders back. "We are going to plant a dead body purporting to be an officer from the Royal Marines off the coast of Huelva for the Spanish fishing boats to find. This officer will carry papers designed to mislead the Germans about where the southern European landings will take place."

"Good Heavens!" murmured Paddy.

The captain observed her solicitously. "Get Mrs. Ridsdale a glass of water, will you, Miss Trehearne? If any of you other ladies feel faint at any stage, do let us know."

Paddy shook her head and gestured for Miss Trehearne to keep her seat. "Heavens, no! It's not that *at all*." She said it loudly and clearly, unwilling to let this gross misjudgment go unchallenged. She couldn't possibly allow these officers—or the young women who were glaring at her for letting the side down—to think she was such a frail creature as to faint at the mere mention of a corpse. "It's just that I believe I recognize this particular plan." And its architect, she thought, but did not say. If Montagu and Cholmondeley wanted to take the credit, she wouldn't embarrass them by disputing their claim. Paddy waved a hand. "Do, please, go on."

As Ewen took up the thread of his story again, Paddy had only half a mind on what he was saying. Oh, this was too ridiculous! That outrageous list of plots Fleming had devised years ago in the *Trout* Memorandum was finally bearing fruit? She rather wished the commander were there to enjoy his triumph. But as usual, once he'd set something in motion he disappeared from view, delegating the work of carrying out his crazy schemes to someone else.

The suspicion occurred to Paddy that Fleming had insisted she take part in the operation simply because she'd mocked and picked apart so many of the wilder plots he'd dreamed up over the years. She narrowed her eyes at the thought, then hurriedly returned her full attention to Montagu's outline of the plan.

The mission had been dubbed "Operation Mincemeat," and Paddy wondered which wag among them had the macabre sense of humor to dream that up. She rather suspected Cholmondeley but couldn't be sure.

While more detailed and intricate than Fleming's hastily dashed-off scheme, the essence of the operation was the same. Its long-awaited approval had perhaps been prompted by an incident in September of the previous year: A British aircraft flying from Britain to Gibraltar crashed off Cádiz, killing everyone on board. One of the passengers had been a courier carrying secret documents that outlined plans for General Eisenhower to arrive in Gibraltar on the eve of Operation Torch's target date. The courier's body washed up on the beach and was recovered by Spanish authorities. It was later determined that the letter on his body wasn't tampered with by German spies, but the British did receive intelligence that the Germans had obtained copies of other documents carried by a different passenger. This showed that at least some intelligence obtained by the Spanish authorities was being passed along to the Germans.

This wasn't surprising to anyone. While technically Spain was neutral, the Spanish authorities tended to assist, or at best turn a blind eye, to German intelligence activities in their country.

The British were also aware that there was a German Abwehr officer by the name of Adolf Clauss in the region of Huelva who would pounce on the news of a British officer's body washing up on his part of the Spanish coast. If that British officer had top-secret, sensitive papers on his person, the German spy would do his utmost to persuade the Spanish authorities to let him see them. Either that, or German assets who worked within the Spanish institutions would do the job covertly.

"Of course, first, we need a body," Montagu was saying. "Now, that might sound easier than it is. We've had the coroner for the Northern District of London keeping an eye out for the appropriate corpse, but so far he's come up empty-handed. The unfortunate deceased must be the right age and physique for our officer and he must not have died of anything detectable on an autopsy that is inconsistent with a plane crash at sea. Once we do find the right body, we will have to move fast. Refrigeration can only do so much to preserve the corpse and he must not be so thoroughly—*ahem*—decomposed as to arouse suspicions that he's a plant. And then there's the matter of the wallet litter." Montagu turned to prompt his colleague. "Cholmondeley?"

Flight Lieutenant Cholmondeley remained seated to take up his part of the lecture. "Ah, yes! The wallet litter." He glanced at Paddy. "This is where you come in, Mrs. Ridsdale, in case you were wondering. Montagu and I have created what we call a legend for the fictitious Major William Martin, as we have chosen to christen him. A sort of biography, if you will. To persuade the

Germans to believe in the ruse, we must make it absolutely watertight. Major Martin will become as real to all of us as he must appear to the Germans."

Cholmondeley started ticking off his fingers. "Martin has a family and a sweetheart called Pam to whom he has become engaged. He has an active social life and has recently enjoyed some leave in Pam's company. He has a worrisome bank overdraft, and further overextended himself by buying his Pam a very handsome engagement ring . . ." He looked around. "D'you see what we're doing? Once we find the body, we will purchase Martin's uniform, and one of us will be wearing it about the place so as to give it that 'lived-in' look."

"I'm going to inhabit the character of Major Martin behind the scenes," added Montagu. "Fine-tune every last detail. It's got to be pitch-perfect. One wrong element, the Germans will smell a rat, and it's over." He leaned in and fixed his gaze on Paddy. "You, Mrs. Ridsdale, will play the part of Pam."

A cry of disappointment went up from the other women present, but Montagu held up a hand. "Now, now. We can't have anyone who actually works here go undercover as Pam in case they are traced back to the NID. Besides, you are all working to capacity already."

Paddy chuckled. "All right, then. I'm game. What must I do?"

Cholmondeley gazed at her from behind his round, black-rimmed spectacles. "Martin's body must have all of the bits and pieces on it that a man collects in daily life, plus those that he treasures and keeps close to him wherever he may be. *You* must live the life Pam would have lived with her fiancé while he's on leave, before he makes that fateful journey from which, tragically, he is never to return."

He paused, as if to underline this small dramatic flourish. Then he added, "You, Mrs. Ridsdale, are to go to the cinema, buy two tickets and keep the stubs. In the post office, you make a fuss about the telegram you're waiting for from your boyfriend." Cholmondeley's voice took on a lighter tone. "His name is William Martin and he's a major in the Royal Marines. Isn't that simply *topping*?"

Paddy blinked. Cholmondeley had done a very good impression of a young upper-class girl, which was so incongruous she was hard put not to laugh.

His voice returned to normal. "At the jeweler's you agonize over engagement rings and pick out ones you like so you can show your fiancé. Make a real show of indecision, drive the shop assistants mad. That sort of thing."

Paddy's thumb pressed the back of her own wedding rings. "That all sounds straightforward, except for one thing. Is there a reason I must do all the play-acting? I mean, could we not collect this wallet litter, as you call it, without my needing to take on the persona of this Pam?"

"It's a necessary precaution," said Montagu. "The Germans are meticulous. If they get first-class intelligence dropping into their laps like a ripe plum, they're likely to think it was too easily obtained. They are going to be suspicious. So they will do everything they can to investigate and verify every single clue that we leave on Martin's person."

Miss Trehearne spoke up. "Do you mean to say, sir, that there are German spies running around England doing this kind of investigative work?"

"No, no, no," said Montagu, huffing a little. "Well, not that we know of. But we must behave as if there *is* someone on the ground who can follow up and check each and every lead we give them."

"Like a murder mystery when a suspect provides an alibi," said Paddy thoughtfully. "The detective has to retrace the suspect's steps and try to disprove their story. I see."

"Your job, Mrs. Ridsdale, is to make sure those witnesses *do* remember you when asked." Montagu threw out a hand. "We'd also like you to write love letters from Pam to Major Martin, full of the pathos of lovers parting ways in wartime. I daresay you know the style of thing. There'll be some key points of information we'd like you to incorporate—our Pam works in the War Office, for example, but we'll brief you separately on those. As for the sentiments, I'm sure you can improvise."

"I see." Paddy rather relished the idea of being a field agent, however briefly. But she must make sure Julian never caught wind of what she was up to—particularly not those love letters! A quivery little qualm unfurled like a seedling in the pit of her stomach, but she ignored it. This was all for the good of the country, for the success of Operation Husky, and for those thousands of men they hoped to save. If he knew, surely Julian would understand.

"Now," said Montagu. "The first thing we need to do is to find a photograph of our Pam." He raised an eyebrow at Paddy. "How do you fancy a little field trip, Mrs. Ridsdale?"

* * *

The field trip turned out to be a short one, no farther than to the offices of MI-5's section B1B. This was located at 58 St. James's Street, a literal stone's throw from several of Britain's most prestigious gentlemen's clubs.

Paddy knew from her time at Room 39 that B1B was responsible for gathering, filing, and analyzing intelligence gathered from captured German spies and anything else to do with running agents under the Double-Cross System. It was also where Jean worked as a secretary. Paddy wondered if their paths would cross on this visit.

The offices themselves had the same hushed air that prevailed at White's or Boodle's—a great contrast to the cramped environs of Room 13 or the bustle of Room 39. As Paddy and Montagu headed toward their destination, however, the noise of several typewriters all hammering away at once grew louder and louder.

"Right. Here we are." Montagu opened the door for Paddy and they went inside. "The secretarial pool."

Paddy had the impression of frenetic activity, young women typing or sorting through yellow carbon copies and dockets, darting here and there to deliver a memorandum or file a report. All of this was presided over by a wiry middle-aged woman with salt-and-pepper hair scraped back into a bun.

"Miss Leggett," said Montagu, holding out his hand. "How do you do?"

She pursed her lips, ignoring his gesture. "All right, girls!" She clapped her hands twice, and silence fell. "Stop what you're doing and listen to what Captain Montagu has to say."

The secretaries immediately downed tools and turned shining, expectant faces to the captain. Paddy slid a glance at Montagu and noticed a pink tinge at the tops of his ears. She smiled to herself, scanning the assembly for Jean. And there she was, bright of eye, bushy of tail, full lips trembling as if she was about to burst out laughing at this unexpected encounter.

"Now, ladies," said Montagu, "you will recall I asked a favor of you last week. Do you have your photos ready? Will you bring them here, please?"

As an aside to Paddy, he added, "This snap of our Major Martin's Pam must be the kind of picture of his girlfriend a young officer would keep close to his heart. I'm sure you know the kind of thing I mean."

Eagerly, the young women fished photographs out of their purses and surged forward. Paddy raised her eyebrows as quite a commotion ensued. It seemed every girl in the secretarial pool wanted to be the one whose photograph was found on the body of the officer whose life had been cut short so tragically. Some wailed that they didn't have anything appropriate with them and could the captain possibly wait for them to go home on leave? But Montagu laughingly shook his head. "I'm afraid this can't wait, my dear."

They collected enough pictures of pretty young women to give them ample choice. For her part, Paddy was relieved Montagu hadn't asked her to participate in this rather demeaning beauty parade. She could easily imagine how the men back at Room 13 would pore over this lineup and rank each girl according to all sorts of criteria. *Ugh.*

Montagu collected the pictures and slipped them tidily into

an envelope. When Jean came up to them with a photograph of her own, she moved forward and proffered it hesitantly. "I don't know if you can use this," she said in a deliberately matter-of-fact tone that didn't fool Paddy for an instant, "but you're welcome to it if you can."

The captain's eyes widened a little and his ears turned redder when he looked from Jean's hopeful face to the slightly risqué picture she'd handed him. Jean was wearing a swimsuit, holding a towel up to her chest, as if caught in the act of drying herself after a dip in the nearby river, her lovely hair tousled and blown by the wind. The photograph was natural, beautiful, and managed to be both innocent and alluring at the same time.

That's it, thought Paddy. *No question. That's the one.* Even better because the black-and-white photograph of Jean bore a superficial resemblance to Paddy herself.

As they were leaving, Jean hurried to catch up with them, ignoring Miss Leggett's sharp command not to run. "Fancy seeing you here!" she said, panting and laughing. She gave Paddy a hug and a kiss on the cheek. Then she said to Montagu, "Good luck with the operation, Captain."

"*Miss* Leslie!" The outraged accents of Miss Leggett from the other end of the room made Jean pull a face.

"You'd best get back or you'll be in hot water, by the sounds of it," said Paddy.

"Oh, don't mind the Spin," whispered Jean. "I don't!" But with a little wave and a dimpled smile, she turned and ran back to her post.

"Lovely girl," murmured Montagu, looking after her. "Friend of yours, I take it?"

"Yes, we met in Bordeaux during the British evacuation," said Paddy.

"Ah." The captain nodded. "I'd say, wouldn't you, Mrs. Ridsdale, that Miss Leslie's photograph will most likely prove the winner of our little beauty pageant." He paused, then repeated, "Lovely girl. Perhaps we might all get together for a drink sometime."

CHAPTER FOURTEEN

London, England
April 1943

Paddy

More than a month had passed since Paddy's hasty induction at Room 13 and everything was in place for Operation Mincemeat to begin. They just needed a suitable corpse to arrive at the mortuary.

Only when the fictional Major Martin's body came into the coroner's morgue could Paddy's part in the plan be set in motion. Until then, she was suspended in an odd limbo of anticipation. She kept herself busy, as ever, with all of the domestic concerns she had taken over from her mother and with her various committees and voluntary positions assisting the war effort. But at least half her mind, and sometimes all of it, was on Operation Mincemeat. So very many things could go wrong.

During that time, Paddy had come to realize how privileged her position in Room 39 with Ian Fleming had been. There, she'd been privy to decisions with momentous consequences, and was encouraged to debate and discuss them with Godfrey and Fleming. She saw herself as more of a facilitator and mediator between the two men than someone who actually took part in the decision-making, but at least she knew much of what went on at the highest level. As long as she didn't waste anyone's time and chose her moment judiciously, both Godfrey and Fleming welcomed her occasional contributions as a matter of course.

By contrast, in Operation Mincemeat, she would be an active participant. That was exciting in its own right, but she was also just one small cog in a very large and complex wheel. Much as she liked and respected Montagu and Cholmondeley, it was clear that neither man had the least intention of involving her in the operation's planning. They would most likely have been astonished at the very idea.

After her initial visit to Room 13, Paddy was never invited back. There was a reason behind this, of course. If she was to work in the field, she needed to have no discernible contact with the Admiralty. That was partly why they'd chosen her for this role. She was no longer NID personnel, and the change of surname upon her marriage made it more difficult to trace her back to her previous employment there.

It was difficult not to feel as if she'd been rather left out in the cold, however, and she often found herself speculating on what was going on in that tiny, airless basement room at the Admiralty. The only interaction she did have with the other participants in Mincemeat was on the social scene. She often met up with Jean of an evening when Julian was otherwise engaged. And lately, where Jean went, often Captain Montagu followed.

The friendship between Montagu and Jean had progressed rapidly since Paddy's visit to Section B1B in the captain's company. As Paddy had predicted, Jean's photograph was, indeed, chosen to be discovered nestled close to Major William Martin's heart when he washed up at Huelva. More than that, Jean and Montagu had taken to calling each other "Pam" and "Bill," after their fictional characters.

"You know Captain Montagu's married with children, don't you?" Paddy had said to Jean, having observed this friendship with rising concern.

"Oh, yes, I know," said Jean, fixing her hair. "But it's not like *that*, Paddy. It's all perfectly innocent."

"Maybe on your part," said Paddy darkly, thinking of the glow in Montagu's eyes when his gaze rested on his "Pam." "All this running around together calling each other pet names can't lead anywhere good. What if his wife finds out?"

"Oh, she knows all about me," said Jean with a shrug. "Besides, she's in Canada, and he's awfully lonely. I feel sorry for him, that's all." She broke into laughter that held a note of self-consciousness. "Oh, don't look at me like that. He's years and years too old for me."

"Well, just don't break his heart," said Paddy, her mind on the practical. "We need him sound of mind and spirit, at least until Mincemeat's done."

Now, as they ate a light supper in one of the booths at the Gargoyle Club, Charles Cholmondeley leaned in to say to Jean,

"Something I've been meaning to ask—did you get back any copies of that photograph of you in the swimsuit from that old boyfriend of yours? Best ask for the negatives, too."

"Oh, yes, I did ask, just like you told me," said Jean. "Tony was so hurt, but I was firm with him. I said, 'My new boyfriend doesn't like that you have such a saucy photograph of me, and he's asked me to get it back.' Tony said it's at his digs and he'll have to find it. But I'm sure he'll return it. He's a decent sort, really."

"In the Grenadier Guards, isn't he?" said Cholmondeley, and when she nodded, he added, "Well, let me know if he gives you any trouble. We can't have other copies floating about. If this Tony sees action and gets captured or killed with that photograph in his pocket, well . . . we'd be sunk."

One of the officers Paddy recognized from Room 13 suddenly appeared at Montagu's elbow and bent to murmur into his ear. One thick eyebrow shot up. Montagu's eyes lit and he was on his feet, full of apologies to Jean. "Mrs. Ridsdale," he said to Paddy, "we're called away on a rather delicate matter. I wonder if you might accompany us?" He jerked his head at Cholmondeley, who dabbed at his lips with a napkin and rose at once.

Paddy turned to Jean. "Sorry! Will you be all right if I leave you?"

"Of course," said Jean. "I know plenty of people here." She made a shooing motion with her hands. "Off you go. Don't keep them waiting."

Paddy frowned. Was it just her imagination, or did Jean seem relieved about the change of subject? She must ask her friend about that when she saw her next. Was this Tony person giving her more trouble than she let on?

As she descended in the rickety elevator with the two men from Room 13, Paddy asked, "Is it . . . ?"

Cholmondeley nodded. "We're off to the mortuary. Let's hope we have our man this time."

A thrill of excitement shot through her but she quickly tamped it down. She ought not to feel jubilant about a man's death or the use to which they planned to put his body—even if their plan might save thousands of other men's lives.

At the St. Pancras morgue they were met by the coroner, who rejoiced in the name Sir Bentley Purchase.

There was a strong smell of formaldehyde inside the mortuary that didn't entirely cover up another, less clinical smell. As Paddy followed the men down a dingy corridor, her stomach turned a full, sickening somersault and her senses swam. She clutched at the wall to steady herself and gave a vigorous shake of her head, then pulled her scarf up to cover her nose and mouth.

What was wrong with her? She'd worked in a hospital for long enough to have smelled much worse. Luckily, the men weren't paying any attention to her, so she took a moment to breathe in and out slowly through her nostrils. Her stomach settled somewhat, and she hurried after the others.

The examination room was tiled in white, and the body was laid out on the table, a white sheet covering his face.

"Here's your man," said the coroner. "Welsh. Former miner by the name of Glyndwr Michael. Thirty-four years of age." Sir Bentley twitched back the sheet so that it uncovered the man to the waist.

Paddy struggled not to recoil. The body's skin was an awful

gray color, the eyes sunken, mouth open, facial muscles slack. The stench of death was strong.

The men used handkerchiefs to cover their noses and mouths but otherwise seemed unaffected by the sight or smell of the corpse. Either that, or they were very good actors.

"Cause of death?" Cholmondeley asked.

"We believe the poor fellow suicided," Sir Bentley replied. "He was brought in suffering from phosphorous poisoning. Rat poison, basically. Terrible way to go usually, but he ingested a relatively small amount. Still, it took him two days to die." The coroner scratched his chin. "Do you know, roughly a quarter of the deaths we get here are suicides. Many of them from another part of the country. It's as if they come to London to die."

They were silent a moment while they thought about this. "Family?" said Montagu.

"None that would be in any way concerned that he's gone. He was a vagrant, poor fellow. Probably not of sound mind."

What a horribly lonely thought. That a man could perish and no one would miss him, no one at all. A rush of sadness flooded Paddy's chest. She said a short, silent prayer for this Glyndwr Michael. Partly out of respect and pity, but partly also as a sort of litany to get her mind off the horrible lurching of her stomach, and the suffocating sensation of only breathing in putrid air.

"And you think the poison won't be detected on an autopsy?" said Montagu.

"Not a chance," said the coroner. "There are always traces of phosphorous in any human body, and phosphorous dissipates over time. In my opinion, it would take a very skilled chemist to detect that the phosphorous in this particular corpse was at an abnormal level." He handed Montagu a folder. "Here's my full report."

The two officers from Room 13 looked at each other, then Montagu nodded. "Right. I'll go over this in more detail, of course, but it looks like we've finally found our man."

"I can't give you a lot of time, you'll understand," said Sir Bentley. "We can't freeze the body or his fluids will expand and cause other damage. We can keep him at four degrees Centigrade. That will slow down the decomposition, but it won't arrest it entirely."

"How long do we have, then?" Cholmondeley asked.

"I can give you three months."

Montagu glanced at Paddy. "Bearing up all right there, Mrs. Ridsdale? I wanted you to have a fair idea of what your fellow looks like, in the, er, in the flesh. Take a good look, and then we'd best get the photographer in."

Swallowing hard, Paddy approached Glyndwr Michael. She concentrated on his face, the dark hair, the moustache, then she cleared her throat. "His eyes? What color were they?"

"Brown." Thank goodness the coroner didn't offer to open his eyelids and show her.

The only other features of note were Michael's hands. They were not the hands of an officer in the Royal Marines but roughened by manual labor and shadowed with ingrained coal dust. "You said he worked in the mines?" She looked up at the coroner.

"Yes, that's right. Back in his hometown in Wales."

Paddy looked at Montagu. "Won't his hands rather give him away?"

Montagu cleared his throat. "After even a small amount of time in the water, I, er, imagine that won't be a problem."

"Yes," said Sir Bentley, less squeamish, or perhaps simply a little less tactful. "Nibbled by the fishes, won't he? The fingers will be the first to go."

Bile surged into Paddy's throat. She forced it down. Back when she'd worked at the hospital, she'd claimed to have a cast-iron stomach, maintaining that it was just a matter of willpower to get through the most difficult and disgusting parts of being a nurse. Now, she regretted her insensitivity toward the less hardy trainees among her cohort. There seemed to be no amount of willpower that would get her through much more of this sort of talk, certainly not in the presence of a cadaver that appeared to be decomposing before her very eyes.

When she could speak again, she said tightly, "I think I've seen enough for my purposes, thank you, gentlemen. I'll wait for you outside." Making herself walk at a slow, measured pace, with her head held high, Paddy left them to it.

But not before she heard Sir Bentley give a huff of laughter. "That's the fair sex for you, bless 'em. Not cut out for this sort of work."

Paddy wanted to charge back in there and kick Sir Bentley Purchase in the shins, but her need for fresh air was far greater. She hurried along the corridor and kept going until, finally, she reached the outdoors and dragged in blessed lungfuls of fresh night air.

It was so unlike her, this weakness, and she bitterly resented that Sir Bentley had correctly assumed the reason for her abrupt departure. Tactfully, when Montagu and Cholmondeley rejoined her, neither man made reference to it.

She waited for quite some time, and when the two officers emerged from the morgue, they told her why.

"Couldn't get a decent photograph of the chap," said Montagu. "No matter how you slice it, he just looks dead."

"As a doornail," Cholmondeley agreed. "We couldn't even convincingly prop up his head without someone holding it."

Paddy must have looked puzzled, because Montagu said, "For his identity card, you know. There's nothing for it. We'll need the photograph of someone alive who looks like our man."

That might prove difficult. Glyndwr Michael had an unusually shaped face, lean to the point of emaciation, with a very pointed chin. Paddy mentally went through the men of her acquaintance. She couldn't think of anyone who might fit the bill.

"Trip to the registry in order, I think." Montagu nodded at Paddy. "Another job for you, Mrs. Ridsdale. We'll motor up to Blenheim day after tomorrow if that suits."

Paddy agreed without hesitation.

"Well. All in all, a good night's work," said Montagu, flicking the coroner's report with his fingertip.

"Now, the game's afoot," said Cholmondeley, all but twirling his waxed moustache with glee.

A surge of excitement overtook Paddy's queasiness. Yes. The game was afoot. And this time, she would be a player in it.

Paddy managed to beat Julian home that evening. Relieved that she had a little time to compose herself before she had to act as if she hadn't just viewed a dead body, Paddy went up to their bedroom and took a bath. Guilty but determined, she used up the greater part of a small cake of soap, scrubbing the smell of death from her body. But the scent seemed to linger in her nostrils even after she'd made herself a cup of cocoa and hopped into bed.

The hot, unsweetened cocoa seemed to calm the squalls in her stomach. From the drawer in her bedside table, she pulled out her diary and a pen. Then she sighed. Not much she could put into writing about what had happened to her that evening.

She frowned, flipped back a few pages, then forward again. She'd been right. That squeamishness at the morgue had *not* been like her at all. And here was the explanation, staring up at her from the pages of her diary. A significant date had come and gone without her noticing. She'd missed her last period. Three weeks ago, in fact.

Pregnant. She was going to have a baby. Paddy clutched the diary to her chest and burst into laughter that was half joyful, half horrified.

Julian came into the bedroom then, whipping off his hat and kicking off his shoes. He stopped, his blond hair sticking up every which way, as he eyed her in puzzlement. "What's so funny?"

Paddy stared at him. Automatically, she said, "Nothing. I was just reading over my diary."

He cocked his head, as if waiting for more, but she couldn't think what recent incident might have produced such mirth, so she simply smiled back at him and raised an eyebrow in an effort to look mysterious.

And why, she thought, had she instinctively lied to Julian about the baby? True, it was early days. Anything might happen, and many women she knew didn't tell their husbands for a little while. But that wasn't the reason she'd temporized just now, was it?

She turned the question over in her mind. Was she afraid that if she told Julian she was pregnant, it would become all too real? And if it became real, then she might have to rethink her role in Operation Mincemeat.

Just a little while longer, she bargained silently, as Julian got into bed beside her. *Just until my part in Operation Mincemeat is complete.*

* * *

Petrol rationing must not have troubled Captain Montagu very much because he drove them both in a sporty little Aston Martin up to Blenheim Palace, near Oxford. He drove with the top down and yelled comments to her now and then over the roar of the wind, but he didn't talk about the operation at all. For Paddy's part, she was doing her best not to gag as the petrol fumes kept filling her nostrils whenever they came to a stop. She'd brought a dry biscuit with her as a precaution, but somehow she didn't like to nibble at it in front of the captain.

They motored through the old market town of Woodstock and soon reached a checkpoint, at which the guard glanced at their passes and exchanged a few pleasantries with Montagu, before waving them through.

Paddy had been to the Duke of Marlborough's residence before the war, and as they drove through the park surrounding the Churchills' country seat, she suffered a shock.

All over what used to be the Great Court, there were prefabricated Nissen huts, row upon row of them, and military vehicles of every description had turned the area immediately outside the palace entrance into a carpark. Paddy could only imagine what the duke must think about this ugliness marring the house's elegant facade.

"Military Intelligence. MI-5," said Montagu, as they pulled up and got out of the car. "Or most of it, anyway. They were at Wormwood Scrubs prison for a while at the start of the war, but it was bombed out, so they thought it best to remove to the country."

A memory stirred at the back of Paddy's mind, but she shook it off. She needed to focus on the job at hand. They passed through another checkpoint, and she raised her eyebrows. So they were entering the palace itself?

"This way." Montagu ushered her up the steps and inside. The Great Hall soared high above them, as did tower upon tower of filing cabinets. Paddy's gaze traveled from the marble floor up the fluted Corinthian columns to the small minstrels' gallery, then up again, to the classical marble statues looking down upon them, then higher still, to the oval painting of a classical scene on the ceiling. Such an imposing entryway seemed like the very last place one ought to find the hustle and bustle of an intelligence service office.

"This is the registry," said Montagu with a nod to one of the young women flitting about importantly with stacks of files and papers. "All of the service personnel files are kept here, along with files on persons of interest. We'll stick to MI-5 personnel today. There's sure to be someone . . ."

He smiled at a young woman with a clipboard who came to greet them. "Morning, Miss Horton. Where have you put us? Ah! I see."

The young woman led them to a table in the corner on which several stacks of files awaited them. Montagu indicated that Paddy should take a seat, and he sat down beside her. "Now, you will remember what our friend looks like, won't you, Mrs. Ridsdale. I'm afraid the material is too sensitive to allow you to have a photograph of him with you for reference, but it's really the shape of the face and the moustache that we need." He placed a hand on one stack of files. "These are the personnel files of every man of approximately the right age from MI-5. If we don't find our Major Martin there, we'll be obliged to move on to other services."

Paddy said, "Right, sir. I'll do my best."

"I'll leave you to it. Need to go up to Oxford and see a man about some smalls," said Montagu cryptically. "I'll call back for you in a couple of hours."

Paddy nodded and turned to the stacks of files. She needed to find a very specific sort of face—narrow with a very sharp chin. Not many men could pass for Glyndwr Michael.

Paddy stumbled on several surprises among the MI-5 personnel files. Tempting though it was to glance through the dossiers of some of the men she knew, she refrained. One file she came across tempted her, though. So Brian Howard had been working at MI-5?

And then the puzzle pieces fell into place. Montagu's mention of MI-5's former home at Wormwood Scrubs prison. Brian Howard saying that he and Jean had escaped from *jail* together. *Really!* thought Paddy. Brian was the absolute limit.

So it had been MI-5 who had given Brian the sack last year. Perhaps that was for the best. While she imagined he'd be quite adept at ferreting out dirty secrets, she wouldn't bet on either his work ethic or his discretion. She set his file in the ever-growing rejection pile.

By the time Montagu came back for her, Paddy had six possible Major Martins, but there was one clear standout, with the same narrow face and pointy chin, as well as the small moustache.

When he saw the photograph, Montagu said, "By Jove! What a beauty. Well done, Mrs. Ridsdale. I think we have our man."

CHAPTER FIFTEEN

London, England
April 1943

Paddy

So you *were* hiding something the other evening at the Gargoyle Club. I thought so," said Paddy. Jean had one of her rare days of leave and Paddy had decided to treat her to tea at Claridge's.

It was a bright spring day and they'd each chosen a twinset and pearls for their outing. Jean's was a camel color that set off her fair skin and emphasized the tawny highlights in her hair. Paddy had opted for ice blue. They looked no different from any of the other young women present. Paddy doubted, however, that any of the other young women were talking about floating corpses and the interesting items that might be found on them by Nazi spies.

"Not hiding something, exactly," said Jean, plaiting her fingers together. "Only, Tony's still sweet on me, you see, and I never *quite* ended it between us, so—"

"—you didn't ask him for the photograph back," said Paddy.

"No, I did. I *did*!" Jean said, curls bobbing as she vigorously nodded her head. "But he looked at me as if he were a puppy and I'd just kicked him. I didn't have the heart to insist."

"Well, you simply must," said Paddy. "Talk to him again. End it kindly but firmly and demand the picture back. The negative, too."

"I wish it were that simple." Jean sighed.

"It is precisely that simple," said Paddy, picking up her purse. "Come on. We'll do it right now."

"But—"

"You said he's on leave, didn't you? Let's start at his flat and go from there."

They drew a blank at Tony's flat and at the Hurlingham Club, too.

By the time they'd tried a few other likely places, it was getting toward the dinner hour, but Paddy refused to give up. "What clubs does he frequent of an evening?"

"Oh, the usual." Jean shrugged. "The Tropicana, the Four Hundred. Places like that."

"Why don't we go back to mine to change for dinner, and you can ring around to see if you can find out where he'll be tonight."

After several phone calls, Jean discovered that Tony was most likely to be at the 400 Club that evening. "Splendid!" said Paddy. "We'll dine there and lie in wait."

Both women hurried to get ready. Julian came in while Paddy was affixing one sparkling diamond earring in place. "Hello, darling." She reached up to kiss him, one hand on his shoulder, and smiled.

He raised his eyebrows as if surprised at her impulsive show of affection, then pulled her close and kissed her properly. She emerged from that embrace confused and a little flustered by the searching expression in Julian's eyes as he gazed down at her.

Guilt at her own duplicity came rushing back. From the moment she'd begun keeping the secret about her pregnancy from him, she'd felt like a fraud whenever he touched her. The only reason she'd kissed him wholeheartedly just now was that in her concern over Jean and the problem of Tony and the photograph, Paddy had forgotten about her own subterfuge. Julian's reaction showed that he'd noticed both her recent coolness and the sudden change.

Keeping her smile, she said, "Well, this *is* nice. But I thought you weren't coming home until late tonight or I would have canceled my plans." She reached up to smooth back his hair. "Jean's here. We're about to go out."

His shoulders slumped a little. She knew how much he looked forward to their rare quiet evenings together. Paddy rubbed his arm. "Sorry, darling. Why don't you come with us? We're only going to the Four Hundred."

She made the offer expecting it to be declined, but Julian said, "Yes. Why not? It's been too long since I took my wife dancing."

As the women waited for Julian to change, Jean said, "Do you think it's a good idea to bring Julian along? Maybe we should try Tony another day."

"This really can't wait, Jean," said Paddy, thinking of poor Glyndwr Michael slowly rotting away in the fridge at the St. Pancras morgue. "Besides, for all you know, Tony might be shipping out any day now, and you'll have lost your chance."

"No. You're right." Jean squared her shoulders and jutted out her chin. "I simply must."

The 400 Club was presided over by a fatherly individual called Mr. Rossi, a great friend to all the young debutantes who came swimmingly into his care. "Mrs. Ridsdale," he said, smiling down at her. "Happy to see you this evening."

He greeted Jean and Julian, and they all checked their coats and moved through to the dining room. Jean was on edge and didn't eat much. Paddy realized that, by now, she herself was quite faint from hunger. But when the meal came, one whiff of it made her stomach churn.

She pushed her plate away.

"I thought you were hungry," said Julian.

"It's the fish," said Paddy, wishing she could eat it without smelling it as well. "I think it might be off."

She tore small chunks off her bread roll and ate them, hoping to appease both her husband and her unruly stomach. That seemed to work, so she finished her roll and then started on Julian's. Jean gave her an odd look, and Julian leaned down to sniff suspiciously at her meal. "You have a sensitive nose, my dear. It smells fine to me. Should I send it back?"

"No, don't do that," said Paddy, wishing she hadn't chosen that excuse. "It's just me. I had food poisoning from haddock once. Sometimes I simply can't stomach it, that's all. It was foolish to order it."

She wished a waiter would come and take it away. Why were

smells so much stronger these days? It was as if nature kept working against her.

At last, the meal was over. Paddy had been maintaining a cheerful flow of conversation while keeping an eye out for Tony, although she had no clear memory of what he looked like. Jean always had a string of boyfriends—or maybe "a web of them" might be a more accurate term. She never seemed to favor one above the next and was to be seen with any one of them on any given evening. Like many young women of their age, Jean saw no point in settling down until she absolutely had to. Until she found the man she wanted as a husband, she wasn't going to limit herself to just one beau.

Several of Julian's acquaintances stopped at their table, and Julian invited them to join their party. Paddy did her best to converse intelligently while keeping half her mind on retrieving Jean's photograph.

Suddenly, Jean clutched Paddy's arm. "There he is."

Paddy was on her feet. "Do excuse us for a moment, Julian." She leaned down to murmur in his ear. "Jean's having a bit of trouble with one of her boyfriends. I said I'd help her sort it out."

He nodded, but he hadn't really been listening, absorbed as he was in a hot political debate, so she patted his cheek and left the table with Jean.

They arrived at the spot Jean had seen Tony, only to find that he'd taken to the dance floor. MJ, who was there with Brian Howard, gave them an airy wave as Tony cut in and spun her in a circle.

"He's a regular Fred Astaire, isn't he?" Paddy murmured, but

Jean didn't hear her above the music. She was staring after the pair with an odd look on her face.

"Are you all right?" Paddy asked her.

Jean shook her head. "No. No, I don't suppose I am."

Paddy waited.

"I rather liked Tony, you know," said Jean. "I quite thought . . . Well, never mind. I have to get that photo back, and I can't tell him why, so that's that, isn't it?"

Surprised, Paddy said, "Do you mean you're sweet on him?"

"Oh, I don't know," said Jean with a sigh. "It's just that when I went to ask him for the picture, he seemed so cut up about it. I suddenly thought, what if Tony's the one? What if I'm destroying my future happiness over a photograph?"

"But it's not over just a photograph," said Paddy. "Anyway, if it's meant to be, he wouldn't let a spat over something like that put him off."

"I suppose not," said Jean. "But—"

"You told him there was someone else?" said Paddy.

Jean nodded. "I think that might be why he refused to give it back."

That did complicate matters, but it couldn't be helped. "Here he is now." Tony was heading straight for them with a very determined look on his face.

He was a handsome, ginger-haired fellow, one of those few redheads fortunate enough to tan easily. His bright blue eyes glanced at Paddy, then his gaze shifted to her friend.

He held out his hand to Jean with a tortured expression that would have done Laurence Olivier proud. "Dance with me."

Before Jean could respond, Paddy said, "Don't mind if I do," and put her hand in Tony's, offering him her most dazzling smile.

All resemblance to Olivier's Heathcliff vanished. Tony stuttered and blushed, and with a look of half apology, half chagrin at Jean, he allowed himself to be commandeered. Now firmly installing herself as captain of this particular ship, Paddy steered Tony to the far side of the dance floor, so he couldn't keep an eye on Jean. As they danced the foxtrot at a very correct distance apart, Paddy went to work. "Well, you don't *look* like a cad," she said thoughtfully, startling him out of his attempts to search for Jean over her shoulder.

"I beg your pardon?" he said, his neck literally stiffening in offense.

"It's just that I rather thought you would be," said Paddy, moving fluidly with the music. She loved dancing. It was a pity she was here on the floor with Tony instead of Julian, but hopefully her business with the Grenadier Guard would be concluded soon. "The way you've treated Jean, I mean."

"Now, see here," said Tony, "if Jean says I behaved badly toward her, boot's on the other leg, if you want to know." He huffed a little. "All the fellows are mad for her, and she just picks and chooses as she pleases, without a single *thought—*"

"Yes, but the point is, if she didn't pick you, then you should simply retire gracefully from the lists, shouldn't you?" said Paddy. "What's this I hear about your hanging on to a picture of her? Quite a risqué one, too."

His mouth flattened. "Oh, that. Well, I suppose that's not really cricket. Truth is, I would have given it back to her, but the thought of some other chap having it . . . No!"

What would Tony say if he knew this "other chap" was a corpse?

Paddy thought for a moment. "If I solemnly swear to you that I shall see to it no other man alive will be in possession of that photograph, will you give it back to her? The negative, too? Her family are all extremely prudish, you see, and if they ever saw that picture . . ." She smiled up at Tony. "I'm sure you wouldn't want her to be embarrassed." She smoothed his lapel and patted it. "Be a gentleman, Tony. Give it back to her. You never know. You might win enough points with her to get the real thing, rather than just the photograph."

"Really?" His eagerness was so boyish despite his enormous size that she almost laughed. "Do you really think so? Has she said something to you?"

Paddy winked. "Now that would be telling tales out of school. But you won't ever get anywhere with Jean if she feels she can't trust you, you know."

He put his shoulders back and gave a sharp nod. "All right. I'll bring it around to her at MJ's later this evening." He jutted his chin as if facing down some imagined enemy. "Just received orders, you know. It's my last night in London."

Goodness, they'd caught him just in time. It sounded like he'd be shipping out soon. Paddy said as much to Jean when she caught up with her after their dance.

"Oh, well done!" said Jean when she heard about Paddy's success. "And you didn't even need to resort to violence. Remember that fellow at Bordeaux?"

"*Once!* That was once!" protested Paddy, laughing. "I don't *always* resort to violence. The negotiation with Tony was very diplomatically done, I'll have you know. Although I might well have given him a tiny bit of false hope . . ." She eyed her friend. "I do trust you'll be kind to him when next you meet, Jean. He seemed a pretty decent sort, all things considered."

"Well, I'd best be off to wait for him at MJ's," said Jean. She gave Paddy a quick, impulsive hug. "Thank you, dearest! I'll be sure to keep the photo safe until I can give it back to Bill again."

"Bill?" Paddy frowned. "Oh, you mean Captain Montagu."

Jean made a moue and then stuck her tongue out. "Yes, Captain Montagu!" Blithely, as if the fate of thousands had never rested on her slim shoulders, Jean hurried off to join her other friends.

Suddenly Paddy felt fatigue drag at her body. Drat this pregnancy! It really did play havoc with one's stamina.

She turned to find Julian at her elbow. "Alone and palely loitering?" he inquired, taking her hand and tucking it into the crook of his arm.

"I do feel a bit like a young knight, now that you mention it," Paddy said, thinking of the rather toothless dragon she'd just managed to vanquish. "But a valiant one." She smiled up at him. "And not heartsick at all."

He didn't return her smile. "Who was that fellow you were dancing with before?"

Then she'd been correct. Julian hadn't been listening to her when she'd told him where she was going. "Oh, that was Tony. A beau of Jean's who needed to be set straight."

"You looked rather like you were charming him silly," observed Julian. Before she could argue the point, he added brusquely, "Shall we go? I've been wishing myself at home for the past half hour."

Paddy agreed out of guilt as much as from a similar wish to be snuggled up with a hot drink in a soft bed. As they made their way home, however, Julian's reticence disturbed her. He was generally the most gregarious of men, at home in any company. He'd seemed to be enjoying himself with his political friends. Until her dance with Tony, that was.

Could Julian be jealous? His dislike of Ian Fleming notwithstanding, Julian had never displayed a hint of jealousy before—particularly not with such trivial cause. At another time, she might have teased him about this sudden fit of possessiveness, but then she remembered that odd moment of uncertainty between them that evening, when she'd returned his kiss without a thought in her head for floating corpses or the secret life that might well be growing inside her. The sapient look in his eye.

What right did she have to rib him about a small fit of groundless jealousy? Rather than ease the tension with an amusing anecdote as she might have done if she had a clear conscience, Paddy let the silence grow between them until it loomed far too large to break.

Would she come to regret agreeing to take part in Operation Mincemeat?

Well, it was too late to turn back now.

CHAPTER SIXTEEN

London, England
April 1943

Friedl

*B*efore she left Estoril in the summer of 1941, Friedl tried several times to tell Popov about her encounter with Kühlenthal. He was so charmingly attentive, however, that she couldn't bring herself to spoil the mood. If he noticed an uncharacteristic reticence in her manner, he didn't comment on it. The strain of keeping her secret was so great that by the time he drove her to the airport, she was more than ready to part from him.

After that, she didn't see Popov for many months. He was in Washington, D.C., it was said, no doubt trying to persuade the Americans to join the war effort. After that, their meetings grew shorter and ever more infrequent, their mutual passion more explosive and desperate—on her part, at least. Despite Friedl's determination to act as if Popov meant nothing to her, London was bleak and miserable without him, and the spy game lost much of its former luster.

Friedl continued her work for Tar under the direction of a young officer, William Luke, and a German operative who went by the unlikely name of Susan Barton. The latter seemed to think Friedl vapid and pointless, and some perverse imp of mischief made Friedl play up to Susan's opinion of her. The two of them couldn't get along, and Friedl yearned for the easy camaraderie of her days with Joan Miller, Billy Younger, and the spymaster, M.

After Kühlenthal's warning at Estoril, Friedl had been on tenterhooks anticipating his next move. Again, she waited for word to come that her services were needed and waited in vain. Now almost two years since she'd met him on Tamariz Beach, it didn't seem likely he would ever make contact. Which was absolutely fine by her. In the intervening period, Friedl received word that her mother had died. She grieved for her gentle parent who had been ill for many years, but she was relieved that the suffering was over. It also meant that Kühlenthal no longer had any kind of hold over Friedl.

One evening, she encountered Tar at a party in Mayfair, where he managed to buttonhole her despite her attempts to avoid private conversation. Tar was disconcertingly perceptive, and she regretted that she hadn't told him about Kühlenthal's approach at Estoril. Had she known Kühlenthal would never even attempt to bring her into play she certainly would have done so.

"Missing Tricycle these days, eh?" said Tar, nodding to the waiter to pour more champagne into Friedl's glass.

She shrugged. "I find plenty to amuse me."

"Well, it's only been a couple of months, I suppose," said Tar, nodding.

A couple of months? Friedl shrugged, determined not to let him know that this pointed remark was a stab in the chest. "I haven't seen Popov since December."

There was a disquieting gleam in Tar's eye. Mildly, he replied, "Duško came to London in February, but it was a flying visit." He cleared his throat, then lifted his chin and raised his eyebrows, as if to catch the attention of someone behind her. "Do excuse me, will you, Miss Stöttinger? There's someone I must speak with."

Relieved, Friedl nodded and waved him away. She sipped at her champagne. So. Duško had been in London and he had not been in touch with her. Too busy, was he? She doubted it. In the first flush of their affair, nothing could have kept him from her side. The sensation of losing her grip on something precious intensified.

Those magical nights in Estoril . . . She closed her eyes and wished she could have her time with him over again. If only she hadn't gone to the beach alone the following morning, she might not have encountered Kühlenthal.

Did Popov know? Had he deliberately distanced himself from her for that reason? More likely, he had simply grown bored with her.

"You seem far away," said a deep voice from behind her, in an accent one heard more and more in London these days.

Friedl turned, and a handsome man in about his midthirties smiled down at her. "Is it a good place? May I join you?"

Her gaze swept from the top of his neatly barbered dark head to the toes of his gleaming black Oxfords. He was tall, broad-shouldered, solid as oak. Whether it was from better nourishment or genes, they simply seemed to grow American men bigger than their European counterparts.

He was smooth, this one, with Ivy League written all over him, but he had a million-dollar smile, and buckets of what Joan Miller would call "S.A." Friedl answered with a half-truth. "I was thinking about a beach in Portugal. At Estoril. Do you know it?"

"The Portuguese Riviera. I've heard of the place but never been. Tell me about it. My name's Don Calder, by the way."

They spent the rest of the party together, talking as easily as if they'd been friends for years, and Friedl felt neither rushed nor imposed upon when Calder offered to take her home.

"Oh, you have a car," said Friedl as he escorted her to his vehicle. Diplomatic plates. Calder had said he was an economist attached to the embassy, but as she well knew, all kinds of occupations could be covers for spies in wartime England. Did he ever have dealings with Tarlair Ltd.?

"I borrowed it," said Calder, holding the door open for her. He drove himself, and she noted with approval the way his big hands gripped the shiny black steering wheel as they crept through the dim London streets. When he pulled up outside the mews where she lived and let her out of the car, she expected him to make some excuse to come up. By now, Friedl had developed quite a reputation in London society, and allowing a gentleman to see her home usually gave out a certain signal few ignored.

The American was attractive and she liked him very much.

Ordinarily she would not hesitate to take him upstairs to her boudoir. But when Calder took off his hat and moved toward her, instinct made Friedl take one decided step back. She couldn't. Not tonight. Not with Duško Popov still dominating her thoughts.

Besides, she liked this American. Too much to sleep with him and discard him again when Popov crooked his finger. But perhaps not enough to resist Duško's call whenever it might come. What a hopeless case she was! This charming, amusing man seemed poised to become serious about her. If so, he deserved better.

"Well, good night, Mr. Calder," she said from an impersonal distance, not even offering to shake his hand. "It's been lovely."

Calder hesitated, turning his hat over and over. Then he nodded, as if accepting the tacit rebuff. "Good night, Miss Stöttinger," he said, and his tone was somber. "It's been a pleasure meeting you. I'll telephone you, if I may."

For once, she would not be selfish and impulsive. For once, she would think about someone else. "No," said Friedl. "Let's just say we enjoyed this evening together and leave it at that, all right?" She made herself turn and walk away.

He waited until she went inside. As she went upstairs, the possibility that Calder might be spying on her crossed her mind. Diplomatic number plates . . . She stooped to lift the loose coping on her doorstep and felt for the key she'd hidden beneath it, then unlocked her door and went inside. Dropping her purse and wrap as she moved through the apartment, she didn't switch the light on immediately, but went to the window to peer through a chink in the blackout curtains. Calder's car had already gone.

She tapped a lacquered fingernail against her lips. If the American was gathering intelligence on her, he wouldn't have taken her polite dismissal as final. He would have found some excuse to come up. That was certainly how Popov operated.

Popov . . . He hadn't contacted her in all this time, although she still sent her carefully vetted letters from "Mrs. Ivy Trevallion" to the address in Lisbon he'd given her. Nothing personal in those, of course. Would it be strictly business between them from now on?

She could make up any number of excuses to salve her own pride, but the fact of the matter was that for Popov, these days Friedl was out of sight, and most definitely out of mind.

* * *

Friedl was drunk. Maudlin drunk. She'd ended up at MJ's place after curfew, as she often did these days, in the company of a motley band of writers, artists, poets, and spies.

MJ's mother welcomed them all with expansive if careless bonhomie. She was an eccentric lady who kept a collection of dollhouses in the family chapel, and even wrote stories about the dollhouses' inhabitants. Brian had taken Friedl on a tour of the chapel once. He knew all of the dolls' names and seemed to take very seriously the entire notion of them having a secret life when clumsy humans were not about. But one never knew with Brian. He might be in deadly earnest or laughing at you behind those melancholy brown eyes.

In the drawing room, someone put on a record and Friedl slung an arm around Brian's neck. Cheek to cheek, they slow-danced to "We'll Meet Again," a song that seemed to have been written specifically to make her cry. She cuddled closer. So comforting to be held by a man and know he had not the remotest interest in sleeping with her.

"What a touching picture we must present," slurred Brian as if to counter her thoughts. "Daddy would be so relieved."

"Parents do not like me," said Friedl, nestling her head into the crook of his shoulder. Now *that* was a thought. Did Duško have family back in Serbia? She didn't know the answer and rather felt she should. "I bet they don't like you, either."

Brian shook with silent laughter. "Very true, pet. Very true." He sighed. "Poor Toni. I do hope he's all right without me."

"Your darling Anton will be just fine," Friedl stated with firm certainty, though in fact, she had no idea. "He will miss you terribly, of course, but he's waiting patiently until this dreadful war is over, and then he'll run back into your arms."

They danced on in silence. Someone tapped Brian on the shoulder as if to cut in but Friedl clung closer. "Tell him to go away," she said.

"Piss off, there's a good chap," said Brian to the interloper. They danced on.

"Bastards," said Brian after a long silence. "Can't believe those utter cretins at Five sacked me."

"Did they, darling?" Friedl had been waiting for him to bring it up. "What on earth for?"

"For using things I learned in the course of my service to blackmail people."

Friedl blinked. She had assumed MI-5 had dismissed him

for insubordination, or laziness, or perhaps even bungling an operation. But then, probably those things might not get Brian sacked. It was typical of the British that they preferred not to confront incompetent people if they could help it. They simply set them aside and sidelined them until they gave up and went away. Brian, who had never actually served at MI-5 in any official capacity beyond "asset," could have been cut loose without fuss at any time. But blackmail? She didn't like to believe it of him.

"Whom did you blackmail, darling? I'm sure they were all nasty people."

"Oh, a couple of cabinet ministers, that's all. And a bishop. That's the thing that utterly infuriates me," said Brian, warming to his theme. "These upright citizens, they commit all manner of sins in secret, and then the hypocrites revile a chap like *me* simply for loving someone good and kind like Toni . . ." He stopped, his throat working, and a rush of sympathetic tears burned behind Friedl's eyes.

"*And* MI-5 protects the villains," Brian added. "Not out of the goodness of their hearts, though. Oh, no! It's so that *they* can be the ones to have a hold over the cabinet ministers and bishops, you see. It's not blackmail when it's for the good of king and country."

"You didn't actually extort money from them, did you, darling?" said Friedl.

"Of course not," said Brian, but she couldn't tell whether he was lying. "I was simply teasing them a little."

They were quiet for a while, then he said, "You know what it's like . . . Well, you know a bit. I mean, it can't be easy being German in wartime London."

Friedl shrugged. She suffered abuse here and there from ignorant people, but by and large, her friends and acquaintances were cosmopolitan enough not to hold her nationality against her. And besides, she made sure that she was so cheerful and such good company, that they soon forgot her origin and joined in the fun. "Billy used to say I use a charm offensive," said Friedl.

"Whereas I simply use an offensive offensive," said Brian.

Friedl chuckled, then quickly sobered. The fear came over her that one day, Brian's "teasing," as he called it, might get him arrested or badly beaten or even killed, but there was no reasoning with him, she knew that. Just as there was no reasoning with her over Popov.

A tear rolled down her cheek and dripped off her nose onto Brian's lapel. "Sorry, darling. I'm ruining your lovely coat."

Brian waved away her apology. "We are a dismal pair." He sighed. "But you know what, Friedl? At least you're not ashamed to show how you feel. All these stiff upper lips the rest of us carry around all the time . . . It's not natural. We're a nation of icebergs, we English."

"I would like to be like that," Friedl murmured. If only she didn't fall in love so easily and so thoroughly and so often, she could avoid the misery of being hurt like this. And she could forget all about that fascinating, wayward, maddening spy.

"Well, *hello*," Brian murmured, his tone sliding from disgruntlement to frank appreciation.

Friedl lifted her head from his shoulder and looked around.

A very large, redheaded fellow paused on the threshold to the drawing room, scanning the crowd. Then he moved impetuously to tap Jean Leslie on the shoulder. Like Friedl, Jean had become quite a fixture at MJ's lately. She worked for the War Office in some capacity, though Friedl didn't know what.

"Hmm. Lucky Jean," murmured Brian.

"They don't seem too friendly," said Friedl, watching as Jean held out her hand and the redhead practically slapped a slim envelope into it. He said another few words to her and stalked off.

Jean gazed after him for several seconds, her shoulders tense. Surreptitiously she wiped the back of her hand over one eye as if to dash away a tear, then turned back to her group of friends with a brilliant smile pasted to her face.

CHAPTER SEVENTEEN

London, England
April 1943

Paddy

"What's this about an appointment in Harley Street, darling?" said Julian as Paddy walked in to breakfast one morning. Traditionally, she never took more than a cup of tea at this hour, but she liked to sit with Julian and read the papers together before he left for the War Office. These days, her stomach rebelled if she didn't at least eat a slice of bread or a dry biscuit first thing.

Paddy shot an accusing glance at her mother, who blinked back at her in mild surprise. Edith spread her hands. "The receptionist rang yesterday to ask if you would mind changing it to Thursday. I'm afraid I said I didn't know anything about it. Everything all right, dear?"

"Just a routine checkup," said Paddy brightly, before she could stop to consider whether now might be the perfect time to break the good news. But really, until she saw the doctor, her pregnancy was pure speculation on her part.

That was her story, and she was sticking to it.

Her mother's sharp eyes took in Paddy from her head to her toes, then she settled back in her chair, as if satisfied with a conclusion she'd made but had no intention of voicing. Well, if Edith had concluded correctly, it seemed she intended to keep her own counsel, at least until she and Paddy were alone.

Julian seemed content with Paddy's explanation, although if he stopped to think about it, he would be bound to recall that his wife was routinely as healthy as a horse and avoided doctors at all costs. If only she'd thought to come up with some relatively minor but pressing malady that would explain her uncharacteristic behavior! Too late now. Gosh, she'd be a hopeless spy if it meant one constantly had to lie to one's loved ones like this.

Julian finished his tea, then rose from the table and bent to kiss her. Touching her cheek with a fingertip, he said, "Bye, darling. Shouldn't be too late tonight, I don't think."

Paddy lingered at the breakfast table, pretending to finish the crossword Julian had begun, but the print blurred before her eyes. She had far too much on her mind: guilt over lying to Julian, yes, but more pressing, a long list of items she must procure over the next few days for Major Martin's wallet litter. Time was of the essence, so she'd decided to cross off several items today. First, a visit to the jeweler's to buy Pam an engagement ring. That would be no hardship, at least.

As soon as the front door closed behind Julian, her mother

gazed at Paddy across the breakfast table. "When are you going to tell him?"

For one, fraught second, Paddy thought she meant about Operation Mincemeat. But of course, Edith had guessed about the baby. "Early days, Mother," said Paddy. "I'll tell him when I'm sure." She sighed. "At least, you know Julian will want to wrap me in cotton wool once he hears the news. I simply want a tiny bit longer to be free. There's something—several things—I need to accomplish here before he packs me off to Ireland."

"Well, don't overdo it trying to prove yourself, will you?" said Edith, getting up from the table. "Pregnant women need plenty of rest. And plenty of nourishment, too. I'll send over to Dublin for a hamper."

Paddy repressed the urge to beg Edith not to do anything out of the ordinary, so as to rouse Julian's suspicions, but that would only make Edith wonder why on earth Paddy was so determined to keep the news from him. Instead, she smiled. "That sounds marvelous."

Edith squeezed her shoulder and dropped a kiss on the crown of her head. "Lovely news, darling. Julian will be so proud of you."

Paddy pressed her mother's hand and smiled up at her. When Edith had gone, however, she thought, *What a strange way to phrase it.* How could one take pride in what was essentially a natural human function?

But she had to admit, it was rather a comfort that someone else knew what she was going through. The nausea, the tiredness—all of it was frustrating to the point of aggravation to a person so ordinarily full of vigor. It made Paddy even more determined to carry out her duties for Operation Mincemeat to the best of her ability.

Choosing the engagement ring for Major Martin's flighty girlfriend, Pam, was one of the more enjoyable tasks she'd been given. Paddy loved beautiful jewels as much as the next woman, so it was an excellent excuse to visit one of London's premier jewelers, S. J. Phillips in New Bond Street.

"You'll go in and do your spiel about the major and love's young dream and all that," said Montagu, as they headed toward the jeweler's from the Tube station where they'd met. "The only tricky part comes when I steal the blank invoice."

"I must make absolutely sure that everyone's eyes are on me while you take a page out of the invoice book," said Paddy. "I can do that."

"Right," said Montagu. "You go in first."

Remembering her own rings just in time, Paddy delayed on the pretext of browsing the pieces displayed in the bow window of the shop. Bending to inspect a handsome silver épergne adorned with peacocks and tigers, she put her left hand in the pocket of her coat and eased off her engagement and wedding rings with her thumb until they dropped off, landing in the bottom of the pocket. Rubbing at the slight indent the rings had made at the base of her finger, she walked confidently to the entrance, pushed open the door, and stepped inside.

Paddy gazed around her with unfeigned pleasure at the mahogany cabinets and glass-topped table displays, their brass fittings as brightly polished as the gems and ornaments they contained. Along with jewelry of every description, there were dinner services in silver and fine china, snuff boxes, cigar boxes, and Fabergé photo frames. There were parures of diamonds— emerald collars, sapphire pendants. A pretty sapphire-and-diamond bracelet caught her eye. But there was little point in pining after the contents of this shop. Maybe one day, after the war was finally won, she'd bring Julian here. Now, she needed to get down to business.

She scanned the room and found it: a discreet, elegant counter, tidily set out with a jeweler's loupe, pens, a stack of tissue paper, tape, scissors, a case containing, she surmised, the tools of the jeweler's trade . . . and Montagu's target, a small invoice pad, the header elegantly printed with the shop's address.

Montagu would come in soon. Paddy pasted an eager, Pam-like expression on her face and rushed over to the display of diamond rings. This cabinet was located some distance from the counter, conveniently enough for Paddy and Montagu's purpose.

The gentleman who came to assist her was all smooth politeness. "Beautiful, aren't they?"

"Oh, yes!" breathed Paddy, setting her large purse on top of the glass showcase. "I do call that very fine."

"Are you looking for something in particular? Something to mark a happy occasion, perhaps?"

"Is it that obvious?" Paddy rolled her eyes and giggled. "I must be glowing from top to toe." She leaned in, as if what she was about to say was confidential, although how could it be when she was about to divulge it to a complete stranger? "My boyfriend proposed last night! Isn't that too, too marvelous? Only he's very busy—my Bill's a major in the Royal Marines, you know—so he asked me to come along and pick something out."

"Ah." The jeweler smiled. "Well, I'd be most happy to assist you, miss."

"Do call me Pam," said Paddy, although it was stretching the bounds of probability that even Major Martin's slightly ditzy girlfriend would seek to be on first-name terms with a jeweler. But, make herself memorable, Cholmondeley had said . . .

Just then, a middle-aged woman walked in from the back room holding a clipboard and pen. She sported a short, crimped bob and a disapproving expression. A pity she wasn't younger and more easily drawn into the debate. Paddy would have to improvise.

Adopting the character of Pam with gay abandon, she waxed lyrical over the manifold admirable qualities possessed by her Major Martin, until the jeweler managed to interject smoothly, "As to that, we have several suitable pieces you might wish to see . . ."

He unlocked the cabinet between them and, with the air of an elegant conjurer of magnificent treasures, took out several beds of velvet, studded with rows and rows of diamond solitaires.

Paddy oohed and aahed as she pored over them, quizzing the jeweler minutely about each one. But she needed to settle on a particular ring, and decided that she might as well do the right thing by Pam. "Do you have anything . . . *larger*?" she asked, her eyes wide, her voice a whisper.

Impassively, the jeweler brought out two more velvet beds. "This one!" She pointed to a brilliant-cut diamond that must surely be worth a year of the major's pay. The ring was duly slipped onto her finger. "This is it!"

She held her hand out in front of her, tilting it this way and that to catch the light. Then she pouted and hunched her shoulders. "Oh, I simply don't know! It's such a big decision, isn't it? I mean I shall be wearing it for the *rest of my life* . . ." Suddenly Paddy felt a pang in her chest. The fictional Major Martin would perish at sea in just a few days' time. Pam would never be his bride, much less wear the major's ring forever.

The bell over the door jangled as Montagu walked in from the street. Without glancing at any of the occupants, he paused at a cabinet at the front of the shop. That was Paddy's cue. She looked over at the assistant, who seemed to be noting down serial numbers on her clipboard. Paddy smiled at the jeweler. "Do you think your colleague would give me the benefit of her advice?" She waved her hands self-deprecatingly. "Oh, I don't mean anything by it, you understand. It's just that I'd like another woman's opinion, if you know what I mean. Excuse me?" she called over to the other assistant. "Would you tell me which of these you think best, please?"

But the woman with the clipboard was wholly absorbed in her task. Either that, or deliberately ignoring her. Paddy rather thought the latter was the case, so she tried again. "*If* you don't mind?" Beneath the sweetness was a distinct note of command. *Oops.* Very un-Pam-like. Bit of Paddy seeping through there.

The jeweler intervened at this point. Smilingly, he said to Paddy, "I understand perfectly. Miss Walker?" he called. "Will you spare us a moment?" Then he looked over at Montagu and tried unsuccessfully to catch his eye. "Be with you in a trice, sir."

"Just browsing, thank you," said Montagu gruffly. His inspection was taking him, bit by bit, toward the counter where the invoice book was.

Or it had been. Miss Walker picked up the invoice book and brought it with her over to Paddy and the jeweler, rather than leaving it unattended. Perhaps it was simply habit. She couldn't have expected to clinch the sale there and then.

Thinking quickly, Paddy waited until the woman approached the display cabinet and placed the invoice book on the display case next to the trays of rings. Seeing her chance, Paddy turned toward the assistant, managing with one swipe of her purse to knock three of the four ring trays flying.

"Oh, no!" she said, watching the jeweler and his assistant dive for the rings. "How clumsy of me!"

Before she joined the pair who were scrabbling about on the floor trying to collect the scattering rings as they rolled underneath various pieces of furniture, Paddy picked up the invoice book and passed it to Montagu, who had come up behind her.

By the time the jeweler, Miss Walker, and Paddy had found all of the rings and fitted them back into place, Montagu had returned the invoice pad and left the shop.

"I am *so* sorry!" Paddy apologized for the hundredth time. "Do, please forgive me."

"That's quite all right, miss," said the jeweler, his smile undimmed, although his assistant couldn't quite hide her annoyance.

Still, Miss Walker cheered up when Paddy said, "I will definitely choose the large one. This one here." She pointed to the solitaire she'd picked out earlier. "Would you write down the details for me so that I can tell him precisely? Oh, and we'd like it engraved, too. Thanks most awfully."

Clutching the little card with the description and price of Pam's ring, Paddy left the shop and walked at what she hoped was a natural pace back to the station. She didn't relax until Montagu joined her.

"Goodness!" She laughed breathlessly. Lowering her voice, she added, "I feel as if I just participated in a diamond heist rather than the theft of one piece of paper."

"A very important piece of paper, nonetheless," murmured Montagu. "Quick thinking to knock over those trays."

"They'll certainly remember our Pam now," said Paddy, handing him the card with the ring's description and price on it.

"That they will," Montagu agreed, tucking the card into his wallet. "And how are those love letters coming along, Mrs. Ridsdale?"

Truth be told, Paddy wasn't the most romantic creature on the planet, and composing these letters had become a bit of a bête noire. Every time she attempted to pour out Pam's feelings for her Bill, they fell terribly flat.

When she'd moaned about her troubles to Jean, her friend had shrugged. "Just imagine it's Julian." But that was no good. Aside from the fact Paddy would rather die than write genuine personal sentiments for those dreadful Nazis to slaver over—not to mention the ribbing she'd get from the men at the Admiralty should they read them—her relationship with Julian simply wasn't like that. She'd made several attempts at Pam's romantic outpourings and destroyed each and every one, but she wasn't going to let Montagu know the trouble she was having.

"Nearly done," she said crisply. "Just some finishing touches to add."

"Excellent," said Montagu. "Good work today, Mrs. Ridsdale. Quick thinking, perfect execution. You're a natural field agent. Fleming was right about you."

Paddy smiled back at him. Praise like that made all of the subterfuge at home worthwhile. The air smelled of rain, and drops began dotting their heads and shoulders, so she said, "Better run. I didn't bring an umbrella!"

On the whole, Paddy was quite pleased with herself when she arrived home, having accomplished several other tasks on the list. She only wished the weight of those unwritten letters didn't feel like such an albatross around her neck.

She took off her wet coat and hung it on the stand in the hall to dry. As she went upstairs, unpinning her hat, she scolded herself for being so ridiculous. Ordinarily she wasn't one to put off a responsibility, no matter how irksome. "Just get it done," she told herself.

Tossing her hat down on her bed, she went to the sitting room that adjoined the bedroom and sat down at her desk to begin. She scribbled a short note to start with, then stopped to read it over, tapping her lips with the lid of her pen. Awful stuff. Really, this was excruciating!

"Hello, darling." Julian's voice made her jump and put a hand to her chest.

"Oh, you startled me!" Heart hammering, Paddy shoved

Pam's love note beneath the blotter and turned in her chair. She hoped she didn't look as guilty as she felt.

With a spurt of nervous laughter that held an edge of anger, she said, "What are you doing, sneaking up on me in the middle of the day?"

Julian frowned, perhaps at her tone, which was admittedly more accusatory than affectionate. "I came home to see if you were all right." He tilted his head. "You never go to the doctor. It's been worrying me all day."

So he *had* noticed. She ought never to underestimate him, and this was a timely reminder. However, she had prepared for this. "Well, it's just a slightly embarrassing complaint, if you must know." She made a moue. "Nothing to worry about, but not a subject for the breakfast table—or for the boudoir, for that matter."

He seemed to accept this, perhaps because Paddy was hardly the type to confess to weakness of any kind, much less a humiliating one. His expression lightened and she realized he was relieved. Clearly he had no thought in his head about a possible pregnancy.

Heart melting, she stood up and went to him. "Did you come home just for that? How lovely you are." She reached up to touch his cheek. He caught her hand and kissed the palm, and her eyes widened a little at the familiar gleam in his. She gave a gurgle of laughter. "Oh, we can't!" One of the disadvantages of living in a large house with plenty of staff was that one of them might come in at any moment. Besides, going to bed with Julian immediately after lying to him like that felt sordid. She was no Mata Hari, after all.

"No," he said regretfully, taking both her hands in his. "I must get back. It's just—" He broke off, and an expression she had never seen before crossed his face, only to vanish. "I—I hope you feel better, whatever it is."

She tried a little half-heartedly to get him to stay longer but the truth was, the look that had passed over Julian's face like a dark cloud across the sun had disconcerted her. He'd been a little moody lately, but surely she hadn't said or done anything to anger or hurt him just now. What on earth was wrong? Had her guilt been written all over her face?

When he was gone, Paddy went back to her desk. The absolute last thing she felt like doing now was pretending to be Pam gushing over her loving fiancé. Still, she blew out a long breath and drew toward her a piece of letter paper Cholmondeley had provided. With a dogged determination that could hardly be less conducive to romantic feeling, she wrote line after line of terrible, florid prose.

* * *

"Gosh, look at the time!" Paddy muttered. She'd been wrestling with Pam's love letters all afternoon, resorting to scribbling out several versions on foolscap purloined from Julian's study, as she was in danger of running out of the writing paper Cholmondeley had supplied.

"You are being too ridiculous!" she told herself. How harshly would the Germans judge these letters anyway? The quality of the prose was hardly going to be their primary concern. And in any case, she simply couldn't do any better than she'd done.

She copied out the letters she'd drafted in fair hand on the proper stationery. The question of what to do with all of the reams of foolscap she'd gone through was a bit of a conundrum. She couldn't tear them into small pieces and flush them down the toilet as she'd done with her other attempts. It was April and not cold enough for a fire, and she couldn't risk burning these papers in case Julian smelled the smoke when he came in and asked her about it. She'd have to hide them somewhere until she could destroy them safely.

Eventually, she settled on taking them up to the attic and tucking them in among her research notes from her first year at the Sorbonne, which she had packed up and sent home, thinking they might come in handy one day. She never could have imagined that the only use to which she would put these notes was as cover for a top-secret mission. She'd burn the practice love letters as soon as she got the chance.

Paddy tidied up her desk, then went back to her room to get ready for the evening.

Her maid, Berry, greeted her with "I've laid out the emerald-green silk, Mrs. Ridsdale."

"Thank you," said Paddy absently, her mind still buzzing with possible phrases she might have included in the letters, and how she might tactfully suggest to Montagu that they get someone else to undertake this particular task. She was washing up, using a scrap of precious soap, when she realized her left hand felt oddly naked.

Paddy flexed her fingers and stared down at them, horror flooding her chest. She wasn't wearing her wedding rings! Her mind flew back over the day. That's right! She'd left them in her coat pocket. Which was hanging on the coat stand by the front door. *If* it hadn't been removed by one of the maids for airing and brushing, that was.

And what if that maid found her rings—or worse, they fell out somewhere in the house?

Berry interrupted these panicked thoughts. "Captain Ridsdale has just come in, ma'am. Shall I do your hair now?"

"Oh, thank you, Berry. Yes." As the maid worked swiftly with a brush and rollers, Paddy licked her lips. She was in her underwear and dressing gown. She couldn't slip down to the hall very easily looking like that. Not until her hair and makeup was done and she was dressed—by which time Julian would be wanting to leave. Could she trust Berry to find the rings for her without gossiping about it? The alternatives seemed much worse.

Fleming's words came back to her. *You have to trust someone, or you don't get anything done.*

In a low voice, Paddy said to her maid, "When you've finished this—"

"Evening, Berry." Julian came into the bedroom, flinging his cap and the evening paper on the armchair by the fireplace. As he started toward Paddy, she plunged her left hand into the folds of her dressing gown, hiding the evidence of her deceit just before Julian bent to kiss her cheek. "Hello, darling."

"Good evening, sir." The maid gave him one of her rare smiles and picked up his cap, bustling off with it to his dressing room.

"All right, Paddy?" Julian said lightly. "You look lost in thought."

"Just daydreaming," said Paddy, her palms beginning to perspire. There went any opportunity she'd have to ask Berry to fetch her rings without Julian hearing. She would have to brazen it out. "I've heard good things about this play." She frowned. Had she heard good things? What on earth *was* the play they were going to see tonight? She couldn't think. She needed to come up with an excuse about the missing wedding rings.

She and Julian were supposed to be going to the theater, then dinner at Quaglino's with a party of friends, and on to dancing at one of the clubs. It was a pretty standard program, but it annoyed Paddy because she knew all of it would exhaust her. And she wouldn't be able to get away with nibbling on a bread roll at Quaglino's, not if she wanted to keep her secret.

"Oh? Jolly good." Julian disappeared into his dressing room and Berry moved to deal with Paddy's hair.

She'd have to say she'd put the rings in for cleaning. If he asked, that was. First thing in the morning, she would do precisely that, so it wouldn't be quite so much of a lie.

Berry seemed to take forever with Paddy's hair. Then, when Paddy finally stepped into her evening gown, the maid began muttering to herself as she struggled with the tiny buttons that marched up the back.

"What is it?" The fabric seemed to pull a little uncomfortably about her middle. Oh dear! Then when Berry got to the buttons between the shoulder blades, she whispered, "Ma'am, I hate to say this, but I think we shall have to choose a different gown."

Paddy peered down at her chest. It had swelled even more than her belly in the past weeks. There'd been a note of excitement in Berry's voice that told Paddy she'd guessed the cause of her weight gain. After all, what with rationing and scarcity, who actually gained weight these days?

Over her shoulder, Paddy whispered, "Don't say anything yet, will you, Berry? I want to keep it a surprise."

"Mum's the word, ma'am," Berry whispered back. "I'll take the Balenciaga down and press it quickly. That's more forgiving."

Paddy grabbed her maid's wrist as inspiration struck. Weight gain. The perfect explanation for her removing her wedding rings. Paddy whispered, "While you're there . . . My fingers have been swelling up as well—isn't it too awful?—and I took my rings off and put them in my coat pocket today and then I left them there! Would you be a dear and bring them up? Thank you. And remember, no telling!"

"Of course, ma'am." Eyes aglow at the happy news, Berry helped Paddy out of the too-tight gown and hurried off with its substitute. "Back in a trice."

Paddy released a pent-up breath and sat down at her dressing table to await Berry's return. She picked up her purse and made sure it held all the essentials, then shut the clasp again and quickly returned her left hand to her pocket as Julian walked in.

He was all shaven and suited and ready, except for his bow tie hanging loose around his neck. She hoped he wouldn't ask her to tie it for him, as he so often did. He'd be sure to notice the absence of her wedding rings.

She picked up her powder puff and dusted it over her nose—unnecessarily, but she wanted to look like she was busy so he wouldn't ask for her assistance.

He didn't request her help, but he did stand behind her, stooping to look in her dressing table mirror while he tied his bow tie. Guilt oozed through Paddy's veins like oil.

Please hurry! she silently begged her maid.

"Well, I'm ready." Julian grabbed the evening paper and settled in to read in the armchair by the fireplace.

"Sorry, darling. I'm running a bit behind." Paddy wanted to take the rollers out of her hair but to do that she'd have to use both hands.

Berry came in then, and with a quick shake of her head, told Paddy she'd been unable to locate her rings. *Oh, no!* What excuse could she use if Julian noticed their absence?

That she'd put them in for cleaning was the obvious one, of course, but then what if the rings had been lost in the house somewhere or were subsequently found and handed to her in front of Julian? She'd be caught out in her lie.

One thing at a time, she thought. *One thing at a time.* Curbing the impulse to blurt out her excuse before he even asked her about it, Paddy forced herself to remove her hand from her pocket and act normally. Thank goodness she was wearing gloves for most of the evening. If only the rings could be found in her absence, she might still make it through.

As they were leaving for the theater, Paddy glanced at the coat rack by the door. It was, of course, empty. She had to restrain herself from fleeing downstairs to question the staff about it herself.

However, although Paddy had her excuses ready and well-rehearsed in her mind, she was not called upon to use them. Julian didn't notice the absence of rings on her fingers. She wasn't seated near him at dinner, which was the only time she took off her gloves that evening. Perhaps she might simply put on her rings again in the morning with him none the wiser.

The relief when she arrived home again to find her wedding band and solitaire in the little china dish next to her cosmetics was almost overwhelming. Berry must have found them!

Quickly, before Julian came back in from his dressing room, Paddy slipped them on again. They felt a little tight, as if guilt had indeed made her fingers swell in punishment for her subterfuge. Or was that really a part of pregnancy, this thickening all over? Would she need to get her rings resized before too long?

In the morning, however, her fingers felt fine again. Thank goodness! She held up her hand by the window, so that the sunlight struck tiny rainbows off each facet of her diamond solitaire. She must take care not to make another slip like the one she'd made yesterday.

Deceiving the Nazis was one thing. Deceiving her husband was quite another.

CHAPTER EIGHTEEN

London, England
April 1943

Paddy

"You will let me be there for the final push, won't you, sir?" Paddy asked Cholmondeley when she'd handed over the love letters and the rest of the wallet litter she'd been asked to collect.

Once Cholmondeley and Montagu had gathered together everything they needed to plant on Glyndwr Michael's body, they would dress him in his uniform and put him in a specially sealed canister. From the St. Pancras morgue, Major Martin would be transported to the submarine that would eventually launch his body into the Mediterranean off the coast of Huelva for the fishing boats to find.

Montagu had engaged Jock Horsfall, Britain's fastest racing car driver—who also happened to work as a chauffeur for MI-5— to speed the major to his destination. Once the body was out of cold storage, time was most certainly of the essence.

Cholmondeley shrugged. "I've no objection, but all the fun will take place in the early hours of the morning. How will you explain your absence at that hour to your husband?"

"Oh, never mind that. I'll think of a way." Paddy didn't feel quite as confident as she sounded about that part, but she needed to be there to see the culmination of all of their preparation. It would be too great an anticlimax if her career with the NID ended on her handing over a few ticket stubs and receipts, not to mention those dreadful love letters.

"In that case, of course you can be there," said Cholmondeley. "Who knows? We might be glad of your help."

Distinctly more thrilled at the prospect of viewing Glyndwr Michael's body the second time than she had been on the first occasion, Paddy thanked the flight lieutenant. Seeing off "Major Martin" from the morgue would give her a sense of finality. She would be able to shut the door on her former life with satisfaction and step into her new role as a mother and wife.

Now, if only she could think of an excuse to take off overnight on short notice . . . The simplest option was to use as her alibi someone who was already in on the operation—Jean, of course. Would it be too much of a stretch to say that Jean's former boyfriend was now bothering her in Dorchester and Paddy was going down there to sort him out? Even to her, that sounded like she might be taking things a bit far, but as she couldn't come up with a better excuse, she went with that one.

"But it's really none of your business, is it, Paddy?" Julian said, frowning. "Surely Jean's a big girl, and she's got her mother and other friends on the spot who can help her. Men friends, too. Sounds like what the fellow needs most is a punch on the nose."

"Yes, but I do feel partly responsible," said Paddy. "Clearly my intervention last time didn't do the trick. He seemed like a pleasant fellow and I gave him the benefit of the doubt, but in fact, I might well have made things worse. And you know me. If something is broken, I have to fix it." She reached up to kiss him on the cheek. "It will only be one night. You won't even notice I'm gone."

From the shuttered look that came over his face, Paddy could see that Julian was far from placated. With the knowledge of her own culpability gnawing away at her conscience, Paddy could only be grateful that he didn't argue the point further.

Ordinarily she'd prefer to have a stand-up row rather than this festering silence. Ordinarily, she'd provoke Julian until she got it, too, and they'd kiss and make up and both be the better for it. However, on this occasion, she knew she was in the wrong—at least, she knew she was being deceitful as far as her trip to Dorchester went—which made his silence on the subject a blessing rather than a curse. She felt like a weasel taking advantage of him this way, but she wasn't quite guilty enough to forgo the pleasure of kitting out Major Martin for his final voyage.

After that, she silently promised, the operation would be finished as far as she was concerned. She would tell Julian about the baby, and everything would be perfect.

It wasn't only Julian who was displeased with her. Paddy's determination not to tell Julian about her pregnancy even after a visit to the doctor confirmed it had caused friction with her mother, and going away on top of that . . . Edith did not approve, and she made that abundantly clear.

"Paddy, I never thought I'd say this of you, but you're being selfish. That's all there is to it." Edith was knitting furiously, her needles click-clacking her disapproval like Morse code.

"I know." Might as well admit it to herself as well as her mother. She could have refused the mission quite easily and no one would have thought the worse of her. It wasn't as if someone else couldn't have taken her place. She didn't absolutely need to help dress Major Martin, either. But the opportunity to do something worthwhile, something that truly mattered to the war— she couldn't sit on the sidelines.

Quietly, she said, "Mother, there is something—something very important to me—that I simply must do. I promise that when I have done it, I will tell Julian about the baby."

Edith stared at her very hard, then closed her lips and kept knitting. Her voice hit a higher register. "It's not another man, is it, dear?"

Paddy gasped, then gave a horrified laugh. "Good Heavens, no! I can't believe you would dream of such a thing."

"Well, it does happen, you know," said Edith. "And you were a great favorite with all the men at the Admiralty. You got on so well with Commander Fleming, in particular, and everyone talks about his devastating charm . . ."

Edith didn't mean to accuse Paddy of an affair with Ian Fleming, surely! Paddy opened her mouth to give a sharp retort, then shut it again. The thought hit her anew that she never would be in a position to tell her mother why she was keeping the news about the baby to herself. Lamely, she said, "Nothing could be further from the truth. I should hope you know me better than that."

Edith reached forward and rubbed her knee. "I'm sorry, darling. It's just that it's so unlike you to be secretive, Paddy."

"Well, I hate being coddled," said Paddy. "And I've changed my mind about leaving London, too. Now that the awful nausea is over, I feel much more myself."

"Yes, I must say in your case, it's true what they say about expectant mothers' skin," said Edith. "You're positively radiant. Although I do wish you'd eat more. You're not even showing yet."

"I've expanded so much I hardly fit into anything anymore," protested Paddy. "Berry has had to make alterations."

Edith dropped her hands into her lap. "Tell him, dear. Sooner rather than later. After all, nothing is more important than the people who love you, when all is said and done."

* * *

On Paddy's second visit to the St. Pancras morgue, Sir Bentley showed her the trick of dabbing a strong-smelling liniment under her nostrils to help mask the smell of death. That, and the fact that her stomach had settled down considerably since the early days of pregnancy, meant she was able to march into that mortuary with confidence that she could last for the duration of their work there without being vilely sick.

Major William, as she now liked to think of him, had been stored at four degrees Centigrade for the past month or so, but when they walked in, he had been taken out of storage and was awaiting them on a metal slab.

"*If* you don't mind, Mrs. Ridsdale . . ." said Montagu, with a gentle cough.

Paddy dutifully turned her back while the men unshrouded Glyndwr Michael and transformed him into Major William Martin.

"We were in a bit of a tight spot about the underwear," said Cholmondeley cheerfully in between grunts as they struggled to clothe the uncooperative corpse. "No one wanted to give up what precious little they had, what with rationing and all. But we knew a chap up at Oxford who died recently. They let us raid his collection. And a fine collection it was, too. Watch it!"

"Whoops! Sorry, old man." Paddy wasn't sure whether Montagu was talking to his colleague or the corpse. "Socks." He muttered. "Where the devil did I put his socks? Needs garters, too."

"Can I help?" asked Paddy.

"Yes, yes, you can turn around now, Mrs. Ridsdale. He's quite decent," said Sir Bentley with a bluff chuckle.

She sorted through the box of tricks they'd brought with them but didn't find the socks. "Sorry. No socks here. No garters, either."

"Worse comes to worst . . ." Cholmondeley lifted his own booted foot. But Montagu was scrabbling around in Major Martin's pockets, then came up triumphant. "Here they are!"

While the men were busy with the major's feet, Paddy went over the wallet litter, ticking off an itemized list and laying everything out neatly and in appropriate categories on the table that had been brought in for the purpose. She didn't know what, exactly, Major William's briefcase contained, but all the wallet litter was open for her inspection. She glanced at the love letters and noticed they were not the ones she had written, after all, but said nothing. Had they asked someone else to do a better job? She couldn't blame them, and just hoped they'd destroyed all of hers.

She went over everything again. There was the invoice for the engagement ring she'd picked out, complete with the authentic S. J. Phillips header. There was a packet of Player's Navy Cut cigarettes, a book of stamps with a couple missing, a pencil stub, keys, matches, a used bus ticket (one of Paddy's contributions). There was also a silver cross and a St. Christopher's medallion on a silver chain. She couldn't help but wonder if the medallion had been included for the sake of irony. St. Christopher was the patron saint of travelers, after all.

"The deuce!" Montagu muttered, grunting with effort. "Can't get his boots on."

"They were made to measure," said Cholmondeley. He checked his notes and then the boots themselves. "Didn't we try them on him before? They should be fine."

"Ah." Sir Bentley Purchase nodded, viewing the offending appendages sagely. "His feet have expanded due to the cold."

"They've bloody frozen is what they've done," said Montagu, panting with the effort of trying to jam the boot on the stiffened foot.

"Could we thaw them out a bit?" asked Paddy, cringing inwardly at the suggestion. "Just enough to put the boots on?" The men stared at her. "I could try to track down an electric heater?"

Montagu looked at Cholmondeley, then they both nodded. "Do it."

Surprising them all, Sir Bentley offered to fetch a heater from the common room. "Back in a jiffy!"

The rising stench as the major's feet were thawed out did not affect Paddy as it had on the first occasion she'd visited, which was rather a source of satisfaction. While Sir Bentley supervised the heating procedure, Paddy, Montagu, and Cholmondeley filled the major's pockets and pocketbook with all of the wallet litter they'd collected.

"Last, but definitely not least, the photo of our Pam," said Montagu, beaming down at the picture of Jean in the swimsuit. The photo was creased and worn, as if the major had taken it out to gaze at it lovingly every now and then. Paddy was quite sure no play-acting was involved in Montagu's fondling of that photo. He really was quite smitten. Pam's picture was duly tucked away close to Major William's heart.

When finally the Royal Marine officer was fully clothed and equipped, right down to his boots, Paddy said, "Might we say a quick prayer? I think we ought, don't you?"

So they bowed their heads and Montagu recited the solemn words of the funeral prayer, or what he could remember of them, anyway. Silently, Paddy said a few words of her own, thanking the unknown Glyndwr Michael for his unwitting sacrifice. Then she left the men to prepare him for his final journey.

CHAPTER NINETEEN

London, England
May 1943

Friedl

"What do you mean, they want me in Portugal?" The shock turned Friedl's blood to ice. She was unprepared, even though she'd been dreading this moment for months. Finally, here was the summons from Kühlenthal, arriving in the manner she'd least expected—via MI-5.

"The message came from Tricycle, you might be interested to know," said Tar. A yellow envelope next to his elbow was marked in red. "Y File. This file when in transit must be in a closed envelope, addressed personally to the officer." He slid some papers from the envelope and began leafing through. "You are to fly out to meet him in Estoril tomorrow night. Once you've completed a little job for us."

From his tone, Tar was bored with the entire subject of Friedl and whatever interest she might receive from officers of German intelligence. She knew better.

This moment was important and she had a decision to make.

She could assume Tar knew about her encounter with Kühlenthal on the beach in Estoril. But if she confessed now, it would be too little, too late in any case. She'd already have raised suspicions by remaining silent on the subject for so long—suspicions that would not be allayed by such a belated confession. Alternatively she could keep it to herself on the off chance that no one knew about that meeting under the early morning Portuguese sun. She *might* get away with it.

If Kühlenthal was sending her instructions via Popov, it meant that whatever he told her to do would be vetted and manipulated by the British.

If, as she suspected he might, Kühlenthal required some definitive proof of her loyalty when she was on the spot in Estoril . . . Well, then, she'd be in Estoril, wouldn't she? And she'd decide when the time came who was the bigger threat—and who might give her better protection.

That Popov had not brought news of Kühlenthal's request in person told its own tale. That cost her a pang but she put the pain away for the moment. Her nerves could stand only one crisis at a time, with Tar shuffling papers and pretending not to observe every minute change of expression his news might bring to her face.

All of this passed through her mind in seconds. "And what little job is that?" she asked, since it seemed he was waiting for her to inquire.

Tar picked up a file and handed it to her. She leafed through. An itemized list of tickets, invoices, receipts. A grainy copy of a photograph . . . Her eyes widened. It was a picture of Jean Leslie.

Friedl's gaze flicked up to Tar. "But I know her," she said, indicating the photo.

He smiled thinly. "Actually, you don't. This charming young lady is Pam, fiancée to a certain Major William Martin, whose body has been found off the coast of Huelva in Spain. Your job, Friedl, is to investigate all of the everyday documents that were found on the major's body by the Spanish, then covertly copied by the Germans. Understand?"

"Yes, I think so," said Friedl slowly.

Tar handed her another slim file. "This is the information you will provide to Kühlenthal about the results of your digging. I want you to rewrite all of it, appropriately worded in your inimitable style, of course. Then memorize it. William Luke will help you. You must be absolutely pitch-perfect when you meet with Kühlenthal. The timing's tight, so I can only give you until tomorrow evening before you fly out."

Friedl's mouth went dry. She wasn't a trained operative. How on earth could she remain cool under Kühlenthal's interrogation with such scant preparation? What if he decided she was lying and resorted to extreme methods? In Estoril, anything might happen to her.

"Might I not simply send him the written report, as I've done with the others?" she asked. Then she thought of an angle that might appeal more to Tar's sense of logic. "Isn't it rather dangerous for you to send me? If I'm blown, Tricycle might well be blown along with me."

Tar nodded. "We've weighed the risks, but if it comes off, the benefits are far greater. We believe you're up to the task." He folded his hands on his desk. "It's not enough for you to memorize the essentials listed in this brief, you know. You must actually visit all of the places in your report and question the jewelry shop owners, film ticket sellers, and the like, so that you can add the right amount of authenticity to your account. You must investigate this matter as earnestly as if you were in fact working for the Germans. You must make detailed notes so that we can embellish the facts you will eventually pass on to the Abwehr. Always easiest to lie when the lie is based on the truth."

"In effect, I'll be trailing this couple's movements like a gumshoe detective," said Friedl. The idea didn't appeal.

"That's right. But you have less than twenty-four hours in which to do it, I'm afraid. William Luke will take you through the most important leads to follow up."

"And Duško—I mean, Tricycle?" She tried to inject a casual note into her voice.

She didn't fool Tar for a second, of course. "He's your excuse for being in Estoril. He'll be close at hand, as will a handful of other operatives, in case anything goes wrong. You'll communicate with the Abwehr via the roulette table at the Estoril Casino. Chips on a certain number means a certain thing, and so on. But Luke will brief you on all of that."

After she'd returned to her flat with the files concealed at the bottom of a shopping bag, Friedl flicked through the information Tar had given her. Her entire body thrummed with fear, but as always, at the edge of fear was excitement. Such was the power of Duško Popov that the anticipation of meeting him again lent all of this intrigue extra piquancy.

She was to meet with William Luke in her flat at 4 P.M. But first, she needed to get hold of a gun. The cosh Joan had ordered for her was scant protection, particularly in Estoril. Many older men she knew owned service revolvers from the Great War, but she needed something that was easily concealed. Weapons like that were far more difficult to come by.

There was nothing for it. She would have to steal Joan's. After all, Friedl's own need was greater, wasn't it? It was certainly more immediate. And M would replace Joan's little toy without trouble.

It seemed a dirty trick to play on a friend, but surely Joan would understand.

She'd have to be quick, leaving enough time to master the documents Tar had given her and begin her pseudo-investigation into Major William Martin and his Pam.

She thought about that photograph of Jean Leslie in the file Tar had given her. Tonight she would track Jean down at one of the clubs and see what she could find out. Always better to go into a mission knowing more than one's handler was willing to tell.

It took Friedl the better part of the night before she found Jean at the Gargoyle Club. Her friend was with a group of people Friedl didn't know, but that didn't stop Friedl adroitly detaching the younger woman from them and getting her alone in one of the booths.

"*Liebling!*" Friedl greeted her quarry and gave her a kiss on each cheek. "Come have a little drink with me. It's been too long since we caught up."

She knew that Jean was rather in awe of her and she wasn't above using that to her advantage. More than a decade younger and possessing an innocence about the ways of the world that Friedl didn't think she'd ever had, the girl suspected no ulterior motive when Friedl sat down with her to gossip.

After several cocktails, and even more confidences from Friedl about her own interesting and varied love life, Jean must have felt emboldened to ask, "Are you still seeing that Popov fellow? I haven't seen him for an age."

That effectively wiped the smile from Friedl's face. She sighed. "I'm afraid he's forgotten all about me." This was partly true in the ways that mattered, and it hurt to say it, but she was endeavoring to establish trust, so she needed to make the sacrifice.

Jean nodded sympathetically. "I've just been through a rather horrid breakup myself. Well, I suppose to be honest, I didn't know how much I liked him until . . ." She shrugged and sighed. "Too late now."

"Not that strapping young redhead who accosted you at MJ's the other evening, darling? Oh, you poor thing. What happened?"

"Nothing, really." The girl smiled a little tremulously. "Just the same old story, I'm afraid."

Friedl put her hand on Jean's shoulder. "*Liebling*. Tell Friedl all about it."

But the younger woman shook her head and gave a determined laugh. "Oh, I'll be all right, don't worry about me."

The band struck up a lively tune and Jean glanced around, as if expecting to be asked to dance. Friedl was running out of time. "You seem a little tired tonight, darling. The War Office working you too hard?"

Again, Jean was tight-lipped. "Oh, no more than usual. And how is your job with Dennis Wheatley going? I never hear about Billy anymore."

The conversation wasn't heading in the direction Friedl needed it to take. She did her best to keep up a stream of chatter, both inconsequential and probing, so as to try to lead her friend into similar confidences, but no matter how tangentially she brought up war work, Jean deflected each and every question. She ought to stop or even someone as naïve as Jean would get suspicious.

One of the men from MJ's set came up to them and asked Jean to dance. Friedl waved her away. "Go, go. Enjoy yourself!"

Jean left her purse with Friedl and tripped off with her partner. Friedl quickly swiped Jean's purse and opened it under the table. She searched it by feel, keeping her attention on the couple whirling around the dance floor. Lipstick. Compact, handkerchief. Yes, yes, yes. All of the usual accoutrements, and something else . . . an envelope. An envelope that was already open.

Her gaze still fixed on the dance floor, Friedl slid her fingertips inside the envelope. With shaking hands, she pulled out the contents and glanced down.

A photograph. The same one of Jean that had been found on

the body of that Royal Marine. And something else . . . A negative. It was too dark in the club to see what the negative was, but she'd have to guess it was of the same photograph. Right. She would take that and hope Jean would think she'd simply lost it somewhere.

She was about to tuck the photograph back into the envelope and transfer the negative to her own purse when MJ slid into the banquette opposite and Brian Howard landed on the seat beside Friedl. "We need your opinion on a subject of the *utmost* importance, my dear," Brian announced.

Whatever it was that Brian deemed so vital, Friedl scarcely heard it. Fortunately Brian and MJ were too busy arguing to actually let her get a word in edgewise anyway. Clumsy with fear, Friedl made several blind attempts to return the photograph to the envelope before she succeeded.

But as she snapped shut Jean's purse, she dropped the negative. Biting back a cry of frustration, she set the purse next to her on the banquette, and was just about to drop something ostentatiously so as to pick both it and the negative up from the floor, when Brian turned to her. "Friedl? You must settle the dispute."

She had absolutely no idea what he was talking about. But before she could answer, Brian was calling over to a waiter. "Bring us three of your *filthiest* martinis, my dear. Oh, and here's Dylan now. Make that four."

As more people crowded around the booth, Friedl felt increasingly desperate, imagining the negative crushed under someone's heel and ground into the sticky nightclub floor.

Jean came back to retrieve her purse for a visit to the powder room and Friedl prayed she wouldn't notice the missing negative. If only Brian and MJ's crowd would go away, but they seemed to have settled in for the duration.

There was nothing for it. "Brian, would you move a little, please, *liebling*? I have something in my shoe."

He wasn't listening, still engaged in a heated debate, so Friedl gave Brian a little shove and ducked beneath the table. She couldn't see a thing except the outlines of various legs and shoes, so she had to feel about the floor for the negative.

Finally, her fingers touched the film, just as Dylan Thomas ducked his head under and said, "Is this a new game, Friedl? Can anyone play?"

She jumped, hitting her head on the underside of the table, and nearly snarled back at him, but she couldn't let him suspect anything, so she said, "Just something in my shoe that was giving me trouble, darling. No games here."

She palmed the negative and waited for an opportune moment to slip the scrap of film into her purse. She hadn't figured out yet what use it might be to her. But it was something, at any rate.

Estoril, Portugal
May 1943

Friedl

$\mathcal{F}$riedl tried to calm her nerves enough to take a nap on her flight to Lisbon, but her trip to Portugal this time was as different from her lovers' tryst with Popov as it was possible for it to be. From the moment she'd learned of this new mission from Tar, she'd been on edge. She hadn't slept a wink the previous night, reading over and over the notes in the file Tar had given her, a painful task for someone who had never liked rote learning at school. However, her fear of Kühlenthal and what he might do to her if she slipped up on any particular was sufficient motivation to study hard.

Trailing after the movements of the apocryphal Pam had been too stultifying for words. But she'd done it. She'd annotated Tar's file and dutifully memorized the extra details. She ought to feel prepared. Instead, exhaustion and anxiety warred inside her, the one urging her to sleep like the dead, the other making her mind race too fast to let her rest.

Her meeting with Kühlenthal was set for Estoril rather than Madrid, where he was based. It was thought that Friedl might draw more attention in the Spanish capital than in a place she'd holidayed before in Popov's company.

She'd expected it to be painful to revisit the Hotel Palàcio, but her brain was so full of information and instructions, all bound up tightly with fear, that she didn't have the capacity to deal with heartbreak as well. Or maybe she was over him, finally. She would like to believe that.

Friedl changed into a sea-green silk gown, transferring Joan Miller's pistol to her evening bag. To her credit, Joan had seen through Friedl's admittedly half-hearted attempt to steal the weapon almost immediately. But whether she sensed that this time Friedl's fear had reached an entirely new pitch, or whether she knew about Friedl's forthcoming mission, something had made Joan relent. With a severe admonition not to get caught in possession of the weapon, Joan gave her the tiny pistol and some ammunition as well. "But I won't lie to M," she warned Friedl. "If he asks about it, I'll tell him I gave it to you."

As instructed, Friedl went to the casino early that evening and played roulette. Feeling apprehensive and on edge, she was only slightly comforted by the fact that Joan's pistol was safely tucked away in her purse.

After half an hour, a beautiful young blonde approached the table. She placed a small stack of chips on each of black 24 and red 25.

That was the signal Friedl had been instructed to watch for. The next bets would tell her the time and place for the rendezvous. The time would be in sequence: day, hour. The place would be one of three designated destinations, each one a different number on red. As the bets were placed for each successive spin of the wheel, Friedl's concentration was so fierce that once she had all the details, she had to force herself to blink and look away.

She checked her watch. The meeting time was in an hour and a half on a street a block away from the hotel. No sign of Popov yet, but perhaps he was keeping his distance this time. Nothing untoward had happened since Friedl's arrival, so there was no need to send out a distress signal via the roulette table to whatever British operative might be watching her. Gathering her chips, Friedl rose from the table and cashed them in. Then she went back to the Palàcio to change.

Before letting herself into her hotel room, Friedl checked for signs that someone had been there before her. She crouched low and saw that the tiny piece of tape she'd stuck across the door jamb had been broken.

She stopped breathing. Someone had been in her room. Perhaps Popov. Perhaps the maids. Perhaps someone not so friendly. Automatically, she drew Joan's tiny pistol from her purse, then stopped. She'd be stupid to go in alone. For all she knew, a professional killer might be lying in wait.

She hesitated, and in the silence she could hear her own breathing, feel the pounding of her heart. The best strategy would be to ask Mr. Black or one of the staff to accompany her, just to be sure.

She was about to turn away when the door opened, making her whirl and raise the pistol, arms straight but relaxed, left hand bracing the right, ready to shoot.

Popov stood there, arms folded, looking faintly amused. "It's been a while, I know, but is that really necessary?"

Friedl lowered her weapon, her heart beating hard and fast. "Duško! You scared me. Do you—"

She broke off as Popov's hand came up, palm out, to stop her. He shook his head and put a finger to his lips, pointed toward the ceiling and then to his ear. Then he beckoned her inside.

Someone had planted a bug to listen in on their conversation? Her eyes widened and her gaze darted to the ceiling, but she failed to see anything out of the ordinary. Well, she wouldn't, would she?

In a casual tone, Popov said, "How was your flight, my dear? I'm sorry I wasn't there to greet you."

"Oh, it was fine," said Friedl lamely, allowing him to take her wrap. So much for the dramatic, passionate reunion that had played out dozens of times in her head. She forced herself to answer Popov's questions as if it were quite like old times, but it was difficult to act naturally. She was acutely aware of their every word being heard, recorded, and analyzed somewhere else in the hotel. Maybe even in the room next door? And by which side? The Germans? The British? Both?

"You must be tired," said Popov, his tone solicitous, his eyes encouraging her to play along as he gently relieved her of both pistol and purse and set them on the sideboard. "How about you freshen up? Change into something more comfortable and join me for a drink on the terrace?"

"Yes. Yes, I'll do that." But when she didn't move to obey his suggestion, Popov gripped her elbow and pulled her with him into the en suite bathroom. He turned on the bath faucet and it took her a moment to realize why. The sound of the water would mask their conversation.

Duško lit a cigarette, blew out smoke, and put one hand in his pocket. As ever, he looked like he'd just stepped out of an advertisement for his Savile Row tailor. "Friedl, we need to talk."

Inwardly, she winced. His words brought memories of their first days together flooding back. Had he said them deliberately to evoke those tender emotions? She wouldn't put it past him.

She wrapped her arms around herself. "I don't have much time."

"I know. And you're not going to like what I have to say, but I must say it." He hesitated. "Don't go to that rendezvous tonight."

She gazed at him, and the confusion she'd felt since he appeared at her door began to wear off. "You don't think I'm up to it."

"Oh, I think you're equal to anything," said Popov. "I know you rather better than you think, my dear."

Her head jerked up. "And what's that supposed to mean?"

"I don't believe you're on anyone's side but your own, Fräulein Stöttinger," said Popov. "That being the case, I don't trust you to meet with Kühlenthal tonight. You see, my fate is rather tied to yours at this point. And I'll be damned if I'll let you destroy everything I and many others have risked our necks for."

She was flabbergasted. "Tar himself instructed me to do this. Believe me, I had far rather have stayed in England. Do you think I want to see that horrible man again?"

"Is that so? Then what about your little rendezvous on the beach the last time you were here? You never mentioned that to Tar, did you?"

So he had known about that. She bit her lip. Was that why he'd cut off contact with her? "I panicked. I was worried Tar might misinterpret it if I told him. I was stupid not to report it." She ought to have guessed they'd find out. Tar had known about Kühlenthal's first approach, after all.

"You could have told me about it that very day." Popov's eyes were cold. Whatever feelings he might have had for her, she saw no evidence of them now.

How could she explain it to him? There *was* no acceptable explanation. She'd kept the meeting secret because she'd intended to do what Kühlenthal asked of her. She hadn't seen any other way to ensure her mother's safety.

"Why didn't you pass on your suspicions to Tar, in that case?" she said uneasily.

"I did," said Popov. His blunt answer dashed over her like a bucket of iced water. He drew on his cigarette, blew out smoke. "No one was more surprised than I when he agreed to let you come here."

The rushing water was beginning to fray her nerves. How could they resolve such a complex matter in the time it took to run a bath?

Popov turned his gold lighter over, end on end. "Tar has faith that you'll do the right thing. I'm not so sure. I'm not at all certain it wouldn't be best to simply drown you in that bath right now to eliminate what I believe to be an unacceptable risk."

The bath was filling rapidly with steaming hot water. Suddenly, Friedl realized that Duško stood between her and the door. She was frozen with fear, so it wouldn't matter even if he weren't blocking her escape. "You wouldn't," she whispered. Not after all they'd been to each other.

"Wouldn't I?" He drew on his cigarette and the smoke swirled around him in the confined space. Then he pitched the cigarette into the sink and shoved his lighter in his pocket. "You might be surprised at what I would do."

Friedl's stomach churned. She'd believed he cared for her but tonight, he was all icy ruthlessness. Try as she might, though, she simply couldn't believe that all of the work she'd done, all of the sacrifices she'd made, would end with her drowning in a bath at the Hotel Palàcio. Perhaps a bottle of pills would be forced down her throat as explanation. A troubled soul, that Friedl Stöttinger, spurned by the man she loved . . .

She started toward the door but Popov caught her. Pulling her against him, he put a hand under her chin to tilt her head up, but she flinched away. "Look at me. *Look* at me." With a muttered expletive, he bunched a hand in the hair at the nape of her neck, forcing her head back so she couldn't avoid his gaze. This time, his signature expression of disgust was aimed at her. That hurt far more than his rough treatment. She fought the urge to shut her eyes and block out that contemptuous look, willed herself not to cry.

"I know you, Friedl." The man who had once spoken to her so caressingly now gritted out his words between clenched teeth. "And I know you have some clever plan up your sleeve to play both sides to see if you can find an advantage. But before you destroy an operation that could save thousands of lives, ask yourself whether you'll be able to live with that, and what your life will be worth if you save yourself at their expense."

Popov had always been the consummate gentleman, never laying a finger on her in anger. This side of him, so hard and brutal, rocked the world off its axis. She tried for a caressing tone. "Duško, darling, I swear it's not what you think."

He was unmoved. "Try again."

She struggled to think of a counterattack. "People have been listening to us. They know why I'm here. My sudden disappearance would cast suspicion on you in many quarters, wouldn't it?" His grip tightened and she gasped. "Duško, you're hurting me."

The fierce light in his eyes died. He let her go so abruptly that she stumbled back. "Clever Friedl. You're right, of course. I can't eliminate you as a threat—not here and now, at any rate. I can only trust that when it comes down to it, you'll do the right thing."

He waited for a moment, perhaps to see how she'd respond. She opened her lips to reply but no sound came out. With a snort of disgust, he turned and walked out of the en suite, his expensive loafers clicking on the entryway tiles. There was a pause. Then the heavy outer door to the hotel room opened and shut.

Friedl's legs wobbled. She fell to her knees on the floor and vomited into the toilet. When she was done, she wiped her mouth and dragged herself shakily to her feet. With a shudder, she turned off the bath taps, yanked the plug chain, and let the water drain away.

Thousands of lives? She didn't have a clue what Popov was talking about. No one had seen fit to explain to her why she was to hand over all of this information to Kühlenthal. She thought of the small piece of insurance she'd brought: the negative of Jean Leslie's photo was rolled up in the false bottom of a lipstick William Luke had given her. The lipstick had contained a suicide pill, but Friedl was brought up Roman Catholic and she hadn't wanted that thing anywhere near her, so she'd flushed it down the lavatory the first chance she'd got.

She hurried out to the sitting room to make sure Popov had gone. The room was empty, and the silence seemed to have a sense of finality about it. He wouldn't be back—at least not before she left for her rendezvous. She glanced at the sideboard. Joan's pistol was gone, too.

Friedl went to the drinks trolley, unstoppered the brandy decanter, and slopped some of the amber liquid into a glass. She downed it in two gulps and poured some more.

Her nerves were shot, and the most difficult part of the night had yet to begin. She looked at the clock. Barely half an hour until she had to meet Kühlenthal. She hurried to her bedroom to change.

Still trembling from Popov's words as much as his rough treatment, she gazed at the clothes she'd brought with her, which had been unpacked and hung up by the hotel maid. When one was attending a rendezvous that might well end in torture and death, what on earth was one to wear?

She smiled a little sourly at herself for this piece of frivolity. Perhaps the British brand of insouciance so admired by Popov was rubbing off on her.

Trousers seemed like a practical choice, but might it be better to wear something a little more feminine when dealing with a man like Kühlenthal? Hurriedly, she decided on a compromise: a plain woolen skirt cut on the bias, a black twinset, and pearls.

At least that won't show the blood, whispered a macabre voice in her head.

With shaking hands, she touched up her makeup and made sure she had that special lipstick in her purse before she left for the rendezvous.

It wasn't far. Friedl walked out of the hotel into the street and around the block. A small dark car—a Fiat, she thought it was—flashed its lights once, momentarily blinding her. When her eyes had adjusted again to the darkness, Friedl walked up to the vehicle. She recognized the driver. It was the young woman who had played roulette at the casino an hour or so before. Friedl saw a man in the back seat, so she opened the door and slid into the cramped space beside him.

The occupant of the back seat was not Kühlenthal, but a younger man—a lieutenant, if his uniform was any guide. "The major was called away suddenly," said the man, who did not give his name. "Your report?"

"It's here." Friedl handed him the file that she and William Luke had fabricated so diligently in London that very day.

The lieutenant flicked through the file, then looked back at her. "Major Kühlenthal has requested that you join him immediately, Miss Stöttinger."

"Join him?" repeated Friedl. "In Madrid? Now?" She hadn't expected that.

"In Berlin, Miss Stöttinger," he replied. "Major Kühlenthal wants you to present your findings in person to German High Command."

CHAPTER TWENTY

Estoril, Portugal
May 1943

Friedl

*A*s the Fiat pulled away from the curb, Friedl felt the last vestige of control slip from her grasp. *Berlin*? That had not been part of the plan—at least, not the plan Tar had disclosed to Friedl. Instinct made her protest. "I never agreed to that!"

"It hardly matters what you agreed," said the young officer as the car gathered speed. "Major Kühlenthal has ordered me to bring you to Berlin, and to treat you with the utmost courtesy as his honored guest. It is up to you whether you wish to cooperate, Fräulein Stöttinger. The way I see it, you can come as his guest or as my prisoner. It's all the same to me."

Friedl had an urge to scramble for the door handle and take her chances falling from a moving vehicle. But the cold muzzle of a gun pressed to her side and all thoughts of escape fled before abject fear. She held her breath, her pulse beating so wildly it was as if she could hear it.

Think, Friedl, think! They couldn't kill her, could they? They needed her alive—at least until she'd given them her report in Berlin. She forced a strained laugh. "All right, *liebling.* Put that nasty thing away. If it's Major Kühlenthal's wish that I come to Berlin, then of course that is what I'll do."

"Sensible of you." He did as she asked, holstering his gun in a sort of harness inside his jacket. Still within easy reach if she made any sudden moves, she observed. Well, she wasn't stupid enough to try. Her friendly traveling companion picked up her report and felt about in his pockets, then came up with a small flashlight roughly the size of a pen and flicked it on.

The Fiat sped along, heading back toward Lisbon. To the airport or to a private landing strip used for covert operations? She supposed she'd find out when they arrived.

She struggled to steady her breathing, even though her chest felt tight and her every nerve ending was electrified with fear. Might the British scoop her up at the airport before she was transferred to the plane? They were sure to be following her, although she noted several countersurveillance measures the female driver of the Fiat took, presumably to shake any tails they might have picked up in Estoril. The wild idea of throwing herself from the moving vehicle recurred, only to be dismissed. They were traveling too fast.

But if a British agent was following them and discovered where she was headed, they would be bound to conclude that the information she carried was so vital, German High Command wanted to interrogate her about it in person. Or would they conclude that Friedl had been a triple agent working for the Germans all along?

Would they stop her getting on that plane? After all, if she told the Germans the truth—whether as a result of willingness or torture—it would scupper the plan, whatever it was. According to Popov, thousands of lives would be lost.

Why, oh why, had Tar let her go to Estoril in the first place? The question had been nagging at her since Popov had first challenged her about her allegiance. How could Tar be confident about what she might do when she wasn't even sure of that herself?

Useless to pursue that line of thought. Regardless of what the British might do, she needed her own plan. Berlin wasn't a safe place for her, even if she did manage to convince Kühlenthal and the rest of them that she was working for the Third Reich. Having run away from her homeland with an Orthodox Jew, and with a sister related by marriage to the head of MI-6, there would always be a question mark over her, a stain on her character, as far as the Nazis were concerned.

She needed to convince them not only that her allegiance was with them, but also that she was useful enough to send back to England again. If she remained in Berlin, who knew what might happen?

Clearly verification of Major Martin's identity and movements was urgently required in Berlin. She might reasonably deduce that since Kühlenthal had discovered the existence of the floating dead man and managed to steal a look at the documents the major carried, the Abwehr officer was biased toward believing them. This would be Kühlenthal's own little intelligence coup, shoring up his status against the continual backbiting and jockeying for position that went on among the Nazi hierarchy. Perhaps it might even be cause for promotion.

But what would German High Command believe? Friedl didn't know much about the British operation, but from her investigations, she was well aware that Major Martin existed only on paper. What she didn't know was precisely what sensitive information was being conveyed to the Germans via this deception. Popov had said the ruse could save thousands of lives, so the intelligence the false major carried must be momentous.

She remembered something her father had said once, in a rare moment of candor. "The truth? The truth doesn't matter. What matters is what Hitler wants to believe."

Very well, she told herself, trying to think it out step by step. Assume Kühlenthal wants to convince Hitler that Major Martin is real. What then?

The fact that Kühlenthal was relying on Friedl to verify something so important pointed to the possibility that he didn't have anyone more reliable in the field. At least, no one with the ability to fly to Estoril at short notice like this. Had it not been for Friedl's insistence on accompanying Popov to Estoril for that brief pleasure jaunt, would she find herself in this fix now?

Self-recrimination and fear rose up again inside her. Useless emotions, both of them. *Get a grip on yourself, Friedl, or you really will be dead.*

She slid a glance at her silent companion, who continued to leaf through her report, holding the flashlight to illuminate the neatly typewritten pages. Seeing him fully absorbed in his task, Friedl tried to reason further.

Logic told her that the only way she could know how to play her own hand in this game was to take a peek at what the Germans held in theirs. If Hitler was disposed to believe the intelligence that was coming his way from Kühlenthal, then her mission might well succeed. But if the Abwehr poked holes in the Major Martin story, then what? Friedl would be tortured and killed if she stuck with Tar's version.

The thought made her palms sweat. She no longer found any comfort in the small piece of camera film secreted in the false bottom of her lipstick. Duško's scathing lecture echoed in her mind; she still felt the whiplash burn of his disgust. He'd been right. She had intended to betray the British if that became necessary to save her own skin. The negative wasn't proof of any kind, but it did lend credence to the story that she knew Jean personally, and that she also knew Jean wasn't Major Martin's Pam. If the Abwehr believed her, an investigation of Jean Leslie would soon prove that what Friedl told them was true.

Friedl clenched her jaw. Well, Popov had been right about her but he'd been wrong about her, too. It came to her that moment with a piercing, cold clarity: no matter what danger she faced, she could never be the one to send thousands of men to their deaths.

The plain, inescapable fact was that Nazism was evil. She thought of her husband and all his people had suffered under

Hitler's decrees, of every country overrun by Axis powers, their citizens kept in terrible subjugation. She thought of men like Brian Howard and his lover, Anton, given the choice between prison and castration. She thought of her homeland, and of Germany, of the good and kind people she'd grown up with all living in fear under the heel of the Nazi jackboot. And she thought of Britain, the small nation that had fought with such do-or-die grit, refusing to bow down to tyranny.

After Popov's threats, Friedl knew just how much was riding on the deception in which she was playing a part. She'd never thought of herself as the kind of person who would make a noble sacrifice, but perhaps one never truly knew one's mettle until one faced the ultimate test.

Friedl drew a deep breath and let it out slowly. She'd been prepared to give a small recital in front of an audience of one at Estoril, before being whisked back to the safety of England. Now she was going to act a part for German High Command in the heart of enemy territory.

It would need to be the greatest performance of her life.

Berlin, Germany
May 1943

The flight to Berlin was over in the blink of an eye. Friedl had thought she was too anxious to sleep, but either the nervous tension that hadn't left her since Tar had given her this "little job" to do had simply exhausted her, or they'd slipped something into her coffee. Either way, she woke up again only as they started to descend.

Drowsily, she looked around her. The officer who had collected her at the airport was staying close, even though there were no other passengers on board the small plane besides the female driver.

Ach du lieber! Her head ached and her mouth felt like it had been stuffed full of cotton wool. She wished she had a toothbrush, at least.

Automatically, Friedl reached for her purse and took out her compact. She powdered her nose, then palmed the lipstick with Jean's negative in it. She'd drop it somewhere once they landed. Somewhere it would never be found.

"Best brace yourself." The lieutenant spoke loudly into her ear over the noise of the engines. "We're about to land."

They alighted from the plane and crossed the tarmac toward a black Mercedes-Benz. This must be a private airfield. There was only one large hangar in sight. The air was crisp and cool, a contrast to Estoril's warmth. Friedl shivered. As she climbed into the waiting automobile, she stooped as if to adjust her shoe. With a feeling of throwing away her last lifeline, she dropped her lipstick with the negative inside it in front of the back wheel.

It was still dark as they sped through the Berlin streets. Friedl hadn't been to Berlin for years, but she recognized the impressive buildings of the Tiergarten in the dawning light of a new day, and when they pulled up at the checkpoint outside the Bendlerblock, she didn't feel surprise.

High flying, indeed. This was the headquarters of both German High Command and the Abwehr. Festooned liberally with swastika flags, the imposing U-shaped building was heavily guarded by men with helmets and machine guns that gleamed in the dawn light.

Once inside, Friedl was forced to surrender her purse. "But I need that," she protested.

"It will be returned to you in good time, Miss Stöttinger," said her escort. "Follow me."

As they moved through the entrance hall, Friedl felt dwarfed. The sheer scale of the building seemed designed to make mere mortals feel insignificant in the face of temporal power, much in the way that cathedrals were built to strike awe of God into men. The ceiling of the atrium was so high above her, it seemed to belong in the heavens.

There was something exceedingly cold about this building, as if it leeched the warmth from the very soul. Or was that her overactive imagination?

Their footsteps echoed as she followed Kühlenthal's subordinate up two flights of stairs. They continued along a corridor to an anteroom, where a young woman sat working at her desk, even at this early hour.

Kühlenthal's man didn't say anything but the secretary lifted the receiver of a black telephone and put it to her ear. "Yes. Yes," she said. "They're here." She looked up, not at Friedl, but at the lieutenant. "You're to take a seat, please."

Now that she stood, if not in the heart of Nazi power, certainly in one of its other vital organs, a sense of unreality gripped Friedl. How on earth had it come to this?

Friedl plucked up courage. Here was another woman who would surely understand. "Please. I need to freshen up. Is there a powder room I could use?"

"There is not," came the unsympathetic reply. "You are to wait here until you're called."

Friedl saw it was useless to argue. They waited so long in silence that she thought she'd go mad, so she began mentally to recite the lyrics of all the songs she knew to try to calm her nerves.

Finally the secretary's telephone buzzed and she was directed to go in.

Friedl rose unsteadily to her feet. The secretary opened the massive door for her and she moved through, trying to look excited and impressed rather than terrified to be there.

The office into which she was shown was more like a drawing room than a place of work, so she gathered that the person who sat behind the handsome mahogany desk—which seemed like the length of a cricket pitch away from the door—was a man of some importance. Unsurprisingly, on the wall behind him hung an enormous portrait of Hitler.

Trying very hard to keep calm, Friedl lifted her head and walked the full length of the room. On her approach, she saw Kühlenthal rise and turn to greet her. She'd never thought she'd be glad to see his face, but better the devil you know . . .

The devil she *didn't* know, the officer in command of the impressive desk, was a slight man of below-average height, hardly a figure who suited the proportions of this office. He had thin lips and sparse, severely brushed-back hair. A pair of round spectacles added an air of studiousness. He looked intelligent, she thought. A bad sign.

She saw that the bespectacled officer had a file open in front of him and remembered that she'd left her report in the hands of Kühlenthal's underling, who hadn't come in with her or given her the report to hand over.

What should she do now? Wait and watch, she thought. No need to volunteer anything until she saw which way the wind blew.

"Ah!" said Kühlenthal, rubbing his hands together as if at the prospect of a tasty meal. "Miss Stöttinger, our star agent. *Heil Hitler!*"

The words nearly stuck in her throat. "*Heil Hitler*," she snapped out, raising her arm to precisely the correct angle of the Nazi salute. She'd better do a good job of acting the part, or she'd be wishing for that suicide pill she'd flushed down the lavatory back in London.

"Allow me to introduce Colonel von Rönne," said Kühlenthal.

She smiled and nodded to the colonel but he simply stared back at her, his eyes impassive and unblinking behind his shining spectacles. "You've been living in London since before the war began, I hear. Most unusual." He turned his head to regard Kühlenthal. "One might almost say, unprecedented, to meet one of our British-based operatives face-to-face."

Kühlenthal beamed in response, but Friedl wasn't at all sure the colonel had meant the remark as a compliment. Memories of similar conversations with her father flooded back. His sarcasm, his rigorous attention to detail, his insistence on perfection at all times. Well before adolescence, she had decided that the best way to counter his crushing irony was to accept such sentiments as sincere. A habit that had led her father to believe she was stupid, but it was better than earning his wrath by arguing or standing up for herself. It was also better than taking every slight and veiled insult to heart, as Lisi had done.

Now, Friedl tried to see what charm could achieve. "It is an honor to serve the Führer. I am overjoyed to be back in the Fatherland again."

That received no warmer response. As if she hadn't spoken, von Rönne said to Kühlenthal, "I have your report, Major. Is there anything Miss Stöttinger can usefully add, or will we simply be going over the same ground?"

Kühlenthal tilted his head. "As to that, I have only this minute set eyes on Miss Stöttinger myself. If you'll permit—"

"Yes, yes, go away and compare notes. If there's anything significant to add from Miss Stöttinger's report, or any evidence to contradict what you've already passed on, you can advise me."

"So you think the intelligence is credible?" said Kühlenthal, looking very like a dog begging for treats from his master. He all but wagged his tail.

"It's too early to conclude one way or the other," said von Rönne repressively. "But yes, it does indeed look to me as if the intelligence from Madrid is sound." He fixed Kühlenthal with a hard stare. "Make sure you leave nothing ambiguous in that report. Ambiguity only causes confusion. The Führer likes his intelligence reports to be clear-cut. *Verstehen Sie?*

"Yes! Yes, I understand." Kühlenthal saluted and clicked his heels, barking out an enthusiastic "*Heil Hitler*" before shepherding Friedl toward the door.

Friedl exhaled a measured breath of relief as she hurried to keep pace with Kühlenthal's long strides. She'd made it through one circle of hell unscathed, but she knew she couldn't afford to relax. That was when men like von Rönne pounced.

"Wait!"

And there it was. Both she and Kühlenthal halted and turned back. Fear was a hard pulse in Friedl's throat.

"I'd like to see Miss Stöttinger alone for a moment."

Friedl sensed that Kühlenthal would have liked to protest but he was too scared of von Rönne to do so. "Of course, Colonel." With a jerk of his head, he indicated that Friedl should return to the desk.

Plastering an avidly obsequious expression on her face, Friedl walked back toward the man who would decide her fate.

CHAPTER TWENTY-ONE

London, England
May 1943

Paddy

When Paddy saw Jean a few weeks after her visit to the morgue, she told her as much as she could about preparing Major Martin for his final voyage. She skipped the part about thawing the corpse's feet, however. Some things were better left unsaid.

"They didn't use the love letters I wrote after all that," Paddy remarked. "And I took so much trouble over them, too." It was just as well, really, but she did wish she hadn't been forced into such subterfuge at home if the results of her efforts were to be discarded in such a cavalier manner. "Did Montagu ask you to do it in the end?"

Jean shook her head, eyes alight with mischief. "You'll never guess who did write them. The Spin!"

"Miss Leggett?" said Paddy, recalling the dour woman who presided over the Section B1B secretarial pool. "*No!*"

"Yes! You know we call her the Spin because she's such a dried-up old wick of a spinster. Dreadfully unkind, of course, but she's so utterly awful to us girls. Even when she's in a good mood she always looks as if she's just eaten a lemon. Anyway, old Spin must have quite the imagination because those letters she wrote sound like they came straight out of a romance novel, don't they? Bill—Captain Montagu, I mean—gave me a peek."

Paddy made a face. "I didn't get the chance to read them in detail, but I'll take your word for it. Goodness, I hope they burned the ones I wrote. Anyway, the long and the short of it is that it all went off without a hitch. Or much of one," she added, thinking of the kerfuffle over the frozen feet. "I wonder where our Major Martin is now."

"I wish I'd been there, too," said Jean. "It all sounds so exciting."

"You were my alibi, don't forget," said Paddy. "I told Julian you were still having trouble with Tony."

"Oh! Tony," said Jean. Her cheeks flushed and she bit her lip.

"What?" Paddy demanded.

Jean shifted uneasily. "What do you mean, what?"

"I mean what are you looking so guilty about?"

"Well, it's too late now, isn't it?" said Jean. "What's done is done."

Paddy was aghast. "You mean you didn't get the photo back? After all we did to get it?"

"No, I did! At least, Tony gave me back the photo, and the negative, too." Jean's mouth trembled. "But then I lost the negative."

Paddy threw up her hands. "How on earth did that happen?"

Drawing out the details was like trying to get blood out of a stone. Good Heavens, what a comedy of errors! "You know the original photograph is making its way into German hands via the body of Major Martin even as we speak."

"Yes, I do, and it's *killing* me!" said Jean, hitting her chest with a clenched fist. "I know I had the negative with me when I went to the Gargoyle Club because that's where I saw Captain Montagu." She licked her lips. "I'd taken the negative to get a blown-up version of the photograph for him, and I'm positive that the negative and the smaller snapshot Tony gave me back were in the envelope in my purse when I arrived at the club. But when I looked again, the snapshot was there but the negative was gone."

Paddy refrained from commenting on Jean's ongoing flirtation with Captain Montagu. Now was not the time. "You must *think*," she said, gripping Jean's hands tightly. "Who was there that night? Who might have searched your purse?"

"Don't you think I've racked my brains over it?" cried Jean. "I always leave my purse behind when I dance, so it could have been anyone." She listed off the people she'd been with that night.

Paddy frowned and thought over the likely suspects. There were quite a few. "What about Brian Howard?"

"He was there, but I've already asked him and he insists he doesn't have it."

Paddy breathed hard out of her nostrils. "And you believe him."

"Well, yes I do, Paddy, because if he did have that negative, he would have orchestrated some huge, elaborate tease with it by now. He would have done something horridly outrageous like make it into a billboard or take out an advertisement in the *Times* or something. I tried to ask him more about the whole thing, but he's like an eel when he wants to be difficult, and I didn't like to seem too anxious. He can smell desperation a mile away, and then he'd never let the matter rest."

Paddy eyed her. "I don't know how you can be so calm about it."

"Well, I'm not. I can't sleep at night, if you must know! And I can't tell Cholmondeley because I swore black and blue that Tony wouldn't be a problem and that I'd destroy the evidence immediately."

Instead, she had created yet another version of that photograph to give to Montagu. "You must tell Cholmondeley," Paddy said. "There might be something he could do."

"There is someone else I think might have it." Jean wrung her hands. "Oh, but she wouldn't, would she? I mean, she has always been so kind to me. And besides, she . . . No, I can't believe it."

"Who?" demanded Paddy. "Now is not the time to protect your friends out of some sense of misplaced loyalty, Jean. If you know something . . ."

"Well, it's just that Friedl was asking me all sorts of questions at the Gargoyle that evening. I didn't tell her anything about the operation, of course. But I left my purse with her when I went to dance, so . . ."

"Who is this Friedl person?" Paddy wanted to know, but her friend didn't answer.

"Can I use your telephone?" asked Jean. "I'll ring MJ to get her address. If anyone knows, she will."

Paddy sat anxiously by while Jean asked MJ about their mutual acquaintance. When she rang off, Jean said, "Friedl's in a nursing home, of all places. Sprained her ankle, apparently."

"Which nursing home?" Paddy asked, taking down the details. This was turning into a wild-goose chase. They needed to see this Friedl person as soon as possible, and who knew how long it might take for a sprained ankle to mend? Paddy hoped that wherever Friedl might be, she could make it there and back in a day. She didn't fancy lying to Julian again.

But the name . . . Friedl Stöttinger . . . Wasn't it German? Paddy didn't like the sound of this at all. Back at the briefing morning in Room 13, Montagu had bluffly reassured them that there weren't any German spies in England, and that all of Paddy's play-acting was just in case . . . But if Friedl was a spy and she had that negative in her possession, what might it mean for Operation Mincemeat?

Paddy said, "As much as I'd hate you to get into trouble, I think we must tell Cholmondeley about this latest development. If you don't want to face Montagu, I quite understand, but one of them ought to be informed."

"Please, can't we just visit Friedl first?" pleaded Jean. "MJ gave me the nursing home's address. At least, I'm afraid I won't be able to go up until the weekend. I have to work tomorrow."

A little grimly, Paddy answered, "Don't worry. I'll handle it."

Fortunately, the nursing home where Friedl was staying wasn't actually in the country but in St. Albans, an easy distance from London. Paddy took the train up the next day and walked from the station.

The place Friedl had chosen to recuperate from her injury was a small, private establishment surrounded by what might once have been pretty garden beds but was now dug up and used exclusively for vegetable growing. Peeping out from behind the large, Tudor-style house was an ornamental lake with a rather forlorn-looking crane standing frozen among the weeping willows, as if posing for a photograph.

The house seemed to have escaped requisition by the military somehow, and when she was shown inside, the faint, mewling cries of a very small baby told Paddy that this was a home for new mothers as well as convalescents. Personally, Paddy would far prefer to give birth at Claridge's Hotel, as her mother had done. The interior of this place was dim and depressing.

At the reception desk, Paddy asked for Miss Friedl Stöttinger. The receptionist, an efficient-looking individual in tweeds and pearls, looked up the register. "Oh, that's right! We do have a booking in that name, but I'm afraid Miss Stöttinger is not here."

Paddy's heart sank. "You mean she's already left?"

"I mean she never came," said the receptionist. "She was due the day before yesterday, but she didn't check in, and our attempts to reach her by telephone have been unsuccessful."

"That is odd," said Paddy. "Her friends think she's here. I hope no accident has befallen her." Not on top of the sprained ankle. Or were both the injury and the sojourn at the nursing home part of some kind of ruse?

The receptionist blinked. "Goodness, I hadn't thought of that."

The telephone rang then, and the receptionist excused herself. Paddy thanked her and left.

"What now?" she said to herself. She supposed she would have to tell Cholmondeley what had happened. From the moment Jean mentioned Friedl's name, Paddy had known this was the kind of possible security breach they couldn't ignore.

She arranged to meet Cholmondeley the following day, and after patiently responding to several pointless pleasantries from the cheerful intelligence officer, Paddy blurted out the news.

True to form, the flight lieutenant looked unfazed by this latest development. "Oh, I shouldn't think we need to worry about that," he said, waving his pipe in a manner that struck Paddy as irresponsibly blasé. "Still. What are the odds, eh?"

She supposed he meant that it was highly unlikely that such a set of circumstances would come about—that this particular photograph should fall into the hands of an enemy alien. It was true, Jean had been spectacularly unlucky.

Paddy tried to persuade him to share her concern. "But this Friedl person—she's German, and as far as I can tell from what I hear on the grapevine, she's profascist as well." Paddy had made it her business to make subtle inquiries about Friedl when she'd telephoned Brian to ask for her home address.

"A *nursing home*?" Brian had said incredulously when Paddy passed on what Friedl had told MJ. "In *St. Alban's*? My *dear*, Friedl would rather have her leg chopped off." He had obligingly furnished her with Friedl's address, however, so she thanked him and rang off.

"I understand your concern," Cholmondeley said to her now, thoughtfully twiddling the end of his waxed moustache. "But leave it with me. I'm sure all will be well."

He gave Paddy the distinct impression that he intended to do nothing whatsoever about the matter. "But—"

Smoothly, Cholmondeley said, "If we'd known beforehand, of course we'd have switched the photographs. But there's not a lot we can do about it now, Mrs. Ridsdale. The die is cast. Major Martin has been launched into the deep. Now we must simply watch and wait."

And gamble on the fact that Friedl Stöttinger either did not realize the true significance of the photograph or wasn't an enemy agent after all, thought Paddy. But what possible other reason could she have for quizzing Jean about her war work like that?

On her way home, Paddy thought of Admiral Godfrey and Commander Fleming and the habit they'd instilled in her of never leaving anything to chance that might be anticipated and dealt with efficiently. She came to a decision. Cholmondeley might wish her to forget the matter, but she simply couldn't leave this particular end loose and dangling, especially when it might turn into a lit fuse that could blow Operation Mincemeat sky high.

A strong sense of duty and the ingrained need to finish what she'd begun drowned out the warnings of her inner voice. Paddy would take the initiative. She would confront this Friedl Stöttinger and retrieve the negative. They couldn't risk it falling into the wrong hands.

She prayed it hadn't already done precisely that.

* * *

"Going somewhere, darling?" Julian popped his head around the door as Paddy was putting on her hat.

Paddy jumped and tried not to look guilty. Why did every such question feel like an accusation these days? "Yes, didn't I tell you? I've got a women's auxiliary meeting tonight. Hopefully it won't run late."

It had been some weeks since Paddy had lied to Julian for what she'd hoped would be the final time. A stab of shame made her avoid his gaze and pretend to hunt through her makeup kit for something. Randomly, she chose a lipstick that was the wrong color, uncapped it, stared at it blankly, then put the cap back on again.

God forbid that she should be proficient at lying to her husband but she was a little annoyed that she still became so flustered whenever it was necessary.

She needed to get that negative back from Friedl—if indeed it was in the German woman's possession. Paddy had decided to duck out of the women's auxiliary meeting early that evening and pay a visit to Friedl Stöttinger's flat. She only prayed she wouldn't be too late.

Whatever happened with Friedl Stöttinger, tonight Paddy would tell Julian about the baby. She would leave the Naval Intelligence Division behind, once and for all.

"I feel as if I never see you these days," said Julian now, reminding her of the occasions he'd said the same during their courtship when she'd worked for the Admiralty. He put his hands on her shoulders and kneaded them gently.

She made herself smile up at him and squeeze his hand. "I am sorry, darling. It's a bit of a tiresome obligation, but I can't pass it off to anyone else. I'll be back as soon as I can."

Twilight had fallen when Paddy arrived at Friedl's mews flat near Claridge's Hotel. It was dark enough to conceal Paddy's features from any casual observer, yet not so late that she wouldn't be back in plenty of time to spend the rest of the evening with Julian. But just as MJ had warned her, when Paddy visited the German woman's flat, she found that Miss Stöttinger wasn't at home, and if the mail stacked on her doormat was any indication, she hadn't been there for a few days. But if she wasn't home and she wasn't in St. Albans, where was she?

Paddy knocked on Friedl's door once again and waited. She listened, but no movement came from within and no light seeped beneath the door. With a quick glance around, Paddy opened her purse and took out two hairpins she'd fashioned specifically for the purpose, then stooped to inspect the lock.

Who would have guessed that talking her way into a couple of the training sessions for Ian Fleming's intelligence commandos would come in handy?

She hadn't been allowed to participate actively in the lock-picking class (taught by an actual housebreaker and safe-cracking expert) and she didn't have the proper tools, but she knew the theory. Besides, they always did it with hairpins in the movies, didn't they?

But as she inserted the makeshift lock picks into the keyhole and judiciously wiggled them about, the task seemed much more difficult than it had appeared when demonstrated by the professional. After scratching and prodding without success, Paddy huffed a sigh and removed the hairpins, glancing back down the stairs to check whether anyone was about.

She tried the lock once more, but whatever knack you needed to be a housebreaker, she clearly didn't have it.

Paddy sighed, exasperated at such a tame ending to her admittedly short career as a field operative. But she'd promised herself that she'd let this go if she didn't succeed in retrieving Jean's photograph tonight.

A small pot plant by the door caught her eye. What if . . . She crouched down and peered through the fronds of the little fern, but there was no key hidden conveniently in the soil, and none in the saucer or under it, either.

But when she went to replace the plant, she saw it. A tile on the edge of the doorstep had lost its grouting and been knocked askew. Without difficulty, she removed the tile and stifled a delighted spurt of laughter. There, gleaming dully in the dim light, was a key. She unlocked the door, replaced the key, the pot plant, and the mail, and went inside.

In the small sitting room, Paddy switched on a lamp, deeming it safe enough, since the blackout curtains would mask any light from the street. She looked about her. This wouldn't take long.

Friedl's set of rooms was tiny, and other than a surfeit of clothing and an enviable collection of cosmetics and scents, she didn't have an awful lot of material possessions. There was a stack of magazines and a book or two by Dennis Wheatley, of all people. Paddy held each one by the spine and fanned through the pages, hoping against hope for Jean's negative to fall out. Nothing.

With all of the obvious places covered, Paddy turned her attention to the tiny kitchenette, opening tins and feeling along empty cupboard shelves and under surfaces in vain. Her heart was pounding. She was trying to be quick, but she was all fingers and thumbs.

A key scraped in the lock. Paddy froze, then instinct sent her scrambling to hide behind the sofa. The door opened and quick footsteps crossed the floor. The shush of a discarded coat or other garment hitting the floor met Paddy's straining ears.

When the footsteps proceeded into the bedroom, Paddy got to her feet, and started to make a beeline for the door. She'd nearly reached it when she realized. The lamp! She'd left it on. Friedl would have known as soon as she walked into the flat that someone was there.

It crossed Paddy's mind that instead of diving for a hiding place, it would have been far better to have confronted Friedl and demanded the photo's return. Paddy was about to make her presence known and do just that, when the hair on the nape of her neck prickled.

She started to turn but saw a blur of movement from the corner of her eye, then felt a hard blow to her temple. The world seemed to spin and turn a fuzzy gray, then her knees buckled and she dropped to the floor.

CHAPTER TWENTY-TWO

Berlin, Germany
May 1943

Friedl

"Are you a patriot, Miss Stöttinger?" Colonel von Rönne held up a hand to forestall her answer. "Ah. That's right. You're Austrian. So it hardly matters if you are or not."

Friedl refrained from the obvious retort. Everyone conveniently forgot that the Führer himself was Austrian by birth. "I am loyal to the Third Reich, if that's what you mean."

"Are you?" said von Rönne. "Then why did you leave?"

She thought of her husband. Of the hate and prejudice that had driven them from their home, and that old anger flared up again. She couldn't talk about any of it to this man. No one rose high in the ranks of this regime unless they hated Jews as much as Hitler did. Instead, she attempted a deflection. "Major Kühlenthal recruited me to work in England—"

"*Please.*" The colonel smiled thinly. "Let us not pretend you couldn't run rings around that dandified buffoon if you chose. Your very presence here is evidence of that."

He was giving her far too much credit. Her heart plummeted. But what had she expected? Anyone in von Rönne's position got there because he didn't fall for every trick in the book. "Then you don't find the major's report credible?"

There was a pause. "Let's say I have yet to be convinced. Our intelligence officers are working around the clock to verify the information from the body. If what they find contradicts what you've written in your report, well . . ." He spread his hands. "Things will not end well for you, I'm afraid."

She tried to swallow but her throat was too dry. Now was the moment. She could still back out.

Survive, instinct told her.

Thousands of lives, Popov had said.

"Tell me about your father, Miss Stöttinger," invited von Rönne, quite as if he were a psychoanalyst and she his patient.

By now, Friedl had been thrown off-balance so many times that she felt seasick. But at least in talking about her late father, a loyal member of the Nazi Party, she had little to fear.

Don't relax, she told herself. There would be no respite until she was back home in London. And even then . . .

Friedl was exhausted and afraid, and von Rönne led her into the interrogation down such a winding path, full of diversions along the way, that when he began to question her about Major Martin, it seemed like yet another natural digression.

"So when the British asked you to spy for them, what did you say?" von Rönne asked, as if inquiring about her response to a party invitation.

"They didn't," said Friedl. There. She'd committed herself. *Ach du lieber,* what had she done? She swallowed and made herself continue. "My sister Lisi protected me from that. Her brother-in-law . . . well, I'm sure you know what he does. Lisi convinced him I didn't have what it takes to be a spy."

And so it went on. After what seemed like hours, Friedl's throat ached from talking, from going over her story again and again. Von Rönne took her through her investigations into Major Martin chronologically, in reverse order, and then fired questions at her at random.

Friedl was shaking, lightheaded, almost delirious with fear. But she'd made her choice. There was no going back now and no room for error. If they found out she was lying, she was dead. Worse than dead.

"May I have a glass of water, please?" It was the third time she'd asked. There was a tall carafe of water on his desk and two tumblers, as if placed there to taunt her. She was tempted to grab them and help herself, but some strange compulsion prevented her. Without doing anything physically threatening, von Rönne made her feel cowed, powerless, and very alone.

"You can have water when you've told me all I want to know," answered von Rönne, also for the third time, in a measured, calm tone, as if he were a teacher gently admonishing a pupil. He glanced down at the file in front of him, light glinting off his spectacles. Then he began the interrogation all over again.

A sense of unreality settled over Friedl. She sat on a comfortable leather chair in a light, airy, wood-paneled room with a rich Persian rug at her feet. There were no shackles on her wrists, no one was beating her, yet she felt like a prisoner all the same. She *was* a prisoner under interrogation. It had come about so insidiously, beginning with quite a pleasant conversation about her father, her family, life in England, escalating so gradually that if she hadn't been on high alert, she'd have been taken unawares.

Sometimes it seemed as if the colonel believed every lie she told him. At others she sensed he was under no illusion at all.

Friedl could have laughed at herself for her ridiculous hubris, trusting that she could handle these people. Well, Kühlenthal in Estoril, she might have handled. The head of German military intelligence at the imposing Bendlerblock in Berlin was a different proposition altogether.

Hours passed—or what seemed like hours—until Friedl's voice had diminished to little more than a croak. Despite her dehydration, she desperately needed the bathroom. It would be too humiliating if she was obliged to release her bladder on this green leather chair. She repeated her answers like an automaton, willing her physical needs to go away.

The sun was high in the sky over Berlin and throwing long patches of sunshine onto the wall behind von Rönne when Friedl's voice finally gave out. She gazed yearningly at the carafe on the colonel's desk. The tiny rainbows of light thrown by the glass danced and blurred before her eyes.

"Water," she whispered. "Please."

He considered her. Then he took a key from his pocket, unlocked the top drawer of his desk, and slid it open. From the drawer, he removed her purse.

Friedl's eyes widened as he undid the clasp and tipped the contents onto his desk. She forced herself to remain still and silent while he arranged each object in a neat line along the blotter before him. And there, neatly in formation like a good little soldier, lay the dummy lipstick she'd left to be crushed under the wheel of the Mercedes that had collected her from the airport. The lipstick that contained Jean's negative. Someone must have seen her drop it and retrieved it. How had she failed to notice?

Seconds ticked by before von Rönne selected the first item to inspect. He clicked open her gold powder compact and took out the puff, set it aside. He pulled out a side drawer of his desk and hunted through it until he drew out a letter opener, its blade glinting. He ran the point of the letter opener around the mirror of her compact and jimmied it until the small reflective circle fell out. Nothing there. He did the same with the powder, levering out the pale disc to look beneath. Nothing. He replaced the mirror and the powder with movements so delicate and precise that the powder disc remained largely intact. *Don't bother*, she wanted to tell him. *I'll never use that compact again. Not even if I have to go barefaced for the rest of the war.*

Von Rönne frowned, rubbing together his fingers and thumb. Unhurriedly, he took out his handkerchief and dusted powder from his hands, then from the blotter on his desk. He refolded his handkerchief precisely and returned it to his pocket.

Next, he picked up her open purse and pinched the silk inner lining between finger and thumb. With the letter opener, he stabbed a hole in the pale, shiny fabric. Having made that incursion, he sliced through the stitching in several precise movements, then lifted the lining out in one ragged-edged piece. He turned the purse upside down and shook it. Nothing. The lining was folded neatly and returned to the purse.

Next, her fountain pen was taken apart and reassembled, her card case inspected closely, as was her cigarette case, the cigarettes inside it, her lighter, the handle of her hair comb, and even her handkerchief. He used the latter to polish his fingerprints off the rest and returned each item to her ruined purse.

By this point, Friedl's nerves were stretched to the breaking point. Von Rönne's movements were as slow and measured and as digressive as his interrogation. She longed for it to be over, nearly grabbed the dummy lipstick and removed its false bottom herself, just to get the discovery over with.

Suddenly, she realized that this was the reaction he sought. Von Rönne was playing with her. Her purse had already been searched. The colonel knew what that lipstick contained. He was not a man who left something like that to chance. Like a cat with a mouse, he was taunting her, leaving the lipstick with Jean's negative in it until last to build the suspense to an unbearable pitch. She would have been better off coolly thinking up an explanation for its presence than sweating on its discovery.

At last, he unscrewed the false half of her lipstick and shook it. Friedl held her breath. Nothing fell out.

Fighting the urge to burst into hysterical, relieved laughter, Friedl dug her fingernails into her palms and waited. Had someone else removed the negative? Someone who was keeping it from von Rönne for their own purposes, perhaps?

Frowning, the colonel bent his head and peered inside the false bottom. He took off his spectacles and set them aside, then squinted again into the small barrel. Another hunt in his desk drawer produced a pair of silver tweezers. After much poking and prodding at the inner edge of the lipstick barrel, von Rönne breathed out a small, satisfied sigh. He tweezed the negative free.

Colonel von Rönne held the snippet of film with Jean's photograph on it up to the light. Then he looked at Friedl. "I think . . . Yes, really, Miss Stöttinger, I think you must explain this to me."

* * *

Friedl stared at the negative and her mind went blank.

"Fräulein?" prompted von Rönne

Come on, Friedl. She must pull herself together. Considering all the lies she'd told already, there was no going back now. After withstanding the rest of von Rönne's interrogation, she couldn't balk at this last hurdle.

"Oh, is that where that was?" Her voice was so raspy, she wasn't sure it would hold out for the entire explanation. "Please, may I have some water?" she whispered. "I've almost lost my voice."

Von Rönne stared at her. Then he nodded, indicating that she should help herself.

Licking her dry lips, Friedl followed von Rönne's example, taking her time over pouring herself water. She offered him some, which he refused. She gulped down the first tumblerful, feeling as if she was trying to swallow around a rock that was lodged in her throat. It hurt, but she kept going and greedily poured herself some more before the colonel could stop her.

Finally, nursing her second glass of water, and with the pressure in her bladder now at crisis level, Friedl cleared her throat a couple of times and forced herself to continue. "Well, I was in such a rush to leave for the airport yesterday, I forgot about it."

Von Rönne waited, clearly believing he'd given her more than enough rope with which to hang herself. She needed no assistance from him at this point.

"I stole the negative, you see," said Friedl. "From Pam. The fiancée. She was busy making me a cup of tea, and while she was distracted, I rifled through her handbag." This was true enough in its essentials. "She mentioned she'd had the photograph blown up and framed for Major Martin since he liked it so much. A sort of engagement present, I suppose. I took the negative thinking it would be corroborating evidence—at least, it proves I made contact with Pam."

"But why not include it with your report?" von Rönne asked the obvious question. "Why conceal it like this?"

Friedl glanced around, then leaned forward. "I wasn't sure whom to trust."

His eyebrows lifted. "You mean you didn't trust Kühlenthal with this piece of evidence?"

She shrugged. "I thought that at least if I had that piece of film securely hidden, I could produce it to lend credence to my story when I needed to." She spread her hands. "I am an ambitious woman, Colonel. I didn't want Kühlenthal taking all the credit."

There was a pause. Von Rönne turned his head to stare out of the window for some time, before he turned to look at the negative again. "So Kühlenthal knows nothing about this?"

Friedl shook her head. "You're the only one I've told."

Von Rönne was silent. Then he said, "The trouble is, Miss Stöttinger, that I simply don't believe you."

"But—"

He held up a hand. "As I said before, the Führer likes intelligence to be clear-cut." He picked up the negative. "This muddies the waters in a way that helps no one." He turned the negative in his hand until he held it by the edge between finger and thumb. Then he flicked his lighter and set fire to the corner, dropping the burning scrap of film into his ashtray.

A strong, chemical smell filled Friedl's nostrils. She felt faint and dizzy and thoroughly confused. "But why—"

"You won't mention this negative to anyone, Miss Stöttinger," said von Rönne. An order, not a request. He clicked the clasp shut on her purse and set it on the desk in front of her. "That will be all. You'll take the next flight back to Lisbon."

Friedl simply stared. She was lost for words, every last vestige of wit and energy absolutely spent. It would have taken very little to have made her spill every secret she knew right then and there, even if it meant her immediate arrest.

"My secretary will show you to a room where you can freshen up and wait," said von Rönne. "Don't speak to anyone. Not a word until you are back in England again."

If her voice hadn't deserted her, she would have assured him of her obedience. At his nod of dismissal, Friedl put down her glass and picked up her thoroughly defiled purse. She got to her feet on wobbly legs, clutching at the chair back for support. The distance to the door seemed three miles, and her senses swam once or twice as she shuffled toward it, but finally she made it. At the door, she was tempted to look back to make sure von Rönne wasn't still playing with her. Would he call her name at the last minute and begin the interrogation all over again? His remark about sending her back on the next flight didn't ring true.

In fact, the reaction of von Rönne to her story had been so capricious, so illogical and unexpected, that it felt as if the slightest untoward movement or word might reverse his decision and have her arrested or executed on the spot.

Nevertheless Friedl dug into the last reserves of grit she possessed and made herself reach for the brass door handle without a backward glance. There was a moment, when she struggled to push open the heavy door, that she thought she might burst into tears. But at last, the door gave way, and she could walk out of that office.

She wouldn't breathe easily again until she was safely back home in her London flat.

London, England
May 1943

"Good Heavens, Friedl!" Joan Miller was among the first to greet her when Friedl stepped off the plane from Lisbon. "What on earth happened to you over there?"

Friedl badly wanted to throw her arms around Joan and burst

into tears. "I'm a little tired, *liebling*," she said instead, walking with her over to the awaiting car. "Do you think they'll let me go home before it all starts again?"

The answer was no, of course. Friedl fell asleep on the drive to London, her head on Joan's shoulder. All too soon, Joan's voice recalled her from slumber. They seemed to have reached their destination. The car door opened and a hard-faced individual who had more than a whiff of Special Branch about him indicated that Friedl should get out.

Friedl glanced at Joan over her shoulder and tried to sound amused. "What? Do they think I'm going to attack someone?"

"This is Peter. Just routine security. Don't worry." Joan smiled reassuringly, but she didn't seem to be getting out as well. Friedl suppressed the urge to beg her friend not to leave her with these people.

As Friedl alighted from the car, she recognized her surroundings. She was stepping out into the colonnade of the Ritz Hotel.

Automatically, she put a hand to her hair. She must look a perfect fright. At least it was early evening and she would be less likely to run into anyone she knew.

"Follow me, please," said Peter.

She straightened her spine and marched into the hotel after him. They passed through the foyer, and Friedl noted that a burly individual who did not look at all like a hotel porter was dealing with her suitcase. She was to be staying overnight at the Ritz, then. They must anticipate that this debrief would take a while.

She shivered. The opulence of the accommodation MI-5 had chosen was no indication of how they would treat her. She'd heard this was where the intelligence services often interrogated double agents and foreign defectors. In other words, the forthcoming debrief could go either way.

They went up in the elevator and turned down a hallway. When they came to the door to the suite at the end of the corridor, Peter said to her, "Arms out, please."

Friedl had to ask him to repeat the direction before she understood. As she held out her arms to be patted down, it said a lot for her level of fatigue that she couldn't even summon a flirtatious remark.

Apparently satisfied that she didn't conceal any weapons on her body, Peter took her purse from her and then turned to knock on the door.

It opened to reveal Tar. That was a familiar face, at least. He smiled. "Good evening, Miss Stöttinger. Good to see you back in one piece. What a time of it you've had, eh?"

So far, so good.

When she reached the sitting room, she saw that C was also present—hence the security, she realized. Stewart Menzies. Head of the Secret Intelligence Service and incidentally, her sister Lisi's brother-in-law. Far from being reassured by his presence, Friedl's heart began to pound. Her sojourn in Berlin had catapulted her from lowly asset status to an agent whose debrief warranted the attention of the intelligence chief himself.

"Before we begin, may I powder my nose?" She needed time to collect herself.

"Of course," said C, raising his eyebrows, as if surprised that she'd need to ask. He turned his head and nodded at Peter, who had been rifling through the contents of her purse. The Special Branch officer kept the lipstick with the false bottom but handed her the rest.

The mirror in the en suite revealed that her face was pale, her hair a bit of a mess. Friedl was surprised that after the ordeal she'd been through, she didn't look ten times more haggard. The thought occurred that it might be better for her if she had appeared wan and damaged. Would they believe that at Bendlerblock she'd been treated as a suspect rather than as a friend? Would anyone credit that von Rönne hadn't believed her story but had still let her go? The truth sounded utterly implausible, but she was far too overwrought even to contemplate telling more lies.

Friedl set her purse on the bathroom counter, turned on the faucet, and splashed her face. With trembling hands, she sorted through her ruined cosmetics and recalled her vow never to use them again. She stared at the compact, which had been handled with such delicate, deadly precision by von Rönne, and shuddered. The comb she did use out of desperation and vanity, pinning her hair into a simple French twist. Then she clasped her purse shut and rejoined the others.

Friedl had to hand it to the British. This interrogation was far more comfortable and friendly than the grilling she'd received from von Rönne. They ordered a delicious meal to be brought. Friedl was ravenous and hardly noticed what she ate, but with regret, she refused the wine. She needed her wits about her for this.

After an hour or more of after-dinner banter, Friedl had had enough. With a forced smile, she said, "Gentlemen, I know why I'm here. I will happily tell you everything, but I have one condition."

They blinked at her in surprise, as if she were a dog who'd started to talk.

"Oh, you do, do you?" Tar permitted himself a slight smile. "And what might that be?"

"That you allow me to become a British citizen once the war is over. I think that after all this I've earned the right."

"Well, now, Friedl," said C, leaning forward and folding his hands together. "That all rather depends on what you have to say."

CHAPTER TWENTY-THREE

London, England
May 1943

Friedl

When Friedl finally arrived back at her flat the following evening after a full day's interview with Tar and C, all she wanted was to crawl beneath the covers. She burst into her apartment and headed for her soft, warm bed, stripping as she went.

It wasn't until she reached the bedroom that she realized. The lamp in the sitting room. She never would have left it on like that.

A soft scuffle made her freeze and turn her head to stare toward the sound. Was someone there? One of Wolkoff's followers? Or an officer from British intelligence, perhaps. Had her interrogators' smiles been hiding their disbelief? Maybe Popov had convinced Tar that Friedl was a triple agent, after all.

Heart pounding, Friedl reached over and eased open her bedside table drawer. She snatched up her cosh and crept to the doorway of her bedroom, straining to listen.

The sound of footsteps galvanized her. She rushed out, cosh raised, and brought it down hard on the head of the intruder.

When she looked closely at the woman lying unconscious on the rug, Friedl realized her mistake. At some point in the course of her attack, she'd half registered that the trespasser was a diminutive figure—hardly the type of heavy Anna Wolkoff or the security services would send to do their wet work. But Friedl had been so full of fear and nervous energy that she hadn't stopped to think, nor to consider how foolhardy it had been to go on the offensive like that. If her adversary *had* been a professional, she'd have been the one who ended up unconscious on the floor. Or worse.

Now it seemed she'd coshed quite an ordinary-looking young woman. A girl, really, no older than Jean Leslie.

Friedl stooped to check the woman's pulse and found it strong and steady. *Thank goodness!* Huffing out a breath of relief, she went to telephone Joan Miller. Hopefully it would be the last time she'd need her friend to bail her out of trouble.

When Joan arrived, she said, "Oh, Friedl, no! What on earth happened?"

After hearing Friedl's story, Joan commented, "Well, at least you didn't shoot her. Where *is* my pistol, by the way? I'm sure they didn't let you near C with it. Oh, never mind. Here, help me lift her onto the couch."

When they had settled Friedl's victim as comfortably as they could, Friedl said, "Smelling salts." She fetched the sal volatile from the bathroom and returned to find her friend searching the victim's purse. Joan fished out an identity card and scanned it. "Ridsdale. Hmm."

"Do you know her?"

"She's one of ours," said Joan, taking the smelling salts from Friedl. "Let's see what she has to say."

* * *

A pungent smell brought Paddy sharply to her senses with a gasp. Her nostrils burned and there was a rushing sound in her ears. A pretty young woman with dark hair was bending over her.

When Paddy tried to scramble up, a great throb of pain radiated from her temple right down into her jaw and the back of her neck. She fell back with a cry. How had she come to be like this? Trying to think physically hurt.

The woman smiled. "Don't worry, Mrs. Ridsdale. You're perfectly safe. My name is Joan and I'm going to help you."

Then it came back. Searching the flat, the stunning blow. Who had hit her? Gingerly, Paddy touched what was now becoming quite an egg on the back of her skull. "My head . . ."

A tall, blond woman with a heavy accent—who must, of course, be Friedl—addressed her. "Well, what do you expect when you go around breaking into people's apartments like that?"

Indeed. Bereft of her usual quickness, Paddy could only stare up at her, trying to come up with a plausible excuse.

"Never mind that now," said Joan in a sweet, cultured voice. "Mrs. Ridsdale, you need to stay calm and still for a little while."

"Oh, but I can't. I must get back." Again, Paddy struggled to sit up but the crushing pain in her head made her whimper and sink into the cushions, fighting the urge to vomit.

"Please do as I say," said Joan. She glanced at Friedl. "Perhaps she needs to see a doctor."

"No! No doctor." Paddy's voice came out in a thready whisper, not because she was afraid, but because all the energy seemed to have drained from her body. Even talking took quite an effort and made her head pound harder. She swallowed. "This is all . . . a complete misunderstanding."

"Yes?" said Joan, tilting her head. "I don't know how that can be. You broke into my friend's apartment and were searching it like a criminal. A criminal who happened to bring her purse with her identity card inside it." Joan smiled a little at Paddy's chagrin. "Mrs. Ridsdale, I know who you are and who you work for, so please don't be alarmed." Her brow furrowed. "But you look very pale. Perhaps you do need a doctor."

"No, I—" Then Paddy felt a wet warmth beneath her. She was bleeding. "The baby!" Fretfully, she placed her palms over her abdomen as if that would keep her child safe. "No, not the baby. Oh, no!" There was a burning sensation behind her eyes and the throbbing in her head increased.

"*Baby?*" Friedl echoed, sounding incredulous.

Joan took Paddy's hand in a firm clasp. "Don't worry, Mrs. Ridsdale. We'll take care of you."

But Paddy was so appalled and confused, she could only repeat, "Julian . . . The baby . . ." Oh, why couldn't she think? *Pull yourself together, Paddy!*

"Let's get you to the hospital," said Joan calmly. "Try not to worry now, Mrs. Ridsdale. You're going to be all right."

But she couldn't know that, could she? Paddy bit her lip,

struggling not to drown in the fear and remorse that flooded her chest. She needed to do everything she could to protect her baby. She would fight to keep this child with every last breath.

* * *

What followed terrified Paddy more than the evacuation from France, more than the bombs that had rained down on London or the incendiary device on her roof, more than the terrible realization that she'd been caught breaking into a possible enemy agent's flat. The bleeding had been minimal, thank goodness, but she developed a fever and had to be kept under close observation while it was brought under control.

Those fretful hours were filled with hot, dank nightmares and chills that racked her body. In lucid moments her mind raced from one dire prediction to the next. She wanted Julian. She wanted her mother, too, but no one except the medical staff was allowed to see Paddy for another twenty-four hours after the fever subsided. In between bouts of fitful sleep, she had more than enough time to dread the forthcoming reunion with Julian. He'd become suspicious and unhappy with her even before he'd learned about her pregnancy. He must have been shocked and hurt to have found out about the baby from a stranger, and in such distressing circumstances, as well.

When he was finally allowed to see her, Julian's face was pale and drawn. The enormity of what she'd done to him hit home then like never before.

Had she lost him forever? Paddy, who had not given in to tears throughout the entire war, couldn't contain her grief. A whimper burst from her. Then a great, anguished sob. *Please. Please don't say I've lost him. Not after all this.*

Julian's face underwent a transformation—a softening—so complete, he seemed like a different man. "Oh, my dear. My poor, darling Paddy."

In three strides he was at her bedside, bending to gather her gingerly in his arms.

"I'm so sorry!" Paddy wept into Julian's shoulder and clung to him tightly. "It's all my fault." And the worst of it was, she could never tell him why.

"No, no, darling," he said vehemently. "Never." He kissed her forehead and smoothed back her hair.

"Please forgive me." She had no right to ask it of him, particularly not now, when she was looking so pathetic and his sympathy was stirred. Not when she was still lying to him.

"My darling Paddy, there is nothing to forgive."

But she didn't believe him. How could she? And how could she live with the fact that it was only her deceit over what she'd been doing to get herself coshed on the head that prevented him from truly blaming her for her recklessness?

Days passed before Paddy was allowed to leave the hospital. By some miracle, they'd kept the baby safe. She was out of danger now, but her doctor had ordered her to stay in bed for another two weeks and to take it easy for the remainder of her pregnancy.

The forced inactivity following her hospital stay made Paddy restless to the screaming point. Apart from everything else, she was burning to know the outcome of Operation Mincemeat.

Had the body been found? Had the Spanish allowed the Germans access to the documents they'd discovered? If not, had the Germans found a way to extract the intelligence covertly? And had that information gone up the chain of command? Most important, did Hitler believe the narrative the British had so carefully constructed?

Of most immediate concern to Paddy, however, was the question of what Friedl Stöttinger had done with Jean's negative. Like Cholmondeley, Joan Miller had as good as told her not to trouble her pretty head over it. And if Joan truly did work at the War Office and she knew Friedl, as she'd claimed, then Paddy supposed all might be well in that department. She had to pray that was the case.

Paddy scoured the newspapers daily but found not a single clue to the success or failure of Operation Mincemeat. She wished she could talk to Montagu and Cholmondeley, or even Jean. Since Paddy had canceled her engagements for the next couple of weeks, she had no opportunity to track down any of the officers who might be in a position to know. In the meantime, she had little to do but mull over her horrible feeling of guilt toward her husband.

At first, Julian had been gentle and attentive, but as Paddy's health improved, the pain in his gaze when it rested on her slowly hardened into a sort of feigned indifference. That hurt Paddy more than the blow to the head.

She almost wished Julian had berated her over keeping the baby a secret. Somehow, that might have lessened her feeling of guilt. At least, she didn't regret taking part in Operation Mincemeat, but she did regret keeping the news about her pregnancy to herself for so long. And what had she been thinking, to put herself and the baby in danger by breaking into the flat of a possible enemy agent? That she knew best, as usual. How utterly wrong she'd been.

Well, if she sought punishment for her crimes, she was certainly getting it. Once Paddy was up and about again, Julian began to avoid being alone with her. He left early for work and dined at one of his clubs more often than not. Once, he came home very drunk. She heard him stumbling about in his dressing room and waited for a chance to talk, hoping that it might be a case of in vino veritas and finally they could have it all out in the open—or most of it, anyway. Perhaps he might actually talk to her about what was on his mind instead of bottling it up for fear it would upset her and somehow put the baby at risk.

But he didn't come to bed at all that evening. From that night on, Julian began sleeping in his dressing room routinely after coming home late. Needing her rest more and more these days, Paddy gave up trying to stay awake for his return.

"You don't think Julian has another woman, do you?" said Edith one morning with her characteristic bluntness. If even Paddy's mother had noticed their estrangement, it was serious, indeed.

"What? Of course not." Julian simply wasn't that sort of man. Not like Ian Fleming, who couldn't remain faithful to a woman if his life depended on it. "He simply isn't the type."

"Well," replied Edith, with a healthy dose of skepticism in her tone, "I'm sure you know best, dear."

Paddy wasn't so certain anymore that she did. What if Julian, civil but increasingly distant from her, found understanding and sympathy in the arms of another woman? A woman with the kind of sweet and pliable nature that Paddy had never possessed? A woman who would never put a secret war operation ahead of her husband and child, who would dutifully pass her days in the country, safely distant from the stresses and horrors of war.

Well, she still didn't believe Julian would stray, but one thing was certain: if the two of them continued to grow apart like this, they might never manage to bridge that gap again.

They couldn't avoid the subject any longer. She needed to have it out with him. Now that she was back on her feet and less an object of pity, she could have a proper stand-up row with him. She owed him that.

* * *

To armor herself for the battle royal with Julian, Paddy put on a full face of makeup and had Berry arrange her hair. She dressed in a cornflower-blue tea gown that fell gracefully over her small pregnancy bump, then went to find Julian in his study.

This room was formerly a parlor at the front of the house and had been dedicated to Julian's use when he and Paddy moved in. He had certainly made it his own, decorating it with various artifacts collected during his brief sojourn in Japan before the war.

These days, it wasn't the done thing to profess such affinity for the Japanese, of course, but Julian had been so enchanted by the country when he'd been stationed there that even the nation's entry into the war on the side of the Axis powers hadn't dimmed his admiration.

He was leafing through a collection of lithographs that he'd begun to catalog when Paddy walked in. "Julian," she said, stepping into the room and shutting the door behind her. "We need to talk."

"Can it wait, Paddy?" He didn't look up from his task, and that told its own tale.

"I'm afraid it can't." She willed him to give her his full attention, but he kept staring at the lithograph in his hand. Craning her neck, she saw that it depicted a stormy sea. "It's important, Julian. Will you put that away and sit down with me, please?"

After a slight hesitation, he complied. They sat down together on the sofa by the fireplace, but Julian did not sling an arm around her affectionately as he had always done in the past. He angled his body away from her, crossing one long leg over the other, which effectively moved him as far from her as possible while still sitting on the same piece of furniture.

All right. She deserved this. "I want to apologize," she said, twisting her fingers together. "I shouldn't have kept the news about the baby to myself for so long."

Julian regarded her impassively. "I'm sure you had your reasons," he said at last.

So he was going to be stubborn about it. She licked her lips. "Well, at first it was because I wasn't sure and I didn't want to get your hopes up."

"And later?"

"Later, I just . . ." *I was working on a secret mission for Naval*

Intelligence, she wanted to say. Instead, she said, "Well, I didn't want to leave London. Or you. Ireland seemed so very far away."

Julian looked incredulous. "If you hadn't wanted to leave, you could have just said so. I'm hardly a Bluebeard, my dear. And you're not exactly a shrinking violet, either, might I remind you."

"Well, when you're an expectant mother it's all different," said Paddy, driven against the ropes. "People make you feel guilty for not putting the baby before everything else, and I wanted to carry on as normal for as long as I could."

"By 'people,' I gather you mean me," said Julian, flushing. "And I suppose you're going to tell me that you would just as likely have fainted and ended up in hospital if you'd been in Ireland, as well."

Paddy opened her mouth to retort, then shut it again. She never would have been coshed on the head if she hadn't been busy searching Friedl Stöttinger's apartment.

"Julian," she said, "you *know* how much I hate to admit it when I'm wrong." She threw her shoulders back and lifted her chin. "Well, I was wrong! I should have told you. I should have taken things easier. I mean, I truly don't wish to spend the rest of the war in Ireland away from you, but if that's what you want—"

"Do you think that's really the trouble between us?" said Julian. "Not telling me about the baby?"

Paddy stared at him. "Well . . . isn't it?"

"No!" Julian flung out a hand. "It's that I hardly know my own wife anymore. You delayed telling me about the baby, but that's not all you've concealed from me lately, is it?"

Suddenly Paddy was walking across a narrow bridge that

might crumble beneath her at any moment. Cautiously she said, "What on earth are you talking about?"

Julian counted off his fingers. "First, I surprise you at home after hearing about that mysterious doctor's appointment, and it's abundantly clear the surprise is unwelcome. *Then* I find you're also not wearing your wedding rings. What sort of conclusion can any man draw from that?" She might have spoken if she'd known what to say, but he went on. "And to top it off, you go somewhere overnight with some half-baked excuse about needing to rescue Jean from some boyfriend or other. I mean, just who is this fellow you've been writing love letters to?"

Paddy was so stunned, she could only stare. Julian went to his desk and picked up a piece of foolscap. He held it out to her.

Automatically she took the page and bent her gaze to read. Her heart stopped as she scanned the words. A few, incriminating lines of "Pam's" love letter to Major Martin. A love letter that hadn't even been used at the end of the day.

"One of the maids found it beneath the blotter on your desk. Naturally, she assumed it was for me." He paused. "But you never write love letters, do you, Paddy? At least, not any that I've received."

Heat rushed to her cheeks. How utterly stupid and careless and *unprofessional* of her to accidentally leave this somewhere anyone might find it! And how hurt Julian must have been.

The corner of her husband's mouth quirked upward in a sardonic smile. "Who is it, Paddy? Not Fleming. Please, not him."

"No, no, of course not!" exclaimed Paddy, horrified. "Listen, Julian. I can't explain it all to you, but please, please believe me.

This is not what it looks like. None of it is. I would *never* do something like that."

"You can't explain," Julian repeated flatly.

Miserably, Paddy shook her head.

"And I'm simply supposed to trust you." Julian rubbed a hand over his eyes. Suddenly, he looked very tired.

The statement hung between them. Paddy drew a deep breath and chose her words carefully. "If you are willing to put this behind us now, I promise you—*promise* you, Julian—that you will never have cause to be suspicious of me ever again."

He was silent for a long time. Then he got up and went to his desk. He shoved a hand in his trouser pocket and picked up one of the lithographs he'd been inspecting when she'd come in, then put it back again.

Still with his back to her, he said in a subdued tone, "Then am I never to know what all this was about?"

She hesitated. Would it be so very bad to give him the truth? He must have pretty high security clearance in his own right, and anyway, Julian wouldn't tell another soul if she did let him in on the secret. Her marriage, their happiness, their *life*, hung in the balance.

But she'd signed the *Official Secrets Act* and she'd given her word to Admiral Godfrey, to Fleming, and to Montagu as well that she would never divulge the work she'd done for the NID. Oaths like that meant something. She'd never dreamed that this secret would be likely to cost her Julian's love, but in the end, if what they had together couldn't survive this, then it wasn't a very strong foundation to begin with.

"No, Julian," she said. "It's not my secret to tell. But I love you more than anything in the world. I have never broken our marriage vows. I have never looked at another man, and I never will."

She hesitated. Perhaps it was unfair of her to say this, but she had to. "I want you to know how important it is to me that you believe me, that you take it on faith that I am the woman you know and love. I have made mistakes and concealed the truth from you, but I am not lying about this. I love you, Julian. *Please*." Paddy felt that this was her last chance to get through to him. "Please have faith in me."

The silence when she'd finished was the longest Paddy had ever known. She wanted to put her arms around him, but a physical expression of affection felt like cheating. Julian had to decide, once and for all, whether he was prepared to let the past lie.

"Very well," he whispered. "I'll try."

Paddy went to him then and touched his shoulder. "You won't regret it, darling. I'll spend the rest of my life making sure of that."

Julian gripped her hand, then turned to face her, and his expression was so full of anguish and love, it made her heart turn over. He opened his arms and she threw herself into them. He enfolded her in a tight embrace, as if he would never let her go.

CHAPTER TWENTY-FOUR

London, England
August 1943

Friedl

There was a problem with Friedl's request for British citizenship. She was informed that the British government had no plans to naturalize any German double agents once the war was over. If the agents continued in service, that was different. In Friedl's case, with her usefulness waning already, it was almost certain that her petition would be denied. The Germans were no longer paying her for information, and the security services seemed to have little further use for her. Yet she couldn't obtain any other kind of paid employment on a German passport. She was completely stuck.

To his credit, M advocated strongly for her, pointing out that it was entirely due to MI-5's requirement that Friedl renounce her Austrian citizenship in order to work for them that she was in this predicament. The plea fell on deaf ears.

"I'll keep trying," he told her, "but I can't say it will be resolved until the war is over. And even then . . ." He rubbed his large nose. "I am sorry. I wish I had better news."

Although von Rönne had released Friedl after that short stint at Bendlerblock, she now considered her cover blown. That being the case, there was little likelihood that the British would continue to use her as a double agent. She said as much to Tar when she met him at a dinner party at Lady Bonham Carter's, which the prime minister himself would attend.

Tar begged to differ. "All the intelligence we've received indicates otherwise. For one thing, Tricycle is still in play."

"He is?" Friedl's shoulders dropped. What a relief! Despite the way he'd treated her, she hadn't wanted to expose Popov as a double agent for the British. The very first thing she'd done when she reached Lisbon was to beg them to get Popov out. But from what Tar was saying, it seemed Popov had been right to keep a cool head about the matter. Popov was safe—or as safe as a double agent could be. Despite his harsh treatment of her in Estoril, relief flooded her chest.

"I understand if von Rönne didn't want to muddy the waters with anything that might seem to contradict what Hitler wanted to believe," murmured Friedl, conscious of any other guests who might be listening. "But why would he leave Tricycle in play?"

Tar shrugged. "The tide of the war has turned, Miss Stöttinger. Mussolini's been deposed. The Italians are being driven against the ropes. Perhaps von Rönne wants to be on the right side of history. End the war with his country still in one piece."

If that were the case . . . Friedl shuddered at how lucky she'd been. "Had von Rönne been loyal to Hitler, I might have been executed as an enemy agent."

"Well, not necessarily," said Tar. "You will recall Kühlenthal's eagerness to sell the story to German High Command. It's entirely possible that he would have garnered sufficient support among the yes men that surround Hitler to have persuaded him the intelligence was real. And none of the Abwehr fact-checkers seem to have come up with anything contradictory, either."

"But how can you be so sure the operation succeeded?" Friedl still wasn't entirely clear about what the operation had been.

Tar's eyes twinkled. "Let's just say the proof was in the pudding." Which made absolutely no sense to her. But before she could ask for illumination, Tar had excused himself and moved on.

Friedl was soon surrounded by acquaintances. She sipped champagne, laughed and chattered with them as if she had not recently risked her life on a secret mission in Berlin.

Well, Popov had been right about her, but he had been wrong, too. At the final hour, she had not betrayed the British or Popov, either. At least, not willingly.

Commander Fleming came in then, and Friedl immediately excused herself. She wasn't entirely sure what his role in the intelligence services might be, but perhaps he had influence and could help her with her little citizenship problem. He seemed like a useful man to know.

The commander greeted her with apparent pleasure, but when she started talking to him about her naturalization, he began to look bored. "Why don't you let me take you home afterward and we can discuss it there?"

Inwardly, Friedl sighed. This man was certainly no Duško Popov. "Tempting though that offer is, *liebling*, I am otherwise engaged tonight."

But Fleming wasn't even listening. Someone across the room had caught his eye and he nodded in response. "Seems I'm being summoned." He relieved Friedl of her drink and set it down with his on an occasional table. "You ought to come along, too."

Was this about her involvement with the fake Major Martin? Friedl saw several other guests file out of the drawing room. All very mysterious. She shrugged and followed the commander.

"Well, hello there!" A touch on her elbow made Friedl turn. The American diplomat she'd met a few months before was gazing at her with delight and wonder, as if she were a goddess descended to earth.

"Mr. Calder." She smiled with real pleasure, remembering that he'd seen her home from a party one evening and accepted her rebuff with very good grace. She'd had the impression that beneath his amusing banter, Calder's interest in her had been sincere. At the time she'd been too much in thrall to Duško Popov to think seriously about anyone else. Now . . .

"I'm surprised you remember me," she said. "It's been a while."

"Four months, in fact," replied the American with flattering promptness. "I've thought of you often." He rubbed his chin ruefully. "Truth is, Miss Stöttinger, I just couldn't get you out of my mind."

Friedl knew what that was like. Well, Duško's spell had been broken that horrible night in Estoril. She was free to love again.

London, England
June 1943

Paddy

"How very sad!" exclaimed Paddy's mother at the breakfast table one morning. "Leslie Howard died. He was in a plane that was shot down by the Luftwaffe over the Bay of Biscay."

"Oh, no!" said Paddy, willing herself not to tear up at the news that a film star who was, in reality, a complete stranger to her, had been killed. She found herself weeping at the slightest provocation these days. Really there was no end to the delights of pregnancy. She particularly loathed being a watering pot, and Julian often teased her about it, deliberately reading sad stories to her just to watch those unaccustomed tears flow.

Julian's willingness to put the past behind them had gone a long way toward healing their rift. Paddy dared to hope that once the baby arrived, all the pain and resentment of the recent months would disappear completely. Without telling Julian the truth about Operation Mincemeat there was no way she could think of to erase any doubts he might still harbor about her loyalty. Her plea for Julian's trust had not fallen on deaf ears, however. He must have known how uncharacteristic it was for her to be sneaking around with another man.

"It's rather upsetting," Edith was saying with a quaver in her voice as she scanned the newspaper article. "Not that one knows Leslie Howard personally, of course."

"But it feels as if one does after all the films he was in." Paddy moved to read the headlines over her mother's shoulder. "I must have seen *The Scarlet Pimpernel* five times."

"You said you thought Ashley in *Gone with the Wind* was a terrific drip," observed Julian, looking up briefly from the financial section of the *Times*.

"Well, the character was, but that's not to say Howard didn't play the role well," said Paddy, scanning the film star's obituary. "In fact, I . . ." She broke off, staring down at the newsprint.

"In fact, you . . ." Julian prompted. But Paddy didn't answer. Her attention had snagged on a smaller death notice opposite the article about the actor.

Major William Martin.

The Royal Marine's body had been found.

The oddest sensation came over her. Not quite the shock and sadness of a bereavement—never that—but a feeling of melancholy and deep pity for the man who had all unwittingly sacrificed himself for their unconventional mission. Glyndwr Michael had served a higher purpose in death than he had in life. At least, that was how Paddy saw it. The man himself might have thought quite differently. However that might be, she hoped and prayed that his contribution hadn't been in vain.

Desperate to know the outcome, Paddy fought the urge to race around to the Admiralty and demand to see Ewen Montagu at once.

"Paddy?" Julian's voice recalled her to the present. He chuck-led. "Wandering in the clouds again?"

It was true that another effect of expecting a baby was a dread-ful woolly-headedness that sometimes descended over her brain and made her dreamy and forgetful. Julian seemed to find these occasional lapses as delightful and endearing as her tendency to weep, but they drove Paddy mad.

This hadn't been one of those lapses, but she could hardly explain that to Julian. "Oh!" she said. "Ah . . ." What had they been talking about? That's right. Leslie Howard in *Gone with the Wind*. "In fact, I didn't like that movie half as much as everyone else seemed to."

If only she could find out what was going on with Major Martin! Now that she was up and about again, Paddy burned to speak with someone from the Admiralty who might tell her. However, since Julian's accusations, she'd felt rather like a young lady from the Victorian age who needed a chaperone every-where she went. Like Caesar's wife, she must be above reproach. No tripping off to the Gargoyle Club with Jean to meet up with Montagu and Cholmondeley, and certainly no private conversa-tions with Commander Fleming, either. Not that Julian himself imposed these restrictions on her. It was her own guilt that set the constraints.

For more than a month, Paddy continued to scour the news-papers for clues. The Allied invasion of Sicily had finally begun, but security measures meant that news articles didn't discuss troop movements or other specifics, so she couldn't deduce whether the Germans had fallen for Operation Mincemeat or not. She quizzed Jean, but her friend knew no more than she did herself. Jean seemed not to have seen much of her "Bill" since the operation concluded. Whether that was due to the photograph incident or Montagu's wife objecting to their flirtation, Paddy didn't know and didn't ask.

It wasn't until August that Paddy came across anyone who might tell her what was going on. She and Julian were invited to a very important dinner with very important people, including the prime minister himself.

The evening began inauspiciously from Paddy's point of view. When she and Julian arrived, the first person they ran into was none other than Commander Fleming, who was walking up the front steps at the same time, accompanied by Muriel Wright.

Fleming nodded to them both. "Evening, Mrs. Ridsdale. Captain Ridsdale."

Julian returned the greeting pleasantly enough and Paddy gave an inward sigh of relief. She nodded to Fleming. "Commander."

"Hello, you!" Muriel hugged Paddy and kissed her cheek. She smelled of lily of the valley. "Splendid to see you up and about again. Have you talked to Jean lately? She mentioned she'd be here tonight."

As the two couples handed their coats to the butler, Paddy itched to collar her former commanding officer and pepper him with questions about Operation Mincemeat, but with Julian present such behavior would be tactless in the extreme. Instead she devoted her attention to Muriel as they followed their escorts into the drawing room.

"You look smashing," said Paddy. Muriel's willowy form was clad in a Grecian gown of ivory silk with a plunging neckline and an even lower back.

"I do, don't I?" Muriel heaved a sigh. "Not that *he'd* notice."

Paddy didn't know what to say to that. She'd spoken her mind about Fleming to Muriel long ago but it hadn't done a particle of good. She'd learned to hold her peace.

They watched as Fleming promptly abandoned his companion to buttonhole Lord Mountbatten, then Paddy linked arms with Muriel. "Let's get you a drink."

Their hostess greeted them and introduced them to several other guests. Julian gravitated toward his uncle and a few other Conservative Party stalwarts, so he was in his element. When Paddy saw Ewen Montagu walk in, she nearly jumped out of her skin with excitement. Tonight, she would find out whether the mission was a success or perish in the attempt.

Unfortunately, getting Montagu alone was difficult. He was a popular figure, always surrounded by other people. It took her the best part of half an hour, but she finally managed to maneuver herself into a small group that included Montagu. Julian was there, too, but Paddy could contain herself no longer.

"I hear you've been *fishing* recently, Captain Montagu," she murmured under cover of another conversation.

"Fishing?" echoed the captain, his thick black brows jamming together. His expression lightened. "Oh. Ah! Yes. Fishing. Helps me relax."

"And wasn't there a *particular* kind of fish you were hoping to catch?" said Paddy under her breath. "Did it take the bait?"

A sparkle lit his eye and he bowed. "It did, indeed, Mrs. Ridsdale. It did, indeed. Swallowed it rod, line, and sinker, in fact."

They'd done it! Jubilation flooded Paddy, swirling up from her chest, rushing down to her toes. They'd convinced the Germans about Major William, and Pam, and the invasion point—all of it! It was so unlikely, so fantastical, she could scarcely believe it was true. She wanted to cheer and jump for joy, grab Jean and Cholmondeley and even Ian Fleming and perform a victory conga line around the room.

But she couldn't do any of that, could she? No one would ever know what she'd done, and that was just how it should be.

At that moment, she caught Commander Fleming's eye across the crowded room. He nodded to her, as to a colleague, and raised his glass in a silent toast. Forcing herself not to grin like a loon, she coolly nodded back. His ridiculous idea had succeeded. British Naval Intelligence had taken on the German Abwehr and won!

A young man appeared at Montagu's elbow and murmured something into his ear. The captain's eyebrows rose. "He does? Yes, yes, of course." Montagu looked across the room at Cholmondeley and gave a jerk of his chin. By now the two of them seemed to communicate via some kind of telepathy. The flight lieutenant tipped an imaginary hat at Montagu and excused himself from his circle.

As Cholmondeley joined them, Montagu addressed Julian. "Might we borrow your wife for a moment, Ridsdale? Mrs. Ridsdale, will you join us?" Before her husband could answer, Montagu turned away, ushering Paddy toward the door. Paddy glanced back at Julian and mouthed *Sorry*, but she was glowing from head to toe with excitement, so she was worried her silent apology might fall flat. But no, Julian wasn't annoyed. Eyes alight with curiosity, he gave her a small, encouraging wave.

In a salon off the drawing room, Paddy found herself in the midst of several people she recognized as having been crowded around that table in Room 13 on the morning of her first brief-ing. Fleming stood apart from the rest, leaning on the chimney piece, smoking and looking as if he'd rather be elsewhere. At the center of them all sat Winston Churchill, his round cheekbones rosy and the ash of his cigar climbing steadily toward his stubby fingers.

Paddy's skin tingled with anticipation as other guests drifted in a handful at a time. Clearly, they were waiting for everyone to arrive before the prime minister made an announcement. She wished the stragglers would hurry up.

Churchill was cackling at something Charles Cholmondeley had said to him when Jean arrived, grinning from ear to ear. She gripped Paddy's hands. "Isn't it exciting? The prime minister!"

A glamorous-looking blonde slipped in and slinked her way across the room to stand next to Fleming, who immediately of-fered her a cigarette and then a light. Paddy gasped. Friedl Stöt-tinger. "What on earth is *she* doing here?" And how did she know Fleming?

"Well, now you know," said Jean with a relieved sigh. "Friedl's working for us."

Paddy stared at Jean. "So that's why you didn't seem terribly worried about her having the negative of your photo."

Jean shrugged. "Well, I was, because I thought it might get back to Captain Montagu that I'd been careless. But I knew Friedl was on our side. At least, when she stole that negative I did wonder, but it's all turned out all right now, hasn't it?"

Paddy gazed across at Friedl, who was even now conversing animatedly with Fleming, causing the corners of his eyes to crinkle with amusement. It made sense, didn't it? Jean was part of the Double-Cross section, so she was bound to know about the agents who worked for them. "But wait a minute. Didn't Friedl have a code name? How did you know who it was?"

"Oh, I didn't hear about her at work," said Jean, shrugging. "Brian Howard told me. He knows everything about everyone."

When finally all were assembled, and the pocket doors to the salon were closed, Churchill drove his walking stick into the floor a couple of times, calling for attention. The hubbub of noise cut off. The prime minister looked around him. "Ladies and gentlemen," he announced, "it is my duty and pleasure to inform you that Sicily has fallen!"

Shouts of victory and jubilation rang out. Jean and Paddy turned and hugged each other, laughing until the tears ran down their faces. It was several minutes before the prime minister could reclaim everyone's attention. "I called you all here to commend you on a sterling operation, carried out with the utmost professionalism and that special brand of derring-do that we Britons pride ourselves we do best."

"Hear hear!" muttered the men.

"We don't have the final numbers," Churchill continued, "but rest assured, Operation Mincemeat saved many thousands of lives."

There were more speeches after that, and Paddy finally heard the entire story from Cholmondeley. The mad race with Major Martin to Scotland in a specially modified van to meet the submarine, the solemn disposal of the body at sea. The autopsy carried out by the Spanish, and several fraught days when it seemed the Spanish Admiralty were not going to allow the Germans access to Major Martin's effects after all. Then the wait while German High Command investigated and deliberated.

As it turned out, Friedl Stöttinger was the one who had been ordered to verify all the wallet litter Paddy had so carefully collected. Was that why she'd purloined Jean's negative?

So when Paddy had been searching for her in St. Albans, Friedl had been on her way to Berlin! Paddy approached Miss Stöttinger and made her apologies. "I am frightfully sorry to have got the wrong end of the stick," she said. "I was convinced you must be working for the Germans."

Friedl blew out smoke and waved her cigarette holder in absolution. "That's quite all right, *liebling*. How were you to know? But I'm the one who should apologize, yes? That was a very nasty blow to the head. I was a little jumpy that night, you understand."

Commander Fleming regarded them both with amusement. "Count yourself lucky, Mrs. Ridsdale. If what I hear is true, Friedl's weapon might well have been a gun."

At dinner, Paddy tried to concentrate on what was being said to her, but she was conscious that Julian must be wondering why she had been invited along to meet Churchill privately. He was seated in the vicinity of the prime minister at dinner, and like the others around him, Julian was avidly listening to the great raconteur speak.

Paddy, farther down the table, strained to hear what the prime minister said, but all she caught was the occasional word here and there.

For the rest of the dinner, she correctly divided her attention between the guests on either side of her, but she burned to know what was going through her husband's mind. Had he thought her inclusion in that small gathering of NID personnel a mere throwback to her employment in Room 39? Might he begin to suspect the truth? But the truth was so unlikely—how could he possibly connect her writing love letters with an operation for the NID?

"Ladies?" Their hostess indicated it was time to leave the men to their port and cigars. Paddy rose from the table, lightly touching Julian's shoulder as she moved past. He smiled up at her over his shoulder.

As she left the dining room, she heard the words erupt from Churchill's mouth in a rumble like thunder. "Then came the message we'd been waiting for. Mincemeat swallowed. Rod, line, and *sinkah*!"

"Golly!" Jean murmured to Paddy as they reapplied their lipstick in the ladies' retiring room. "Did you hear that?"

Paddy didn't know whether to laugh or throw something. After all she'd been through to keep Operation Mincemeat secret even from Julian, the prime minister—*the prime minister*—had spilled the beans!

Jean rolled her eyes. "Captain Montagu says Churchill has been rather dining out on the story since the invasion. I mean, it's absolutely the PM's cup of tea, isn't it?" She shrugged. "Now that the Allies have taken Sicily, I suppose it doesn't matter too much."

Paddy blinked. "But I nearly—" She couldn't reveal to anyone the strife her involvement in the operation had brought to her marriage, but she ought to be furious that a story she would have taken to the grave had become fodder for dinner party conversation. Somehow she couldn't summon the appropriate degree of anger, however. Churchill's indiscretion might well have tipped off Julian about Paddy's part in the business, and that could only be a good thing.

Later that evening, when finally she and Julian were alone again together and in bed, Julian gathered her into his arms and rested his chin on the top of her head. "That was it, wasn't it, Paddy?" he said. "Or should I call you Pam?"

She shifted her head on his chest and took his hand in hers but remained silent.

Fortunately, Julian seemed content to have the entire conversation with himself. "*That's* why you couldn't tell me about the letters. Of course, I should have realized, but . . . by Jove, what a bizarre plot! How could anyone have guessed?"

Paddy tilted her head to look up at him. Far from being annoyed, Julian was tickled by the whole thing. Pride shone from his gaze as he smiled down at her, smoothing her hair back from her face. "And you never said a single word."

"I could just about strangle Winston," Paddy grumbled. "Give him a good story to tell and national security goes out the window."

Julian threw his head back and laughed and Paddy laughed, too.

Suddenly, Julian sobered, and his grip on her hand tightened. "I'm so sorry, darling. I should never, ever, have doubted you." He bent and kissed her with a passion that she'd thought had been lost between them forever. Paddy let herself sink into happiness and wallow in it, finally free from the burden of secrecy and guilt she'd carried inside her for months.

All was right with the world. At least, as right as it could be until the war was won.

London, England
July 1953

Paddy

It was a hot summer's day with a sky as blue as a robin's egg and not a whisper of a breeze as Paddy and Jean sat together on the back terrace of Number 12 The Boltons. They sipped Pimm's and fanned themselves with their floppy straw hats while they watched three little girls play on the lawn.

Paddy smiled. Her daughter was showing Jean's nieces the very spot in the garden where the incendiary bomb had landed after Paddy had shoved it off the roof on that unforgettable evening in 1943.

At nine years old, Penelope Ridsdale was bidding fair to become as redoubtable as her mother ever was. It was perhaps typical of any child of Paddy's that Penelope had come into the world on a December evening in the midst of an air raid, squalling her head off with rage, tiny fists fighting some invisible foe.

The Germans had promised reprisals for the recent British raids on Berlin, and the bombings on the night of Penelope's birth were among the first of a renewed effort to blast London to kingdom come. But the war had been over for many years now. Despite the scars that would always remain with them and the rest of their generation, life had returned to normal. Britain was free.

"All right, darlings?" Jean called, but the girls simply waved and ran off into the trees. Jean's elder niece was two years younger than Penelope and the other was two years younger again, but the three of them got along very well—as long as they let Penelope lead them in their games.

Ostensibly Jean had brought the girls over that afternoon to play, but as Paddy soon discovered, her friend had an ulterior motive: she was dying to discuss Ian Fleming's ridiculous spy novel, *Casino Royale*.

"Have you read it?" demanded Jean.

"No, of course not." Paddy wished very much that she spoke the truth. But how could anyone who knew Fleming resist? People of her acquaintance hardly talked about anything else.

Paddy had fought the urge to read the thriller for as long as she could, but finally curiosity won. Much as she disliked the thought of putting even a penny of royalty money in Fleming's pocket, she'd purchased a copy. She'd hidden it from Julian until one day he'd caught her engrossed in the silly book.

"Snap!" said Julian, producing his own well-thumbed copy. They both laughed.

"I don't know how you can be so dismissive about it," Jean was saying now. "You're in it, after all. Miss Moneypenny! It's you. Everyone says so."

"I can't imagine why they'd think that," said Paddy, although it certainly wasn't the first time she'd been asked about it. Everyone from Room 39 was convinced she was the model for the spymaster M's private secretary.

"'Miss Moneypenny would have been alluring if not for the cool intelligence in her eyes,'" Jean misquoted in a deep, dramatic voice. "Or something like that. Come on, Paddy! It *must* be!"

"Or she could be simply a made-up character—as the characters in most novels are," Paddy replied.

But it was as if Jean couldn't hear her. "I've been going over and over it, trying to work out who everyone is. I mean, he's used the code name 'M,' but Bond's chief isn't at all like our M, is he?"

"I really have no idea." Paddy's tone said that she didn't care, either. But of course she knew precisely who had inspired the character of M. It was almost certainly Admiral Godfrey, but she couldn't tell Jean so. The *Official Secrets Act* still prevented her from discussing her work for the NID.

"But did Fleming actually *do* all of those things he writes about?" said Jean, undeterred by Paddy's feigned lack of interest in the topic. "Is Bond modeled on him, do you think?"

"I'm sure *he'd* like everyone to think so!" Paddy couldn't resist retorting. She fanned herself more vigorously and tried to change the subject. "*Ugh!* Is there no end to this heat?"

"And then there's the girlfriend, that Vesper Lynd," Jean said. "Do you think it's meant to be Friedl?"

"Good gracious, I hope not." Friedl Stöttinger had married

an eminently respectable American diplomat and now traveled with him to foreign postings, their two sons in tow.

"Well, she's definitely not Muriel," said Jean. "I thought so at first, but in the end, she wasn't like her at all."

Paddy felt the pang of loss and regret that always squeezed her chest when Muriel was mentioned. While at home in bed during an air raid in 1944, Muriel was hit on the head by a piece of flying masonry and killed. Fleming himself had been called in to identify her body. Paddy could only imagine how he'd felt.

As for Fleming's dreams of seeing active service while leading his own commando unit, as far as Paddy was aware, they had never come to pass. Godfrey had been right—the commander was too valuable to risk capture. Fleming might not have been as skilled in field work and hand-to-hand combat as the hero of his salacious thriller, but in his own way he was a force to be reckoned with at the NID. Working for him had been a challenge Paddy wouldn't have missed for anything. And if not for the commander, she would never have had the privilege of becoming a field agent herself, albeit briefly, in one of the greatest and most eccentric intelligence deceptions of all time.

The words Fleming had written about Miss Moneypenny passed through her mind. Paddy decided she rather liked the sound of them. To be desired by Ian Fleming was no great thing, after all. But to have earned his respect as a colleague . . . Well, she'd take that compliment in the spirit in which it was meant.

Acknowledgments

Writing this book has been a joy from start to finish, and I want to thank my wonderful editor, Lucia Macro, for enthusiastically jumping on the crazy train of Operation Mincemeat with me and for her excellent editorial advice. It takes many people to publish a novel, and my heartfelt thanks go to the entire team at William Morrow, in particular Amelia Wood, Bianca Flores, and Asanté Simons. My gratitude also to HarperCollins Canada and HarperCollins Australia—Michael White, Kimberley Allsopp, and Erin Dunk, it's been a pleasure to work with you.

To my dynamo agent, Kevan Lyon, thank you for the expertise, care, and attention you give to me and my books. Taryn Fagerness, thank you for your energetic representation in foreign markets.

Writing would be a lonely business without the advice and support of other writers. My gratitude to Denise Frost, Anna Campbell, to the fabulous Lyonesses, and most especially to

Stephanie Marie Thornton and Victoria Schnitzerling for their wonderfully insightful critiques.

It was such a serendipitous thrill to discover that my friend and fellow author, Alison Stuart / A.M. Stuart, has a family connection to Room 39 in George Penkivil "Pen" Slade K.C., who worked there during the Second World War. Alison generously sent me a fascinating memoir written about Pen by his son, Christopher, which proved to be a valuable resource.

Unfortunately, due to the pandemic, I was unable to travel to research this book. Many thanks to another delightful fellow author, Madeline Martin, who shared with me photographs and information from her own investigations on the Portuguese Riviera.

My love and gratitude to my parents, Ian and Cheryl, for their enthusiastic support and editorial suggestions on the messy first draft of this book, and to Allister and Adrian, who are so patient with me when I become wrapped up in a story. Adrian, thank you for pointing out plot holes and helping me brainstorm solutions.

As always, to my dear friends, Lucy, Jason, Yasmin, Vikki, and Ben, thank you for your stalwart friendship and support. I don't know what I'd do without you!

About the author

About the book

Read on

Insights,
Interviews
& More...

Meet Christine Wells

Bill Tsiknaris

CHRISTINE WELLS writes historical fiction featuring strong, fascinating women. From early childhood, she drank in her father's tales about the true stories behind popular nursery rhymes, and she has been a keen student of history ever since. She began her first novel while working as a corporate lawyer, and has gone on to write about periods ranging from Georgian England to post–World War II France. Christine is passionate about helping other writers learn the craft and business of writing fiction, and she enjoys mentoring and teaching workshops whenever her schedule permits. She loves dogs, running, holidays at the beach, and browsing antique shops. She lives with her family in Brisbane, Australia. ᦔ

Truth Is Stranger than Fiction

Amazingly, Operation Mincemeat was one of the most effective intelligence deceptions of the Second World War. It saved thousands of Allied lives and subsequently made the Germans overly suspicious of genuine intelligence that came their way.

The plan was to float a dead body dressed as a British Royal Marine off the coastal town of Huelva, Spain, in the almost certain knowledge that the Germans would get their hands on any documents found on the corpse, either via the Spanish authorities or by less direct methods. Of course, Major Martin's briefcase, which was handcuffed to him so it wouldn't float away, contained misinformation about the Allies' intended invasion point for southern Europe.

The success of the operation depended on a series of fortunate events, including the willingness of Hitler to believe in the intelligence obtained from Major Martin's body and the eagerness of Major Karl-Erich Kühlenthal to ignore inconvenient details and even lie in order to carry off this personal intelligence coup. But the clincher seemed to have been the recommendation of one of the Abwehr's chief intelligence officers, Colonel Baron Alexis von Rönne. Von Rönne was later accused of being involved in the 1944 plot to assassinate

Hitler and was horrifically hanged by the throat from a meat hook. The colonel was a devout Christian who disagreed with the tenets of Nazism. His motivation for misleading Hitler about the reliability of the Mincemeat intelligence is unknown, but it is speculated that he was actively working against Hitler at this stage of the war.

What struck me particularly was how many different versions of the Mincemeat story had been told over the years, even by those who participated in it. Ewen Montagu's own account, *The Man Who Never Was*, did not give the whole truth because of the ongoing need for secrecy regarding many aspects of the operation. It was only recently that the true identity of the man whose body became Major William Martin was found to be Glyndwr Michael, although that might have been more of a political omission than a security-conscious one.

The 1956 movie, also titled *The Man Who Never Was*, embellished the story heavily, as movies tend to do, including a dreadful made-up subplot about the hapless girl who pretended to be Pam. (Interestingly, Ewen Montagu played a cameo role in this film). *The Goon Show* even had an episode called "The Man Who Never Was." At the time of writing, a feature film starring Colin Firth and Matthew Macfadyen is set to tell the story yet again. *Operation Mincemeat*, to be released in April 2022 in the United Kingdom and Australian cinemas and in May on Netflix in the United States, ▶

Truth Is Stranger than Fiction *(continued)*

is based on Ben Macintyre's excellent book of the same name.

In this novel, I have added my own twist to the tale, focusing on the roles of the women involved.

The meeting of Paddy Bennett, Jean Leslie, and Ian Fleming at Bordeaux did not happen in the manner described, although Fleming did take charge of the evacuation from Point Verdon, and Jean and her mother were among the British evacuees scrambling to leave the country after the fall of Paris. Paddy was studying architecture at the Sorbonne at around this time, so I hope I will be forgiven the license I have taken in bringing them all together here.

I moved the date of Fleming's *Trout* Memorandum from 1939 to 1940 so that Paddy could be privy to its contents.

Paddy's visits to the St. Pancras mortuary and to MI-5 with Ewen Montagu are fictional, but I wanted to have her on the spot to show the elaborate preparations that took place. It is likely that Paddy was in the early stages of pregnancy when she was running around London collecting wallet litter for Major Martin. Her daughter, Penelope Ridsdale, was born at home during an air raid on December 10, 1943. It is also true that poor Glyndwr Michael's feet had frozen solid and needed to be thawed before his boots could be put on. I have compressed the time between Michael's death and when the operation started and delayed dressing him for the purposes of this novel.

I have taken the greatest liberty with Friedl's story. While Friedl Stöttinger was an Austrian double agent working for the British, there is no suggestion that she was involved in Operation Mincemeat directly or that she was ever tempted to betray Britain. She did have a torrid affair with Duško Popov, but her intelligence activities were confined to reporting on fifth column activities in Britain and later working in Popov's circuit as a fake informant. She never went to Estoril with Popov, nor to Berlin. Popov retained a high opinion of her abilities as an intelligence agent and never doubted her loyalty as he did in this novel. ᴖ

Dramatis Personae

FRIEDL

Friedl Gärtner, née Stöttinger, was approached by the Abwehr (but probably not by Kühlenthal) to spy for the Nazis before she settled in England in about 1937. Her sister, Liesel, was married to Ian Menzies, the brother of Stewart Menzies, who was head of MI-6. Friedl became a double agent for the British, working first with Maxwell Knight ("M") and Joan Miller for MI-5, and later joining Duško Popov's circuit under the aegis of Stewart Menzies ("C") and Thomas Argyll Robertson ("Tar").

Friedl did not, however, accompany Popov to Estoril or go to Berlin to report on the movements of Major Martin and his Pam. In fact, Popov was the agent tasked with monitoring the Abwehr's reception of Mincemeat on the Iberian Peninsula, and one of his contacts reported back on the reaction in Berlin.

The incidents described at the Estoril casino are drawn from Popov's memoir, *Spy/Counterspy*, and *Into the Lion's Mouth* by Larry Loftis. Popov often changed names and places in his memoir, but it was clear from cross-referencing his account with Joan Miller's memoir that Popov's "Gerda" and Friedl were the same person. Friedl and Popov conducted a passionate affair while also spying for Britain.

Popov described Friedl as "charming, beautiful, sexy. And intelligent" and

better at her job than he was at his.
This assessment was at odds with the
dismissive notes in her file from some of
her superiors in the intelligence services.
I still can't quite understand why she
ended up with the code name "Gelatine,"
which was said to have arisen from
people calling her a "Jolly Little Thing,"
but that's the spy world for you.

The question of Friedl's status after
the war was a fraught one. She wanted
to marry the American diplomat Donald
Calder, but he would have had to leave
the diplomatic service if he married a
German national, which the passport
MI-5 arranged for her said she was.
In the end, love prevailed. The couple
married after the war, and there are
records of them moving to different
diplomatic postings with their two sons
in tow.

JEAN

Jean Leslie was the girl in the swimsuit
whose photograph would be found
nestled close to Major Martin's heart.
Jean's trouble over retrieving the negative
and copy of the photograph, Friedl's theft
of the negative, and Paddy's subsequent
investigation of Friedl are pure fiction,
inspired by Charles Cholmondeley's
warning to Jean that she had better ask
the friend who took the photos to destroy
any copies. In real life, Jean obeyed
this directive, apparently causing poor
Tony of the Grenadier Guards some
heartache. Jean must have kept the ▶

negative, however, because she had the photograph enlarged, inscribed it with a sentimental message, and gave it to Ewen Montagu. Jean was perhaps not as flighty in real life as she appears in this novel, but she seems to have been more than willing to play along with Montagu's little fantasy about Bill and Pam.

JOAN

Joan Miller and Friedl were friends and colleagues. In her memoir, *One Girl's War*, Joan describes Friedl's antics, including winding up in jail after being mistakenly arrested as a lady of the night on more than one occasion. Joan also recounts her own ill-fated love affair with Maxwell Knight (a.k.a. "M"). Incidentally, M did purchase a cosh and a tiny gun for Joan because her undercover field work had placed her on several blacklists.

JULIAN

Following in the footsteps of his uncle, the former prime minister Stanley Baldwin, Julian Ridsdale entered politics after the war and was member for Harwich for thirty-eight years, ably assisted by Paddy, who acted as his private secretary. Julian was knighted in 1987.

All the marital troubles caused by Paddy's activities for the Admiralty are my invention. In fact, Julian must have been aware of Paddy's involvement in Mincemeat at the time because he reportedly joked about being jealous of this fellow to whom his wife was writing love letters. They appear to have been a devoted, happy couple, and I apologize for the strife I created between them in the name of dramatic tension.

The question of who actually wrote those love letters seems to be somewhat in dispute. News reports have Paddy claiming that honor, and if the quote has been accurately attributed to her, one rather thinks she ought to know. In his book *Operation Mincemeat*, Ben Macintyre maintains that it was not Paddy, but MI-5's Hester Leggett (unkindly nicknamed "the Spin") who penned those pages of unbridled sentimentality. I have tried to accommodate both versions here.

The real women portrayed in this novel might have crossed paths at various stages, but the friendship among Paddy, Jean, and Muriel Wright in this novel is my invention.

FLEMING

Commander Ian Fleming was extremely effective as Rear Admiral Godfrey's personal assistant during the Second World War, even if he might have yearned to take a more active part in the missions he designed. Operation Mincemeat was Fleming's suggestion, although perhaps not an original one, as it had been used in a popular mystery of the time. Fleming later came full circle, going on to create one of the world's most successful and ▶

enduring franchises in James Bond. He used his background knowledge of intelligence work to give Bond a grounding in fact—fantastical though that fact often was.

POPOV

One source of inspiration for the character of James Bond was clearly Duško Popov, although Popov himself expressed doubt that Bond would have lasted more than forty-eight hours as a real spy.

One of the most important schemes Popov undertook for the British was to convince the Germans that he would launder money for them so that they could pay their overseas informants in the correct currency. In fact the British had already executed, turned, or imprisoned all Nazi agents on British soil and set up a fake network of spies to report misinformation to the Abwehr. With typical British irony, MI-6 used German funds to finance their own operations.

Popov, as the intermediary, often carried large amounts of cash on him while in Estoril. On the occasion described in this book, Fleming was said to be shadowing Popov in Estoril to make sure the MI-6 money got where it was meant to go. While Fleming himself claimed to have had the idea for the first James Bond novel, *Casino Royale*, on another visit to the Estoril casino and Popov's own account of his bluff with MI-6 money might have been apocryphal, it does make for an excellent story.

MURIEL

The original "Bond girl," Muriel Wright was a tragic figure. Beautiful and aristocratic, a model, champion skier and polo player, she was madly in love with Fleming, but he treated her badly. In 1944, Muriel was killed in a bomb blast by a piece of masonry that flew through her window, and her death affected Fleming deeply. One of his friends remarked that the trouble with Fleming was, you had to die before he realized he cared. When Fleming killed off Bond's wife, Tracy Draco, in *On Her Majesty's Secret Service*, he might well have drawn on his experience of Muriel's death.

BRIAN

Brian Howard was a member of that set of "Bright Young Things" immortalized in the novels of Evelyn Waugh. He seemed to me to be a sad figure in many ways, a wasted talent whose waspish tongue was perhaps a defense mechanism against the horrible treatment meted out to openly homosexual men in that era. He was said to have been prone to using the tidbits he picked up for MI-5 to blackmail the people concerned. However, I am not aware that he blackmailed cabinet ministers or bishops in particular. ▶

PADDY

Paddy Ridsdale was made a Dame of the British Empire in 1991 for her wartime service, which involved a stint working in Room 39 for several officers, including Commander Fleming. Later, Paddy would pretend to be Pam for Operation Mincemeat, even though she no longer worked at the Admiralty. More recently, at age seventy-five, the redoubtable Paddy hit the newspapers when she fended off a mugging by kicking her assailant in the groin, commenting that her years of ballet gave her the requisite flexibility. It is that spirit, along with Paddy's keen mind, which I have tried to convey in this novel.

While several women have been mentioned as having inspired the creation of Miss Moneypenny in Ian Fleming's James Bond novels, to my mind Paddy Ridsdale best fits the bill. Intelligent, cool, elegant, determined, and well respected by her colleagues, Paddy denied mooning over Fleming the way Moneypenny did over Bond. But the Bond novels are pure fantasy, after all, and perhaps Fleming was indulging in a little wish fulfilment there . . .

MINOR PLAYERS

Edith Bennett, Paddy's mother, was the daughter of an Irish judge and among the first cohort of women to graduate from Trinity College, Dublin with a medical degree in 1906.

Karl-Erich Kühlenthal was related to Admiral Wilhelm Canaris, the head of the German Abwehr, but he had a dark secret—his grandmother was Jewish. He was therefore doubly anxious to ingratiate himself with his superiors and desperate to take credit for the intelligence "triumph" of the information gleaned from Major William Martin's body.

Due to the undercover work and testimony of Friedl Stöttinger and Joan Miller, **Anna Wolkoff** was sentenced to ten years' imprisonment for attempting to assist the enemy.

Marie-Jaqueline Lancaster, Dylan Thomas, and **Lucian Freud** were all madcap friends of Brian Howard, and MJ was well acquainted with Cambridge spies Guy Burgess and Anthony Blunt from working at MI-5. MJ also edited a fascinating book about Brian called *Brian Howard: Portrait of a Failure.*

Dennis and **Joan Wheatley, Billy Younger, Thomas Argyll Robertson** ("**Tar**"), **Stewart Menzies, Liesel Menzies, Susan Barton, Pen Slade, William Luke,** and **Donald Calder** were all real people, as were **Patricia Trehearne, Charles Cholmondeley,** and **Ewen Montagu** from Room 13.

Sir Bentley Purchase was the delightfully Dickensian name of the coroner who helped find a suitable body for the operation. ▶

Dramatis Personae *(continued)*

George Black was the manager of the Hotel Palàcio, which was a hotbed of spies in World War II. Apparently years later, when the hotel was renovated, the ceilings of the rooms were found to be riddled with listening devices. The bar of the hotel is now known as the "Spy Bar" because Ian Fleming and Popov, among other spies, used to drink there.

Lady Bonham Carter, briefly mentioned as the hostess of the dinner party attended by Churchill, was an intimate friend of the prime minister, but she did not host a dinner to celebrate the success of Operation Mincemeat, as far as I'm aware. She was the grandmother of actress Helena Bonham Carter. Incidentally, it was said that Churchill rather "dined out" on the story of Mincemeat, a joke on the Germans that was surely too rich to be kept to himself. The prime minister's indiscretion seemed a neat way to resolve Paddy's dilemma and restore peace to the Ridsdales' world. ◐

Reading Group Guide

1. Strong female friendships feature in this novel. In what ways do you see yourself and your friends in the characters?

2. Secrecy was a necessity in wartime Britain. In Paddy's shoes, how far would you have gone to keep your role in Operation Mincemeat secret? Are there some things husbands don't need to know?

3. Friedl decides to put her life on the line, lying to German High Command in order to help save thousands of Allied soldiers. What would you have done when faced with that dilemma?

4. In the twenty-first century, a woman like Paddy Bennett might well be running Room 39 rather than working there as a secretary. However, the Second World War gave women career opportunities they had never had before. How were the women in your family affected by World War II?

5. Friedl is an ambiguous character. Do you think she was basically a good person? Why? ▸

Reading Group Guide *(continued)*

6. Duško Popov and Ian Fleming were both brilliant at their wartime occupations and both treated women badly. Do these kinds of men still have appeal in the modern age?

Further Reading

Baker, Phil, *The Devil Is a Gentleman:
    The Life and Times of Dennis Wheatley*
Bright Astley, Joan, *The Inner Circle:
    A View of War at the Top*
De Courcy, Anne, *Debs at War:
    1939–1945*
Dorling, Captain Taprell, *The Hurlingham
    Club 1869–1953*
Fleming, Ian, *Casino Royale*
Hemming, Henry, *M: Maxwell Knight,
    MI5's Greatest Spymaster*
Jeffery, Keith, *MI6: The History of the
    Secret Intelligence Service 1909–1949*
Lancaster, Marie-Jaqueline, ed., *Brian
    Howard: Portrait of a Failure*
Loftis, Larry, *Into the Lion's Mouth:
    The True Story of Duško Popov:
    World War II Spy, Patriot, and the
    Real-Life Inspiration for James Bond*
Macintyre, Ben, *Double Cross*
Macintyre, Ben, *For Your Eyes Only:
    Ian Fleming and James Bond*
Macintyre, Ben, *Operation Mincemeat:
    The True Spy Story That Changed the
    Course of World War II*
McLachlan, Donald, *Room 39*
Miller, Joan, *One Girl's War*
Miller, Russell, *Codename Tricycle:
    The True Story of the Second World
    War's Most Extraordinary Double
    Agent*
Montagu, Ewen, *The Man Who Never
    Was: World War II's Boldest
    Counterintelligence Operation*
O'Connor, Bernard, *Agent Fifi and the
    Wartime Honeytrap Spies* ▶

Further Reading (*continued*)

Pearson, John, *The Life of Ian Fleming*
Popov, Duško, *Spy/Counterspy: The Autobiography of Duško Popov* (foreword by Ewen Montagu)
Schüler, C. J., *Writers, Lovers, Soldiers, Spies: A History of the Authors' Club of London 1891–2016*
Smith, Michael, *The Debs of Bletchley Park and Other Stories*
Smyth, Denis, *Deathly Deception: The Real Story of Operation Mincemeat*
Sweet, Matthew, *The West End Front*
Waugh, Evelyn, *Vile Bodies*
West, Nigel, *MI5: British Security Service Operations, 1909–1945* ◠